DOWN TO EARTH . . .

There was a sense of sadness and finality about almost everything that he did in these last days. Sometimes it puzzled Duncan; he should be excited, anticipating the great adventure that only a handful of men on his world could ever share.

He was certain that a year's absence would pass swiftly enough, among the wonders and distractions of Earth.

So why this melancholy?

If he was saying farewell to the things of his youth, it was only for a little while, and he would appreciate them all the more when he returned . . .

<u>When he returned.</u>

That was the real problem. The Duncan Makenzie who was now leaving Titan would never return.

He was heading sunward in search of knowledge, of power, of maturity—and, above all, in search of the successor which his own world could never give him.

Reviewers agree:
IMPERIAL EARTH IS

"Scintillating . . . consummate . . . precise technical detail . . . This book has more plot and human interest than Clarke's previous opus Rendezvous with Rama."

—The Washington Post

"Readers will generally agree that this is Clarke's best book."

—Lester del Rey

"Chilling . . . amusing . . . engaging readable . . . Clarke manages to build suspense . . . and to weave it into a plea, at the climax, for further exploration of deep space. Five years from now when you've put the Bicentennial ashtrays in the attic for the grandchildren, you'll be able to reread Imperial Earth with pleasure."

—The Baltimore Sun

Also by Arthur C. Clarke
published by Ballantine Books:

EARTHLIGHT

EXPEDITION TO EARTH

PRELUDE TO SPACE

REACH FOR TOMORROW

RENDEZVOUS WITH RAMA

TALES FROM THE "WHITE HART"

CHILDHOOD'S END

IMPERIAL EARTH

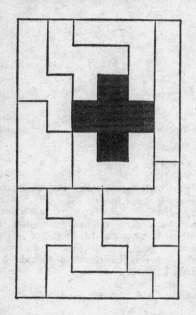

Arthur C. Clarke

A Del Rey Book

BALLANTINE BOOKS • NEW YORK

A Del Rey Book
Published by Ballantine Books

Library of Congress Catalog Card Number: 75-30595

ISBN 0-345-31561-8

This edition published by arrangement with
Harcourt Brace Jovanovich, Inc.

Manufactured in the United States of America

First Ballantine Books Edition: November 1976
Eighth Printing: January 1984

First Canadian Printing: December 1976

Cover art by Stanislaw Fernandes

For a lost friend

"Remember them as they were; and
write them off."
—Ernest Hemingway

CONTENTS

IV TITAN

For every man has business and desire.
—HAMLET, Act I, Scene 4

Part I

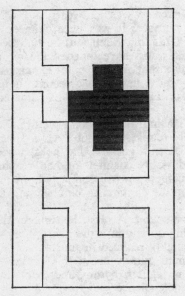

Titan

I

A SHRIEK IN THE NIGHT

Duncan Makenzie was ten years old when he found the magic number. It was pure chance; he had intended to call Grandma Ellen, but he had been careless and his fingers must have touched the wrong keys. He knew at once that he had made a mistake, because Grandma's viddy had a two-second delay, even on Auto/Record. This circuit was live immediately.

Yet there was no ringing tone, and no picture. The screen was completely blank, with not even a speckling of interference. Duncan guessed that he had been switched into an audio-only channel, or had reached a station where the camera was disconnected. In any case, this certainly wasn't Grandma's number, and he reached out to break the circuit.

Then he noticed the sound. At first, he thought that someone was breathing quietly into the microphone at the far end, but he quickly realized his mistake. There was a random, inhuman quality about this gentle susurration; it lacked any regular rhythm, and there were long intervals of complete silence.

As he listened, Duncan felt a growing sense of awe. Here was something completely outside his normal, everyday experience, yet he recognized it almost at once. In his ten years of life, the impressions of many worlds had been inprinted on his mind, and no one who had heard this most evocative of sounds could ever forget it. He was listening to the voice of the wind, as it sighed and whispered across the lifeless landscape a hundred meters above his head.

Duncan forgot all about Grandma, and turned the volume up to its highest level. He lay back on the couch, closed his eyes, and tried to project himself into the unknown, hostile world from which he was protected by all the safety devices that three hundred years of space technology could contrive. Someday, when he had passed his survival tests, he would go up into that world and see with his own eyes the lakes and chasms and low-lying orange clouds, lit by the thin, cold rays of the distant sun. He had looked forward to that day with calm anticipation rather than excitement—the Makenzies were noted for their lack of excitement—but now he suddenly realized what he was missing. So might a child of Earth, on some dusty desert far from the ocean, have pressed a shell against his ear and listened with sick longing to the music of the unattainable sea.

There was no mystery about the sound, but how was it reaching him? It could be coming from any of the hundred million square kilometers lying above his head. Somewhere—perhaps in an abandoned construction project or experimental station—a live microphone had been left in circuit, exposed to the freezing, poisonous winds of the world above. It was not likely to remain undetected for long; sooner or later it would be discovered and disconnected. He had better capture this message from the outside while it was still there; even if he knew the number he had accidentally called, he doubted if he could ever establish the circuit again.

The amount of audio-visual material that Duncan had stored under MISC was remarkable, even for an inquisitive ten-year-old. It was not that he lacked organizing ability—that was the most celebrated of all the Makenzie talents—but he was interested in more things than he knew how to index. He had now begun to discover, the hard way, that information not properly classified can be irretrievably lost.

He thought intently for a minute, while the lonely wind sobbed and moaned and brought the chill of space into his warm little cubicle. Then he tapped out APHA INDEX* WIND SOUNDS* PERM STORE #.

From the moment he touched the # or EXECUTE key, he had begun to capture that voice from the world above. If all went well, he could call it forth again at any time by using the index heading WIND SOUNDS.

3

Even if he had made a mistake, and the console's search program failed to locate the recording, it would be *somewhere* in the machine's permanent, nonerasable memory. There was always the hope that he might one day find it again by chance, as was happening all the time with information he had filed under MISC.

He decided to let the recording run for another few minutes before completing the interrupted call to Grandma. As luck would have it, the wind must have slackened at about the time he keyed EXECUTE, because there was a long, frustrating silence. Then, out of that silence, came something new.

It was faint and distant, yet conveyed the impression of overwhelming power. First there was a thin scream that mounted second by second in intensity, but somehow never came any closer. The scream rose swiftly to a demonic shriek, with undertones of thunder—then dwindled away as quickly as it had appeared. From beginning to end it lasted less than half a minute. Then there was only the sighing of the wind, even lonelier than before.

For a long, delicious moment, Duncan savored the unique pleasure of fear without danger; then he reacted as he always did when he encountered something new or exciting. He tapped out Karl Helmer's number, and said: "Listen to *this*."

Three kilometers away, at the northern end of Oasis City, Karl waited until the thin scream died into silence. As always, his face gave no hint of his thoughts. Presently he said: "Let's hear it again."

Duncan repeated the playback, confident that the mystery would soon be solved. For Karl was fifteen, and therefore knew everything.

Those dazzling blue eyes, apparently so candid yet already so full of secrets, looked straight at Duncan. Karl's surprise and sincerity were totally convincing as he exclaimed: "You didn't recognize it?"

Duncan hesitated. He had thought of several obvious possibilities—but if he guessed wrongly, Karl would make fun of him. Better to be on the safe side . . .

"No," he answered. "Did *you*?"

4

"Of course," said Karl, in his most superior tone of voice. He paused for effect, then leaned toward the camera so that his face loomed enormous on the screen.

"It's a *Hydrosaurus* on the rampage."

For a fraction of a second, Duncan took him seriously—which was exactly what Karl had intended. He quickly recovered, and laughed back at his friend.

"You're crazy. So you don't know what it is."

For the methane-breathing monster *Hydrosaurus rex* was their private joke—the product of youthful imaginations, inflamed by pictures of ancient Earth and the wonders it had brought forth near the dawn of creation. Duncan knew perfectly well that nothing lived now, or had ever lived, on the world that he called home; only Man had walked upon its frozen surface. Yet if *Hydrosaurus* could have existed, that awesome sound might indeed have been its battle cry, as it leaped upon the gentle *Carbotherium,* wallowing in some ammonia lake . . .

"Oh. *I* know what made that noise," said Karl smugly. "Didn't you guess? That was a ram-tanker making a scoop. If you call Traffic Control, they'll tell you where it was heading."

Karl had had his fun, and the explanation was undoubtedly correct. Duncan had already thought of it, yet he had hoped for something more romantic. Though it was perhaps too much to expect methane monsters, an everyday spaceship was a disappointing anticlimax. He felt a sense of letdown, and was sorry that he had given Karl another chance to deflate his dreams. Karl was rather good at that.

But like all healthy ten-year-olds, Duncan was resilient. The magic had not been destroyed. Though the first ship had lifted from Earth three centuries before he was born, the wonder of space had not yet been exhausted. There was romance enough in that shriek from the edge of the atmosphere, as the orbiting tanker collected hydrogen to power the commerce of the Solar System.

In a few hours, that precious cargo would be falling sunward, past Saturn's other moons, past giant Jupiter, to make its rendezvous with one of the fueling

5

stations that circled the inner planets. It would take months—even years—to get there, but there was no hurry. As long as cheap hydrogen flowed through the invisible pipeline across the Solar System, the fusion rockets could fly from world to world, as once the ocean liners had plied the seas of Earth.

Duncan understood this better than most boys of his age; the hydrogen economy was also the story of his family, and would dominate his own future when he was old enough to play a part in the affairs of Titan. It was now almost a century since Grandfather Malcolm had realized that Titan was the key to all the planets, and had shrewdly used this knowledge for the benefit of mankind—and of himself.

So Duncan continued to listen to the recording after Karl had switched off. Over and over again he played back that triumphant cry of power, trying to detect the precise moment when it was finally swallowed up in the gulfs of space. For years it would haunt his dreams; he would wake in the night, convinced that he had heard it again through the roof of rock that protected Oasis from the hostile wilderness above.

And when at last he fell back into sleep, he would always dream of Earth.

2

DYNASTY

Malcolm Makenzie had been the right man, at the right time. Others before him had looked covetously at Titan, but he was the first to work out all the engineering details and to conceive the total system of orbiting scoops, compressors, and cheap, expendable tanks that could hold their liquid hydrogen with minimum loss as they dropped leisurely sunward.

Back in the 2180's, Malcolm had been a promising young aerospace designer at Port Lowell, trying to make aircraft that could carry useful payloads in the tenuous Martian atmosphere. In those days he had been Malcolm Mackenzie, for the computer mishap that had irrevocably changed the family name did not occur until he emigrated to Titan. After wasting five years in futile attempts at correction, Malcolm had finally co-operated with the inevitable. It was one of the few battles in which the Makenzies had ever admitted defeat, but now they were quite proud of their unique name.

When he had finished his calculations and stolen enough drafting-computer time to prepare a beautiful set of drawings, young Malcolm had approached the Planning Office of the Martian Department of Transportation. He did not anticipate serious criticism, because he knew that his facts and his logic were impeccable.

A large fusion-powered spaceliner could use ten thousand tons of hydrogen on a single flight, merely as inert working fluid. Ninety-nine percent of it took no part in the nuclear reaction, but was hurled from the jets unchanged, at scores of kilometers a second, imparting momentum to the ships it drove between the planets.

There was plenty of hydrogen on Earth, easily available in the oceans; but the cost of lifting megatons a year into space was horrendous. And the other inhabited worlds—Mars, Mercury, Ganymede, and the Moon—could not help. They had no surplus hydrogen at all.

Of course, Jupiter and the other Gas Giants possessed unlimited quantities of the vital element, but their gravitational fields guarded it more effectively than any unsleeping dragon, coiled round some mythical treasure of the Gods. In all the Solar System, Titan was the only place where Nature had contrived the paradox of low gravity and an atmosphere remarkably rich in hydrogen and its compounds.

Malcolm was right in guessing that no one would challenge his figures, or deny the feasibility of the scheme, but a kindhearted senior administrator took it upon himself to lecture young Makenzie on the political and economic facts of life. He learned, with remarkable speed, about growth curves and forward discounting and interplanetary debts and rates of depreciation and technological obsolescence, and understood for the first time why the solar was backed, not by gold, but by kilowatt-hours.

"It's an old problem," his mentor had explained patiently. "In fact, it goes back to the very beginnings of astronautics, in the twentieth century. We couldn't have commercial space flight until there were flourishing extraterrestrial colonies—and we couldn't have colonies until there was commercial space transportation. In this sort of bootstrap situation, you have a very slow growth rate until you reach the takeoff point. Then, quite suddenly, the curves start shooting upward, and you're in business.

"It could be the same with your Titan refueling scheme—but have you any *idea* of the initial investment required? Only the World Bank could possibly underwrite it. . . ."

"What about the Bank of Selene? Isn't it supposed to be more adventurous?"

"Don't believe all you've read about the Gnomes of Aristarchus; they're as careful as anyone else. They *have* to be. Bankers on Earth can still go on breathing if they make a bad investment. . . ."

But it was the Bank of Selene, three years later, that put up the five megasols for the initial feasibility study. Then Mercury became interested—and finally Mars. By this time, of course, Malcolm was no longer an aerospace engineer. He had become, not necessarily in this order, a financial expert, a public-relations adviser, a media manipulator, and a shrewd politician. In the incredibly short time of twenty years, the first hydrogen shipments were falling sunward from Titan.

Malcolm's achievement had been an extraordinary one, now well documented in dozens of scholarly studies, all respectful, though some of them far from flattering. What made it so remarkable—even unique— was the way in which he had converted his hard-won expertise from technology to administration. The process had been so imperceptible that no one realized what was happening. Malcolm was not the first engineer to become a head of state; but he was the first, his critics pointed out sourly, to establish a dynasty. And he had done so against odds that would have daunted lesser men.

In 2195, at the age of forty-four, he had married Ellen Killner, recently emigrated from Earth. Their daughter, Anitra, was the first child to be born in the little frontier community of Oasis, then the only permanent base on Titan, and it was several years before the devoted parents realized the cruel jest that Nature had played upon them.

Even as a baby, Anitra was beautiful, and it was confidently predicted that when she grew up she would be completely spoiled. Needless to say, there were as yet no child psychologists on Titan; so no one noticed that the little girl was too docile, too well behaved—and too silent. Not until she was almost four years old did Malcolm and Ellen finally accept the fact that Anitra would never be able to speak, and that there was really no one at home in the lovely shell their bodies had fashioned.

The fault lay in Malcolm's genes, not Ellen's. Sometime during his shuttling back and forth between Earth and Mars, a stray photon that had been cruising through space since the cosmic dawn had blasted his hopes for the future. The damage was irreparable, as Malcolm discovered when he consulted the best genetic surgeons of four worlds. It was a chilling thought that he had actually been lucky with Anitra; the results could have been far, far worse. . . .

To the mingled sorrow and relief of an entire world, Anitra had died before she was six years old, and the Makenzie marriage died with her in a flurry of grief and recrimination. Ellen threw herself into her work, and Malcolm departed on what was to be his last visit to Earth. He was gone for almost two years, and in that time he achieved much.

He consolidated his political position and set the pattern of economic development on Titan for the next half-century. And he acquired the son he had now set his heart upon.

Human cloning—the creation of exact replicas of another individual from any cell in the body except the sex cells—had been achieved early in the twenty-first century. Even when the technology had been perfected, it had never become widespread, partly because there were few circumstances that could ever justify it.

Malcolm was not a rich man—there had been no large personal fortunes for a hundred years—but he was certainly not poor. He used a skillful combination of money, flattery, and more subtle pressures to attain his goal. When he returned to Titan, he brought with him the baby who was his identical twin—but half a century younger.

When Colin grew up, there was no way in which he could be distinguished from his clone father at the same age. Physically, he was an exact duplicate in every respect. But Malcolm was no Narcissus, interested in creating a mere carbon copy of himself; he wanted a partner as well as a successor. So Colin's educational program concentrated on the weak points of Malcolm's. Though he had a good grounding in science, he specialized in history, law, and economics. Whereas Malcolm was an engineer-administrator, Colin was an administrator-engineer. While still in his twenties, he was acting as his father's deputy wherever it was legally admissible, and sometimes where it was not. Together, the two Makenzies formed an unbeatable combination, and trying to draw subtle distinctions between their psychologies was a favorite Titanian pastime.

Perhaps because he had never been compelled to fight for any great objective, and had had all his goals formulated before his birth, Colin was more gentle and easygoing than Malcolm—and therefore more popular. No one outside the Makenzie family ever called the older man by his first name; few called Colin anything else. He had no real enemies, and there was only one person on Titan who disliked him. At least, it was assumed that Malcolm's estranged wife, Ellen, did so, for she refused to acknowledge his existence.

Perhaps she regarded Colin as a usurper, an unacceptable substitute for the son who could never be

10

born to her. If so, it was indeed strange that she was so fond of Duncan.

But Duncan had been cloned from Colin almost forty years later and by that time Ellen had passed through a second tragedy—one that had nothing to do with the Makenzies. To Duncan, she was always *Grandma* Ellen, but he was now old enough to realize that in his heart she combined two generations, and filled a void that earlier ages would have found it impossible to imagine or believe.

If Grandma had any real genetic relationship with him, all trace of it had been lost centuries ago on another world. And yet, by some strange quirk of chance and personality, she had become for him the phantom mother who had never even existed.

3

INVITATION TO A CENTENNIAL

"**A**nd who the hell is George Washington?" asked Malcolm Makenzie.

"Middle-aged Virginia farmer, runs a place called Mount Vernon—"

"You're joking."

"I'm not. No relation, of course—old George was childless—but that's his real name, and he's perfectly genuine."

"I suppose you've checked with the embassy."

"Of course, and got a fifty-line print-out of his family tree. Most impressive—half the American aristocracy for the last hundred years. Lots of Cabots and Du Ponts and Kennedys and Kissingers. And before that, a couple of African kings."

"It may impress *you*, Colin," interjected Duncan, "but now that I've glanced at the program, it all seems a little childish. Grown men pretending to be historical

11

figures. Are they *really* going to throw tea into Boston Harbor?"

Before Colin could answer, Grandfather Malcolm stepped in. A discussion among the three Makenzies —which was something seldom overheard by outsiders—was more in the nature of a monologue than an argument. Because their three personas differed only through the accidents of background and education, genuine disagreements among them were virtually unknown. When difficult decisions had to be made, Duncan and Colin would take opposing viewpoints and debate them before Malcolm—who would listen without saying a word, though his eyebrows could be very eloquent. He seldom had to give a judgment, because the two advocates usually reached a synthesis without much difficulty; but when he did, that was the end of the matter. It was quite a good way to run a family—or a world.

"I don't know about the tea, which would certainly be a waste at fifty solars a kilo, but you're being too hard on Mr. Washington and his friends. When *we* have five hundred years behind us, we'll be justified in a little pomp and ceremony. And never forget— the Declaration of Independence was one of the most important historical events of the last three thousand years. *We* wouldn't be here without it. After all, the Treaty of Phobos opens with the words: *When in the course of human events, it becomes necessary for one people . . .*"

"Quite inappropriate in that context. On the whole, Earth was heartily glad to get rid of us."

"Perfectly true, but don't ever let the Terrans hear it."

"I'm still confused," said Duncan rather plaintively. "Just what does the good general want from us? How can we raw colonials contribute to the proceedings?"

"He's only a professor, not a general," replied Colin. "They're extinct, even on Earth. As I see it, a few nicely composed speeches, drawing whatever parallels you can find between our historical situations. A certain exotic charm—you know; a whiff of the frontier, where men still live dangerously. The usual barbarian virility, so irresistible to decadent

Terrans of all sexes. And, not least, a low-keyed yet genuine gratitude for the unexpected gift of an open Earth-Titan return ticket with all expenses for a two-month stay. That solves several of our problems, and we should appreciate it."

"Very true," Duncan replied thoughtfully, "even though it wrecks our plans for the next five years."

"It doesn't wreck them," said Colin. "It advances them. Time gained is time created. And success in politics—"

"—depends upon the masterful administration of the unforeseen, as you are so fond of saying. Well, this invitation is certainly unforeseen, and I'll try to master it. Have we sent an official thank you?"

"Only a routine acknowledgment. I suggest that you follow it up, Duncan, with a personal note to President—er—Professor Washington."

"They're both right," said Malcolm, rereading the formal invitation. "It says here: 'Chairman of the Quincentennial Celebration Committee, and President of the Historical Association of Virginia.' So you can take your choice."

"We've got to be very careful about this, or someone will bring it up in the Assembly. Was the invitation official, or personal?"

"It's not government to government, I'm happy to say, since the Committee sponsored it. And the fax was addressed to the Honorable Malcolm Makenzie, *not* to the President." The Honorable Malcolm Makenzie, also President of Titan, was clearly pleased at this subtle distinction.

"Do I detect in this the fine hand of your good friend Ambassador Farrell?" asked Colin.

"I'm sure the idea never occurred to him."

"I thought as much. Well, even if we are on firm legal grounds, that won't stop the objections. There will be the usual cries of privilege, and we'll be accused once again of running Titan for our personal benefit."

"I'd like to know who started the word 'fiefdom' circulating. I had to look it up."

Colin ignored the older man's interruption. As Chief Administrator, he had to face the day-to-day

13

problems of running the world, and could not afford the slight irresponsibility that Malcolm was beginning to show in his old age. It was not senility—Grandfather was still only a hundred and twenty-four —but, rather, the carefree, Olympian attitude of one who had seen and experienced everything, and had achieved all his ambitions.

"There are two points in our favor," Colin continued. "No official funds are involved, so we can't be criticized for using government money. And let's have no false modesty—Earth will *expect* a Makenzie. It might even be regarded as an insult if one of us didn't go. And as Duncan is the only possibility, that settles the matter."

"You're perfectly correct, of course. But not everyone will see it that way. All the families will want to send their younger sons and daughters."

"There's nothing to stop them," Duncan interjected.

"How many could afford it? *We* couldn't."

"We could if we didn't have some expensive extras in mind. So can the Tanaka-Smiths, the Mohadeens, the Schwartzes, the Deweys . . ."

"But not, I believe, the Helmers."

Colin spoke lightly, but without humor, and there was a long silence while all three Makenzies shared a single thought. Then Malcolm said slowly: "Don't underrate Karl. We have only power and brains. But he has genius, and that's always unpredictable."

"But he's crazy," protested Duncan. "The last time we met, he tried to convince me that there's intelligent life on Saturn."

"Did he succeed?"

"Almost."

"If he's crazy—which I doubt, despite that famous breakdown—then he's even more dangerous. Especially to *you,* Duncan."

Duncan made no attempt to answer. His wiser and older twins understood his feelings, even if they could never fully share them.

"There is one other point," said Malcolm thoughtfully, "and it may be the most important of all. We may have only ten years in which to change the whole basis of our economy. If you can find an answer to this problem on your trip—even a *hint* of an answer!—you'll be a hero when you come home. No one will criticize any of your other activities, public or private."

"That's a tall order. I'm not a magician."

"Then perhaps you'd better start taking lessons. If the Asymptotic Drive isn't pure magic, I don't know what it is."

"Just a minute!" said Colin. "Isn't the first A-Drive ship going to be here in a few weeks?"

"The second. There was that freighter, *Fomalhaut.* I went aboard, but they wouldn't let me see anything. *Sirius* is the first passenger liner—she enters parking orbit—oh—in about thirty days."

"Could you be ready by then, Duncan?"

"I very much doubt it."

"Of course you can."

"I mean *physiologically*. Even on a crash program, it takes months to prepare for Earth gravity."

"Um. But this is far too good an opportunity to miss—everything is falling into place beautifully. After all, you were born on Earth."

"So were you. And how long did *you* take to get ready when you went back?"

Colin sighed.

"It seemed like ages, but by now they must have improved the techniques. Don't they have neuroprogramming while you sleep?"

"It's supposed to give you horrible dreams, and I'll need all the sleep I can get. Still, what's good for Titan . . ."

He had no need to complete the quotation, which had been coined by some unknown cynic half a century ago. In thirty years, Duncan had never really doubted this old cliché—once intended to wound, now virtually adopted as a family motto.

What was good for the Makenzies was indeed good for Titan.

4

THE RED MOON

Of the eighty-five known natural satellites, only Ganymede, lord of the Jovian system, exceeds Titan in size—and that by a narrow margin. But in another respect Titan has no rivals; no other moon of *any* planet has more than a trace of atmosphere. Titan's is so dense that if it were made of oxygen, it would be easy for a man to breathe.

When this fact was discovered, late in the twentieth century, it presented the astronomers with a first-class mystery. Why should a world not much larger than the Earth's totally airless Moon be able to hold on to *any* atmosphere—particularly one rich in hydrogen, lightest of all gases? It should long ago have leaked away into space.

Nor was that the only enigma. Like the Moon, almost all other satellites are virtually colorless, covered with rock and dust shattered by ages of meteoric bombardment. But Titan is *red*—as red as Mars, whose baleful glare reminded men in ancient times of bloodshed and of war.

The first robot probes solved some of Titan's mysteries, but, as is always the case, raised a host of new problems. The red color came from a layer of low, thick clouds, made from much the same bewildering mixture of organic compounds as the Great Red Spot of Jupiter. Beneath those clouds was a world more than a hundred degrees hotter than it had any right to be; indeed, there were regions of Titan where a man needed little more than an oxygen mask and a simple thermofoil suit to move around in the open. To everyone's great surprise, Titan had turned out to be the most hospitable place in the Solar System, next to Earth itself.

16

Part of this unexpected warmth came from the greenhouse effect, as the hydrogenous atmosphere trapped the feeble rays of the distant sun. But a good deal more was due to internal sources; the equatorial region of Titan abounded in what, for want of a better phrase, might be called cold volcanoes. On rare occasions, indeed, some of them actually erupted liquid water.

This activity, triggered by radioactive heat generated deep in the core of Titan, spewed megatons of hydrogen compounds into the atmosphere, and so continually made up for the leakage into space. One day, of course, the bruised reserves—like the lost oil fields of Earth—would all be gone, but the geologists had calculated that Titan could hold the vacuum of space at bay for at least two billion years. Man's most vigorous atmospheric mining activities would have only a negligible influence on this figure.

Like the Earth, Titan has distinct seasons—though it is difficult to apply the word "summer" where the temperature at high noon seldom climbs to fifty below. And as Saturn takes almost thirty years to circle the sun, each of the Titanian seasons is more than seven Terran years in length.

The tiny sun, taking eight days to cross the sky, is seldom visible through the cloud cover, and there is very little temperature difference between day and night—or, for that matter, between Poles and Equator. Titan thus lacks climate; but it can, on occasion, produce its own quite spectacular brand of weather.

The most impressive meteorological phenomenon is the so-called Methane Monsoon, which often—though not invariably—occurs with the onset of spring in the northern hemisphere. During the long winter, some of the methane in the atmosphere condenses in local cold spots and forms shallow lakes, up to a thousand kilometers square but seldom more than a few meters deep, and often covered with fantastically shaped bergs and floes of ammonia ice. However, it requires the exceedingly low temperature of minus a hundred and sixty to keep methane liquefied, and no part of Titan is ever that cold for very long.

17

A "warm" wind, or a break in the clouds—and the methane lakes will flash suddenly into vapor. It is as if, on Earth, one of the oceans were to evaporate, abruptly increasing its volume hundreds of times and so completely changing the state of the atmosphere. The result would be catastrophic, and on Titan it is sometimes scarcely less so. Wind speeds of up to five hundred kilometers an hour have been recorded —or to be accurate, estimated from their aftereffects. They last only for a few minutes; but that is quite long enough. Several of the early expeditions were annihilated by the monsoon, before it became possible to predict its onset.

Before the first landings on Titan, at the beginning of the twenty-first century, some optimistic exobiologists had hoped to find life around the relatively warm oases that were known to exist. This hope was slow to fade, and for a while it was revived by the discovery of the strange wax formations of the famous Crystal Caves. But by the end of the century, it was quite certain that no indigenous life forms had ever existed on Titan.

There had never been any expectation of finding life on the other moons, where conditions were far more hostile. Only Iapetus and Rhea, less than half the size of Titan, had even a trace of atmosphere. The remaining satellites were barren aggregates of rock, overgrown snowballs, or mixtures of both. By the mid-2200's, more than forty had been discovered, the majority of them less than a hundred kilometers in diameter. The outer ones—twenty million kilometers from Saturn—all moved in retrograde orbits and were clearly temporary visitors from the asteriod belt; there was much argument as to whether they should be counted as genuine satellites at all. Though some had been explored by geologists, many had never been examined, except by robot space probes, but there was no reason to suppose that they held any great surprises.

Perhaps one day, when Titan was prosperous and getting a little dull, future generations would take up the challenge of these tiny worlds. Some optimists had talked of turning the carbon-rich snowballs into or-

bital zoos, basking beneath the warmth of their own
fusion suns and teeming with strange life forms.
Others had dreamed of private pleasure domes and
low-gravity resorts, and islands in space for experiments in super-technology life styles. But these were
fantasies of a Utopian future; Titan needed all its
energies now to solve its coming crisis, in this demimil-
lennial year of 2276.

5

THE POLITICS OF TIME AND SPACE

Then only two Makenzies were talking
together, their conversation was even more terse and
telegraphic than when all three were present. Intuition, parallel thought processes, and shared experience filled in gaps that would have made much of
their discourse wholly unintelligible to outsiders.

"Handle?" asked Malcolm.

"We?!" retorted Colin.

"Thirty-one? Boy!"

Which might be translated into plain English as:

"Do you think he can handle the job?"

"Have you any doubts that *we* could?"

"At thirty-one? I'm not so sure. He's only a boy."

"Anyway, we've no choice. This is a God-sent—
or Washington-sent—opportunity that we can't afford
to miss. He'll have to get a crash briefing on Terran
affairs, learn all that's necessary about the United
States . . ."

"That reminds me—what *is* the United States these
days? I've lost count."

"Now there are forty-five states—Texas, New Mex-
ico, Alaska, and Hawaii have rejoined the Union, at
least for the Centennial year."

"Just what does that mean, legally?"

"Not very much. They pretend to be autonomous,

but pay their regional and global taxes like everyone else. It's a typical Terran compromise."

Malcolm, remembering his origins, sometimes found it necessary to defend his native world against such cynical remarks.

"I often wish we had a little more Terran compromise here. It would be nice to inject some into Cousin Armand."

Armand Helmer, Controller of Resources, was not in fact a cousin of Malcolm's, but a nephew of his ex-wife, Ellen. However, in the closed little world of Titan everyone except recent immigrants was related to everybody else, and the designations "uncle," "aunt," "nephew," "cousin" were tossed around with cheerful inaccuracy.

"Cousin Armand," said Colin with some satisfaction, "is going to be very upset when he learns that Duncan is on his way to Earth."

"And what will he do about it?" Malcolm asked softly.

It was a good question, and for a moment both Makenzies brooded over the deepening rivalry between their family and the Helmers. In some ways, it was commonplace enough; both Armand and his son, Karl, were Terran-born, and had brought with them across a billion kilometers that maddening aura of superiority that was so often the hallmark of the mother world. Some immigrants eventually managed to eradicate it, though the process was difficult. Malcolm Makenzie had succeeded only after three planets and a hundred years, but the Helmers had never even tried. And although Karl had been only five years old when he left Earth, he seemed to have spent the subsequent thirty trying to become more Terran than the Terrans. Nor could it have been a coincidence that all his wives had been from Earth.

Yet this had been a matter of amusement, rather than annoyance, until only a dozen years ago. As boys, Duncan and Karl had been inseparable, and there had been no cause for conflict between the families until Armand's swift rise through the technological hierarchy of Titan had brought him into a position of power. Now the Controller did not bother

20

to conceal his belief that three generations of Makenzies were enough. Whether or not he had actually coined the famous "What's good for the Makenzies . . ." phrase, he certainly quoted it with relish.

To do Armand justice, his ambitions seemed more concentrated on his only son than on himself. That alone would have been sufficient to put some strains on the friendship between Karl and Duncan, but it would probably have survived paternal pressures from either direction. What had caused the final rift was still something of a mystery, and was associated with a psychological breakdown that Karl had experienced fifteen years ago.

He had emerged from it with all his abilities intact, but with a marked change of personality. After graduating with honors at the University of Titan, he had become involved in a whole range of research activities, from measurements of galactic radio waves to studies of the magnetic fields around Saturn. All this work had some practical relevance, and Karl had also played a valuable role in the establishment and maintenance of the communications network upon which Titanian life depended. It would be true to say, however, that his interests were theoretical rather than practical, and he sometimes tried to exploit this whenever the old "Two Cultures" debate raised its hoary head.

Despite a couple of centuries of invective from both sides, no one really believed that Scientists, with a capital S, were more cultured (whatever *that* meant) than Engineers. The purity of theoretical knowledge was a philosophical aberration which would have been laughed out of court by those Greek thinkers who had had it foisted on them more than a thousand years earlier. The fact that the greatest sculptor on Earth had begun his career as a bridge designer, and the best violinist on Mars was still doing original work in the theory of numbers, proved exactly nothing one way or the other. But the Helmers liked to argue that it was time for a change; the engineers had run Titan for long enough, and *they* had the perfect replacement, who would bring intellectual distinction to his world.

21

At thirty-six, Karl still possessed the charm that had captivated all his peers, but it seemed to many—and certainly to Duncan—that this was now underlined by something hard, calculating, and faintly repellent. He could still be loved, but he had lost the ability to love; and it was strange that none of his spectacular marriages had produced any offspring.

If Armand hoped to challenge the Makenzie regime, Karl's lack of an heir was not his only problem. Whatever the Seven Worlds might say about their independence, the center of power was still on Earth. As, two thousand years ago, men had once gone to Rome in search of justice, or prestige, or knowledge, so in this age the Imperial planet called to its scattered children. No man could be taken seriously in the arena of Solar politics unless he was personally acquainted with the key figures of Terran affairs, and had traced his way at least once through the labyrinth of the terrestrial bureaucracy.

And to do this, one *had* to go to Earth; as in the days of the Caesars, there was no alternative. Those who believed otherwise—or pretended to—risked being tagged with the dreaded word "colonial."

It might have been different if the velocity of light were infinite; but it was a mere billion kilometers an hour—and therefore, real-time conversation would be forever impossible between Earth and anyone beyond the orbit of the Moon. The global electronic village which had existed for centuries on the mother world could never be extended into space; the political and psychological effects of this were enormous, and still not fully understood.

For generations, earth-dwellers had been accustomed to being in each other's presence at the touch of a button. The communications satellites had made possible, and then inevitable, the creation of the World State in all but name. And despite many earlier fears, it was a state still controlled by men, not by machines.

There were perhaps a thousand key individuals, and ten thousand important ones—and they talked to each other incessantly from Pole to Pole. The decisions needed to run a world sometimes had to be made in minutes, and for this the instantaneous feedback of face-to-face conversation was essential. Across a reaction of a light-second, that was easy to arrange, and for three hundred years men had taken it for granted that distance could no longer bar them from each other.

But with the establishment of the first Mars Base, this intimacy had ended. Earth could talk to Mars— but its words would always take at least three minutes to get there, and the reply would take just as long. Conversation was thus impossible, and all business had to be done by Telex or its equivalent.

In theory, this should have been good enough, and usually it was. But there were disastrous exceptions— costly and sometimes fatal interplanetary misunderstandings resulting from the fact that the two men at the opposite ends of the circuit did not really know each other, or comprehend each other's ways of thought, because they had never been in personal contact.

And personal contact was essential at the highest levels of statesmanship and administration. Diplomats had known this for several thousand years, with their apparatus of missions and envoys and official visits. Only after that contact, with its inevitable character evaluation, had been made, and the subtle links of mutual understanding and common interest established, could one do business by long-distance communications with any degree of confidence.

Malcolm Makenzie could never have achieved his own rise on Titan without the friendships made when he had returned to Earth. Once he had thought it strange that a personal tragedy should have led him to power and responsibility beyond all the dreams of his youth; but unlike Ellen, he had buried his dead past and it had ceased to haunt him long ago.

When Colin had repeated the pattern, forty years later, and had returned to Titan with the infant Duncan, the position of the clan had been immensely strengthened. To most of the human race, Saturn's largest moon was now virtually identified with the Makenzies. No one could hope to challenge them if he could not match the network of personal contacts they had established not only on Earth, but everywhere else that mattered. It was through this network, rather than official channels, that the Makenzies, as even their opponents grudgingly admitted, Got Things Done.

And now a fourth generation was being prepared to consolidate the dynasty. Everyone knew that this would happen eventually, but no one had expected it so soon.

Not even the Makenzies. And especially not the Helmers.

6

BY THE BONNY, BONNY BANKS OF LOCH HELLBREW

In the past, Duncan had always cycled to Grandmother Ellen's home, or taken an electric cart whenever he had to deliver some household necessity. This time, however, he walked the two-kilometer tunnel from the city, carrying fifty kilos of carefully distributed mass—which, however, only gave him ten kilos of extra weight. Had he known that such characters had once existed, he might have felt a strong affinity with old-time smugglers, wearing a stylish waistcoat of gold bars.

Colin had presented him with the complex harness of webbing and pouches, with a heartfelt "Thank God I'll never have to use it again! I knew I had it around somewhere, but it took a couple of days to find. It's only too true that the Makenzies never throw anything away."

Duncan found that it needed both hands to lift the harness off the table; when he unzipped one of the many small pouches, he found that it contained a pencil-sized rod of dull metal, astonishingly massive.

"What is it?" he asked. "It feels heavier than gold."

"It is. Tungsten superalloy, if I remember. The

24

total mass is seventy kilos, but don't start wearing it all at once. I began at forty, and added a couple of kilos a day. The important thing is to keep the distribution uniform, and to avoid chafing."

Duncan was doing some mental arithmetic, and finding the results very depressing. Earth gravity was *five* times Titan's—yet this diabolical device would merely double his local weight.

"It's impossible," he said gloomily. "I'll never be able to walk on Earth."

"Well, *I* did—though it wasn't easy at first. Do everything that the doctors tell you, even if it sounds silly. Spend all the time you can in baths, or lying down. Don't be ashamed to use wheelchairs or prosthetic devices, at least for the first couple of weeks. And never try to run."

"Run!"

"Sooner or later you'll forget you're on Earth, and then you'll break a leg. Like to bet on it?"

Betting was one of the useful Makenzie vices. The money stayed in the family, and the loser always learned some valuable lesson. Though Duncan found it impossible to imagine five gravities, it could not be denied that Colin had spent a year on Earth and had survived to tell the tale. So this was not a bet that promised favorable odds.

Now he was beginning to believe Colin's prediction, and he scarcely noticed the extra mass—at least when he was moving in a straight line. It was only when he tried to change direction that he felt himself in the grip of some irresistible force. Not counting visitors from Earth, he was probably now the strongest man on Titan. It was not that his body was developing new strength; rather, it was recovering latent powers which had been slumbering, waiting for the moment when they would be called forth. In a few more years, what he was now attempting would be too late.

The four-meter-wide tunnel had been lasered, years ago, through the rim of the small crater which surrounded Oasis. Originally, it had been a pipeline for the ammoniated petrochemicals of the aptly named Loch Hellbrew, one of the region's chief natural resources. Most of the lake had gone to feed the industries of Titan; later, the tapping of the moon's internal heat, as part of the local planetary engineering project, had caused the remainder to evaporate.

There had been a certain amount of quiet grumbling when Ellen Makenzie had made her intentions clear, but the Department of Resources had pumped the remaining hydrogen-methane fog out of the tunnel, and now carried its oxygen, to the annual annoyance of the auditors, on inventory as part of the city's air reserve. There were two manually operated bulkheads, as well as the city's own backup seals. Anyone went beyond the second bulkhead at his own risk, but that was negligible. The tunnel was through solid rock, and since the pressure inside was higher than ambient, there was no danger of Titanian poisons leaking inward.

Half a dozen side tunnels, all of them now blocked, led out of the main passageway. When he had first come here as a small boy, Duncan had filled those sealed-off shafts with wonder and magic. Now he knew that they merely led to long-abandoned surge chambers. Yet though all the mystery was gone, it still seemed to him that these corridors were haunted by two ghosts. One was a little girl who had been known and loved by only a handful of pioneers; the other was a giant who had been mourned by millions.

There had been endless jokes about Robert Kleinman's name, for he was almost two meters tall, and porportioned accordingly. And his talents had matched his physique; he had been a master pilot at the age of thirty, despite the difficulty of fitting him into standard space equipment. Duncan had never considered him particularly good-looking, but in this matter he was outvoted by a small army of women—including Ellen Makenzie.

Grandma had met Captain Kleinman only a year after the final parting with Malcolm; she may have been on an emotional rebound, but *he* certainly was not. Yet thereafter the Captain had never looked at another woman, and it had become one of those love affairs famous on many worlds. It had lasted throughout the planning and preparations for the first expedition to Saturn and the fitting-out of the *Challenger* in orbit off Titan. And as far as Ellen Makenzie was concerned it had never died; it was frozen forever at the moment when the ship met its mysterious and still inexplicable doom, deep in the jet streams of the South Temperate Zone.

Moving rather more slowly than when he had started his walk, Duncan came to the final bulkhead. On Grandma's hundredth birthday, the younger members of the family had painted it in brilliant fluorescent colors, which had faded not at all in the last dozen years. Since Ellen had never referred to it, and never heard questions which she did not wish to answer, there was no way of discovering if she appreciated the gift.

"I'm here, Grandma," Duncan called into the antique intercom which had been presented to her by some anonymous admirer long ago. (It was still clearly marked "Made in Hong Kong," and had been dated *circa* 1995. Shameful to relate, there had been one attempt to steal it, though since theft was virtually unknown on Titan, this was probably only a childish prank or an anti-Makenzie gesture.)

There was, as usual, no reply, but the door unlatched at once and Duncan walked through into the tiny foyer. Grandma's electrocycle occupied the place from which it had not moved for years. Duncan checked the battery and kicked the tires, as he always did with great conscientiousness. No need for any pumping or charging this time; if the old lady suddenly felt the impulse to descend upon the city, there was nothing to prevent her.

The kitchen, which was a unit lifted intact from a small orbital passenger shuttle, was a little tidier than usual. Presumably one of the voluntary helpers had just made her weekly visit. Nevertheless, the usual sickly sour smell of slow culinary disintegration and inadequate recycling was heavy in the air, and Duncan held his breath as he hurried through into the living room. He never accepted more than a cup of coffee from Grandma, and feared accidental poisoning if he ever sampled the products of her robot reconstituter. But Ellen seemed to thrive on it; over the years she must have established some kind of symbiosis with her kitchen. It still lived up to the manufacturer's "fail-safe" guarantee, even though it did produce the most peculiar odors. Doubtless Grandma never noticed them. Duncan wondered what she would do when the final disaster occurred.

The main living room was as crowded as ever. Against one wall were the shelves of carefully labeled rocks—a complete mineralogy of Titan and the other examined moons of Saturn, as well as samples from each of the rings. As long as Duncan could remember, there had been just one section empty, as if, even now, Grandma was still waiting for Kleinman to return.

The opposite wall was more sparsely occupied with communications and information equipment, and racks of micromodules which, if completely saturated, could have held more knowledge than all the libraries of Earth up to the twenty-first century. The rest of the room was a compact little workshop, most of the floor space being occupied by the machines that had fascinated Duncan throughout his childhood, and that he would associate with Grandma Ellen as long as he lived.

There were petrological microscopes, polishing and cutting tools, ultrasonic cleaners, laser knives, and all the shining paraphernalia of gemologist and jeweler. Duncan had learned to use most of them, over the years, though he had never acquired more than a fraction of his grandmother's skill and almost wholly lacked her artistic talents. What he did share, to a much greater extent, were her mathematical interests, exemplified by the small computer and associated holographic display.

The computer, like the kitchen, was long overdue for retirement. But it was completely autonomous, so Grandma did not have to rely in any way upon the immensely larger storage facilities in the city. Although her computer had a memory scarcely larger than that of a human brain, it was sufficient for her rather modest purposes. Her interest in minerals had led her, inevitably, to crystallography, then to group theory, and then to the harmless obsession that had dominated so much of her lonely existence. Twenty years ago, in this same room, she had infected Duncan with it. In his case, the disease was no longer virulent, having run its course in a few months; but he knew, with amused tolerance, that he would suffer occasional relapses throughout his life. How incredible that five perfectly identical squares could create a universe that neither man nor computer would ever be able to explore fully. . . .

Nothing in the familiar room had changed since his last visit, three weeks ago. He could even imagine that Grandma had not moved; she was still sitting at her worktable, sorting rocks and crystals, while behind her the read-out screen intermittently flashed solutions of some problem the computer was analyzing. She was, as usual, wearing a long gown that made her look like a Roman matron, though Duncan was quite sure that no Roman matron's dress ever appeared quite so disheveled or, to be perfectly frank, so overdue for the laundry. While Duncan had known her, Ellen's care of her equipment had never extended to her personal appearance.

She did not rise, but tilted her head slightly so that he could deliver his usual affectionate kiss. As he did so, he noticed that the external world, at least, had been touched by change.

The view from Grandma's picture window was famous—but by reputation only, since few indeed had been privileged to see it with their own eyes. Her home was partly countersunk into a ledge overlooking the dried-up bed of Loch Hellbrew and the canyon that led into it, so it presented her with a 180-degree panorama of Titan's most picturesque landscape. Sometimes, when storms raged through the mountains, the view disappeared for hours behind clouds of ammonia crystals. But today the weather was clear and Duncan could see for at least twenty kilometers.

"What's happening over there?" he asked.

At first, he had thought it was one of the fire fountains that sometimes erupted in unstable areas; but in that case the city would have been in danger, and he would have heard of it long ago. Then he realized that the brilliant yet smoky column of light burning steadily on the hill crest three or four kilometers away could only be man-made.

"There's a fusor running over at Huygens. I don't know what they're doing, but that's the oxygen burn-off."

"Oh, one of Armand's projects. Doesn't it annoy you?"

"No—I think it's beautiful. Besides, we need the water. Look at those rain clouds . . . *real* rain. And I think there's something growing over there. I've noticed a change in color on the rocks since that flame started burning."

"That's quite possible—the bioengineering people will know all about it. One day you may have a forest to look at, instead of all this bare rock."

He was joking, of course, and she knew it. Except in very restricted areas, no vegetation could grow here in the open. But experiments like this were a beginning, and one day . . .

Over there in the mountain, a hydrogen fusion plant was at work, melting down the crust of Titan to release all the elements needed for the industries of the little world. And as half that crust consisted of oxygen, now needed only in very small quantities in the closed-cycle economies of the cities, it was simply allowed to burn off.

"Do you realize, Duncan," said Grandma suddenly, "how neatly that flame symbolizes the difference between Titan and Earth?"

"Well, they don't have to melt rocks there to get everything they need."

"I was thinking of something much more fundamental. If a Terran wants a fire, he ignites a jet of hydrocarbons and lets it burn. We do exactly the opposite. We set fire to a jet of oxygen, and let it burn in our hydromethane atmosphere."

This was such an elementary fact of life—indeed an ecological platitude—that Duncan felt disappointed; he had hoped for some more startling revelation. His face must have reflected his thoughts, for Grandma gave him no chance to comment.

"What I'm trying to tell you," she said, "is that it may not be as easy for you to adjust to Earth as you imagine. You may know—or *think* you know—what conditions are like there, but that knowledge isn't based on experience. When you need it in a hurry, it won't be there. Your Titan instincts may give the wrong answers. So act slowly, and always think twice before you move."

"I've no choice about acting slowly—my Titan muscles will see to that."

"How long will you be gone?"

"About a year. My official invitation is for two months, but now the trip's being paid for, I'll have funds for a much longer stay. And it seems a pity to waste the opportunity, since it's my only one."

He tried to keep his voice as cheerfully optimistic as he could, though he knew perfectly well the thoughts that must be passing through Grandma's mind. They were both aware that this might be their last meeting. One hundred fourteen was not an excessive age for a woman—but, truly, what did Grandma have to live for? The hope of seeing him again, when he returned from Earth? He liked to think so. . . .

And there was another matter, never to be referred to, yet hovering in the background. Grandma knew perfectly well the main purpose of his visit to Earth, and the knowledge must, even after all these years, be like a dagger in her heart. She had never forgiven Malcolm; she had never accepted Colin; would she continue to accept him when he returned with little Malcolm?

Now she was hunting around, with a clumsiness quite unlike her normal precise movements, in one of the cubbyholes of her work desk.

"Here's a souvenir to take with you."

"What—oh, it's beautiful!" He was not being excessively polite; sheer surprise had forced the reaction from him. The flat, crystal-lidded box he was now holding in his hands was, indeed, one of the most exquisite works of geometrical art he had ever seen. And Grandma could not have chosen any single object more evocative of his youth and of the world that, though he was now about to leave it, must always be his home.

As he stared at the mosaic of colored stones that

exactly filled the little box, greeting each of the familiar shapes like an old friend, his eyes misted and the years seemed to roll away. Grandma had not changed; but he was only ten. . . .

7

A CROSS OF TITANITE

"You're old enough now, Duncan, to understand this game . . . though it's very much more than a game."

Whatever it is, thought Duncan, it doesn't look very exciting. What can you do with five identical squares of white plastic, a couple of centimeters on a side?

"Now the first problem," continued Grandma, "is to see how many *different* patterns you can make, by putting all these squares together."

"While they lie flat on the table?"

"Yes, with the edges matching exactly—overlapping isn't allowed."

Duncan started to shuffle the squares.

"Well," he began, "I can put them all in a straight line like this . . . then I can switch the end one to make an L . . . and the one at the *other* end to make a U. . . ."

He quickly produced half a dozen different assemblies of the five squares, then found that he was repeating himself.

"I think that's all—oh, stupid of me."

He had missed the most obvious figure of all—the cross, or X, formed by putting one square in the middle and the other four surrounding it.

"Most people," said Grandma, "find *that* one first. I don't know what this proves about your mental processes. Do you think you've found them all?"

Duncan continued to slide the squares around, and

eventually discovered three more figures. Then he gave up.

"That's the lot," he announced confidently.

"Then what about *this* one?" said Grandma, moving the squares swiftly to make a figure that looked like a humpbacked F.

"Oh!"

"And this . . ."

Duncan began to feel very foolish, and was much relieved when Grandma continued: "You did fairly well—you only missed these two. Altogether, there are exactly *twelve* of these patterns—no more and no less. Here they are. You could hunt forever—you won't find another one."

She brushed aside the five little squares, and laid on the table a dozen brightly colored pieces of plastic. Each was different in shape, and together they formed the complete set of twelve figures that, Duncan was now quite prepared to admit, were all that could be made from five equal squares.

But surely there must be more to it than this. The game couldn't have finished already. No, Grandma still had something up her sleeve.

"Now listen carefully, Duncan. Each of these figures—they're called pentominoes, by the way—is obviously the same size, since they're all made from five identical squares. And there are twelve of them, so the *total* area is sixty squares. Right?"

"Um . . . yes."

"Now sixty is a nice round number, which you can split up in lots of ways. Let's start with ten multiplied by six, the easiest one. That's the area of this little box—ten units by six units. So the twelve pieces should fit exactly into it, like a simple jigsaw puzzle."

Duncan looked for traps—Grandma had a fondness for verbal and mathematical paradoxes, not all of them comprehensible to a ten-year-old victim—but he could find none. If the box was indeed the size Grandma said, then the twelve pieces should just fit into it. After all, both were sixty units in area.

Wait a minute . . . the area might be the same, but the *shape* could be wrong. There might be no way of

33

making the twelve pieces fit this rectangular box, even though it was the right size.

"I'll leave you to it," said Grandma, after he had shuffled pieces around for a few minutes. "But I promise you this—it *can* be done."

Ten minutes later, Duncan was beginning to doubt it. It was easy enough to fit ten of the pieces into the frame—and once he had managed eleven. Unfortunately, the hole then left in the jigsaw was not the same shape as the piece that remained in his hand —even though, of course, it was of exactly the same area. The hole was an X, the piece was a Z. . . .

Thirty minutes later, he was fairly bursting with frustration. Grandma had left him completely alone, while she conducted an earnest dialogue with her computer; but from time to time she gave him an amused glance, as if to say "See—it isn't as easy as you thought. . . ."

Duncan was stubborn for his age. Most boys of ten would have given up long ago. (It never occurred to him, until years later, that Grandma was also doing a neat job of psychological testing.) He did not appeal for help for almost forty minutes. . . .

Grandma's fingers flickered over the mosaic. The U and X and L slid around inside their restraining frame—and suddenly the little box was exactly full. The twelve pieces had been perfectly fitted into the jig-saw.

"Well, you knew the answer!" said Duncan, rather lamely.

"*The* answer?" retorted Grandma. "Would you care to guess how many *different* ways those pieces can be fitted into their box?"

There was a catch here—Duncan was sure of it. He hadn't found a single solution in almost an hour of effort—and he must have tried at least a hundred arrangements. But it was possible that there might be—oh—a dozen different answers.

"I'd guess there might be twenty ways of putting those pieces into the box," he replied, determined to be on the safe side.

"Try again."

That was a danger signal. Obviously, there was

much more to this business than met the eye, and it would be safer not to commit himself.

Duncan shook his head.

"I can't imagine."

"Sensible boy. Intuition is a dangerous guide—though sometimes it's the only one we have. *Nobody* could ever guess the right answer. There are more than *two thousand* distinct ways of putting these twelve pieces back into their box. To be precise, 2,339. What do you think of that?"

It was not likely that Grandma was lying to him, yet Duncan felt so humiliated by his total failure to find even one solution that he blurted out: "I don't believe it!"

Grandma seldom showed annoyance, though she could become cold and withdrawn when he had offended her. This time, however, she merely laughed and punched out some instructions to the computer.

"Look at that," she said.

A pattern of bright lines had appeared on the screen, showing the set of all twelve pentominoes fitted into the six-by-ten frame. It held for a few seconds, then was replaced by another obviously different, though Duncan could not possibly remember the arrangement briefly presented to him. Then came another . . . and another, until Grandma canceled the program.

"Even at this fast rate," she said, "it takes five hours to run through them all. And take my word for it—though no human being has ever checked each one, or ever could—they're all different."

For a long time, Duncan stared at the collection of twelve deceptively simple figures. As he slowly assimilated what Grandma had told him, he had the first genuine mathematical revelation of his life. What had at first seemed merely a childish game had opened endless vistas and horizons—though even the brightest of ten-year-olds could not begin to guess the full extent of the universe now opening up before him.

This moment of dawning wonder and awe was purely passive; a far more intense explosion of intellectual delight occurred when he found his first very own solution to the problem. For weeks he carried around with him the set of twelve pentominoes in their plastic box, playing with them at every odd moment. He got to know each of the dozen shapes as personal friends, calling them by the letters which they most resembled, though in some cases with a good deal of imaginative distortion: the odd group, F, I, L, P, N and the ultimate alphabetical sequence T, U, V, W, X, Y, Z.

And once in a sort of geometrical trance or ecstasy which he was never able to repeat, he discovered five solutions in less than an hour. Newton and Einstein and Chen-tsu could have felt no greater kinship with the gods of mathematics in their own moments of truth. . . .

It did not take him long to realize, without any prompting from Grandma, that it might also be possible to arrange the pieces in other shapes besides the six-by-ten rectangle. In theory, at least, the twelve pentominoes could exactnly cover rectangles with sides of five-by-twelve units, four-by-fifteen units, and even the narrow strip only three units wide and twenty long.

Without too much effort, he found several examples of the five-by-twelve and four-by-fifteen rectangles. Then he spent a frustrating week, trying to align the dozen pieces into a perfect three-by-twenty strip. Again and again he produced shorter rectangles, but always there were a few pieces left over, and at last he decided that this shape was impossible.

Defeated, he went back to Grandma—and received another surprise.

"I'm glad you made the effort," she said. "Generalizing—exploring every possibility—is what mathematics is all about. But you're wrong. It *can* be done. There are just two solutions; and if you find one, you'll also have the other."

Encouraged, Duncan continued the hunt with renewed vigor. After another week, he began to realize the magnitude of the problem. The number of distinct ways in which a mere twelve objects could be laid out essentially in a straight line, when one also allowed for the fact that most of them could assume at least four different orientations, was staggering.

Once again, he appealed to Grandma, pointing out the unfairness of the odds. If there were only two solutions, how long would it take to find them?

"I'll tell you," she said. "If you were a brainless computer, and put down the pieces at the rate of one a second in every possible way, you could run through the whole set in"—she paused for effect—"rather more than six million, *million* years."

Earth years or Titan years? thought the appalled Duncan. Not that it really mattered . . .

"But you aren't a brainless computer," continued Grandma. "You can see at a glance whole categories that won't fit into the pattern, so you don't have to bother about them. Try again. . . ."

Duncan obeyed, though without much enthusiasm or success. And then he had a brilliant idea.

Karl was interested, and accepted the challenge at once. He took the set of pentominoes, and that was the last Duncan heard of him for several hours.

Then he called back, looking a little flustered.

"Are you *sure* it can be done?" he demanded.

"Absolutely. In fact, there are two solutions. Haven't you found even one? I thought you were good in mathematics."

"So I am. *That's* why I know how tough the job is. There are over a quadrillion possible arrangements to be checked."

"How do you work that out?" asked Duncan, delighted to discover something that had baffled his friend.

Karl looked at a piece of paper covered with sketches and numbers.

"Well, excluding forbidden positions, and allowing for symmetry and rotation, it comes to factorial twelve times two to the twenty-first—*you* wouldn't understand why! That's quite a number; here it is."

He held up a sheet on which he had written, in large figures, the imposing array of digits:

$$1 \quad 004 \quad 539 \quad 160 \quad 000 \quad 000$$

Duncan looked at the number with satisfaction; he did not doubt Karl's arithmetic.

"So you've given up."

"*NO!* I'm just telling you how hard it is." And Karl, looking grimly determined, switched off.

The next day, Duncan had one of the biggest surprises of his young life. A bleary-eyed Karl, who had obviously not slept since their last conversation, appeared on his screen.

"Here it is," he said, exhaustion and triumph competing in his voice.

Duncan could hardly believe his eyes; he had been convinced that the odds against success were impossibly great. But there was the narrow rectangular strip, only three squares wide and twenty long, formed from the complete set of twelve pieces. . . .

With fingers that trembled slightly from fatigue, Karl took the two end sections and switched them around, leaving the center portion of the puzzle untouched.

"And here's the second solution," he said. "Now I'm going to bed. Good night—or good morning, if that's what it is."

For a long time, a very chastened Duncan sat staring at the blank screen. He did not yet understand what had happened. He only knew that Karl had won against all reasonable expectations.

It was not that Duncan really minded; he loved Karl too much to resent his little victory, and indeed was capable of rejoicing in his friend's triumphs even when they were at his own expense. But there was something strange here, something almost magical.

It was Duncan's first glimpse of the power of intuition, and the mind's mysterious ability to go beyond the available facts and to short-circuit the process of logic. In a few hours, Karl had completed a search that should have required trillions of operations, and would have tied up the fastest computer in existence for an appreciable number of seconds.

One day, Duncan would realize that all men had such powers, but might use them only once in a lifetime. In Karl, the gift was exceptionally well developed; from that moment onward, Duncan had learned to take seriously even his most outrageous speculations.

38

That was twenty years ago; whatever had happened to that little set of plastic figures? He could not remember when he had last seen it.

But here it was again, reincarnated in colored minerals—the peculiar rose-tinted granite from the Galileo Hills, the obsidian of the Huygens Plateau, the pseudomarble of the Herschel Escarpment. And there—it was unbelievable, but doubt was impossible in such a matter—was the rarest and most mysterious of all the gemstones found on this world. The X of the puzzle was made of Titanite itself; no one could ever mistake that blue-black sheen with its fugitive flecks of gold. It was the largest piece that Duncan had ever seen, and he could not even guess at its value.

"I don't know what to say," he stammered. "It's beautiful—I've never seen anything like it."

He put his arms around Grandma's thin shoulders —and found, to his distress, that they were quivering uncontrollably. He held her gently until the shaking stopped, knowing that there were no words for such moments, and realizing as never before that he was the last love of her empty life, and he was leaving her to her memories.

8

CHILDREN OF THE CORRIDORS

There was a sense of sadness and finality about almost everything that he did in these last days. Sometimes it puzzled Duncan; he should be excited, anticipating the great adventure that only a handful of men on his world could ever share. And though he had never before been out of touch with his friends and family for more than a few hours, he was certain that a year's absence would pass swiftly enough, among the wonders and distractions of Earth.

So why this melancholy? If he was saying farewell to the things of his youth, it was only for a little while, and he would appreciate them all the more when he returned. . . .

When he returned. That, of course, was the heart of the problem. In a real sense, the Duncan Makenzie who was now leaving Titan would never return; indeed, that was the purpose of the exercise. Like Colin thirty years ago, and Malcolm forty years before that, he was heading sunward in search of knowledge, of power, of maturity—and, above all, of the successor which his own world could never give him. For, of course, being Malcolm's duplicate, he too carried in his loins the fatal Makenzie gene.

Sooner than he had expected, he had to prepare his family for the new addition. After the usual number of earlier experiments, he had settled down with Marissa four years ago, and he loved her children as much, he was certain, as if they had been his own flesh and blood. Clyde was now six years old, Caroline three. They in their turn appeared to be as fond of Duncan as of their real fathers, who were now regarded as honorary members of the Clan Makenzie. Much the same thing had happened in Colin's generation—he had acquired or adopted three families—and in Malcolm's. Grandfather had never gone to the trouble of marrying again after Ellen had left him, but he had never lacked company for long. Only a computer could keep track of the comings and goings on the periphery of the clan; it often seemed that most of Titan was related to it in some way or other. One of Duncan's major problems now was deciding who would be mortally offended if he failed to say good-bye.

Quite apart from the time factor, he had other reasons for making as few farewells as possible. Every one of his friends and relatives—as well as almost complete strangers—seemed to have some request for him, some mission they wanted him to carry out as soon as he reached Earth. Or, worse still, there was some essential item ("It won't be any trouble") they wanted him to bring back. Duncan calculated that he would have to charter a special freighter if he acquiesced to all these demands.

Every job now had to be divided into one of two categories. There were the things that *must* be done before he left Titan, and those that could be postponed until he was aboard ship. The latter included his studies of current terrestrial affairs, which kept slipping despite Colin's increasingly frantic attempts to update him.

Extricating himself from his official duties was also no easy task, and Duncan realized that in a few more years it would be well-nigh impossible. He was getting involved in too many things, though that was a matter of deliberate family policy. More than once he had complained that his title of Special Assistant to the Chief Administrator gave him responsibility without power. To this, Chief Administrator Colin had retorted: "Do you know what power means in our society? Giving orders to people who carry them out—only *if* and when they feel like it."

This was, of course, a gross libel on the Titanian bureaucracy, which functioned surprisingly well and with a minimum of red tape. Because all the key individuals knew each other, an immense amount of business got done through direct personal contact. Everyone who had come to Titan had been carefully selected for intelligence and ability, and knew that survival depended upon co-operation. Those who felt like abandoning their social responsibilities first had to practice breathing methane at a hundred below.

One possible embarrassment he had at least been spared. He could hardly leave Titan without saying good-bye to his once closest friend—but, very fortunately, Karl was off-world. Several months ago he had left on one of the shuttles to join a Terran survey ship working its way through the outer moons. Ironically enough, Duncan had envied Karl his chance of seeing some unknown worlds; now it was Karl who would be envious of him.

He could well imagine Karl's frustration when he heard that Duncan was on his way to Earth. The thought gave him more sadness than pleasure; the Makenzies, whatever their faults, were not vindic-

41

tive. Yet Duncan could not help wondering how often Karl's reveries would now turn sunward, and to the moment long ago when their emotions had been irrevocably linked with the mother world.

Duncan was just sixteen, and Karl twenty-one, when the cruise liner *Mentor* had made her first, and it was widely hoped only, rendezvous with Titan. She was a converted fusion-drive freighter—slow but economical, provided adequate supplies of hydrogen could be picked up at strategic points.

Mentor had stopped at Titan for her final refueling, on the last leg of a grand tour that had taken her to Mars, Ganymede, Europa, Pallas, and Iapetus, and had included fly-bys of Mercury and Eros. As soon as she had loaded some fifteen thousand tons of hydrogen, her exhausted crew planned to head back to Earth on the fastest orbit they could compute, if possible after marooning all the passengers.

The cruise must have seemed a good idea when a consortium of Terran universities had planned it several years earlier. And so indeed it had turned out, in the long run, for *Mentor* graduates had since proved their worth throughout the Solar System. But when the ship staggered into her parking orbit, under the command of a prematurely gray captain, the whole enterprise looked like a first-magnitude disaster.

The problems of keeping five hundred young adults entertained and out of mischief on a six-months' cruise aboard even the largest spaceliner had not been given sufficient thought; the law professor who had signed on as master-at-arms was later heard to complain bitterly about the complete absence from the ship's inventory of hypodermic guns and knockout gas. On the other hand, there had been no deaths or serious injuries, only one pregnancy, and everyone had learned a great deal, though not necessarily in the areas that the organizers had intended. The first few weeks, for example, were mostly occupied by experiments in zero-gravity sex, despite warnings that this was an expensive addiction for those compelled to spend most of their lives on planetary surfaces.

Other shipboard activities, it was widely believed, were not quite so harmless. There were reports of *tobacco*-smoking—not actually illegal, of course, but hardly sensible behaviour when there were so many safe alternatives. Even more alarming were persistent rumors that someone had smuggled an Emotion Amplifier on board *Mentor*. The so-called joy machines were banned on all planets, except under strict medical control; but there would always be people to whom reality was not good enough, and who would want to try something better.

Notwithstanding the horror stories radioed ahead from other ports of call, Titan had looked forward to welcoming its young visitors. It was felt that they would add color to the social scene, and help establish some enjoyable contacts with Mother Earth. And anyway, it would be for only a week. . . .

Luckily, no one dreamed that it would be for two months. This was not *Mentor's* fault; Titan had only itself to blame.

When *Mentor* fell into her parking orbit, Earth and Titan were involved in one of their periodical wrangles over the price of hydrogen, F.O.B. Zero Gravitational Potential (Solar Reference). The proposed 15 percent rise, screamed the Terrans, would cause the collapse of interplanetary commerce. Anything under 10 percent, swore the Titanians, would result in their instant bankruptcy and would make it impossible for them to import any of the expensive items Earth was always trying to sell. To any historian of economics, the whole debate was boringly familiar.

Unable to get a firm quotation, *Mentor* was stranded in orbit with empty fuel tanks. At first, her captain was not too unhappy; he and the crew could do with the rest, now that the passengers had shuttled down to Titan and had fanned out all over the face of the hapless satellite. But one week stretched into two, then three, then a month. By that time, Titan was ready to settle on almost any terms; unfortunately, *Mentor* had now missed her optimum trajectories, and it would be another four weeks before the next launch window opened. Meanwhile, the

43

five hundred guests were enjoying themselves, usually much more than their hosts.

But to the younger Titanians, it was an exciting time which they would remember all their lives. On a small world where everyone knew everybody else, half a thousand fascinating strangers had arrived, full of tales, many of them quite true, about the wonders of Earth. Here were men and women, barely into their twenties, who had seen forests and prairies and oceans of liquid water, who had strolled unprotected under an open sky beneath a sun whose heat could actually be felt. . . .

This very contrast in backgrounds, however, was a possible source of danger. The Terrans could not be allowed to go wandering around by themselves, even inside the habitats. They had to have escorts, preferably responsible people not too far from their own age group, to see that they did not inadvertently kill either themselves or their hosts.

Naturally, there were times when they resented this well-intentioned supervision, and even tried to escape from it. One group succeeded; it was very lucky, and suffered no more than a few searing whiffs of ammonia. Damage was so slight that the foolish adventurers required only routine lung transplants, but after this exploit there was no more serious trouble.

There were plenty of other problems. The sheer mechanics of absorbing five hundred visitors was a challenge to a society where living standards were still somewhat Spartan, and accommodation limited. At first, all the unexpected guests were housed in the complex of corridors left by an abandoned mining operation, hastily converted into dormitories. Then, as quickly as arrangements could be made, they were farmed out—like refugees from some bombed city in an ancient war—to any households that were able to cope with them. At this stage, there were still many willing volunteers, among them Colin and Sheela Makenzie.

The apartment was lonely, now that Duncan's pseudosibling Glynn had left home to work on the other side of Titan; Sheela's other child, Yuri, had been gone for a decade. Though Number 402, Second Level, Meridian Park was hardly spacious by Terran standards, Assistant Administrator Colin Makenzie, as he was then, had selected one of the homeless waifs for temporary adoption.

And so Calindy had come into Duncan's life—and into Karl's.

9

THE FATAL GIFT

Catherine Linden Ellerman had celebrated her twenty-first birthday just before *Mentor* reached Saturn. By all accounts, it had been a memorable party, giving the final silvery gloss to the captain's remaining hairs. Calindy would have sailed through untouched; next to her beauty, that was her most outstanding characteristic. In the midst of chaos— even chaos that she herself had generated—she was the calm center of the storm. With a self-possession far beyond her years, she seemed to young Duncan the very embodiment of Terran culture and sophistication. He could smile wryly, one and a half decades later, at his boyish naïveté; but it was not wholly unfounded. By any standards, Calindy was a remarkable phenomenon.

Duncan knew, of course, that all Terrans were rich. (How could it be otherwise, when each was the heir to a hundred thousand generations?) But he was overawed by Calindy's display of jewels and silks, never realizing that she had a limited wardrobe which she varied with consummate skill. Most impressive of all was a stunningly beautiful coat of golden fur—the only one ever seen on Titan—made from the skins of an animal called a mink. That was typical of Calindy; no one else would have dreamed of taking a fur coat aboard a spaceship. And she had not done so—as malicious rumor pretended—because she had heard

45

it was cold out around Saturn. She was much too intelligent for that kind of stupidity, and knew exactly what she was doing; she had brought her mink simply because it was beautiful.

Perhaps because he could see her only through a mist of adoration, Duncan could never visualize her, in later years, as an actual person. When he thought of Calindy, and tried to conjure up her image, he did not see the real girl, but always his only replica of her, in one of the bubble stereos that had become popular in the '50's.

How many thousands of times he had taken that apparently solid, yet almost weightless sphere in his hands, shaken it gently, and thus activated the five-second loop! Through the subtle magic of organized gas molecules, each releasing its programmed quantum of light, Calindy's face would appear out of the swirling mists—tiny, yet perfect in form and color. At first she would be in profile; then she would turn and suddenly—Duncan could never be sure of the moment when it arrived—there would be the faint smile that only Leonardo could have captured in an earlier age. She did not seem to be smiling at him, but at someone over his shoulder. The impression was so strong that more than once Duncan had looked back, startled, to see who was standing behind him.

Then the image would fade, the bubble would become opaque, and he would have to wait five minutes before the system recharged itself. It did not matter; he had only to close his eyes and he could still see the perfect oval face, the delicate ivory skin, the lustrous black hair gathered up into a toque and held in place by a silver comb that had belonged to a Spanish princess, when Columbus was a child. Calindy liked playing roles, though she took none of them too seriously, and Carmen was one of her favorites.

When she entered the Makenzie household, however, she was the exiled aristocrat, graciously accepting the hospitality of kindly provincials, with what few family heirlooms she had been able to save from the Revolution. As this impressed no one except Duncan, she quickly became the studious anthropologist, taking notes for her thesis on the quaint habits of primitive societies. This role was at least partly genuine, for Calindy was really interested in differing life styles; and by some definitions, Titan could indeed be classed as primitive—or, at least, undeveloped.

Thus the supposedly unshockable Terrans were genuinely horrified at encountering families with three—and even four!—children on Titan. The twentieth century's millions of skeleton babies still haunted the conscience of the world, and such tragic but understandable excesses as the "Breeder Lynching" campaign, not to mention the burning of the Vatican, had left permanent scars on the human psyche. Duncan could still remember Calindy's expression when she encountered her first family of six: outrage contended with curiosity, until both were moderated by Terran good manners. He had patiently explained the facts of life to her, pointing out that there was nothing eternally sacred about the dogma of Zero Growth, and that Titan *really* needed to double its population every fifty years. Eventually she appreciated this logically, but she had never been able to accept it emotionally. And it was emotion that provided the driving force of Calindy's life; her will and beauty and intelligence were merely its servants.

For a young Terran, she was not promiscuous. She once told Duncan—and he believed her—that she never had more than two lovers at a time. On Titan, to Duncan's considerable distress, she had only one.

Even if the Helmers and Makenzies had not been related through Grandma Ellen, it was inevitable that she would have met Karl, at one of the countless concerts and parties and dances arranged for *Mentor's* castaways. So Duncan could not really blame himself for introducing them; it would have made no difference in the end. Yet even so, he would always wonder. . . .

Karl was then almost twenty-two—a year older than Calindy, though far less experienced. He still possessed the slightly overmuscled build of the native-born Terran, but had adapted so well to the lower gravity that he moved more gracefully than most men who had spent their entire lives on Titan. He seemed to possess the secret of power without clumsiness.

And in a quite literal sense, he was the Golden Boy of his generation. Though he pretended to hate the phrase, Duncan knew that he was secretly proud of the title someone had given him in his teens: "The boy with hair like the sun." The description could only have been coined by a visitor from Earth. No Titanian would have thought of it—but everyone agreed that it was completely appropriate. For Karl Helmer was one of those men upon whom, for their own amusement, the Gods had bestowed the fatal gift of beauty.

Only years later, and partly thanks to Colin, did Duncan begin to understand all the nuances of the affair. Soon after his twenty-third birthday, the Makenzies received the last Star Day card that Calindy ever sent them.

"I *still* don't know if I made a mistake," Colin said ruefully as he fingered the bright rectangle of paper that had carried its conventional greetings halfway across the Solar System. "But it seemed a good idea at the time."

"Well, I don't think it did any harm, in the long run."

Colin looked at him strangely.

"I wonder. Anyway, it certainly didn't turn out as I expected."

"And what *did* you expect?"

It was sometimes a great advantage, and sometimes downright embarrassing, to have a father who was also your thirty-year-older identical twin. He knew all the mistakes you were going to make, because he had made them already. It was impossible to conceal any secrets from him, because his thought processes were virtually the same. In such a situation, the only policy that made any sense was complete honesty, as far as that could be achieved by human beings.

"I'm not quite sure. But the moment I saw Calindy, shining like a nova amid all that gloom and chaos down in the old mine workings, I wanted to learn more about her . . . wanted to make her part of my life. *You* know what I mean."

Duncan could only nod his head in silent agreement.

"Sheela didn't mind—after all, I'm not a baby-snatcher! And we both hoped that Calindy would give you someone to think about besides Karl."

"I was already getting over that, anyway. It was much too frustrating."

Colin chuckled, not unsympathetically.

"So I can imagine. Karl was spreading himself pretty thin. Half of Titan was in love with him in those days—still is, for that matter. Which is why we must keep him out of politics. Remind me to tell you about Alcibiades someday."

"Who?"

"Ancient Greek general—too clever and charming for his own good. Or for anyone else's."

"I appreciate your concern," said Duncan, with only a slight trace of sarcasm. "But that increased my problems a hundred percent. As she made quite clear, I was much too young for Calindy, and of course Karl was now interested only in her. And to make matters worse, they didn't even mind me sharing their bed—as long as I didn't get in the way. In fact—"

"Yes?"

Duncan's face darkened. How strange that he had never thought of this before, yet how obvious it was!

"Didn't mind, hell! They *enjoyed* having me there, just to tease me! At least Karl did."

It should have been a shattering revelation, yet somehow it did not hurt as much as he would have expected. He must have realized for a long time, without admitting it to himself, that there was a very definite streak of cruelty in Karl. Certainly his lovemaking often lacked tenderness and consideration; there were even times when he had scared Duncan into something approaching impotence. And to do *that* to a virile sixteen-year-old was no mean feat.

"I'm glad you've realized that," said Colin somberly. "You had to find it out for yourself—you wouldn't have believed us. But whatever Karl did, he certainly paid for it. That breakdown was *serious*. And, frankly, I don't believe his recovery is as complete as the doctors claim."

This was also a new thought to Duncan, and he turned it over in his mind. Karl's breakdown was still a considerable mystery, which the Helmer family had never discussed with outsiders. The romantics had a simple explanation: he was heartbroken over the loss of Calindy. Duncan had always found this too hard to accept. Karl was too tough to pine away like some character in an oldtime melodrama—especially when there were at least a thousand volunteers waiting to console him. Yet it was undeniable that the breakdown had occurred only a few weeks after *Mentor* had, to everyone's relief, blasted Earthward.

After that, there had been a complete change in his personality; whenever Duncan met him in these last few years, he had seemed almost a stranger.

Physically, he was as beautiful as ever—perhaps even more so, thanks to his greater maturity. And he could still be friendly, though there were sudden silences when he seemed to retreat into himself for no apparent reason. But real communication was missing; maybe it had never been there. . . .

No, that was unfair and untrue. They had known many shared moments before Calindy entered their lives. And one, though only one, after she had left.

That was still the deepest pain that Duncan had ever known. He had been inarticulate with grief when they had made their farewells in the shuttle terminus of Meridian, surrounded by scores of other parting guests. To its great surprise, Titan had suddenly discovered that it was going to miss its young visitors; nearly every one of them was surrounded by a tearful group of local residents.

Duncan's grief was also, to no small extent, compounded with jealousy. He never discovered how Karl —or Calindy—had managed it, but they flew up in the shuttle together, and made their final farewells on the ship. So when Duncan glimpsed Calindy for the last time, when she waved back at him from the quarantine barrier, Karl was still with her. In that desolating moment, he did not suppose that he would ever see her again.

When Karl returned on the last shuttle flight, five hours later, he was drawn and pale, and had lost all his usual vivacity. Without a word, he had handed Duncan a small package, wrapped in brightly colored paper, and bearing the inscription LOVE FROM CALINDY.

Duncan had opened it with trembling fingers; a bubble stereo was inside. It was a long time before he was able to see, through the mist of tears, the image it contained.

Much later that same day, as they clung together in mutual misery, an obvious question had suddenly occurred to Duncan.

"What did she give *you*, Karl?" he had asked.

There was a sudden pause in the other's breathing, and he felt Karl's body tense slightly and draw away from him. It was an almost imperceptible gesture; probably Karl was not even aware of it.

When he answered, his voice was strained and curiously defensive.

"It's—it's a secret. Nothing important; perhaps one day I'll tell you."

Even then, Duncan knew that he never would; and somehow he already realized that this was the last night they would ever spend together.

10

WORLD'S END

Ground Effect Vehicles were very attractive in a low-gravity, dense-atmosphere environment, but they did tend to rearrange the landscape, especially when it consisted largely of fluffy snow. That was only a problem, however, to anyone following in the rear. When it reached its normal cruising speed of two hundred kilometers an hour, the hoversled left its private blizzard behind it, and the view ahead was excellent.

But it was not cruising at two hundred klicks; it

was flat out at three, and Duncan was beginning to wish he had stayed home. It would be very stupid if he broke his neck, on a mission where his presence was quite unnecessary, only two days before he was due to leave for Earth.

Yet there was no real danger. They were moving over smooth, flat ammonia snow, on a terrain known to be free from crevasses. Top speed was safe, and it was fully justified. This was too good an opportunity to miss, and he had waited for it for years. No one had ever observed a waxworm in the active phase, and this one was only eighty kilometers from Oasis. The seismographs had spotted its characteristic signature, and the environment computer had given the alert. The hoversled had been through the airlock within ten minutes.

Now it was approaching the lower slopes of Mount Shackelton, the well-behaved little volcano which, after much careful thought, the original settlers had decided to accept as a neighbor. Waxworms were almost always associated with volcanoes, and some were festooned with them—"like an explosion in a spaghetti factory," as one early explorer had put it. No wonder that their discovery had caused much excitement; from the air they looked very much like the protective tunnels built by termites and other social insects on Earth.

To the bitter disappointment of the exobiologists, they had turned out to be a purely natural phenomenon—the equivalent, at a much lower temperature, of terrestrial lava tubes. The head of a waxworm moved, judging from the seismic records, at up to fifty kilometers an hour, preferring slopes of not more than ten degrees. They had even been known to go *uphill* for short distances, when the driving pressure was sufficiently high. Once the core of hot petrochemicals had passed along, what remained was a hollow tube as much as five meters in diameter. Waxworms were among Titan's more benign manifestations; not only were they a valuable source of raw materials, but they could be readily adapted for storage space and even temporary surface housing—if one could get used to the rich orchestration of alliphatic smells.

The hoversled had another reason for speed; it was the season of eclipses. Twice every Saturnian year, around the equinoxes, the sun would vanish behind the invisible bulk of the planet for up to six hours at a time. There would be no slow waning of light, as on Earth; with shocking abruptness, the monstrous shadow of Saturn would sweep across Titan, bringing sudden and unexpected night to any traveler who had been foolish enough not to check his calendar.

Today's eclipse was due in just over an hour, which, unless they ran into obstacles, would give ample time to reach the waxworm. The sled was now driving down a narrow valley flanked by beautiful ammonia cliffs, tinted every possible shade of blue from the palest sapphire to deep indigo. Titan had been called the most colorful world in the Solar System—not excluding Earth; if the sunlight had been more powerful, it would have been positively garish. Although reds and oranges predominated, every part of the spectrum was available somewhere, though seldom for long in the same place. The methane storms and ammonia rains were continually sculpting the landscape.

"Hello, Sled Three," said Oasis Control suddenly. "You'll be out in the open again in five kilometers— less than two minutes at your present speed. Then there's a ten-kilometer slope up to the Amundsen Glacier. From there, you should be able to see the worm. But I think you're too late—it's almost reached World's End."

"Damn," said the geologist who had been handling the sled with such effortless skill. "I was afraid of that. Something tells me I'm *never* going to catch a worm on the run."

He cut the speed abruptly as a flurry of snow reduced visibility almost to zero, and for a few minutes they were navigating on radar alone through a shining white mist. A film of sticky hydrocarbon slush started to build up on the forward windows, and would soon have covered them completely if the driver had not taken remedial action. A high-pitched whine filled the cabin as the sheets of tough plastic started to oscillate at near ultrasonic frequencies, and a fascinating pat-

53

tern of standing waves appeared before the obscuring layer was flicked away.

Then they were through the little storm, and the jet-black wall of the Amundsen Glacier was visible on the horizon. In a few centuries that creeping mountain would reach Oasis, and it would be necessary to do something about it. During the years of summer, the viscosity of the carbon-impregnated oils and waxes became low enough for the glacier to advance at the breath-taking speed of several centimeters an hour, but during the long winter it was as motionless as rock.

Ages ago, local heating had melted part of the glacier and formed Lake Tuonela, almost as Stygian black as its parent but decorated by great whorls and loops where lighter material had been caught in patterns of turbulence, now frozen for eternity. Everyone who saw the phenomenon from the air for the first time thought he was being original when he exclaimed: "Why, it looks exactly like a cup of coffee, just after you've stirred in the cream!"

As the sled raced over the lake, the pattern flickered past in a few minutes, too close for its swirls to be properly observed. Then there was another long slope, dotted with large boulders which could be avoided only by the full thrust of the underjets. This cut speed to less than a hundred klicks, and the sled labored up toward the crest in zigs and zags, the driver cursing and looking every few seconds at his watch.

"There it is!" Duncan shouted.

Only a few kilometers away, coming out of the mist that always enveloped the flanks of Mount Shackelton, was a thin white line, like a piece of rope laid across the landscape. It stretched away downhill until it disappeared over the horizon, and the driver swung the sled around to follow its track. But Duncan already knew that they were too late to achieve their main objective; they were much too close to World's End. Minutes later, they were there, and the sled came to a stop at a respectful distance.

"That's as close as I'm getting," said the driver. "I wouldn't like a gust to catch us when we're skirting the edge. Who wants to go out? We still have thirty minutes of light."

"What's the temperature?" someone asked.

"Warm. Only fifty below. Single-layer suits will do."

It was the first time that Duncan had been out in the open for months, but there were some skills that nobody who lived on Titan ever allowed himself to forget. He checked the oxygen pressure, the reserve tank, the radio, the fit of the neck seal—all those little details upon which his hopes of a peaceful old age depended. The fact that he would be within a hundred meters of safety, and surrounded by other men who could come to his aid in a moment, did not affect his thoroughness in the least.

Real spacers sometimes underestimated Titan, with disastrous results. It seemed altogether too easy to move around on a world where a pressure suit was unnecessary and the whole body could be exposed to the surrounding atmosphere. Nor was there any need to worry about freezing, even in the Titanian night. As long as the thermosuit retained its integrity, the body's own hundred and fifty watts of heat could maintain a comfortable temperature indefinitely.

These facts could induce a sense of false security. A torn suit—which would be immediately noticed and repaired in a vacuum environment—might be ignored here as a minor discomfort until it was too late, and toes and fingers were quietly dropping off through frostbite. And although it seemed incredible that anyone could ignore an oxygen warning, or be careless enough to go beyond his point of no return, it *had* happened. Ammonia poisoning is not the nicest way to die.

Duncan did not let these facts oppress him, but they were always there at the back of his mind. As he walked toward the worm, his feet crunching through a thin crust like congealed candle grease, he kept automatically checking the positions of his nearest companions, in case they needed him—or he needed them.

The cylindrical wall of the worm now loomed above him, ghostly white, textured with little scales or platelets which were slowly peeling off and falling to the ground. Duncan removed a mitten and laid his bare hand on the tube. It was slightly warm and there was a gentle vibration; the core of hot liquid was still pulsing within, like blood through a giant artery. But the worm itself, controlled by the interacting forces of surface tension and gravity, had committed suicide.

While the others busied themselves with their measurements, photographs, and samples, Duncan walked to World's End. It was not his first visit to that famous and spectacular view, but the impact had not diminished.

Almost at his feet, the ground fell away vertically for more than a thousand meters. Down the face of the cliff, the decapitated worm was slowly dripping stalactites of wax. From time to time an oily globule would break off and fall slowly toward the cloud layer far below. Duncan knew that the ground itself was another kilometer beneath that, but the sea of clouds that stretched out to the horizon had never broken since men had first observed it.

Yet overhead, the weather was remarkably clear. Apart from a little ethylene cirrus, nothing obscured the sky, and the sun was as sharp and bright as Duncan had ever seen it. He could even make out, thirty kilometers to the north, the unmistakable cone of Mount Shackelton, with its perpetual streamer of smoke.

"Hurry up and take your pictures," said a voice in his radio. "You have less than five minutes."

A million kilometers away, the invisible bulk of Saturn was edging toward the brilliant star that flooded this strange landscape with a light ten thousand times brighter than Earth's full Moon. Duncan stepped back a few paces from the brink, but not so far that he could no longer watch the clouds below; he hoped he would be able to observe the shadow of the eclipse as it came racing toward him.

The light was going—going—gone. He never saw the onrushing shadow; it seemed that night fell instantly upon all the world.

He looked up toward the vanished sun, hoping to catch a glimpse of the fabled corona. But there was only a shrinking glow, revealing for a few seconds the curved edge of Saturn as the giant world swept inexorably across the sky. Beyond that was a faint and distant star, which in another moment would also be engulfed.

"Eclipse will last twelve minutes," said the hover-sled driver. "If any of you want to stay outside, keep away from the edge. You can easily get disoriented in the darkness."

Duncan scarcely heard him. Something had caught at his throat, almost as if a whiff of the surrounding ammonia had invaded his suit.

He could not take his gaze off that faint little star, during the seconds before Saturn wiped it from the sky. He continued to stare long after it was gone, with all its promise of warmth and wonder, and the storied centuries of its civilization.

For the first time in his life, Duncan Makenzie had seen the planet Earth with his own unaided eyes.

Part II

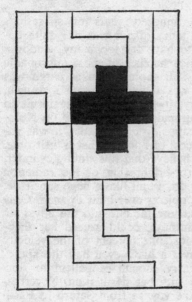

Transit

II

SIRIUS

After three hundred years of spaceships that were mostly fuel tanks, *Sirius* was not quite believable. She seemed to have far too many windows, and there were entrance hatches in most improbable places, some of them still gaping open as cargo was loaded. At least she was taking on *some* hydrogen, thought Duncan sourly; it would be adding insult to economic injury if she made the round trip on a single fueling. She was capable of doing this, it was rumored, though at the cost of doubling her transit time.

It was also hard to believe that this stubby cylinder, with the smooth mirror-bright ring of the radiation baffle surrounding the drive unit like a huge sunshade, was one of the fastest objects ever built by man. Only the interstellar probes, now far out into the abyss on their centuries-long journeys, could exceed her theoretical maximum—almost one percent of the velocity of light. She would never achieve even half this speed, because she had to carry enough propellent to slow down and rendezvous with her destination. Nevertheless, she could make the voyage from Saturn to Earth in twenty days, despite a minor detour to avoid the hazards—largely psychological—of the asteroid belt.

The forty-minute flight from surface to parking orbit was not Duncan's first experience of space; he had made several brief trips to neighboring moons, aboard this same shuttle. The Titanian passenger fleet consisted of exactly five vessels, and as none possessed the expensive luxury of centrifugal gravity, all safety belts were secured throughout the voyage. Any passenger who wished to sample the joys and hazards of weightlessness would have just under two hours to experience it aboard *Sirius,* before the drive started to operate. Although Duncan had always felt completely at ease in free fall, he let the stewards float him, an inert and unresisting package, through the airlock and into the ship.

It had been rather too much to expect the Centennial Committee to provide a single cabin—there were only four on the ship—and Duncan knew that he would have to share a double. L.3 was a minute cell with two folding bunks, a couple of lockers, two seats—also folding—and a mirror-vision screen. There was no window looking out into space; this, the *Welcome Aboard!* brochure carefully explained, would create unacceptable structural hazards. Duncan did not believe this for a moment, and wondered if the designers feared an attempt by claustrophobic passengers to claw a way out.

And there were no toilet facilities—these were all in an adjacent cubicle, which serviced the four cabins around it. Well, it was only going to be for a few weeks. . . .

Duncan's spirits rose somewhat after he had gained enough confidence to start exploring his little world. He quickly learned to visualize his location by following the advice printed on the shipboard maps; it was convenient to think of *Sirius* as a cylindrical tower with ten floors. The fifty cabins were divided between the sixth and seventh floors. Immediately below, on the fifth level, was the lounge, recreation and dining area.

The territory above these three floors was forbidden to passengers. Going upward, the remaining levels were Life Support, Crew Quarters, and—forming a kind of penthouse with all-round visibility—the Bridge. In the other direction, the four levels were Galley, Hold, Fuel, and Propulsion. It was a logical arrangement, but it would take Duncan some time to discover that the Purser's Office was on the kitchen level, the surgery next to the freight compartment, the gym in Life Support, and the library tucked away in an emergency airlock overlapping levels Six and Seven. . . .

During the circumnavigation of his new home, Duncan encountered a dozen other passengers on a similar voyage of exploration, and exchanged the guarded greetings appropriate among strangers who will soon get to know each other perhaps all too well. He had already been through the passenger list to see if there was anyone on board he knew and had found a few familiar Titanian names, but no close acquaintances. Sharing cabin L.3, he had discovered, was a Dr. Louise Chung; but the parting with Marissa still hurt too much for the "Louise" to arouse more than the faintest flicker of interest.

In any event, as he found when he returned to L.3, Dr. Chung was a bright little old lady, undoubtedly on the far side of a hundred, who greeted him with an absent-minded courtesy which, even by the end of the voyage, never seemed to extend to a complete recognition of his existence. She was, he soon discovered, one of the Solar System's leading mathematical physicists, and *the* authority on resonance phenomena among the satellites of the outer planets. For half a century she had been trying to explain why the gaps in Saturn's rings were not exactly where all the best theories demanded.

The two hours ticked slowly away, finally seeming to move with a rush toward the expected announcement: "This is Captain Ivanov speaking at minus five minutes. All crew members should be on station or standby, all passengers should have safety straps secured. Initial acceleration will be one hundredth gravity—ten centimeters second squared. I repeat, one hundredth gravity. This will be maintained for ten minutes while the propulsion system undergoes routine checks."

And suppose it doesn't pass those checks? Duncan asked himself. Do even the mathematicians know what would happen if the Asymptotic Drive started to malfunction? This line of thought was not very profitable, and he hastily abandoned it.

"Minus four minutes. Stewards check all passengers secured."

Now *that* instruction could not possibly be obeyed. There were three hundred twenty-five passengers, half of them in their cabins and the other half in the two lounges, and there was no way in which the dozen harassed stewards could see that all their charges were behaving. They had made one round of the ship at minus thirty and minus ten minutes, and passengers who had cut loose since then had only themselves to blame. And anyone who could be hurt by a hundredth of a gee, thought Duncan, certainly deserved it. Impacts at that acceleration had about the punch of a large wet sponge.

"Minus three minutes. All systems normal. Passengers in Lounge B will see Saturn rising."

Duncan permitted himself a slight glow of self-satisfaction. This was precisely why, after checking with one of the stewards, he was now in Lounge B. As Titan always kept the same face turned toward its primary, the spectacle of the great globe climbing above the horizon was one that could never be seen from the surface, even if the almost perpetual overcast of hydrocarbon clouds had permitted.

That blanket of clouds now lay a thousand kilometers below, hiding the world that it protected from the chill of space. And then suddenly—*unexpectedly,* even though he had been waiting for it—Saturn was rising like a golden ghost.

In all the known universe, there was nothing to compare with the wonder he was seeing now. A hundred times the size of the puny Moon that floated in the skies of Earth, the flattened yellow globe looked like an object lesson in planetary meteorology. Its knotted bands of cloud could change their appearance almost every hour, while thousands of kilometers down in the hydrogen-methane atmosphere, eruptions whose cause was still unknown would lift bubbles larger than terrestrial continents up from the hidden core. They would expand and burst as they reached the limits of the atmosphere, and in minutes Saturn's furious ten-hour spin would have smeared them out into long colored ribbons, stretching halfway round the planet.

Somewhere down there in that inferno, Duncan reminded himself with awe, Captain Kleinman had died seventy years ago, and so had part of Grandma Ellen. In all that time, no one had attempted to return. Saturn still represented one of the largest pieces of un-

63

finished business in the Solar System—next, perhaps, to the smoldering hell of Venus.

The rings themselves were still so inconspicuous that it was easy to overlook them. By a cosmic irony, all the inner satellites lay in almost the same plane as the delicate, wafer-thin structure that made Saturn unique. Edge on, as they were now, the rings were visible only as hairlines of light jutting out on either side of the planet, yet they threw a broad, dusky band of shadow along the equator.

In a few hours, as *Sirius* rose above the orbital plane of Titan, the rings would open up in their full glory. And that alone, thought Duncan, would be enough to justify this voyage.

"Minus one minute . . ."

He had never even heard the two-minute mark; the great world rising out of the horizon clouds must have held him hypnotized. In sixty seconds, the automatic sequencer in the heart of the drive unit would initiate its final mysteries. Forces which only a handful of living men could envisage, and none could truly understand, would awaken in their fury, tear *Sirius* from the grip of Saturn, and hurl her sunward toward the distant goal of Earth.

". . . ten seconds . . . five seconds . . . ignition!"

How strange that a word that had been technologically obsolete for at least two hundred years should have survived in the jargon of astronautics! Duncan barely had time to formulate this thought when he felt the onset of thrust. From exactly zero his weight leaped up to less than a kilogram. It was barely enough to dent the cushion above which he had been floating, and was detectable chiefly by the slackening tension of his waist belt.

Other effects were scarcely more dramatic. There was a distinct change in the timbre of the indefinable noises which never cease on board a spacecraft while its mechanical hearts are operating; and it seemed to Duncan that, far away, he could hear a faint hissing. But he was not even sure of that.

And then, a thousand kilometers below, he saw the unmistakable evidence that *Sirius* was indeed breaking away from her orbit. The ship had been driving into night on its final circuit of Titan, and the wan sunlight had been swiftly fading on the sea of clouds far below. But now a second dawn had come, in a wide swathe across the face of the world he was soon to leave. For a hundred kilometers behind the accelerating ship, a column of incandescent plasma was splashing untold quintillions of candlepower out into space and across the carmine cloudscape of Titan. *Sirius* was falling sunward in greater glory than the sun itself.

"Ten minutes after ignition. All drive checks complete. We will now be increasing thrust to our cruise level of point two gravities—two hundred centimeters second squared."

And now, for the first time, *Sirius* was showing what she could do. In a smooth surge of power, thrust and weight climbed twenty-fold and held steady. The light on the clouds below was now so strong that it hurt the eye. Duncan even glanced at the still-rising disc of Saturn to see if it too showed any sign of this fierce new sun. He could now hear, faint but unmistakable, the steady whistling roar that would be the background to all life aboard the ship until the voyage ended. It must, he thought, be pure coincidence that the awesome voice of the Asymptotic Drive sounded so much like that of the old chemical rockets that first gave men the freedom of space. The plasma hurtling from the ship's reactor was moving a thousand times more swiftly than the exhaust gases of any rocket, even a nuclear one; and how it created that apparently familiar noise was a puzzle that would not be solved by any naïve mechanical intuition.

"We are now on cruise mode at one-fifth gee. Passengers may unstrap themselves and move about freely—but please use caution until you are completely adapted."

That won't take *me* very long, thought Duncan as he unbuckled himself; the ship's acceleration gave him his normal, Titan weight. Any residents of the Moon would also feel completely at home here, while Martians and Terrans would have a delightful sense of buoyancy.

The lights in the lounge, which had been dimmed almost to extinction for better viewing of the spectacle outside, slowly brightened to normal. The few first-magnitude stars that had been visible disappeared at once, and the gibbous globe of Saturn became bleached and pale, losing all its colors. Duncan could restore the scene by drawing the black curtains around the observation alcove, but his eyes would take several minutes to readapt. He was wondering whether to make the effort when the decision was made for him.

There was a musical "Ding-*dong*-ding," and a new voice, which sounded as if it came from a social stratum several degrees above the Captain's, announced languidly: "This is the Chief Steward. Will passengers kindly note that First Seating for lunch is at twelve hundred, Second Seating at thirteen hundred, Last Seating at fourteen hundred. Please do *not* attempt to make any changes without consulting me. Thank you." A less peremptory "Dong-*ding*-dong" signaled end of message.

Looking at the marvels of the universe made you hungry, Duncan instantly discovered. It was already 1150, and he was glad that he was in the First Seating. He wondered how many starving passengers were now converging upon the Chief Steward, in search of an earlier time slot.

Enjoying the sensation of man-made weight which, barring accidents, would remain constant until the moment of mid-voyage, Duncan went to join the rapidly lengthening line at the cafeteria.

Already, his first thirty years of life on Titan seemed to belong to another existence.

12

LAST WORDS

For one moment more, the achingly familiar image remained frozen on the screen. Behind Marissa and the children, Duncan could see the two armchairs of the living room, the photograph of Grandfather (as usual, slightly askew), the cover of the food-distribution hatch, the door to the main bedroom, the bookcase with the few but priceless treasures that had survived two centuries of interplanetary wandering. . . . This was his universe. It held everything he loved, and now he was leaving it. Already, it lay in his past.

It lay only three seconds away, yet that was enough. He had traveled a mere million kilometers in less than half a day; but the sense of separation was already almost complete. It was intolerable to wait six seconds for every reaction and every answer. By the time a reply came, he had forgotten the original question and had started to say something else. And so the attempted conversation had quickly degenerated into a series of stops and starts, while he and Marissa had stared at each other in dumb misery, each waiting for the other to speak. . . . He was glad that the ordeal was over.

The experience brought home to him, as nothing else had yet done, the sheer immensity of space. The Solar System, he began to suspect, was not designed for the convenience of Man, and that presumptuous creature's attempts to use it for his own advantage would often be foiled by laws beyond his control. All his life, Duncan had assumed without question that he could speak to friends or family instantly, wherever he might be. Yet now—before he had even passed Saturn's outer moons!—that power had been taken from him. For the next twenty days, he would share a lonely, isolated bubble of humanity, able to interact with his fellow passengers, but cut off from all real contact with the rest of mankind.

His self-pity lasted only a few moments. There was also an exhilaration—even a freedom—in this sense of isolation, and in the knowledge that he was setting forth on one of the longest and swiftest voyages that any man could make. Travel to the outer planets was routine and uneventful—but it was also rare, and only a very small fraction of the human race would ever experience it. Duncan remembered a favorite Terran phrase of Malcolm's, usually employed in a different context, but sound advice for every occasion: "When it's inevitable, relax and enjoy it." He would do his best to enjoy this voyage.

Yet Duncan was exhausted when he finally climbed into his bunk at the end of his first day in space. The strain of innumerable farewells, not only to his family but to countless friends, had left him emotionally drained. On top of this, there were all the nagging worries of departure: What had he forgotten to do? What vital necessities had he failed to pack? Had all his baggage been safely loaded and stowed? What essential good-byes had he overlooked? It was useless worrying about these matters now that he was speeding away from home at a velocity increasing by twenty-five thousand kilometers an hour, *every* hour, yet he could not help doing so. Tired though he was, his hyperactive brain would not let him sleep.

It takes real genius to make a bed that can be uncomfortable at a fifth of a gravity, and luckily the designers of *Sirius* had not accepted this challenging assignment. After thirty minutes or so, Duncan began to relax and to get his racing thoughts in order. He prided himself on being able to sleep without artificial aids, and it looked as if he would be able to dispense with electronarcosis after all. That was, of course, supposed to be completely harmless, but he never felt properly awake the next day.

You're falling asleep, he told himself. You won't know anything more until it's time for breakfast. All your dreams are going to be happy ones. . . .

A sound like a small volcano clearing its throat undid the good work of the last ten minutes. He was instantly wide awake, wondering what disaster had befallen *Sirius*. Not until several anxious seconds had passed did he realize that some antisocial shipmate had found it necessary to visit the adjacent toilet.

Cursing, he tried to recapture the broken mood and to return to the threshold of sleep. But it was useless; the myriad voices of the ship had started to clamor for his attention. He seemed to have lost control of the analytical portion of his brain, and it was busy classifying all the noises from the surrounding universe.

It had been hours since he had really noticed the far-off, ghostly whistling of the drive. Every second *Sirius* was ejecting a hundred grams of hydrogen at a third of the velocity of light—a trifling loss of mass, yet it represented meaningless millions of gigawatts. During the first few centuries of the Industrial Revolution, all the factories of Earth could not have matched the power that was now driving him sunward.

That incongruously faint and feeble scream was not really disturbing, but it was overlaid with all sorts of other peculiar sounds. What could possibly cause the "Buzz . . . click, click . . . buzz," the soft "thump . . . thump . . . thump," the "gurgle, hissssss," and the intermittent "whee-wheee-whee" which was the most maddening of all?

Duncan rolled over and tried to bury his head in the pillows. It made no difference, except that the higher-pitched sounds got filtered out and the lower frequencies were enhanced. He also became more aware of the steady pulsation of the bed itself, at just about the ten cycles per second nicely calculated to produce epileptic fits.

Hello, *that* was something new. It was a kind of dispirited "ker-*plunk,* ker-*plunk,* ker-*plunk*" that might have been produced by an ancient internal combustion engine in the last stages of decrepitude. Somehow, Duncan seriously doubted that i.c. engines, old or new, were to be found aboard *Sirius*.

He rolled over on the other side—and then became conscious of the slightly cold airstream from the ventilator hitting him on his left cheek. Perhaps if he ignored it, the sensation would sink below the threshold of consciousness. However, the very effort of pretending it wasn't there focused attention upon the annoyance.

On the other side of the thin partition, the ship's plumbing once again advertised its presence with a series of soft thumps. There was an air bubble somewhere in the system, and Duncan knew, with a deadly certainty, that all the engineering skills aboard *Sirius* would be unable to exorcise it before the end of the voyage.

And what was that? It was a rasping, whistling sound, so irregular that no well-adjusted mechanism could possibly have produced it. As Duncan lay in the darkness, racking his brains to think of an explanation, his annoyance slowly grew to alarm. Should he call the steward and report that something had gone wrong?

He was still trying to make up his mind when a sudden explosive change in pitch and intensity left him in no doubt as to the sound's origin. Groaning and cursing his luck, Duncan resigned himself to a sleepless night.

Dr. Chung snored. . . .

Someone was gently shaking him. He mumbled "Go away," then swam groggily upward from the depths of slumber.

"If you don't hurry," said Dr. Chung, "you're going to miss breakfast."

13

THE LONGEST VOYAGE

"This is the Captain speaking. We will be performing a final out-of-ecliptic velocity trim during the next fifteen minutes. This will be your last opportunity for a good view of Saturn, and we are orientating the ship so that it will be visible through the B Lounge windows. Thank you."

Thank *you*, thought Duncan, though he was a little less grateful when he reached B Lounge. This time, too many other passengers had been tipped off by the stewards. Nevertheless, he managed to obtain a good vantage point, even though he had to stand.

Though the journey had scarcely begun, Saturn already seemed far away. The planet had dwindled to a quarter of its accustomed size; it was now only twice as large as the Moon would appear from Earth.

Yet though it had shrunk in size, it had gained in impressiveness. *Sirius* had risen several degrees out of the planet's equatorial plane, and now at last he could see the rings in all their glory. Thin, concentric silver haloes, they looked so artificial that it was almost impossible to believe that they were not the work of some cosmic craftsman whose raw materials were worlds. Although at first sight they appeared to be solid, when he looked more carefully Duncan could see the planet glimmering through them, its yellow light contrasting strangely with their immaculate, snowy whiteness. A hundred thousand kilometers below, the shadow of the rings lay in a dusky band along the equator; it could easily have been taken for an unusually dark cloud belt, rather than something whose cause lay far out in space.

The two main divisions of the rings were apparent at the most casual glance, but a more careful inspection revealed at least a dozen fainter boundaries where there were abrupt changes in brightness between adjacent sections. Ever since the rings had been discovered, back in the seventeenth century, mathematicians like Dr. Chung had been trying to account for their structure. It had long been known that the attractions of Saturn's many moons segregated the billions of orbiting particles into separate bands, but the details of the process were still unclear.

There was also a certain amount of variation within the individual bands themselves. The outermost ring, for example, showed a distinct mottling or beadiness, and a tiny clot of light was clearly visible near its eastern extremity. Was this, Duncan wondered, a moon about to be born—or the last remnants of one that had been destroyed?

Rather diffidently, he put the question to Dr. Chung.

"Both possibilities have been considered," she said. "My studies indicate the former. That condensation may, with luck, become another satellite in a few thousand years."

"I can't agree, Doctor," interjected another passenger. "It's merely a statistical fluctuation in the particle density. They're quite common, and seldom last more than a few years."

"The *smaller* ones—yes. But this is too intense, and too near the edge of the B-ring."

"But Vanderplas' analysis of the Janus problem . . ."

At that moment, it became rather like the shootout in an oldtime Western movie. The two scientists reached simultaneously for their hip computers and then retreated, muttering equations, to the back of the lounge. Thereafter, they completely ignored the *real* Saturn they had come so far to study—and which, in all probability, they would never see again.

"Captain speaking. We have concluded our velocity trim and are reorientating the ship into the plane of the ecliptic. I hope you had a good view—Saturn will be a long way off next time you see it."

There was no perceptible sense of motion, but the great ringed globe began to creep slowly down the observation window. The passengers in front craned

72

forward to follow it, and there was a chorus of disappointed "Ohs" as it finally sank from view below the wide skirting that surrounded the lower part of the ship. That band of metal had one purpose only—to block any radiation from the jet that might stray forward. Even a momentary glimpse of that intolerable glare, bright as a supernova at the moment of detonation, could cause total blindness; a few seconds' exposure would be lethal.

Sirius was now aimed almost directly at the sun, as she accelerated toward the inner planets. While the drive was on, there could be no rear-viewing. Duncan knew that when he next saw Saturn with his unaided eyes, it would be merely a not-very-distinguished star.

A day later, moving at three hundred kilometers a second, the ship passed another milestone. She had, of course, escaped from the planet's gravitational field hours earlier; neither Saturn—nor, for that matter, the Sun—could ever recapture her. The frontier that *Sirius* was crossing now was a purely arbitrary one: the orbit of the outermost moon.

Mnemosyne, only fifteen kilometers in diameter, could claim two modest records. It had the longest period of any satellite, taking no fewer than 1,139 days to orbit Saturn, at an average distance of twenty-one million kilometers. And it also had the longest day of *any* body in the Solar System, its period of rotation being an amazing 1,143 days. Although it seemed obvious that these two facts must be connected, no one had been able to arrive at any plausible explanation of Mnemosyne's sluggish behavior.

Purely by chance, *Sirius* passed within fewer than a million kilometers of the tiny world. At first, even under the highest power of the ship's telescope, Mnemosyne was only a minute crescent showing no visible features at all, but as it swiftly grew to a half-moon, patches of light and shade merged which eventually resolved themselves into craters. It was typical of all the denser, Mercury-type satellites—as opposed to the inner snowballs like Mimas, Enceladus, and Tethys—but to Duncan it now held a special interest. It was more to him than the last landmark on the road to Earth.

Karl was there, and had been for many weeks, with the joint Titan-Terran Outer Satellite Survey. Indeed, that survey had been in progress as long as Duncan could remember—the surface area of all the moons added up to a surprising number of million square kilometers—and the TTOSS team was doing a thorough job. There had been complaints about the cost, and the critics had subsided only when promised that the survey would be so thorough that it would never be necessary to go back to the outer moons again. Somehow, Duncan doubted that the promise would be kept.

He watched the pale crescent of Mnemosyne wax to full, simultaneously dwindling astern as the ship dropped sunward, and wondered fleetingly if he should send Karl a farewell greeting. But if he did, it would only be interpreted as a taunt.

It took Duncan several days to adjust to the complicated schedule of shipboard life—a schedule dominated by the fact that the dining room (as the lounge adjacent to the cafeteria was grandly called) could seat only one third of the passengers at a time. There were consequently three sittings for each of the three main meals—so for nine hours of every day, at least a hundred people were eating, while two hundred were either thinking about the next meal or grumbling about the last. This made it very difficult for the Purser, who doubled as Entertainment Officer, to organize any shipboard activities. The fact that most of the passengers had no wish to be organized did not help him.

Nevertheless, the day was loosely structured by a series of events, at which a good attendance was guaranteed by sheer boredom. There would be a thirty-minute newscast from Earth at 0800, with a repeat at 1000, and updates in the evening at 1900 and 2100. At the beginning of the voyage, the Earth news would be at least an hour and a half late, but it would become more and more timely as *Sirius* approached her destination. When she reached her final parking orbit, a thousand kilometers above the Equator, the delay would be effectively zero, and watches could at last be set by the radio time signals. Those passengers who did not realize this were liable to get into a hopeless state of confusion and, even worse, to miss meal sittings.

All types of visual display, including the contents of several million volumes of fiction and nonfiction, as well as most of the musical treasures of mankind, were available in the tiny library; at a squeeze, it could hold ten people. However, there were two movie screenings every evening in the main lounge, selection being made—if the Purser could be believed —in the approved democratic manner by public ballot. Almost all the great film classics were available, right back to the beginning of the twentieth century. For the first time in his life, Duncan saw Charlie Chaplin's *Modern Times,* much of the Disney canon, Olivier's *Hamlet,* Ray's *Pather Panchali,* Kubrick's *Napoleon Bonaparte,* Zymanowski's *Moby Dick,* and many other old masterpieces that had not even been names to him. But by far the greatest popular success was *If This Is Tuesday, This Must Be Mars*—a selection from the countless space-travel movies made in the days before space flight was actually achieved. This invariably reduced the audience to helpless hysterics, and it was hard to believe that it had once been banned for in-flight screening because some unimaginative bureaucrat feared that its disasters— such as accidentally arriving at the wrong planet— might alarm nervous passengers. In fact, it had just the opposite effect; they laughed too much to worry.

The big event of the day, however, was the lottery on the ship's run, a simple but ingenious device for redistributing wealth among the passengers. All that one had to do was to guess how far *Sirius* had traveled along her heliocentric trajectory during the previous twenty-four hours; any number of guesses was permitted, at the cost of one solar each.

At noon, the Captain announced the correct result.

The suspense was terrific, as he read out the figures very slowly: "Today's run has been two—two—seven —five—nine—zero—six—four—point—three kilometers." (Cheers and moans.) Since everyone knew the ship's position and acceleration, it required very little mathematics to calculate the first four or five figures, but beyond that the digits were completely arbitrary, so winning was a matter of luck. Although it was rumored that navigating officers had been bribed to trim the last few decimal places by minute adjustments to the thrust, no one had ever been able to prove it.

Another wealth-distributor was a noisy entertainment called "Bingo," apparently the main surviving relic of a once flourishing religious order. Duncan attended one session, then decided that there were better ways of wasting time. Yet a surprising percentage of his very talented and intellectually superior companions seemed to enjoy this rather mindless ritual, jumping up and down and shrieking like small children when their numbers were called. . . .

They could not be criticized for this; they needed some such relaxation. For they were the loneliest people in the Solar System; hundreds of millions of kilometers separated them from the rest of mankind. Everybody knew this, but no one ever mentioned it. Yet it would not have taken an astute psychologist to detect countless slightly unusual reactions—even minor symptoms of stress—in the behavior of *Sirius'* passengers and crew.

There was, for example, a tendency to laugh at the feeblest of jokes, and to go into positive convulsions over catch phrases such as "This is the Captain speaking" or "Dining room closes in fifteen minutes." Most popular of all—at least among the men—was "Any more for Cabin 44." Why the two middle-aged and rather quiet lady geologists who occupied this cabin had acquired a reputation for ravening insatiability was a mystery that Duncan never solved.

Nor was he particularly interested; his heart still ached for Marissa and he would not seek any other consolation until he reached Earth. Moreover, with the somewhat excessive conscientiousness that was typical of the Makenzies, he was already hard at work by the second day of the voyage.

He had three major projects—one physical and two intellectual. The first, carried out under the hard, cold eye of the ship's doctor, was to get himself fit for life at one gravity. The second was to learn all that he could about his new home, so that he would not appear too much of a country cousin when he arrived. And the third was to prepare his speech of thanks, or at least to write a fairly detailed outline, which could be revised as necessary during the course of his stay.

The toughening-up process involved a fifteen-minute session, twice a day, in the ship's centrifuge or on the "race track." Nobody enjoyed the centrifuge; not even the best background music could alleviate the boredom of being whirled around in a tiny cabin until legs and arms appeared to be made of lead. But the race track was so much fun that it operated right around the clock, and some enthusiasts even tried to get extra time on it.

Part of its appeal was undoubtedly due to sheer novelty; who would have expected to find *bicycles* in space? The track was a narrow tunnel, with steeply banked floor, completely encircling the ship, and rather like an old-time particle accelerator—except that in this case the particles themselves provided the acceleration.

Every evening, just before going to bed, Duncan would enter the tunnel, climb onto one of the four bicycles, and start pedaling slowly around the sixty meters of track. His first revolution would take a leisurely half minute; then he would gradually work up to full speed. As he did so, he would rise higher and higher up the banked wall, until at maximum speed he was almost at right angles to the floor. At the same time, he would feel his weight steadily increase; the bicycle's speedometer had been calibrated to read in fractions of a gee, so he could tell exactly how well he was doing. Forty kilometers an hour— ten times around *Sirius* every minute—was the equivalent of one Earth gravity. After several days of practice Duncan was able to maintain this for ten minutes without too much effort. By the end of the voyage, he could tolerate it indefinitely—as he would have to, when he reached Earth.

The race track was at its most exciting when it contained two or more riders—especially when they were moving at different speeds. Though overtaking was strictly forbidden, it was an irresistible challenge, and on this voyage there were no serious casualties. One of Duncan's most vivid and incongruous memories of *Sirius* would be the tinkle of bicycle bells, echoing round and round a brightly lit circular tunnel whose blurred walls flashed by only a few centimeters away. . . . And the race track also provided him with a more material souvenir, a pseudomedieval scroll which announced to all who were interested that I, DUNCAN MAKENZIE, OF OASIS CITY, TITAN, AM HEREBY CERTIFIED TO HAVE BICYCLED FROM SATURN TO EARTH, AT AN AVERAGE VELOCITY OF 2,176,420 KILOMETERS AN HOUR.

Duncan's mental preparation for life on Earth occupied considerably more time, but was not quite so exhausting. He already had a good knowledge of Terran history, geography, and current affairs, but until now it had been mostly theoretical, because it had little direct application to him. Both astronomically and psychologically, Earth had been a long way off. Now it was coming closer by millions of kilometers a day.

Even more to the point, he was now surrounded by Terrans; there were only seven passengers from Titan aboard *Sirius,* so they were outnumbered fifty to one. Whether he liked it or not, Duncan was being rapidly brainwashed and molded by another culture. He found himself using Terran figures of speech, adopting the slightly sing-song intonation now universal on Earth, and employing more and more words of Chinese origin. All this was to be expected; what he found disturbing was the fact that his own swiftly receding world was becoming steadily more unreal.

Before the voyage was finished, he suspected that he would have become half-Terran.

He spent much of his time viewing Earth scenes, listening to famous political debates, and trying to understand what was happening in culture and the arts, so that he would not appear to be a complete barbarian from the outer darkness. When he was not sitting at the viddy, he was likely to be flicking through the pages of a small, dense booklet optimistically entitled *Earth in Ten Days*. He was fond of trying out bits of new-found information on his fellow passengers, to study their reactions and to check on his own understanding. Sometimes the response was a blank stare, sometimes a slightly condescending smile. But everyone was very polite to him; after a while, Duncan realized that there was some truth in the old cliché that Terrans were never *unintentionally* rude.

Of course, it was absurd to apply a single label to half a billion people—or even to the three hundred and fifty on the ship. Yet Duncan was surprised to find how often his preconceived ideas—even his prejudices—were perfectly accurate. Most Terrans *did* have a quite unconscious air of superiority. At first, Duncan found it annoying; then he realized that several thousand years of history and culture justified a certain pride.

It was still too early for him to answer the question, so long debated on all the other worlds: "Is Earth becoming decadent?" The individuals he had met aboard *Sirius* showed no trace of that effete oversensibility with which Terrans were frequently charged—but, of course, they were not a fair sample. Anyone who had occasion to visit the outer reaches of the Solar System must possess exceptional ability or resources.

He would have to wait until he reached earth before he could measure its decadence more precisely. The project might be an interesting one—if his budget and his timetable could stand the strain.

79

14

SONGS OF EMPIRE

In a hundred years, thought Duncan, he could never have managed to arrange this deliberately. Masterful administration of the unforeseen, indeed! Colin would be proud of him. . . .

It had all begun quite accidentally. When he discovered that the Chief Engineer bore the scarcely uncommon name of Mackenzie, it had been natural enough to introduce himself and to compare family trees. A glance was sufficient to show that any relationship was remote: Warren Mackenzie, Doctor of Astrotechnology (Propulsion) was a freckled redhead.

It made no difference, for he was pleased to meet Duncan and happy to chat with him. A genuine friendship had developed, long before Duncan decided to take advantage of it.

"I sometimes feel," Warren lamented, not very seriously, "that I'm a living cliché. Did you know that there was a time when all ship's engineers were Scots, and called Mac-something-or-other?"

"I didn't know it. Why not Germans or Russians? They started the whole thing."

"You're on the wrong wavelength. I'm talking about ships that float on water. The first powered ones were driven by steam—piston engines, working paddle wheels—around the beginning of the nineteenth century. Now, the Industrial Revolution started in Britain, and the first practical steam engine was made by a Scot. So when steamships began to operate all over the world, the Macs went with them. No one else could understand such complicated pieces of machinery."

"*Steam* engines? *Complicated?* You must be joking."

"Have you ever looked at one? More to it than you might think, though it doesn't take long to figure it out. . . . Anyway, while the steamships lasted—that was only about a hundred years—the Scots ran them. I've made a hobby of the period; it has some surprising parallels with our time."

"Go on—surprise me."

"Well, those old ships were incredibly slow, averaging only about ten klicks, at least for freighters. So really long journeys, even on Earth, could take weeks. Just like space travel."

"I see. In those days, the countries on Earth were almost as far apart as the planets."

"Well, some of them. The most perfect analogy is the old British Commonwealth, the first and last world empire. For almost a hundred years, countries like Canada, India, and Australia relied entirely on steamships to link them to Britain; the one-way journey could easily take a month or more, and was often a once-in-a-lifetime affair. Only the wealthy, or people on official business, could afford it. And—just like today—people in the colonies couldn't even *speak* to the mother country. The psychological isolation was almost complete."

"They had telephones, didn't they?"

"Only for local use, and only a few even then. I'm talking about the beginning of the *twentieth century,* remember. Universal global communication didn't arrive until the end of it."

"I feel that the analogy is a little forced," protested Duncan. He was intrigued but unconvinced, and quite willing to listen to Mackenzie's arguments—as yet, with no ulterior motive.

"I can give you some more evidence that makes a better case. Have you heard of Rudyard Kipling?"

"Yes, though I've never read anything of his. He was a writer, wasn't he? Anglo-American—sometime between Melville and Hemingway. English Lit's almost unknown territory to me. Life's too short."

"True, alas. But I *have* read Kipling. He was the first poet of the machine age, and some people think he was also the finest short-story writer of his century. I couldn't judge that, of course, but he exactly described the period I'm talking about. 'McAndrew's Hymn,' for example—an old engineer musing about the pistons and boilers and crankshafts that drive his ship round the world. Its technology—not to mention its theology!—has been extinct for three hundred years; but the spirit behind it is still as valid as ever.

"And he wrote poems and stories about the far places of the empire which make them seem quite as remote as the planets are today—and sometimes even more exotic! There's a favorite of mine called 'The Song of the Cities.' I don't understand half the allusions, but the tributes to Bombay, Singapore, Rangoon, Sydney, Auckland . . . make me think of Luna, Mercury, Mars, Titan . . ."

Mackenzie paused and looked just a little embarrassed.

"I've tried to do something of the same kind myself—but don't worry, I won't inflict my verses on you."

Duncan made the encouraging noises he knew were expected. He was quite sure that before the end of the voyage he would be asked for his criticism—translation, praise—of Mackenzie's literary efforts.

It was a timely reminder of his own responsibilities. While the voyage was still beginning, he had better start work.

Exactly ten minutes, George Washington had directed—not a second more. Even the President will be allowed only fifteen, and all the planets must have equal time. The whole affair is scheduled to last two and a half hours, from the moment we enter the Capitol until we leave for the reception at the White House. . . .

It still seemed faintly absurd to travel three billion kilometers to make a ten-minute speech, even for an occasion as unique as a five-hundredth anniversary. Duncan was not going to waste more than the bare minimum of it on polite formalities; anyway, as Malcolm had pointed out, the sincerity of a speech of thanks is often inversely proportional to its length.

For his amusement—and, more important, because it would help to fix the other participants in his mind—Duncan had tried to compose a formal opening, based on the list of guests that Professor Washington had provided. It started off: "Madame President, Mr. Vice President, Honorable Chief Justice, Honorable Leader of the Senate, Honorable Leader of the House, Your Excellencies the Ambassadors for Luna, Mars, Mercury, Ganymede, and Titan"—at this point he would incline his head slightly toward Ambassador Farrell, if he could see him in the crowded gallery—"distinguished representatives from Albania, Austrand, Cyprus, Bohemia, France, Khmer, Palestine, Kalinga, Zimbawe, Eire. . . ." He calculated that if he acknowledged all the fifty or sixty regions that still insisted on some form of individual recognition, a quarter of his time would be expended before he had even begun. This, obviously, was absurd, and he hoped that all the other speakers would agree. Regardless of protocol, Duncan had decided to opt for dignified brevity.

"People of Earth" would cover a lot of ground—to be precise, five times the area of Titan, an impressive statistic which Duncan knew by heart. But that would leave out the visitors; what about "Friends from other worlds"? No, that was too pretentious, since most of them would be complete strangers. Perhaps: "Madame President, distinguished guests, known and unknown friends from many worlds . . ." That was better, yet somehow it still didn't seem right.

There was more to this business, Duncan realized, than met the eye, or the ear. Plenty of people would be willing to give him advice, but he was determined, in the good old Makenzie tradition, to see what he could do himself before calling for help. He had read somewhere that the best way to learn to swim is by being thrown into deep water. Duncan could not swim —that skill being singularly useless on Titan—but he could appreciate the analogy. His career in Solar politics would start with a spectacular splash, and before the eyes of millions.

It was not that he was nervous; after all, he had addressed his whole world as an expert witness during technical debates in the Assembly. He had acquitted himself well when he weighed the complex arguments for and against mining the ammonia glaciers of Mount Nansen. Even Armand Helmer had congratulated him, despite the fact that they had reached opposing conclusions. In those debates, affecting the future of Titan, he had had real responsibility, and his career might have come to an abrupt end if he had made a fool of himself.

His Terran audience might be a thousand times larger, but it would be very much less critical. Indeed, his listeners would be friendly unless he committed the unpardonable sin of boring them.

This, however, he could not yet guarantee, for he still had no idea how he was going to use the most important ten minutes of his life.

15

AT THE NODE

On the seas of Earth, they had called it "Crossing the Line." Whenever a ship had passed from one hemisphere to another, there had been light-hearted ceremonies and rituals, during which those who had never traversed the Equator before were subjected to ingenious indignities by Father Neptune and his Court.

During the first centuries of space flight, the equivalent transition involved no physical changes; only the navigational computer knew when a ship had ceased to fall toward one planet and was beginning to fall toward another. But now, with the advent of constant-acceleration drives, which could maintain thrust for the entire duration of a voyage, Midpoint, or "Turn-around," had a real physical meaning, and a correspondingly enhanced psychological impact. After living and moving for days in an apparent gravitational field,

84

Sirius' passengers would lose all weight for several hours, and could at least feel that they were *really* in space.

They could watch the slow rotation of the stars as the ship was swung through one hundred eighty degrees, and the drive was aimed precisely against its previous line of thrust, to slowly whittle away the enormous velocity built up over the preceding ten days. They could savor the thought that they were now moving faster than any human beings in history—and could also contemplate the exciting prospect that if the drive failed to restart, *Sirius* would ultimately reach the nearest stars, in not much more than a thousand years. . . .

All these things they could do; however, human nature having certain invariants, a majority of *Sirius'* passengers had other possibilities in mind.

It was the only chance most of them would ever have of experiencing weightlessness long enough to enjoy it. What a crime to waste the opportunity! No wonder that the most popular item in the ship's library these last few days had been the *Nasa Sutra,* an old book and an old joke, explained so often that it was no longer funny.

Captain Ivanov denied, with a reasonably convincing show of indignation, that the ship's schedule had been designed to pander to the passenger's lower instincts. When the subject had been raised at the Captain's table, the day before Turnaround, he had put up quite a plausible defense.

"It's the only logical time to shut down the Drive," he had explained. "Between zero zero and zero four, all the passengers will be in their cabins, er, sleeping. So there will be the minimum of disturbance. We *couldn't* close down during the day—remember, the kitchens and the toilets will be out of action while we're weightless. Don't forget that! We'll remind everyone in the late evening, but some idiot always gets overconfident, or drinks too much, and doesn't have enough sense to read the instructions on those little plastic bags you'll find in your cabins—no thanks, Steward, I don't feel like soup."

Duncan had been tempted; Marissa was beginning

to fade, and there was no lack of opportunity. He had received unmistakable signals from several directions, and for groups with all values of n from one to five. It would not have been easy to make a choice, but Fate had saved him the trouble.

It was a full week, and Turnaround was only three days ahead, before he had felt confident enough of his increasing intimacy with Chief Engineer Mackenzie to drop some gentle hints. They had not been rejected out of hand, but Warren obviously wanted time to weigh the possibilities. He gave Duncan his decision only twelve hours in advance.

"I won't pretend this might cost me my job," he said, "but it could be embarrassing, to say the least, if it got around. But you *are* a Makenzie, and a Special Assistant to the Administrator, and all that. If the worst comes to the worst, which I hope it won't, we can say your request's official."

"Of course. I understand completely, and I really appreciate what you're doing. I won't let you down."

"Now there's the question of timing. If everything checks out smoothly—and I've no reason to expect otherwise—I'll be through in two hours and can dismiss my assistants. They'll leave like meteors—they'll all have something lined up, you can be sure of *that* —so we'll have the place to ourselves. I'll give you a call at zero two, or as soon after as possible."

"I hope I'm not interrupting any—ah—personal plans you've made."

"As it happens, no. The novelty's worn off. What are you smiling at?"

"It's just occurred to me," Duncan answered, "that if anyone does meet the pair of us at two o'clock on the morning of Turnaround, we'll have a perfect alibi. . . ."

Nevertheless, he felt a mild sense of guilt as he drifted along the corridors behind Warren Mackenzie. The weightless—but far from sleeping—ship might have been deserted, for there was no occasion now for anyone to descend below the freight deck on Level Three. It was not even necessary to pretend that they were heading for an innocent assignation.

Yet the guilt was there, and he knew why. He was

taking advantage of a friendship for secret purposes of his own, by suggesting that his interest in the Asymptotic Drive was no more than would be expected from anyone with a scientific or engineering background. But perhaps Warren was not as naïve as he seemed; he could hardly be unaware that the Drive posed a threat to the entire economy of Duncan's society. He might even be trying to help, in a tactful way.

"You may be disappointed," said Warren as they passed through the bulkhead floor separating levels Three and Two. "There's not much to see. But what there is is enough to give some people nightmares— which is why we discourage visitors."

Not the most important reason, thought Duncan. The Drive was not exactly a secret; there was an immense literature on the subject, from the most esoteric mathematical papers down to popularizations so elementary that they amounted to little more than: "You pull on your bootstraps, and away you go." But it would be fair to say that Earth's Space Transportation Authority was curiously evasive when it came down to the practical details, and only its own personnel were allowed on the minor planet where the Drive was assembled. The few photos of Asteroid 4587 were blurred telescopic shots showing two cylindrical structures, more than a thousand kilometers long, stretching out into space on either side of the tiny world, which was an almost invisible speck between them. It was known that these were the accelerators that smashed matter together at such velocities that it fused to form the node or singularity at the heart of the Drive; and this was all that anyone *did* know, outside the STA.

Duncan was now floating, a few meters behind his guide, along a corridor lined with pipes and cable ducts—all the anonymous plumbing any vehicle of sea, air, or space for the last three hundred years. Only the remarkable number of handholds, and the profusion of thick padding, revealed that this was the interior of a ship designed to be independent of gravity.

"D'you see that pipe?" said the engineer. "The little red one?"

"Yes—what about it?"

Duncan would certainly never have given it a second glance; it was only about as thick as a lead pencil.

"*That's* the main hydrogen feed, believe it or not. All of a hundred grams a second. Say eight tons a day, under full thrust."

Duncan wondered what the old-time rocket engineers would have thought of this tiny fuel line. He tried to visualize the monstrous pipes and pumps of the Saturns that had first taken men to the Moon; what was their rate of fuel consumption? He was certain that they burned more in every second than *Sirius* consumed in a day. That was a good measure of how far technology had progressed, in three centuries. And in another three . . . ?

"Mind your head—those are the deflection coils. We don't trust room-temperature superconductors. These are still good old cryogenics."

"Deflection coils? What for?"

"Ever stopped to think what would happen if that jet accidentally touched part of the ship? These coils keep it centered, and also give all the vector control we need."

They were now hovering beside a massive—yet still surprisingly small—cylinder that might have been the barrel of a twentieth-century naval gun. So this was the reaction chamber of the Drive. It was hard not to feel a sense of almost superstitious awe at the knowledge of what lay within a few centimeters of him. Duncan could easily have encircled the metal tube with his arms; how strange to think of putting your arms around a singularity, and thus, if some of the theories were correct, embracing an entire universe. . . .

Near the middle of the five-meter-long tube a small section of the casing had been removed, like the door of some miniature bank vault, and replaced by a crystal window. Through this obviously temporary opening a microscope, mounted on a swinging arm so that it could be moved away after use, was aimed into the interior of the drive unit.

The engineer clipped himself into position by the buckles conveniently fixed to the casing, stared through the eyepiece, and made some delicate micrometer adjustments.

"Take a look," he said, when he was finally satisfied.

Duncan floated to the eyepiece and fastened himself rather clumsily in place. He did not know what he had expected to see, and he remembered that the eye had to be educated before it could pass intelligible impressions to the brain. Anything utterly unfamiliar could be, quite literally, invisible, so he was not too disappointed at his first view.

What he saw was, indeed, perfectly ordinary— merely a grid of fine hairlines, crossing at right angles to form a reticule of the kind commonly used for optical measurements. Though he searched the brightly lit field of view, he could find nothing else; he might have been exploring a piece of blank graph paper.

"Look at the crossover at the exact center," said his guide, "and turn the knob on the left—*very* slowly. Half a rev will do—either direction."

Duncan obeyed, yet for a few seconds he could still see nothing. Then he realized that a tiny bulge was creeping along the hairline as he tracked the microscope. It was as if he was looking at the reticule through a sheet of glass with one minute bubble or imperfection in it.

"Do you see it?"

"Yes—*just*. Like a pinhead-sized lens. Without the grid, you'd never notice it."

"Pinhead-sized! *That's* an exaggeration, if ever I heard one. The node's smaller than an atomic nucleus. You're not actually seeing it, of course—only the distortion it produces."

"And yet there are thousands of tons of matter in there."

"Well, one or two thousand," answered the engineer, rather evasively. "It's made a dozen trips and is getting near saturation, so we'll soon have to install a new one. Of course it would go on absorbing hydrogen as long as we fed it, but we can't drag too much unnecessary mass around, or we'll pay for it in performance. Like the old seagoing ships—they used to get covered with barnacles, and slowed down if they weren't scraped clean every so often."

"What do they do with old nodes when they're too

massive to use? Is it true that they're dropped into the sun?"

"What good would that do? A node would sail right through the sun and out the other side. Frankly, I don't know what they do with the old ones. Perhaps they lump them all together into a big granddaddy node, smaller than a neutron but weighing a few million tons."

There were a dozen other questions that Duncan was longing to ask. How were these tiny yet immensely massive objects handled? Now that *Sirius* was in free fall, the node would remain floating where it was—but what kept it from shooting out of the drive tube as soon as acceleration started? He assumed that some combination of powerful electric and magnetic fields held it in place, and transmitted its thrust to the ship.

"What would happen," Duncan asked, "if I tried to touch it?"

"You know, absolutely *everyone* asks that question."

"I'm not surprised. What's the answer?"

"Well, you'd have to open the vacuum seal, and then all hell would break loose as the air rushed in."

"Then I don't do it that way. I wear a spacesuit, and I crawl up the drive tunnel and reach out a finger . . ."

"How clever of you to hit exactly the right spot! But if you did, when your finger tip got within—oh —something like a millimeter, I'd guess—the gravitational tidal forces would start to tear away at it. As soon as the first few atoms fell into the field, they'd give up all their mass-energy—and you'd think that a small hydrogen bomb had gone off in your face. The explosion would probably blow you out of the tube at a fair fraction of the speed of light."

Duncan gave an uncomfortable little laugh.

"It would certainly take a clever man to steal one of your babies. Doesn't it ever give you nightmares?"

"No. It's the tool I'm trained to use, and I understand its little ways. *I* can't imagine handling power lasers—they scare the hell out of me. You know, old

Kipling had it all summed up, as usual. You remember me talking about him?"

"Yes."

"He wrote a poem called 'The Secret of the Machines,' and it has some lines I often say to myself when I'm down here:

"But remember, please, the Law by which we
   live,
We are not built to comprehend a lie,
We can neither love nor pity nor forgive.
If you make a slip in handling us you die!

"And that's true of all machines—all the natural forces we've ever learned to handle. There's no real difference between the first caveman's fire and the node in the heart of the Asymptotic Drive."

An hour later, Duncan lay sleepless in his bunk, waiting for the Drive to go on and for *Sirius* to begin the ten days of deceleration that would lead to her rendezvous with Earth. He could still see that tiny flaw in the structure of space, hanging there in the field of the microscope, and knew that its image would haunt him for the rest of his life. And he realized now that Warren Mackenzie had betrayed nothing of his trust; all that he had learned had been published a thousand times. But no words or photos could ever convey the emotional impact he had experienced.

Tiny fingers began to tug at him; weight was returning to *Sirius*. From an infinite distance came the thin wail of the Drive; Duncan told himself that he was listening to the death cry of matter as it left the known universe, bequeathing to the ship all the energy of its mass in the final moment of dissolution. Every minute, several kilograms of hydrogen were falling into that tiny but insatiable vortex—the hole that could never be filled.

Duncan slept poorly for the rest of the night. He had dreams that he too was falling, falling into a spinning whirlpool, indefinitely deep. As he fell, he was being crushed to molecular, to atomic, and finally to subnuclear dimensions. In a moment, it would all be over, and he would disappear in a single flash of radiation. . . .

But that moment never came, because as Space contracted, Time stretched endlessly, the passing seconds becoming longer . . . and longer . . . and longer —until he was trapped forever in a changeless Eternity.

16

PORT VAN ALLEN

When Duncan had gone to bed for the last time aboard *Sirius,* Earth was still five million kilometers away. Now it seemed to fill the sky—and it was exactly like the photographs. He had laughed when more seasoned travelers told him he would be surprised at this; now he was ruefully surprised at his surprise.

Because the ship had cut right across the Earth's orbit, they were approaching from sunward, and the hemisphere below was almost fully illuminated. White continents of cloud covered most of the day side, and there were only rare glimpses of land, impossible to identify without a map. The dazzling glare of the Antarctic icecap was the most prominent surface feature; it looked very cold down there, yet Duncan reminded himself that it was tropical in comparison with much of his world.

Earth was a beautiful planet; that was beyond dispute. But it was also alien, and its cool whites and blues did nothing to warm his heart. It was indeed a paradox that Titan, with its cheerful orange clouds, looked so much more hospitable from space.

Duncan stayed in Lounge B, watching the approaching Earth and making his farewells to many temporary friends, until Port Van Allen was a dazzling star against the blackness of space, then a glittering ring, then a huge, slowly turning wheel. Weight gradually ebbed away as the drive that had taken them halfway across the Solar System decreased its thrust to zero; then there were only occasional nudges as low-powered thrustors trimmed the attitude of the ship.

The space station continued to expand. Its size was incredible, even when one realized that it had been steadily growing for almost three centuries. Now it completely eclipsed the planet whose commerce it directed and controlled; a moment later a barely perceptible vibration, instantly damped out, informed everyone that the ship had docked. A few seconds later, the Captain confirmed it.

"Welcome to Port Van Allen—Gateway to Earth. It's been nice having you with us, and I hope you enjoy your stay. Please follow the stewards, and check that you've left nothing in your cabins. And I'm sorry to mention this, but three passengers *still* haven't settled their accounts. The Purser will be waiting for them at the exit. . . ."

A few derisive groans and cheers greeted this announcement, but were quickly lost in the noisy bustle of disembarkation. Although everything was supposed to have been carefully planned, chaos was rampant. The wrong passengers went to the wrong checkpoints, while the public-address system called plaintively for individuals with improbable names. It took Duncan more than an hour to get into the spaceport, and he did not see all of his baggage again until his second day on Earth.

But at last the confusion abated as people squeezed through the bottleneck of the docking hub and sorted themselves out in the appropriate levels of the station. Duncan followed instructions conscientiously, and eventually found himself, with the rest of his alphabetical group, lined up outside the Quarantine Office. All other formalities had been completed hours ago, by radio circuit; but this was something that could not be done by electronics. Occasionally, travelers had been turned back at this point, on the very doorstep of Earth, and it was not without qualms that Duncan confronted this last hurdle.

"We don't get many visitors from Titan," said the medical officer who checked his record. "You come in the Lunar classification—less than a quarter gee. It may be tough down there for the first week, but you're young enough to adapt. It helps if both your parents were born . . ."

The doctor's voice trailed off into silence; he had come to the entry marked MOTHER. Duncan was used to the reaction, and it had long ago ceased to bother him. Indeed, he now derived a certain amusement from the surprise that discovery of his status usually produced. At least the M.O. would not ask the silly question that laymen so often asked, and to which he had long ago formulated an automatic reply: "Of course I've got a navel—the best that money can buy." The other common myth—that male clones must be abnormally virile "because they had one father *twice*"—he had wisely left unchallenged. It had been useful to him on several occasions.

Perhaps because there were six other people waiting in line, the doctor suppressed any scientific curiosity he may have felt, and sent Duncan "upstairs" to the Earth-gravity section of the spaceport. It seemed a long time before the elevator, moving out along one of the spokes of the slowly spinning wheel, finally reached the rim; and all the while, Duncan felt his weight increasing remorselessly.

When the doors opened at last, he walked stiff-legged out of the cage. Though he was still a thousand kilometers above the Earth, and his new-found weight was entirely artificial, he felt that he was already in the cruel grip of the planet below. If he could not pass the test, he would be shipped back to Titan in disgrace.

It was true that those who *just* failed to make the grade could take a high-speed toughening-up course, primarily intended for returning Lunar residents. This, however, was safe only for those who had spent most of their infancy on Earth, and Duncan could not possibly qualify.

He forgot all these fears when he entered the lounge and saw the cresent Earth, filling half the sky and slowly sliding along the huge observation windows—themselves a famous *tour de force* of space engineering. Duncan had no intention of calculating how many tons of air pressure they were resisting; as he walked up to the nearest, it was easy to imagine that there was nothing protecting him from the vacuum of space. The sensation was both exhilarating and disturbing.

He had intended to go through the check list that the doctor had given him, but that awesome view made it impossible. He stood rooted to the spot, only shifting his unaccustomed weight from one foot to the other as hitherto unknown muscles registered their complaints.

Port Van Allen circled the globe every two hours, and also rotated on its own axis three times a minute. After a while, Duncan found that he could ignore the station's own spin; his mind was able to cancel it out, like an irrelevant background noise or a persistent but neutral odor. Once he had achieved this mental attitude, he could imagine that he was alone in space, a human satellite racing along the Equator from night into day. For the Earth was waxing visibly even as he watched, the curved line of dawn moving steadily away from him as he hurtled into the east.

As usual, there was little land visible, and what could be seen through or between the clouds seemed to have no relationship to any maps. And from this altitude there was not the slightest sign of life—still less of intelligence. It was very hard to believe that most of human history had taken place beneath that blanket of brilliant white, and that, until a mere three hundred years ago, no man had ever risen above it.

He was still searching for signs of life when the disc started to contrast to a crescent once more, and the public-address system called on all passengers for Earth to report to the shuttle embarkation area, Elevators Two and Three.

He just had time to stop at the "Last Chance" toilet—almost as famous as the lounge windows—and then he was down by elevator again, back into the weightless world of the station's hub, where the Earth-to-orbit shuttle was being readied for its return journey.

There were no windows here, but each passenger had his own vision screen, on the back of the seat in front of him, and could switch to forward, rear, or downward as preferred. The choice was not completely free, though this fact was not widely advertised. Images that were likely to be too disturbing—like the final moments of docking or touchdown—were thoughtfully censored by the ship's computer.

It was pleasant to be weightless again—if only during the fifty minutes needed for the fall down to the edge of the atmosphere—and to watch the Earth slowly changing from a planet to a world. The curve of the horizon became flatter and flatter; there were fleeting glimpses of islands and the spiral nebula of a great storm, raging in silence far below. Then at last a feature that Duncan could recognize—the characteristic narrow isthmus of the California coastline, as the shuttle dropped out of the Pacific skies for its final landfall, still the width of a continent away.

He felt himself sinking deeper and deeper into the superbly padded seat, which spread the load so evenly over his body that there was the minimum of discomfort. But it was hard to breathe, until he remembered the "Advice to Passengers" he had finally managed to read. Don't try to inhale deeply, it had said; take short, sharp pants, to reduce the strain on the chest muscles. He tried it, and it worked.

Now there was a gentle buffeting and a distant roar, and the vision screen flashed into momentary flame, then switched automatically from the fires of reentry to the view astern. The canyons and deserts dwindled behind, to be replaced by a group of lakes —obviously artificial, with the tiny white flecks of sailboats clearly visible. He caught a glimpse of the huge V-shaped wake, kilometers long, of some vessel going at great speed over the water, although from this altitude it seemed completely motionless.

Then the scene changed with an abruptness that took him by surprise. He might have been flying over the ocean once more, so uniform was the view below. Still so high that he could not see the individual trees, he was passing over the endless forests of the American Midwest.

Here indeed was proof of Life, on a scale such as he had never imagined. On all of Titan, there were fewer than a hundred trees, cherished and protected with loving care. Spread out beneath him now were incomputable millions.

Somewhere, Duncan had encountered the phrase "primeval forest," and now it flashed again into his mind. So must the Earth have looked in the ancient days, before Man had set to work upon it with fire and axe. Now, with the ending of the brief Agricultural Age, much of the planet was reverting to something like its original state.

Though the fact was very hard to believe, Duncan knew perfectly well that the "primeval forest" lying endlessly beneath him was not much older than Grandfather. Only two centuries ago, this had all been farmland, divided into enormous checkerboards and covered in the autumn with golden grain. (That concept of seasons was another local reality he found extremely difficult to grasp. . . .) There were still plenty of farms in the world, run by eccentric hobbyists or biological research organizations, but the disasters of the twentieth century had taught men never again to rely on a technology that, at its very best, had an efficiency of barely one percent.

The sun was sinking, driven down into the west with unnatural speed by the shuttle's velocity. It clung to the horizon for a few seconds, then winked out. For perhaps a minute longer the forest was still visible; then it faded into obscurity.

But not into darkness. As if by magic, faint lines of light had appeared on the land below—spiders' webs of luminosity, stretching as far as the eye could see. Sometimes three or four lines would meet at a single glowing knot. There were also isolated islands of phosphorescence, apparently unconnected with the main network. Here was further proof of Man's existence; that great forest was a much busier place than it appeared to be by daylight. Yet Duncan could not help comparing this modest display with pictures he had seen from the early Atomic Age, when millions of square kilometers blazed at night with such brilliance that men could no longer see the stars.

He suddenly became aware of a compact constellation of flashing lights, moving independently of the glimmering landscape far below. For a moment, he was baffled; then he realized that he was watching some great airship, cruising not much faster than a cloud with its cargo of freight or passengers. This was one experience Titan could not provide. He determined to enjoy it as soon as the opportunity arose.

And there was a city—quite a big one, at least a hundred thousand people. The shuttle was now so low that he could make out blocks of buildings, roads, parks, and a stadium blazing with light, presumably the scene of some sporting event. The city fell astern, and a few minutes later everything was lost in a gray mist, lit by occasional flashes of lightning, not very impressive by the standards of Titan. Inside the cabin, Duncan could hear nothing of the storm through which they were now flying, but the vibration of the engines had taken a new note and he could sense that the ship was dropping rapidly. Nevertheless, he was taken completely by surprise when there was a sudden surge of weight, the slightest of jolts—and there on the screen was a sea of wet concrete, a confusion of lights, and half a dozen buses and service vehicles scurrying around in the driving rain.

After thirty years, Duncan Makenzie had returned to the world where he was born, but which he had never seen. . . .

Part III

Terra

17

WASHINGTON, D.C.

"Sorry about the weather," said George Washington. "We used to have local climate control, but gave it up after an Independence Day parade was blocked by snow."

Duncan laughed dutifully, though he was not quite sure if he was supposed to believe this.

"I don't mind," he said. "It's all new to me. I've never seen rain before."

That was not the literal truth, but it was near enough. He had often driven through ammonia gales and could still remember the poisonous cascades streaming down the windows only a few centimeters before his eyes. But this was harmless—no, *beneficent*—water, the source of life both on Earth and on Titan. If he opened the door now he would merely get wet; he would not die horribly. But the instincts of a lifetime were hard to overcome, and he knew that it would require a real effort of will to leave the protection of the limousine.

And it was a genuine limousine—another first for Duncan. Never before had he traveled in such sybaritic comfort, with a communications console on one side and a well-stocked bar on the other. Washington saw his admiring gaze and commented: "Impressive, isn't it? They don't make them any more. This was President Bernstein's favorite car."

Duncan was not too good on American presidents—after all, there had been by now ninety-five of them—but he had an approximate idea of Bernstein's date. He performed a quick calculation, didn't believe the result, and repeated it.

"That means—it's more than a hundred and fifty years old!"

"*And* it's probably good for another hundred and fifty. Of course, the upholstery—real leather, notice —is replaced every twenty years or so. If these seats could talk, they could tell some secrets. As a matter of fact, they often did—but you have my personal assurance that it's now been thoroughly debugged."

"Debugged? Oh, I know what you mean. Anyway, I don't have any secrets."

"Then we'll soon provide you with some; that's our chief local industry."

As the beautiful old car cruised in almost perfect silence under the guidance of its automatic controls, Duncan tried to see something of the terrain through which he was passing. The spaceport was fifty kilometers from the city—no one had yet invented a noiseless rocket—and the four-lane highway bore a surprising amount of traffic. Duncan could count at least twenty vehicles of various types, and even though they were all moving in the same direction, the spectacle was somewhat alarming.

"I hope all those other cars are on automatic," he said anxiously.

Washington looked a little shocked. "Of course," he said. "It's been a criminal offense for—oh—at least a hundred years to drive manually on a public highway. Though we still have occasional psychopaths who kill themselves and other people."

That was an interesting admission; Earth had not solved *all* its problems. One of the greatest dangers to the Technological Society was the unpredictable madman who tried to express his frustrations— consciously or otherwise—by sabotage. There had been hideous instances of this in the past. The destruction of the Gondwana reactor in the early twenty-first century was perhaps the best-known example. Since Titan was even more vulnerable than Earth in this respect, Duncan would have liked to discuss the matter further; but to do so within an hour of his arrival would hardly be tactful.

He was quite sure that if he did commit such a faux

pas, his host would neatly divert the conversation without causing him the slightest embarrassment. During the short time that they had been acquainted, Duncan had decided that George Washington was a very polished diplomat, with the self-assurance that comes only with a family tree whose roots are several hundred years deep. Yet it would have been hard to imagine anyone less like his distinguished namesake, for *this* George Washington was a short, bald, and rather plump brown man, very elegantly dressed and bejeweled. The baldness and plumpness were both rather surprising, since they could be so easily corrected. On the other hand, they did provide a mark of distinction, and perhaps that was the idea. But this was another sensitive subject that Duncan would be well advised to avoid—at least until he knew his host much better. And perhaps not even then.

The car was now passing over a slender bridge spanning a wide and rather dirty river. The spectacle of so much genuine water was impressive, but it looked very cold and dismal on this dreary night.

"The Potomac," said Washington. "But wait until you see it on a sunny day, after that silt's gone downstream. Then it's blue and sparkling, and you'd never guess it took two hundred years of hard work to get it that way. And that's Watergate—not the original, of course; *that* was pulled down around 2000, though the Democrats wanted to make it a national monument. And the Kennedy Center—that is the original, more or less. Every fifty years some architect tries to salvage it, but now it's been given up as a bad job."

So this was Washington, still basking (though not very effectively, on a night like this) in its former glories. Duncan had read that the physical appearance of the city had changed very little in three hundred years, and he could well believe it. Most of the old government and public buildings had been carefully preserved. The result, said the critics, was the largest inhabited museum in the world.

A little later, the car turned into a driveway which led through beautifully kept lawns. There was a gentle beeping from the control panel, and a sign flashed beneath the steering handle: SWITCH TO MANUAL. George Washington took over, and proceeded at a cautious twenty klicks between flower beds and sculptured bushes, coming to a halt under the portico of an obviously very old building. It seemed much too large for a private house, but rather too small for a hotel, despite the fact that it bore the sign, in lettering so elaborate that it was almost impossible to read: CENTENNIAL HOTEL.

Professor Washington seemed to have an extraordinary knack of anticipating questions before they could be asked.

"It was built by a railroad baron, in the late nineteenth century. He wanted to have somewhere to entertain Congress, and the investment paid him several thousand percent. We've taken it over for the occasion, and most of the official guests will be staying here."

To Duncan's astonishment—and embarrassment, since personal service was unknown on Titan—his scanty baggage was seized by two black gentlemen wearing gorgeous liveries. One of them addressed him in a soft, musical language of which he could not comprehend a single word.

"You're overdoing it, Henry," George Washington remonstrated mildly. "That may be genuine slave patter, but what's the point if only you linguistic historians can understand it? And where *did* you get that make-up? I may need some myself."

Despite this appeal, Duncan still found the reply unintelligible. On their way up in a gilded birdcage of a tiny elevator, Washington commented: "I'm afraid Professor Murchison is entering too thoroughly into the Spirit of '76. Still, it shows we've made some progress. A couple of centuries ago, if you'd suggested to him that he play one of his humbler ancestors, even in a pageant, he'd have knocked your head off. Now he's having a perfectly wonderful time, and we may not be able to get him back to his classes at Georgetown."

Washington looked at his plump, brown hand and sighed.

"It's getting more and more difficult to find a *genuine* black skin. I'm no race snob," he added hastily, "but it will be a pity when we're all the same shade of off white. Meanwhile, I suppose you *do* have a slightly unfair advantage."

Duncan looked at him for a moment with puzzled incomprehension. He had never given any more thought to his skin color than to that of his hair; indeed, if suddenly challenged, he would have been hard pressed to describe either. Certainly he had never thought of himself as black; but now he realized, with understandable satisfaction, that he was several shades darker than George Washington, descendant of African kings.

When the door of the hotel suite closed behind him, and it was no longer necessary to keep up appearances, Duncan collapsed thankfully into one of the heavily padded chairs. It tilted backward so voluptuously that he guessed it had been especially designed for visitors from low-gravity worlds. George Washington was certainly an admirable host and seemed to have thought of everything. Nevertheless, Duncan knew that it would be a long time before he felt really at ease.

Quite apart from the drag of gravity, there were dozens of subtler reminders that he was not on his home world. One was the very *size* of the room; by Titanian standards, it was enormous. And it was furnished in such luxury as he had never seen in real life, but only in historical plays. Yet that, of course, was completely appropriate; he was living in the middle of history. This mansion had been built before the first man had ventured beyond the atmosphere, and he guessed that most of its fittings were contemporary. The cabinets full of delicate glassware, the oil paintings, the quaint old photographs of stiffly posed and long-forgotten eminences (perhaps the original Washington—no, cameras hadn't been invented then), the heavy drapes—none of these could have been matched on Titan, and Duncan doubted if their holographic patterns were even stored in the Central Library.

104

The very communications console looked as if it dated back to the last century. Although all the elements were familiar—the blank gray screen, the alphanumeric keyboard, the camera lens and speaker grille—something about the design gave it an old-fashioned appearance. When he felt that he could again walk a few yards without danger of collapse, Duncan made his way cautiously to the console and parked himself heavily on the chair in front of it.

The type and serial numbers were in the usual place, tucked away at the side of the screen. Yes, there was the date—2183. It was almost a hundred years old.

Yet apart from a slight fuzziness of the "e" and "a" on the contact pads, there was practically no sign of wear. And why should there be, in a piece of equipment that did not contain a single moving part?

This was another sharp reminder that Earth was an old world, and had learned to conserve the past. Novelty for its own sake was an unlamented relic of the centuries of waste. If a piece of equipment functioned satisfactorily, it was not replaced merely because of changes in style, but only if it broke down, or there was some fundamental improvement in performance. The home communications console—or Comsole—had reached its technological plateau in the early twenty-first century, and Duncan was prepared to bet that there were units on Earth that had given continuous service for over two hundred years.

And that was not even one tenth of the history of this world. For the first time in his life, Duncan felt an almost overwhelming sense of inferiority. He had not really believed that the Terrans would regard him as a barbarian from the outer darkness; but now he was not so sure.

18

EMBASSY

Duncan's Minisec had been a parting gift from Colin, and he was not completely familiar with its controls. There had been nothing really wrong with his old unit, and he had left it behind with some regret; but the casing had become stained and battle-scarred, and he had to agree that it was not elegant enough for Earth.

The 'Sec was the standard size of all such units, determined by what could fit comfortably in the normal human hand. At a quick glance, it did not differ greatly from one of the small electronic calculators that had started coming into general use in the late twentieth century. It was, however, infinitely more versatile, and Duncan could not imagine how life would be possible without it.

Because of the finite size of clumsy human fingers, it had no more controls than its ancestors of three centuries earlier. There were fifty neat little studs; each, however, had a virtually unlimited number of functions, according to the mode of operation—for the character visible on each stud changed according to the mode. Thus on ALPHANUMERIC, twenty-six of the studs bore the letters of the alphabet, while ten showed the digits zero to nine. On MATH, the letters disappeared from the alphabetical studs and were replaced by $\times$, $+$, $\div$, $-$, $=$, and all the standard mathematical functions.

Another mode was DICTIONARY. The 'Sec stored over a hundred thousand words, whose three-line definitions could be displayed on the bright little screen, steadily rolling over page by page if desired. CLOCK and CALENDAR also used the screen for display, but for dealing with vast amounts of information it was desirable to link the 'Sec to the much larger screen of a standard Comsole. This could be done through the unit's optical interface—a tiny Transmit-Receive bull's-eye operating in the near ultraviolet As long as this lens was in visual range of the corresponding sensor on a Comsole, the two units could happily exchange information at the rate of megabits per second. Thus when the 'Sec's own internal memory was saturated, its contents could be dumped into a larger store for permanent keeping; or, conversely, it could be loaded up through the optical link with any special data required for a particular job.

Duncan was now employing it for its simplest possible use—merely as a speech recorder, which was almost an insult to a machine of such power. But first there was an important matter to settle—the question of security.

An easily remembered word, preferably one that would never be employed in this context, would be the simplest key. Better still, a word that did not even exist—then it could never accidentally trigger the 'Sec's memory.

Suddenly, he had it. There was one name he would never forget; and if he deliberately misspelled it. . . .

He carefully pecked out KALINDY, followed by the sequence of instructions that would set up the memory. Then he unplugged the tiny radiomike, pinned it on his shirt, spoke a test message, and checked that the machine would play it back only after it had been given the correct order.

Duncan had never kept a diary, but he had decided to do so as soon as he arrived on Earth. In a few weeks he would meet more people and visit more places than in the whole of his preceding life, and would certainly have experiences that could never be repeated when he returned to Titan. He was determined to miss nothing that could be helped, for the memories he was storing now would be of inestimable value in the years ahead. How many times in his old age, he wondered, would he play back these words of his youth . . . ?

"2276 June 12. I'm still adapting to Earth gravity, and don't think I'll ever get really used to it. But I can stand for an hour at a time now, without developing too many aches and pains. Yesterday I saw a man actually *jumping*. I could hardly believe my eyes. . . .

"George, who thinks of everything, has arranged a masseur for me. I don't know if that's helped at all, but it's certainly an interesting experience."

Duncan stopped recording and contemplated this slight understatement. Such luxuries were rare on Titan, and he had never before had a massage in his life. Bernie Patras, the amiable and uninhibited young man who had visited him, had shown a remarkable (indeed, startling) knowledge of physiology, and had also given Duncan much useful advice. He was a specialist in treating off-worlders, and recommended one sovereign cure for gravitational complaints. "Spend an hour a day floating in a bath—at least for the first month. Don't let your schedule squeeze this out, no matter how busy you are. If you *have* to, you can do a lot of work in a tub—reading, dictating, and so forth. Why, the Lunar Ambassador used to hold briefings with just his nose and mouth above water. Said he could think better that way. . . ."

That would certainly be an undiplomatic spectacle, Duncan told himself—unique even in this city, which had probably seen everything.

"I've been here three days now, and this is the first time I've had the energy—and the inclination—*and* the opportunity—to put my thoughts in order. But from now on, I swear, I'll do this every day. . . .

"The first morning after my arrival, General George—that's what everyone calls him—took me to the Embassy, which is only a few hundred meters from the hotel. Ambassador Robert Farrell apologized because he couldn't come to the spaceport. He said, 'I knew you'd be in good hands with George—he's the world's greatest organizer.' Then the General left us, and we had a long private talk.

"I met Bob Farrell on his last visit to Titan, three years ago, and he remembers me well—at least, he gave that impression, which I suppose is an art all diplomats have to acquire. He was very helpful and friendly, but I got the feeling that he was sounding me out, and not telling me everything he knew. I realize that he's in an ambiguous position, being a Terran yet having to represent our interests. One day this may cause difficulties, but I don't know what we can do about it, since no native-born Titanian can ever live on Earth. . . .

"Luckily, there are no urgent problems, as the Hydrogen Agreement isn't due for renegotiation until '80. But there were dozens of little items on my shopping list, and I left him with plenty to think about. Such as: why can't we get quicker deliveries of equipment, can anything be done to improve shipping schedules, what went wrong with the new student exchange?—and similar Galaxy-shaking questions. He promised to set up appointments for me with all the people who could straighten these things out, but I tried to hint that I wanted to spend some time looking at Earth. And after all, he's not only our man in Washington but also our representative on Terra. . . .

"He seemed quite surprised when I told him that I expected to stay on Earth for almost a year, but at this stage I thought it best not to give him the main reason. I'm sure he'll guess it quickly enough. When he tactfully asked about my budget, I explained that the Centennial Committee had been a great help, and there was still some Makenzie money in the World Bank which I was determined to use. 'I understand,' he said, 'Old Malcolm's over a hundred and twenty now, isn't he? Even on Earth, leaving as little as possible for the Community Fund to grab is a popular pastime.' Then he added, not very hopefully, that any personal balances could be legally bequeathed to the Embassy for its running expenses. I said that was a very interesting point and I'd bear it in mind. . . .

"He volunteered to give me any assistance on my speech, which was kind of him. When I said I was still working on it, he reminded me that it was essential to have a final draft by the end of June so that all the important commentators could study it in advance. Otherwise, it would be drowned in the flood of verbiage on July Fourth. That was a very good point, which I hadn't thought of; but then I said, 'Won't the other speakers do exactly the same?' And he answered, 'Of course, but I've got good friends in all the media, and there's a great interest in Titan. You're still intrepid pioneers at the edge of the Solar System, carving out a new civilization in the wilderness. There may not be many volunteer carvers around here, but we like to hear about such things.' By that time I felt we'd got to understand each other, and so I risked teasing him: 'You mean it's true—Earth *is* getting decadent?' And he looked at me with a grin and answered quickly: 'Oh no—*we* aren't decadent.' Then he paused, and added: 'But the *next* generation will be.' I wonder how far he was joking. . . .

"Then we talked for ten minutes about mutual friends like the Helmers and the Wongs and the Morgans and the Lees—oh, he seems to know everyone important on Titan. And finally he asked about Grandma Ellen, and I told him that she was just the same as ever, which he understood perfectly. And then George came back and took me to his farm. It was the first chance I had of seeing the open countryside, in full daylight. I'm still trying to get over it. . . ."

19

MOUNT VERNON

"**D**on't take this program too seriously," said General George Washington. "It's still being changed every day. But your main appointments—I've marked them—aren't going to be altered. Especially on July Fourth."

Duncan leafed through the small brochure that the other had handed to him when they entered President Bernstein's limousine. It was a daunting document—stuffed full of Addresses and Receptions and Balls and Processions and Concerts. Nobody in the capital was going to get much sleep during the first few days in July, and Duncan felt sorry for poor President Claire Hansen.

As a gesture of courtesy, in this Centennial year she was President not only of the United States, but also of Earth. And, of course, she had not asked for either job; if she *had* done so—or even if she had been suspected of such a faux pas—she would have been automatically eliminated. For the last century, almost all top political appointments on Terra had been made by random computer selection from the pool of individuals who had the necessary qualifications. It had taken the human race several thousand years to realize that there were some jobs that should never be given to the people who volunteered for them, especially if they showed too much enthusiasm. As on shrewd political commentator had remarked: "We want a President who has to be carried screaming and kicking into the White House—but will then do the best job he possibly can, so that he'll get time off for good behavior."

Duncan put the program away; there would be plenty of opportunity to study it later. Now he had eyes only for his first real look at Planet Earth, on a bright sunny day.

And *that* was the first problem. Never before in his life had he been exposed to such a glare. Though he had been warned, he was still taken aback by the sheer blazing ferocity of a sun almost one hundred times brighter than the star that shone gently on his own world. As the car whispered automatically through the outskirts of Washington, he kept readjusting the transmission of his dark glasses to find a comfortable level. It was appalling to think that there were places on Earth where the sun was even more brilliant than this, and he remembered another warning that had now suddenly become very real. Where the light fell directly on his exposed skin, he could actually *feel* the heat. On Titan, the very concept of "sunburn" was ludicrous; now, it was all too easy to imagine, especially for skin as dark as his.

He was like a newborn child, seeing the world for the first time. Almost every single object in his field of vision was unfamiliar, or recognizable only from the recordings he had studied. Impressions flowed in upon him at such a rate that he felt utterly confused, until he decided that the only thing to do was to concentrate on a single category of objects and to ignore all the rest—even though they were clamoring for his attention.

Trees, for example. There were millions of them—but he had expected that. What he had not anticipated was the enormous variety of their shape, size, and color. And he had no words for any of them. Indeed, as he realized with shame, he could not have identified the few trees in his own Meridian Park. Here was a whole complex universe, part of everyday life for most of mankind since the beginning of history; and he could not utter one meaningful sentence about it, for lack of a vocabulary. When he searched his mind, he could think of only four words that had anything to do with trees—"leaf," "branch," "root," and "stem." And all these he had learned in a totally different context.

Then there were flowers. At first, Duncan had been puzzled by the random patches of color that he glimpsed from time to time. Flowers were not uncommon on Titan—usually as highly prized, isolated specimens, though there were some small groups of a few dozen in the Park. Here they were as countless as the trees, and even more varied. And once again, he had no names for any of them. This world was full of beauties of which he could not speak. Living on Earth was going to have some unanticipated frustrations. . . .

"What was *that!*" he suddenly cried. Washington swung around in his seat to get a fix on the tiny object that had just shot across the roadway.

"A squirrel, I think. Lots of them in these woods —and of course they're always getting run over. That's one problem no one has ever been able to solve." He paused, then added gently: "I suppose you've never seen one before?"

Duncan laughed, without much humor.

"I've never seen *any* animal before—except Man."

"You don't even have a zoo on Titan?"

"No. We've been arguing about it for years, but the

problems are too great. And, to be perfectly frank, I think most people are scared of something going wrong—remember the plague of rats in that Lunar colony. What we're really frightened of, though, are insects. If anyone ever discovered that a fly had slipped through quarantine, there'd be world-wide hysteria. We've got a nice, sterile environment, and we want to keep it that way."

"Hm," said Washington. "You're not going to find it easy to adjust to our dirty, infested world. Yet a lot of people here have been complaining for the last century or so that it's too clean and tidy. They're talking nonsense, of course; there's more wilderness now than there has been for a thousand years."

The car had come to the crest of a low hill, and for the first time Duncan had an extensive view of the surrounding countryside. He could see for at least twenty kilometers, and the effect of all this open space was overwhelming. It was true that he had gazed at much larger—and far more dramatic—vistas on Titan; but the landscapes of his own world were implacably lethal, and when he traveled on its open surface he had to be insulated from the hostile environment by all the resources of modern technology. It was almost impossible to believe that there was nowhere here, from horizon to horizon, where he could not stand unprotected in the open, breathing freely in an atmosphere which would not instantly shrivel his lungs. The knowledge did not give him a sense of freedom, but rather of vertigo.

It was even worse when he looked up at the sky, so utterly different from the low, crimson overcast of Titan. He had flown halfway across the Solar System, yet never had he received such an impression of space and distance as he did now, when he stared at the solid-looking white clouds, sailing through a blue abyss that seemed to go on forever. It was useless to tell himself that they were only ten kilometers away—the distance a spaceship could travel in a fraction of a second. Not even the starfields of the Milky Way had yielded such glimpses of infinity.

For the very first time, as he looked at the fields and forests spread out around him under the open

113

sky, Duncan realized the immensity of Planet Earth by the only measure that counted—the scale of the individual human being. And now he understood that cryptic remark Robert Kleinman had made before he left for Saturn: "Space is small; only the planets are big."

"If you were here three hundred years ago," said his host, with considerable satisfaction, "about eighty percent of this would have been houses and highways. Now the figure's down to ten percent— and *this* is one of the most heavily built-up areas on the continent. It's taken a long time, but we've finally cleaned up the mess the twentieth century left. Most of it, anyway. We've kept some as a reminder. There are a couple of steel towns still intact in Pennsylvania; visiting them is an educational experience you won't forget, but won't want to repeat."

"You said this was a ten-percent built-up area. I find it hard to believe even that. Where is everyone?" Duncan queried.

"There are many more people around than you imagine. I'd hate to think of the mental activity that's going on within two hundred meters of us, at this very moment. But because this parkway is so well landscaped, you probably haven't noticed the surface exits and feeder roads."

"Of course—I still have the old-fashioned picture of Terrans as surface dwellers."

"Oh, we are, essentially. I don't think we'll ever develop the—ah—'corridor culture' you have on the Moon and planets."

Professor Washington had used that anthropological cliché with some caution. Obviously he was not quite sure if Duncan approved of it. Nor, for that matter, was Duncan himself; but he had to admit that despite all the debates that had raged about it, the phrase was an accurate description of Titan's social life.

"One of the chief problems of entertaining off-worlders like yourself," said Washington somewhat ruefully, "is that I find myself explaining at great length things that they know perfectly well, but are too polite to admit. A couple of years ago I took a statistician from Tranquillity along this road, and gave him a brilliant lecture on the population changes here in the Washington-Virginia region over the last three hundred years. I thought he'd be interested, and he was. If I'd done my homework properly—which I *usually* do, but for some reason had neglected in this case—I'd have found that he'd written the standard work on the subject. After he'd left, he sent me a copy, with a very nice inscription."

Duncan wondered how much "homework" George had done on him; doubtless a good deal.

"You can assume my total ignorance in these matters. Still, I should have realized that fusor technology would be almost as important *on* Earth as off it."

"It's not my field, but you're probably right. When it was cheaper and simpler to melt a home underground than to build it above—*and* to fit it with viewscreens that were better than any conceivable window—it's not surprising that the surface lost many of its attractions. Not all, though." He gestured toward the left-hand side of the parkway.

They were approaching a small access road, which merged gently into the main traffic lane. It led into a wood about a kilometer away, and through the trees Duncan could glimpse at least a dozen houses. They were all of different design, yet had common features so that they formed a harmonious group. Every one had steeply gabled red roofs, large windows, gray stone walls—and even chimneys. These were certainly not functional, but many of them served to support complicated structures of metal rods.

"Fake antique," said Washington with some disapproval. "Mid-twentieth-century TV antennas. Oh well, there's no accounting for tastes."

The road was plunging downhill now, and was about to pass under a graceful bridge carring a road much wider than the parkway. It was also carrying considerably more traffic, moving at a leisurely twenty or thirty kilometers an hour.

"Enjoying the good weather," said Washington. "You only see a few madmen there in the winter. And you may not believe this, but there was a time when

115

the *motorways* were the wide roads. They had to be when there was a hundred times as much traffic— *and no automatic steering.*" He shuddered at the thought. "More people were killed on these roads than ever died in warfare—did you know that? And of course they still get killed, up there on the bikeways. No one's ever discovered a way to stop cyclists from wobbling; that's another reason why the road's so wide."

As they dived under the bridge, a colorful group of young riders waved down at them, and Washington replied with a cheerful salute.

"When I was thirty years younger," he said wistfully, "a gang of us set off for California on the Transcontinental Bikeway. No electrocycles allowed, either. Well, we were unlucky—ran into terrible weather in Kansas. Some of us made it, but I wasn't one of them. I've still got a twelve-speed Diamond Special—all carbon fiber and beryllium; you can lift it with one finger. Even now, I could do a hundred klicks on it, if I were fool enough to try."

The big car was slowing down, its computer brain sensing an exit ahead. Presently it peeled off from the parkway, then speeded up again along a narrow road whose surface rapidly disintegrated into a barely visible grass-covered track. Washington took the steering lever just a second before the END AUTO warning light started to flash on the control panel.

"I'm taking you to the farm for several reasons," he said. "Life will soon get hectic for both of us, as more visitors start arriving. This may be the last opportunity we have to go through your program in peace and quiet. Also, out-worlders can learn a lot about Earth very quickly in a place like this. But to be honest—the truth is that I'm proud of the place, and like showing it off."

They were now approaching a high stone wall, running for hundreds of meters in both directions. Duncan tried to calculate how much labor it represented, if all those oddly shaped blocks were assembled by hand—as surely they must have been. The figure was so incredible that he couldn't believe it.

And that huge gate was made of—*genuine* wood,

for it was unpainted and he could see the grain. As it swung automatically open, Duncan read the name-plate, and turned to the Professor in surprise.

"But I thought——" he began.

George Washington looked slightly embarrassed.

"That's my private joke," he admitted. "The real Mount Vernon is fifty kilometers southeast of here. You mustn't miss it."

That last phrase, Duncan guessed, was going to become all too familiar in the months ahead—right up to the day when he reembarked for Titan.

Inside the walls, the road—now firm-packed gravel —ran in a straight line through a checkerboard of small fields. Some of the fields were plowed, and there was a tractor working in one of them—under direct human control, for a man was sitting on the open driving seat. Duncan felt that he had indeed traveled back in time.

"I suppose there's no need to explain," said the Professor, "that all this doesn't belong to *me*. It's owned by the Smithsonian. Some people complain that everything within a hundred kilometers of the Capitol is owned by the Smithsonian, but that's a slight exaggeration. I'm just the administrator; you might say it's a kind of full-time hobby. Every year I have to submit a report, and as long as I do a good job, and don't have a fight with the Regents, this is my home. Needless to say, I am careful to keep on excellent terms with at least fifty-one percent of the Regents. By the way, do you recognize any of these crops?"

"I'm afraid not—though that's grass, isn't it?"

"Well, technically, almost everything here is. Grass includes all the cereals—barley, rice, maize, wheat, oats. . . . We grow them all except rice."

"But why—I mean, except for scientific and archaeological interest?"

"Isn't that sufficient? But I think you'll find there's more to it than that, when you've had a look around."

At the risk of being impolite, Duncan persisted. He was not trying to be stubborn, but was genuinely interested.

"What about efficiency? Doesn't it take a square kilometer to feed one man, with this system?"

"Out around Saturn, perhaps; I'm afraid you've dropped a few zeros. If it *had* to, this little farm could support fifty people in fair comfort, though their diet would be rather monotonous."

"I'd no idea—my God, what's *that?*"

"You're joking—you don't recognize it?"

"Oh, I know it's a horse. But it's *enormous*. I thought . . ."

"Well, I can't blame you, though wait until you see an elephant. Charlemagne is probably the largest horse alive today. He's a Percheron, and weighs over a ton. His ancestors used to carry knights in full armor. Like to meet him?"

Duncan wanted to say "Not really," but it was too late. Washington brought the car to a halt, and the gigantic creature ambled toward them.

Until this moment, the limousine had been closed and they had been traveling in air-conditioned comfort. Now the windows slid down—and Primeval Earth hit Duncan full in the nostrils.

"What's the matter?" asked Washington anxiously. "Are you all right?"

Duncan gulped, and took a cautious sniff.

"I think so," he said, without much conviction. "It's just that—the air is rather—" He struggled for words as well as breath, and had almost selected "ripe" when he gratefully switched to "rich" in the nick of time.

"I'm so sorry," apologized Washington, genuinely contrite. "I'd quite forgotten how strange this must be to you. Let me close the window. Go away, Charlie —sorry, some other time."

The monster now completely dwarfed the car, and a huge head, half as big as a man, was trying to insert itself through the partially open window on Duncan's side. The air became even thicker, and redolent of more animal secretions than he cared to identify. Two huge, slobbering lips drew back, to disclose a perfectly terrifying set of teeth. . . .

"Oh, very well," said Professor Washington in a resigned voice. He leaned across his cowering guest, holding out an open palm on which two lumps of sugar had magically appeared. Gently as any maiden's kiss, the lips nuzzled Washington's hand, and the gift vanished as if inhaled. A mild, gentle eye, which from this distance seemed about as large as a fist, looked straight at Duncan, who started to laugh a little hysterically as the apparition withdrew.

"What's so funny?" asked Washington.

"Look at it from *my* point of view. I've just met my first Monster from Outer Space. Thank God it was friendly."

20

THE TASTE OF HONEY

"I do hope you slept well," said George Washington, as they walked out into the bright summer morning.

"Quite well, thank you," Duncan answered, stifling a yawn. He only wished that the statement were true.

It had been almost as bad as his first night aboard *Sirius*. Then, the noises had all been mechanical. This time, they were made by—*things*.

Leaving the window open had been a big mistake, but who could have guessed? "We don't need air conditioning this time of year," George had explained. "Which is just as well, because we haven't got it. The Regents weren't too happy even about electric light in a four-hundred-year-old house. If you do get too cold, here are some extra blankets. Primitive, but very effective."

Duncan did not get too cold; the night was pleasantly mild. It was also extremely busy.

There had been distant thumpings which, he eventually decided, must have been Charlie moving his thousand kilos of muscle around the fields. There had been strange squeakings and rustlings apparently just outside his window, and one high-pitched squeal, suddenly terminated, which could only have been caused by some unfortunate small beast meeting an untimely end.

But at last he dozed off—only to be wakened, quite suddenly, by the most horrible of all the sensations that can be experienced by a man in the utter darkness of an unfamiliar bedchamber. *Something* was moving around the room.

It was moving almost silently, yet with amazing speed. There was a kind of whispering rush and, occasionally, a ghostly squeaking so high-pitched that at first Duncan wondered if he was imagining the entire phenomenon. After some minutes he decided, reluctantly, that it was real enough. Whatever the thing might be, it was obviously airborne. But what could possibly move at such speed, in total darkness, without colliding with the fittings and furniture of the bedroom?

While he considered this problem, Duncan did what any sensible man would do. He burrowed under the bedclothes, and presently, to his vast relief, the whispering phantom, with a few more shrill gibberings, swooped out into the night. When his nerves had fully recovered, Duncan hopped out of bed and closed the window; but it seemed hours before his nervous system settled down again.

In the bright light of morning, his fears seemed as foolish as they doubtless were, and he decided not to ask George any questions about his nocturnal visitor; presumably it was some night bird or large insect. Everyone knew that there were no dangerous animals left on Earth, except in well-guarded reservations. . . .

Yet the creatures that George now seemed bent on introducing to him looked distinctly menacing. Unlike Charlemagne, they had built-in weapons.

"I suppose," said George, only half doubtfully, "that you recognize these?"

"Of course—I do know *some* Terran zoology. If it has a leg at each corner, *and* horns, it's not a horse, but a cow."

"I'll only give you half marks. Not all cows have horns. And for that matter, there used to be horned horses. But they became extinct when there were no more virgins to bridle them."

Duncan was still trying to decide if this was a joke, and if so what was the point of it, when he had a slight mishap.

"Sorry!" exclaimed George, "I should have warned you to mind your step. Just rub it off on that tuft of grass."

"Well, at least it doesn't smell quite as bad as it looks," said Duncan resignedly, determined to make the best of a bad job.

"That's because cows are herbivores. Though they're not very bright, they're sweet, clean animals. No wonder they used to worship them in India. Hello, Daisy—morning, Ruby—now, Clemence, *that* was naughty—"

It seemed to Duncan that these bovine endearments were rather one-sided, for their recipients gave no detectable reaction. Then his attention was suddenly diverted; something quite incredible was flying toward them.

It was small—its wingspan could not have been more than ten centimeters—and it traced wavering, zigzag patterns through the air, often seeming about to land on a low bush or patch of grass, then changing its mind at the last moment. Like a living jewel, it blazed with all the colors of the rainbow; its beauty struck Duncan like a sudden revelation. Yet at the same time he found himself asking what purpose such exuberant—no, *arrogant*—loveliness could possibly serve.

"What is it?" he whispered to his companion, as the creature swept aimlessly back and forth a couple of meters above the grass.

"Sorry," said George. "I can't identify it. I don't *think* it's indigenous, though I may be wrong. We get a lot of migrants nowadays, and sometimes they escape from collectors—breeding them's been a popular hobby for years." Then he stopped. He had suddenly understood the real thrust of Duncan's question. There was something close to pity in his eyes when he continued, in quite a different tone of voice: "I should have explained—it's a butterfly."

But Duncan scarcely heard him. That iridescent creature, drifting so effortlessly through the air, made

121

him forget the ferocious gravitational field of which he was now a captive. He started to run toward it—with the inevitable result.

Luckily, he landed on a clean patch of grass.

Half an hour later, feeling quite comfortable but rather foolish, Duncan was sitting in the centuries-old farmhouse with his bandaged ankle stretched out on a footstool, while Mrs. Washington and her two young daughters prepared lunch. He had been carried back like a wounded warrior from the battlefield by a couple of tough farm workers who handled his weight with contemptuous ease, and also, he could not help noticing, radiated a distinct aroma of Charlemagne. . . .

It must be strange, he thought, to live in what was virtually a museum, even as a kind of part-time hobby; he would have been continually afraid of damaging some priceless artifact—such as the spinning wheel that Mrs. Washington had demonstrated to him. At the same time, he could appreciate that all this activity made a good deal of sense. There was no other way in which you could really get to understand the past, and there were still many people on earth who found this an attractive way of life. The twenty or so farm workers, for example, were here permanently, summer and winter. Indeed, he found it rather hard to imagine some of them in any other environment—even after they had been thoroughly scrubbed. . . .

But the kitchen was spotless, and a most attractive smell was floating from it. Duncan could recognize very few of its ingredients, but one was unmistakable, even though he had met it today for the first time in his life. It was the mouth-watering fragrance of newly baked bread.

It would be all right, he assured his still slightly queasy stomach. He had to ignore the undeniable fact that everything on the table was grown from dirt and dung, and not synthesized from nice, clean chemicals in a spotless factory. This was how the human race had lived for almost the whole of its history; only in the last few seconds of time had there been any alternative.

For one gut-wrenching moment, until Washington had reassured him, he had feared that he might be served real meat. Apparently it was still available, and there was no actual law against it, though many attempts had been made to pass one. Those who opposed Prohibition pointed out that attempts to enforce morality by legislation were always counterproductive; if meat were banned, everybody would want it, even if it made them sick. And anyway, this was a perversion which did harm to nobody. . . . Not so, retorted the Prohibitionists; it would do irreparable harm to countless innocent animals, and revive the revolting trade of the butcher. The debate continued, with no end in sight.

Confident that lunch would present mysteries but no terrors, Duncan did his best to enjoy himself. On the whole he succeeded. He bravely tackled everything set before him, rejecting about a third after one nibble, tolerating another third, and thoroughly appreciating the remainder. As it turned out, there was nothing that he actively disliked, but several items had flavors that were too strange and complicated to appeal to him at first taste. Cheese, for example— that was a complete novelty. There were about six different kinds, and he nibbled at them all. He felt that he could get quite enthusiastic about at least two varieties, if he worked on it. But that might not be a good idea, for it was notoriously difficult to persuade the Titan food chemists to introduce new patterns into their synthesizers.

Some products were quite familiar. Potatoes and tomatoes, it seemed, tasted much the same all over the Solar System. He had already encountered them, as luxury products of the hydroponic farms, but had always found it difficult to get enthusiastic about either, at several solars a kilogram.

The main dish was—well, interesting. It was something called steak and kidney pie, and perhaps the unfortunate name turned him off. He knew perfectly well that the contents were based on high-protein soya; Washington had confessed that this was the only item not actually produced on the farm, because the

123

technology needed was too elaborate. Nevertheless, he could not manage more than a few bites. It was too bad that every time he tried to take a mouthful, he kept thinking of the phrase "kidney function" and its unhappy associations. But the crust of the pie was delicious, and he polished off more than half of it.

Dessert was no problem. It consisted of a large variety of fruits, most of them unfamiliar to Duncan even by name. Some were insipid, others very pleasant, but he felt that all were perfectly safe. The strawberries he thought especially good, though he turned down the cream that was offered with them when he discovered, by tactful questioning, exactly how it was made.

He was comfortably replete when Mrs. Washington produced a final surprise—a small wooden box containing a wax honeycomb. As long as he could remember, Duncan had been familiar with that term for lightweight structures; it required a mental volte-face to realize that this was the genuine, original item constructed by Terran insects.

"We've just started keeping bees," explained the Professor. "Fascinating creatures, but we're still not sure if they're worth the trouble. I think you'll like this honey—try it on this crust of new bread."

His hosts watched him anxiously as he spread the golden fluid, which he thought looked exactly like lubricating oil. He hoped that it would taste better, but he was now prepared for almost anything.

There was a long silence. Then he took another bite—and another.

"Well?" asked George at last.

"It's—delicious—one of the best things I've ever tasted."

"I'm so pleased," said Mrs. Washington. "George, be sure to send some to the hotel for Mr. Makenzie."

Mr. Makenzie continued to sample the bread and honey, very slowly. There was a remote and abstracted expression on his face, which his delighted hosts attributed to sheer gastronomical pleasure. They could not possibly have guessed at the real reason.

Duncan had never been particularly interested in

food, and had made no effort to try the occasional novelties that were imported into Titan. The few times that any had been pressed upon him, he had not enjoyed them; he still grimaced at the memory of a reputed delicacy called caviar. He was therefore absolutely certain that never before in his life had he tasted honey.

Yet he recognized it at once; and that was only half the mystery. Like a name that is on the tip of the tongue, yet eludes all attempts to grasp it, the memory of that earlier encounter lay just below the level of consciousness. It had happened a long time ago—but *when,* and *where?* For a fleeting moment he almost took seriously the idea of reincarnation. You, Duncan Makenzie, were a beekeeper in some earlier life on Earth. . . .

Perhaps he was mistaken in thinking that he knew the taste. The association could have been triggered by some random leakage between mental circuits. And anyway, it could not possibly be of the slightest importance. . . .

He knew better. Somehow, it was very important indeed.

21

HISTORY LESSON

Of all the old cities, it was generally agreed that Paris and Washington offered the best combination of beauty, culture, history—and convenience. Unlike such largely random aggregations as London and Rome, which had defied millennia of planning, they had been adapted fairly easily to automatic transportation. Could he have risen from his tomb in Arlington, the luckless Pierre Charles L'Enfant would have been proud indeed to have discovered how well he had laid the ground for a technology centuries in his future.

Though an official car was available whenever he wished, Duncan preferred to be as independent as possible. Coming from an aggressively egalitarian society, he never felt quite happy when he was afforded special privileges—except, of course, those he had earned himself. Now that his sprained ankle was no longer paining him he had no excuse for using personal transport, and one could never know a city until one had explored it on foot.

Like any ordinary tourist—and Washington expected the incredible total of five million before the end of July—Duncan rode the glideways and autojitneys, gaping at the famous buildings and remembering the great men who had lived and worked here for half a thousand years. In the five-kilometer-long rectangle from the Lincoln Memorial to the Capitol, and from the Washington Monument to the White House, no changes had been permitted for more than a century. To ride the shuttle down Constitution Avenue and back along Independence, on the south side of the Mall, was to take a journey through time.

And time was the problem, for Duncan could spare only an hour or two a day for sightseeing. His planned schedule had already been wrecked by a factor that he had refused to take seriously, despite numerous warnings. Instead of his usual six, he needed no fewer than ten hours of sleep every day. This was yet another side effect of the increased gravity, and there was nothing he could do about it; his body stubbornly insisted on the additional time, to overcome the extra wear and tear. Eventually, he knew, he would make a partial adaptation, but he could hardly hope to manage with less than eight hours. It was maddening to have come all this way, to one of the most fascinating places on Earth, and to be compelled to waste more than forty percent of his life in unconsciousness.

As with most off-worlders, his first target had been the National Museum of Astronautics on the Mall, because it was here that his own history had begun, that day in July 1969. He had walked past the flimsy and improbable hardware of the early Space Age, and had taken his seat with several hundred other visitors in the Apollo Rotunda just before the beginning of the half-hourly show.

There was nothing that he had not seen many times before, yet the old drama still gripped him. Here were the faces of the first men to ride these crazy contraptions into space, and the sound of their actual voices—sometimes emotionless, sometimes full of excitement—as they spoke to their colleagues on the receding Earth. Now the air shook with the crackling roar of a Saturn launch, magically re-created exactly as it had taken place on that bright Florida morning, three hundred and seven years ago—and still, in many ways, the most impressive spectacle ever staged by man.

The Moon drew closer—not the busy world that Duncan knew, but the virgin Moon of the twentieth century. Hard to imagine what it must have meant to people of that time, to whom the Earth was not only the center of the Universe, but—even to the most sophisticated—still the whole of creation. . . .

Now Man's first contact with another world was barely minutes ahead. It seemed to Duncan that he was floating in space, only meters away from the spidery Lunar Module, bristling with antennas and wrapped in multicolored metal foil. The simulation was so perfect that he had an involuntary urge to hold his breath, and found himself clutching the handrail, seeking reassurance that he was still on Earth.

"Two minutes, twenty seconds, everything looking good. We show altitude about 47,000 feet . . ." said Houston to the waiting world of 1969, and to the centuries to come. And then, cutting across the voice of Mission Control, making a montage of conflicting accents, was a speaker whom for a moment Duncan could not identify, though he knew the voice. . . .

"I believe that this nation should commit itself to achieving the goal, before this decade is out, of landing a man on the Moon and returning him safely to the Earth."

127

Even back in 1969, that was already a voice from the grave; the President who had launched Apollo in that speech to Congress had never lived to see the achievement of his dream.

"We're now in the approach phase, everything looking good. Altitude 5,200 feet."

And once again that voice, silenced six years earlier in Dallas:

"We set sail on this new sea because there is new knowledge to be gained, and new rights to be won, and they must be won and used for the progress of all people. . . ."

"Roger. Go for landing, 3,000 feet. We're go. Hang tight. We're go. 2,000 feet. 2,000 feet . . ."

"And why, some say, the Moon? Why choose this as our goal . . . ? Why, thirty-five years ago, fly the Atlantic? WE CHOOSE TO GO TO THE MOON!"

"200 feet, 4½ down, 5½ down, 160, 6½ down, 5½ down, 9 forward, 120 feet, 100 feet, 3½ down, 9 forward, 75 feet, things still looking good . . ."

"We choose to go to the Moon in this decade because that challenge is one that we're willing to accept, one that we are unwilling to postpone, and one that we intend to win!"

"Forward, forward 40 feet, down 2½, kicking up some dust, 30 feet, 2½ down, faint shadow, 4 forward, 4 forward, drifting to the right a little . . . . Contact light. O.K. engine stopped, descent engine command overide off . . . Houston, Tranquillity Base here. The *Eagle* has landed."

The music rose to a crescendo. There before his eyes, on the dusty Lunar plain, history had lived again. And presently he saw the clumsy, spacesuited figure climb down the ladder, cautiously test the alien soil, and utter the famous words:

"That's one small step for man, one giant leap for mankind."

As always, Duncan listened for that missing "a" before the word "man," and as always, he was unable to detect it. A whole book had been written about that odd slip of the tongue, using as its starting point Neil Armstrong's slightly exasperated "That's what I *intended* to say, and that's what I *thought* I said."

All of this, of course, was simulation—utterly convincing, and apparently life-sized by the magic of holography—but actually contrived in some studio by patient technicians, two centuries after the events themselves. There was *Eagle,* glittering in the fierce sunlight, with the Stars and Stripes frozen motionless beside it, just as it must have appeared early in the Lunar morning of that first day. Then the music became quiet, mysterious . . . something was about to happen. Even though he knew what to expect, Duncan felt his skin crawling in the ancient, involuntary reflex which Man had inherited from his hirsute ancestors.

The image faded, dissolved into another—similar, yet different. In a fraction of a second, three centuries had dropped away.

They were still on the Moon, viewing the Sea of Tranquillity from exactly the same vantage point. But the direction of the light had changed, for the sun was now low and the long shadows threw into relief all the myriads of footprints on the trampled ground. And there stood all that was left of *Eagle*—the slightly peeled and blistered descent stage, standing on its four outstretched legs like some abandoned robot.

He was seeing Tranquillity Base as it was at this instant—or, to be precise, a second and a quarter ago, when the video signals left the Moon. Again, the illusion was perfect; Duncan felt that he could walk out into that shining silence and feel the warm metal beneath his hands. Or he could reach down into the dust and lift up the flag, to end the old debate that had reerupted in this Centennial Year. Should the Stars and Stripes be left where the blast of the takeoff had thrown it, or should it be erected again? Don't tamper with history, said some. We're only *restoring* it, said others. . . .

Something was happening just beyond the fenced-off area, at the very limits of the 3-D scanners. It was shockingly incongruous to see any movement at all at such a spot; then Duncan remembered that the Sea had lost its tranquillity at least two centuries ago. A busful of tourists was slowly circling the landing site, its occupants in full view through the curving glass of the observation windows. And though they could not see him, they waved across at the scanners, correctly guessing that someone on Earth was watching at this very moment.

The interruption should have destroyed the magic, yet it did not. Nothing could detract from the skill and courage of the pioneers; and they would have been happy to know that, where they had first ventured, thousands could now travel in safety and in comfort.

That, in the long run, was what History was all about.

22

BUDGET

"Today I walked at least three kilometers, and was on my feet for over two hours. I'm beginning to feel that life *is* possible on Earth. . . .

"But I must be careful not to overdo it, and I'm still using glideways and transporters most of the time. This means that I've not visited the White House or the Capitol, which can only be entered on foot. But I've been to the Museum of Technology and the National Gallery of Art. They have transport cubicles that you can program yourself, so there's no need to waste time on exhibits that don't interest you. Of course, I could stay in the hotel and take a holovision tour *anywhere,* but that would be ridiculous. I could do that any time, back at home. . . .

"I must remember that I'll be replaying these words twenty, fifty, maybe a hundred years from now, when this visit to Earth is a dim memory. So it may be a good idea to describe a typical day—if there is such a thing!—here at the Centennial Hotel.

"I wake up at six-thirty and listen to the radio

news summary while I'm having my bath. Then I dial the Comsole for any messages that have arrived during the night—usually there are half a dozen. Not many people know I'm here yet, but I've had quite a few offers of hospitality and have been asked to speak to a number of social and cultural groups. I suspect Ambassador Farrell is behind most of these.

"Then I set the news abstractor to print out anything that's happened in my area of interest, and scan the result. That doesn't take long, since I give TITAN as the main heading, and we're *never* in the news. If I want to know what's happening at home, I call the Embassy and get the daily dispatch. Usually that makes me rather homesick, especially when my friends and family are being reported. Which is most days . . .

"At seven-fifteen I go down to breakfast. As there are only a dozen guests—the place won't get crowded until later in June—I have a table to myself. We nod politely at each other, but no one is very sociable at this time in the morning.

"The food and service are excellent, and I'm going to miss both when I get home. Terrans know how to live comfortably—they've had enough time to practice—but it was several days before I realized that the hotel was unusual, maybe unique. It's been set up purely for the duration of the festivities, regardless of expense, just for us VIP guests. Staff has been brought from all over the world—some professional, some voluntary, like those academic clowns who met us when we arrived. (I still see them from time to time, and still can't understand a word they say. Because I'm darker than they are, I think they enjoy making a fool of me.)

"For breakfast—in fact, for all my meals—I try to have something new every day, and this has caused problems. I won't forget my first eggs. . . .

"I asked for them boiled—because that was the first listing—and the waiter said, 'How many minutes, sir?' (I don't think I'll ever get used to being called 'sir' by people who are *not* trying to insult me.) Of course, I had no idea what to answer, so I said 'Medium rare,' which was a phrase I'd picked up at din-

131

ner the night before. The waiter looked at me rather oddly, I thought.

"He came back five minutes later with two eggs sitting in silver cups, and placed them in front of me. I just sat there looking at them; never having seen eggs before, I'd no idea what to do next. And incidentally, they were larger than I'd imagined.

"I'm afraid I might have gone hungry if another guest a couple of tables away hadn't ordered the same thing. I watched him carefully, and discovered that you start by cutting off the top of the shell with a knife. I made a horrible mess of the first egg, but got it right the second time. Later, I found that they'll do this in the kitchen, which saves a lot of trouble. I'll never ask for eggs this way again, but I'm glad I did it once.

"The taste—though not the texture—was perfectly normal. Our chemists have done a good job here, and I'd never have known that it wasn't synthetic. I've since discovered that very few Terrans have ever tasted a real egg, and there are only two or three farms that still produce them. Hens are not very interesting animals it appears.

"I should have mentioned the Menu—it's a most elaborate affair, beautifully printed, and changes every day. I'm keeping a set as a souvenir, though I don't recognize half the items—or understand many of the instructions. I suspect that some are jokes. What does 'No Tipping' mean? And 'Gentlemen are requested to use the cuspidors provided'? What *is* a cuspidor? And why only gentlemen and not ladies? I must ask George.

"After breakfast I go back to my room and deal with the overnight messages. Usually I spend the next two or three hours at the Comsole, talking to people, recording data, transferring items from the main memory to my Minisec, or vice versa.

"Most of this is dull but important; I'm working through a list of contacts that every head of department on Titan has given me. I'm trying to be as tactful as possible, but I'm afraid I'm not going to be

132

very popular by the time I've delivered all these complaints and apologies.

"And I've run into something that complicates business on Earth to an incredible extent. I *knew* about it, but hadn't realized its full implications. It's the problem of Time Zones. . . .

"There are some advantages in belonging to a corridor culture. We're not slaves of the sun, and can set all our clocks to the same time, all over Titan. But on Earth!

"There are four time zones—America, Africa, Asia, Oceania—six hours apart. So when you want to speak to anyone, or make an appointment, you have to know what zone he's in. And when you move from one zone to another, you have to put your watch ahead—or back—six hours.

"It's very awkward and confusing, but it was even worse a couple of centuries ago; then there were *twenty-four* zones, one for every hour of the day! The development of global telecommunications made that situation impossible—not that it's very satisfactory even now. There's talk of going over to a single World Time—probably Absolute Ephemeris Time—and igignoring the day-night cycle, just as we do. But the arguments on both sides are nicely balanced, and no one expects a decision in a hurry. After all, it took several hundred years to get the World Calendar adopted, and *that* was because the Martian and Lunar administrations simply wouldn't put up with Earth's ridiculous months any longer. . . .

"Where was I? Oh, the morning's business. By noon, I usually feel that I need a break, and I spend half an hour in the swimming pool. At first I did this merely to get away from gravity, but now I enjoy it for its own sake. I've even learned to swim, and feel quite confident in the water. When I get home, I'll be a regular visitor to the Oasis pool.

"After that, I go for a quick walk in the hotel grounds. There are more flowers and trees here than I ever imagined, all beautifully kept. It reminds me a little of George's farm, though on a smaller scale. But Earth is a dangerous place, and there are things

I'd not been warned about. Who would have guessed that there were plants with thorns on them—sharp enough to draw blood? I'm going to make very sure they never take me to any really wild places on this complicated old planet.

"And even here in Washington, not everything is under control. Yesterday, just as I was going for a walk, it started to rain. *Rain!* In no time, the streets were wet and glistening; they looked so slippery I should have been afraid to walk on them, but from my window I could see people moving about as if nothing had happened. Some of them weren't even wearing protective clothing. . . .

"After watching for a while, I went down to the lobby and stood under the portico. I had to fight off the bellboys—they tried to get me a car, and couldn't believe I merely wanted to watch the falling water from a safe place. Eventually I managed to make myself believe that it *wasn't* liquid ammonia, and stepped outside for a few seconds, all in the cause of science. Needless to say, I got wet very quickly, and I can't say I really enjoyed it.

"Around thirteen hundred I go to lunch, usually with someone who wants to talk business or politics, or both. There are some wonderful restaurants here, and the great problem is not to eat too much. I've put on a couple of kilos since I arrived. . . . One of the favorite dining places—I've been there several times—is called the Sans Souci, which means "without a care" in Greek or Latin, I'm not sure which. Apparently President Washington himself used to eat there, though I find that hard to believe. One would have thought they'd have had photographs to prove it—stupid!—I keep forgetting—

"I met my first congressmen in the Sans Souci— Representative Matsukawa of Hawaii, Senator Gromeyko of Alaska. It was a purely social get-together; we had no business to discuss. But they were interested in Titan because they both felt that it had some points in common with their states, now temporarily back in the Union. They're quite right—Engineer Warren Mackenzie made the same point, aboard *Sirius*.

To the people who explored the Pacific in canoes, the ocean must have seemed about as large as the Solar System. And the development of Alaska, in its time, must have been as tough a job as getting a foothold on Titan.

"After lunch I do a little sightseeing, then get back to the hotel and carry on with the day's business, until dinnertime. By then, I'm too exhausted to think of anything but bed; the very latest I've been awake is twenty-one thirty. It's going to be quite embarrassing if I don't adapt soon to the local life style. Already I've had to turn down several party invitations because I couldn't afford to miss the sleep. That sort of thing isn't easy to explain, and I hope I've not offended any of the hostesses this city's famous for.

"I *have* accepted one late engagement, because George stressed its importance. This is to speak—in person, not holovision—to a group called the Daughters of the Revolutions. They're mostly elderly ladies ("Queen dragons—but dears when you get to know them," George said) and they're all over the place this Centennial year. Originally they were only concerned with the American Revolution, but later, they became less exclusive. I'm told I'll meet direct descendants of Lenin and Mao and Balunga. What a pity Washington never had any children. . . . I wonder why.

"Because I've given priority to my official mission—I'm still working on that damn speech—I've had almost no time for personal or family business. About the only thing I've been able to do in this direction is to contact the bank and establish my credentials, so that I can use Malcolm's accumulated funds. Even if everything works out according to plan and our estimates are correct, the budget will be tight. My big fear is running out of money and having to go to Finance for more of our precious Terran solars. If that happens, the family will be under attack from all quarters, and it won't be easy to think of a good defense.

"This is one reason why I've done no shopping—

135

that, and the time factor. I won't know how much money I'll have until I'm almost ready to leave! But I have run some of the catalogs through the Comsole, and they're fascinating. You could spend a lifetime —and a million solars a day—sampling the luxuries of Earth. Every conceivable artifact has its tape stored somewhere, waiting to go into a replicator. Since manufacturing costs are essentially zero, I don't understand why some items are so expensive. The capital costs of the replicators must have been written off decades ago, one would have thought. Despite Colin's efforts, I don't really understand Terran economy.

"But I'm learning many things, fast. For example, there are some smart operators around, on the lookout for innocents from space. Yesterday I was going through a display of Persian carpets—antique, not replicated—wondering if I could possibly afford to take a small one back to Marissa. (I can't.) This morning there was a message—addressed to me personally, correct room number—from a dealer in Tehran, offering his wares at very special rates. He's probably quite legitimate, and may have some bargains—*but how did he know?* I thought Comsole circuits were totally private. But perhaps this doesn't apply to some commercial services. Anyway, I didn't answer.

"Nor have I acknowledged some even more personal messages from various Sex Clubs. They were very explicit, and I've stored them as mementos for my old age. After the carpet episode, I was wondering if any would be tailored to my psych profile, which must be on record somewhere—that *would* have made me mad. But it was very broad-band stuff, and the artwork was beautiful. Perhaps when I'm not so busy . . ."

Duncan stopped talking; he was not quite sure why—and then he began to laugh at his hesitation. Could it be that, despite fairly heroic efforts, the Makenzies were puritanical after all? For he had just recalled that, only a kilometer or so from this very

136

spot, a President of the United States had got into perfectly terrible trouble with a tape recorder.

But whether it had been a Roosevelt or a Kennedy, he was not quite sure.

23

DAUGHTERS OF THE REVOLUTIONS

George Washington had been right; they *did* look like dragons. Formidable, tight-lipped ladies, few of them were under seventy, and they sported the most astonishing array of hats, in more shapes and sizes than Duncan would have believed possible. On Titan, hats were as rare as wigs, and even less useful. Not that there was any question of utility with most of this headgear; it was obviously designed to impress or intimidate. It certainly intimidated Duncan.

So did the introductions, though he quickly lost track of all the names being thrown at him. Every one of these ladies, it appeared, boasted ancestors who had played some role in the great revolutions that had shaped the modern world. As he shook hands, and listened to the chairperson's brief comments, he felt that he was being presented with snapshots of history. Most of the audience, of course, traced its involvement back to the birth of the United States, and he had heard vaguely of such places as Yorktown and Valley Forge. But he could only smile with feigned comprehension when hearing of revered ancestors who had fought in the hills with Castro, or accompanied Mao on the Long March, or shared the sealed train with Lenin, or fallen in the final assault on Cape Town. . . .

At last all the introductions—including his own— were completed. Feeling none too sure of himself, Duncan perched on the high chair overlooking his expectant audience.

"Perhaps I should apologize," he began, "for addressing you from a seated position. But as you know, I've spent all my life on a world with only a fraction of Earth's gravity. Believe me, having five times normal weight isn't exactly enjoyable! How would *you* like it if you woke up one morning and found your scales registered—oh—three hundred and fifty kilograms?"

There was a moment of shocked surprise as the audience confronted this startling vision, then a titter ran around the room. Fine, Duncan told himself—I've broken the ice. Then he realized that there was an undertone of something besides good-natured amusement in the sound, as if the listeners were laughing not with him, but *at* him.

He glanced frantically around the audience; then, to his horror, saw that there was a perfectly enormous woman halfway back on the far left. She was the fattest person Duncan had ever seen—and the entire audience seemed to be carefully not looking in her direction.

Well, thought Duncan, I've got nothing more to lose. It can only go uphill from here. He plunged into his prepared speech.

"The history of my world goes back little more than halfway to the event we are all celebrating next month. The first manned ship touched down on Titan in 2015—but the first *permanent* base wasn't established there until considerably later—2046. Even then, it was only a scientific observation post, with the crews rotating back to Earth every few years. There was no thought, in those days, of a self-contained colony that might eventually develop its own culture, just as happened on this continent. In any case, the twenty-first century was too busy dealing with Mars and the Moon to have the energy, or the resources, for activities farther afield."

Could that have been a yawn he spotted there, near the back of the hall? Surely not so soon! He was being morbidly sensitive; that sea of hats was getting him down. Most of the faces beneath them seemed to be reasonably attentive. . . .

But how to make these sleek and elegant matrons —not one of whom, probably, had ever been farther than the Moon—understand the harsh realities of his distant world? It was a challenge, and that was something that no Makenzie could ever resist.

"You may wonder why anyone would want to settle down in a place where the temperature never rises above a hundred below zero, where the atmosphere is poisoned by methane and ammonia, and the sun's so feeble that you can't detect its heat when it shines full on your face. Well, I won't pretend that Titan is an atractive tourist resort—though we have *some* tourists, believe it or not. But it does have certain unique advantages, which is why it's become important in human affairs.

"First of all, it's the *only* place, outside the Earth, where a man can move around on the surface without a full spacesuit. That may surprise you, after what I've just said about the conditions there! I don't deny that we need protection, but it's much less than required on the Moon, or even on Mars. The atmosphere is so dense it allows us to breathe with simple oxygen masks, though we have to be extremely careful to avoid any leaks. If you've ever smelled ammonia, you'll know why. And lightweight thermosuits can cope with the temperature, except in very bad weather.

"Having an atmosphere—even a poisonous one! —makes life easier in dozens of ways. It means that we can use aircraft for long-distance transportation. It protects us from meteorites—not that there are many out there—and from the temperature extremes that a completely airless world would have. And, most important of all—we've got an atmosphere we can *burn,* and use as a source of energy.

"It's just the opposite of the way things are on Earth. Here, you burn hydrogen compounds, and the atmosphere supplies the oxygen. On Titan, we have to provide the oxygen, and we burn *that* in the hydrogen atmosphere. But the final result is the same—heat and energy, to warm ourselves and drive our vehicles

"That hydrogen-rich atmosphere is Titan's greatest asset, and the reason men settled there in the first place. For without hydrogen, our spaceships cannot operate. Our chemical rockets burn it, and our fusion rockets—er—fuse it. Hydrogen is the key to the Solar System.

"And there are only two places where it's easily obtainable. One is right here—in the oceans of Earth. But it's expensive, lifting it out into space against the huge gravity field of your world—the one that's keeping me pinned to this chair right now."

Duncan paused hopefully, and got a few encouraging smiles.

"The other place is Titan. It's a filling station, if you like, halfway to the stars. And because of its low gravity, we can export hydrogen cheaply, to anywhere in the Solar System, using robot tankers carrying up to ten thousand tons. Without us, space travel would be at least four times as expensive as it is now, and interplanetary commerce would be crippled.

"And how we get that hydrogen is interesting. We've been called 'sky miners' because of the way we take it out of the atmosphere. Specialized aircraft—'ramscoops'—fly at high altitude and ever-increasing velocity, collecting hydrogen and liquefying it, then jumping up to orbit when they have a full load. There they rendezvous with the space tankers, deliver the goods, and go back into the atmosphere for more. They stay up for weeks on end, and land only when it's time for servicing, or a change of crew."

Better not overdo the technicalities, Duncan told himself. It was a pity, but he'd be wise to omit the most dramatic part of the whole operation—the fall down to Saturn after the robot tanker had escaped from Titan, and the hairpin loop around the giant planet taking advantage of its gravitational field to launch the precious payload to the customer who was waiting one or two years in the future. And he certainly couldn't do justice to the most spectacular trip in the Solar System—the Saturn sleighride, as it had been aptly christened by one of the few men who had

140

raced across the thousands of kilometers of spinning ice that formed the rings.

Duncan bravely resisted these temptations. He had best stick to history and politics—even though, in this case, both were largely by-product of technology.

"One could make a very interesting comparison," he continued, "between the settlement of Titan and the opening up of *this* continent, three or four hundred years earlier. I'm sure it took the same kind of pioneering spirit, and in our case we're lucky because we have films and tapes and cassettes of the whole period. More than that—some of our pioneers are still around, ready to reminisce at the drop of a hat. In fact, quicker than that, because hats drop slowly on Titan. . . ."

That was rather neat, Duncan told himself, though it was undoubtedly inspired by the view in front of him. Why did they wear the damn things *indoors?* Obviously, they were trying to outdo each other. Most of these creations were not merely useless; they looked as if they would take off in the slightest wind.

A flicker of movement caught Duncan's eye. I don't believe it, he thought. Then he stole another quick glance, hoping his interest would be unobserved.

Either he had taken leave of his senses, which was an acceptable working hypothesis, or there was a live fish swimming around in the third row. It was orbiting in a tiny crystal globe, surrounded by a tasteful display of corals and seashells, on the head of an intense, middle-aged lady who, unluckily, was staring straight at him with popeyed concentration.

Duncan gulped, gave a sickly smile, and stumbled on. He tried to push to the back of his mind the baffling problem of the fish's life-support system. If he stopped to worry about that, he would be tripping over his tongue in no time at all. Where was he? Oh, back with the pioneers, difficult though it was to focus on them in this lavishly decorated and slightly overheated room.

"I'm sure many of you have read Professor Prescott's famous book *With Axe and Laser: A Study of*

Two Frontiers. Though he draws his parallels between America and Mercury, everything that he says is also applicable to Titan.

"As I recall, Prescott argues that Man's conquest of the wilderness on *this* planet was based on three things: the axe, the plow, and fire. He uses these symbolically rather than literally; the axe stands for all tools, the plow for agriculture, and fire for all forms of power generation.

"The axe cut down the forests, shaped homes and furniture. More refined tools manufactured all the other necessities of civilized living, from cups and saucers to aircraft and computers.

"The axe wasn't much use on the Moon, or Mercury —or Titan. What took its place was the power laser. That was the tool that carved out our homes and, later, cities. And it opened up the mineral resources, buried kilometers down in the rocks.

"Of course, we were luckier than the old pioneers, because we did not have to spend endless man-hours making every single object that we needed. All the artifacts of civilization were already stored in the memories of our replicators. As long as we fed in the raw materials, anything we needed—no matter how complex—would be produced automatically in a matter of seconds, and in any quantity we needed. I know we take the replicator for granted, but it would have seemed like magic to our ancestors.

"As for the plow, that too had no place on our world. But by the twenty-second century, it had no place on yours either; we simply took your food technology to the planets. And on Titan, it was easy, much easier than anywhere else in the Solar System. We have enormous deposits of hydrocarbons—waxes, oils, and so forth. Who knows—perhaps one day *we* may be feeding Earth!

"Finally, the third item—fire. Occasionally, we still use it, though, as I explained, we have to provide the oxygen. But, again as on Earth, we get all the power we need from nuclear fusion. We're already heating large areas of Titan and are thinking about major changes to its climate. But as some of these may be be irreversible, we're proceeding very cautiously. We don't want to repeat the mistakes that have been made—elsewhere."

Duncan nearly said "on Earth," but tactfully changed gear just in time. He did a swift scan of the audience, carefully avoiding the fish in the third row. The ladies still seemed to be with him, though one or two hats were nodding suspiciously.

"Yet despite their sophisticated tools, the first generation of *our* pioneers probably had as tough a time as your Pilgrim Fathers. What they lacked in hostile Indians was more than made up for by a hostile environment. Deaths by accident were common; anyone who was careless did not live long on Titan in the early days. . . .

"But, slowly and painfully, we managed to convert our first primitive bases, which had no more than the bare necessities for survival, into fairly comfortable towns, then cities . . . like Meridian, Carbonville, Oasis. True, the largest has a population of only fifty thousand—there are still fewer than a quarter of a million of us on Titan—but, as we all know, quality is more important than quantity."

There were a few smiles at this strikingly original remark, and Duncan felt encouraged to continue, but then he saw something that almost stopped him dead in his tracks.

The smallest member of his audience was showing obvious signs of distress. Back there in the third row, that infernal fish was swimming round and round at an acute angle to the rest of the world. Since Duncan had noticed no alteration in the force of gravity, he could only assume that something had happened to its sense of balance. Even as he watched, it flipped over on its side. . . .

Very close at hand, somebody was talking, using Duncan's voice. Whether the words made any sense, he could not even guess. He was elsewhere, struggling with a problem of life and death.

Should he stop talking, and warn Miss Fishbowl of the impending tragedy of which she was obviously unaware? Perhaps there was still time for her to rush to the nearest animal hospital. That creature might be the last of its species—the only one in the

143

world, doomed to extinction owing to his negligence. . . .

Alas, it was too late. With a final convulsive wriggle, the fish turned belly up and floated motionless in its crystal globe. Duncan had never received a more obvious hint. As quickly as possible he brought his peroration to a close. To his astonishment the applause seemed perfectly genuine.

He hoped he was not mistaken, but in any event he was quite sure of one thing. After *this* ordeal, speaking to the Congress of the United States would be child's play.

24

CALINDY

The package had been delivered to Duncan's room while he was lecturing. It was a small, neatly wrapped cylinder, about fifteen centimeters high and ten across, and he could not imagine what it contained.

He hefted it in his hand a few times; it was fairly heavy, but not heavy enough to be metal. When he tapped it, there was merely a dull, unreverberant thud.

He abandoned futile speculation and tore open the envelope taped around the cylinder.

> *Mt. Vernon Farm*
>
> Dear Duncan,
>
> *Sorry about the delay, but we had a little accident. Charlemagne managed to walk into the hives one night. Luckily—or not, depending on the point of view—our bees don't sting. However, production was badly affected.*
>
> *Remembering your reaction last time, Clara and I thought you might like this souvenir of your visit.*
>
> *Best,*
> *George*

How kind of them, Duncan told himself. When he got through the wrappings, he found a transparent plastic jar, full of golden liquid. The locking mechanism on the screw-top lid baffled him for a moment—it had to be pushed down and *tightened* before it could be opened—but after a few frustrating minutes he had it off.

The smell was delicious, and once again there was that haunting sense of familiarity. Like a small boy, he could not resist dipping in a finger, then savoring the tip with his tongue.

Some delayed-action circuit was operating: deep in the recesses of memory, the most primitive—and potent—of all senses was opening doors that had been locked for years.

His body remembered before his mind. As he relaxed contentedly in a warm glow of sheer animal lust, everything came back to him.

Honey tasted like Calindy. . . .

Sooner or later, of course, he would have contacted her. But he wanted time to adjust, and to feel as much at home on Earth as he could ever be. So he had told himself; but that was not the only reason.

The logical part of his mind had no wish for him to be sucked back into the whirlpool that had engulfed him as a boy. But in matters of the heart, logic was always defeated. In the long run, it could do no more than say: "I told you so. . . ." And by then it was too late.

He had known Calindy's body, but he had been too young to know her love. Now he was a man—and there was nothing that Karl could do to stop him.

The first task was to locate Calindy. He felt some disappointment that she had not already contacted him, for the news of his arrival had been well publicized. Was she indifferent—even embarrassed? He would take that chance.

Duncan walked to the Comsole, and the screen became alive as his fingers brushed the ON pad. Now it was a miracle beyond the dreams of any poet, a charmed magic casement, opening on all seas, all lands. Through this window could flow everything that

Man had ever learned about his universe, and every work of art he had saved from the dominion of Time. All the libraries and museums that had ever existed could be funneled through this screen and the millions like it scattered over the face of Earth. Even the least sensitive of men could be overwhelmed by the thought that one could operate a Comsole for a thousand life-times—and barely sample the knowledge stored within the memory banks that lay triplicated in their widely separated caverns, more securely guarded than any gold. There was an appropriate irony in the fact that two of these buried complexes had once been control centers for nuclear missiles.

But now Duncan was not concerned with the heritage of mankind; he had a more modest objective in view. His fingers tapped out the word INFO, and the screen instantly displayed:

> PLEASE *SPECIFY* CATEGORY
> 01. General
> 02. Science
> 03. History
> 04. Arts
> 05. Recreation
> 06. Geography
> 07. Earth Directory
> 08. Moon Directory
> 09. Planet Directory

and so on for more than thirty subject headings.

As his fingers tapped out 07, Duncan could not help recalling his very first confrontation with the Terran Comsole system. The categories were almost the same as on Titan, but ACTIVATE was on the left-hand side of the keyboard, and the unfamiliar position had made him forget to press it. So nothing had happened for a good five seconds; then a really beautiful girl had appeared on the screen and said sweetly, in a voice to which Duncan could have listened forever: "You seem to be having some difficulty. Have you remembered to press ACTIVATE?"

He had stared at her until she faded out, leaving a dazzling smile that, like the Cheshire Cat, lingered in

146

his memory. Though he had promptly repeated the same mistake five times in a row, she never came back. It was a different girl each time. Oh well, he told himself, they had probably all been dead for years. . . .

When EARTH DIRECTORY came up, he was requested to give Family Name, Given Names, Personal Number, and Last Known Address—Region, Country, Province, Postal Code. But that was the problem—he had not heard from Calindy for five years, and had never known her personal number. It had even been hard to recall her family name; if it had been Smith or Wong or Lee the task would have been hopeless.

He typed out ELLERMAN, CATHERINE LINDEN, and a string of DON'T KNOWS. The Comsole shot back: WHAT INFORMATION DO YOU WANT? Duncan answered: ADDRESS AND VIDDY NUMBER: ACTIVATE

Suppose Calindy had changed her name? Unlikely; she was not the sort of woman who would let herself be dominated by any man, even if she established a long-term relationship with one. Duncan could imagine the man changing his name, rather than the other way around. . . .

He had barely completed this thought when, to his surprise, the screen announced:

ELLERMAN, CATHERINE LINDEN
  North Atlan
  New York
  New York
  Personal: 373:496:000:000
  Viddy: 99:373:496:000:000

The speed with which the system had located Calindy was so amazing that it was several seconds before two even more surprising facts registered in Duncan's mind.

The first was that Calindy had managed to secure a—quite literally—one-in-a-million personal identification. The second was that she had been able to get it incorporated in her viddy number. Duncan would not have believed it possible; Karl had once tried to do the same thing, and even he had failed. Calindy's powers of persuasion had always been remarkable, but he realized that he had underestimated them.

So here she was, not only on this planet, but on this continent—a mere five hundred kilometers away. He had only to tap out that number, and he could look once more into the eyes that had so often smiled at him from the bubble stereo.

He knew that he was going to do it; of that there was never any question. Yet still he hesitated, partly savoring the moment of anticipation, partly wondering just what he was going to say. He had still not decided this when, almost impulsively, he tapped out the fourteen digits that opened up the road to the past.

Duncan would never have recognized her had they met in the street; he had forgotten what years of Earth gravity could do. For long seconds he stared at the image, unable to speak. Finally she broke the silence, with a slightly impatient: "Yes? What is it?"

Before he could answer, Duncan found it necessary to start breathing again.

"Calindy," he said, "don't you remember me?"

The expression in those lustrous eyes changed imperceptibly. Then there was the trace of a smile, though a wary one. Be reasonable, Duncan told himself; she can't possibly recognize you, after fifteen years. How many thousands of people has she met in that time, on this busy, crowded world? (And how many lovers, since Karl?)

But she surprised him, as usual.

"Of course, Duncan—how lovely to see you. I knew you were on Earth, and had been wondering when you'd call."

He felt a little embarrassed, as perhaps he was intended to do.

"I'm sorry," he said. "I was incredibly busy. The Centennial celebrations, you know."

As he stared into the screen, the remembered features slowly emerged from the stranger looking back at him. The impact of the years was not as great as he had supposed; much of the unfamiliarity was purely artificial. She had changed the color of her hair so that it was no longer black, but brown, shot with flecks of gold. The oval of the face was the same, the ivory skin still flawless. When he forgot that image in the bubble stereo, he could see that she was still Calindy —more mature, and even more desirable.

He could also see that she was sitting in a crowded office, with shadowy figures coming and going all around her, and occasionally handing her sheafs of documents. Somehow, he had never imagined Calindy as a busy executive, but he was quite sure that if she had set her heart on the role, she would be a great success. It was obvious, however, that this was no time for tender endearments. The best that he could hope for was to arrange a meeting as soon as possible.

He had come all the way from Saturn; it should not be difficult to span the extra distance between Washington and New York. But, it seemed, there were problems. He even got the impression that there was some hesitation, even reluctance, on Calindy's part. She consulted a very complicated diary, threw several dates at him, and appeared slightly relieved when Duncan found that they clashed with his own appointments.

He was becoming quite disheartened when she suddenly exclaimed: "Wait a minute—are you free next Thursday—and Friday?"

"I think so—yes, I could manage." It was almost a week ahead; he would have to be patient. But *two* days—that sounded promising.

"Wonderful." A slow, mischievous smile spread over her face, and for a moment the old Calindy looked back at him.

"And it's perfect—so *very* appropriate. . . .I couldn't have arranged it better if I'd tried."

"Arranged *what*?" asked Duncan.

"Contact the van Hyatts at this number—they're just outside Washington—and do *exactly* what they tell you. Say that Enigma's asked them to bring you along as my personal guest. They're nice people and you'll like them. Now I really must break off—see you next week." She paused for a moment, then said carefully: "I'd better warn you that I'll be so busy we won't have much time, even then. But I promise you —you'll really enjoy the experience."

Duncan looked at her doubtfully. Notwithstanding

that assurance, he felt disappointed; he also hated to be involved in something over which he had no control. Makenzies organized other people—for their own good, of course, even if the victim did not always agree. This reversal of standard procedure made him uncomfortable.

"I'll come," he said, taking the plunge. "But at least tell me what this is all about."

Calindy gave that stubborn little *moue* which he remembered so well.

"No," she replied firmly. "I'd be violating the motto of my own organization, and even the executive vice-president can't do that."

"What organization?"

"Really?" she said, with a smile of pure delight. "I thought Enigma was rather well known, but this makes it even better. Anyone on Earth will tell you our slogan . . ." She broke off for a second to collect some documents from another harried assistant.

"Good-bye, Duncan—I *have* to rush. See you soon."

"Your slogan!" he almost yelled at her.

She blew him a dainty kiss.

"Ask the van Hyatts. Lots of love."

The screen was blank.

Duncan did not immediately contact the van Hyatts; he waited for a few minutes, until he had emotionally decompressed, then called his host and general adviser.

"George," he said, "have you heard of Enigma Associates?"

"Yes, of course. What about them?"

"Do you know their slogan?"

"We astonish."

"Eh?"

Washington repeated the phrase, slowly and carefully.

"Well, I'm astonished. What does it mean?"

"You might say they're very sophisticated entertainers, or impresarios, working on a highly individual basis. You go to them when you're bored, and want novelty. They analyze your psych profile, run it through their computer banks, and come up with a program to fit the time and money you're prepared to invest. They may arrange for you to live at the North Pole, or take up a new profession, or have an exotic love affair, or write a play, or learn three-dimensional chess. . . . And they rely a great deal on the element of surprise—you never know what they've planned for you until you're already involved. . . ."

"Suppose you don't like their program, and want to pull out?"

"Apparently, that very seldom happens. They know their job—and, moreover, you don't get your money back. But how did you hear about them? I hope *you* aren't bored!"

Duncan laughed.

"I haven't had time for that luxury. But I've just contacted an old friend who's apparently vice-president of the organization, and she's invited me to join a group for a couple of days. Would you advise it?"

"Frankly, that's very difficult to say. How well does she know you?"

"We've not met for fifteen years, since she visited Titan."

"Then whatever program she's invited you to join will be fairly bland and innocuous, especially if it lasts only two days. Your chances of survival are excellent."

"Thank you," said Duncan. "That's all I wanted to know."

The van Hyatts, when he introduced himself to them a little later, were able to fill in a few more details. They were a friendly but rather highly strung couple in late middle age, which was itself some reassurance. Calindy would hardly dump them in the heart of a desert with one canteen of water, or set them climbing Mount Everest. Duncan felt reasonably confident that he could handle whatever was in store for them.

"We've been instructed," said Bill van Hyatt, "to wear old clothes and sturdy boots, and to carry raincoats. It also says here, 'Hard hats will be provided when necessary.' What on Earth is a hard hat?"

The van Hyatts, Duncan decided, had led somewhat sheltered lives.

"A hard hat," he explained, "is a protective helmet of metal or plastic. Miners and construction workers have to wear them."

"That sounds dangerous," said Millie van Hyatt, with obvious relish.

"It sounds like cave-exploring to me. I hate caves."

"Then Enigma won't send you into them. They have your profile, don't they?"

"Yes, but sometimes they decide that what you *don't* like may be good for you. Shock treatment. Remember what happened to the Mulligans."

Duncan never did discover what happened to the Mulligans, as he thought it best not to intervene in what looked to be escalating into a family quarrel. He made hasty arrangements for a rendezvous at Washington airport next Thursday, signed off, and then sat wondering if he had done the right thing.

It was quite some time before he was suddenly struck by a curious omission on Calindy's part—one that both surprised and saddened him.

She had never asked about Karl.

25

MYSTERY TOUR

Only an expert on the history of aeronautics could have dated the vehicle that stood glistening in the late-afternoon light. Like sailing ships, though in less than a tenth of the time, aircraft had reached their technological plateau. Improvements in detail would continue indefinitely, but the era of revolutionary change was long past.

Bill van Hyatt was convinced that this flying machine was at least a hundred years old. "It's powered by rubber bands," he insisted. "When we get inside, there'll be a big windlass and we'll all have to walk round and round, winding it up."

"Thank you, Mr. van Hyatt," said the Enigma representative, who had met them at Washington airport. "That's a very interesting idea. We'll bear it in mind."

There were twenty clients in the party, and they all seemed a little tense and expectant. The only person who was in complete control—in more ways than one —was the man from Enigma. He was a tough, self-assured character ("Just call me Boss—you may think of something else later"); Duncan would have guessed his age at about fifty. They never discovered his real name, but he had that indefinable air of authority that comes only from years of command; van Hyatt advanced the plausible theory that he was a spaceship captain, grounded for some technical misdemeanor. However, he showed no signs of concealing any secret disgrace.

Boss's first order to his customers was completely unexpected, but set the tone of the whole enterprise.

"I must ask you," he said, "to hand over all watches, radios, and communication devices. You won't need them until you get home."

He held up an admonitory hand at the chorus of protests.

"There's a good reason for this—and for any other peculiar requests I may make. Remember, this whole program has been worked out for *your* benefit. If you won't cooperate, you're only cheating yourselves. Cameras and recorders—yes, of course. Use them as much as you like."

There was a general sigh of relief at this. Duncan had noticed that most of his companions were festooned with equipment designed to capture every aspect of their experience. A couple were obviously "tapeworms," those peculiar addicts who went through life accompanied by voice-actuated recorders, so that nothing they said—or heard—was ever lost. Unless they could do this, Duncan had been told, they did not believe that they had really and truly lived. . . .

Such a backward-looking obsession was typically

153

Terran. Duncan could not imagine anyone on *his* world trying to encapsulate his whole life so that whenever he wished he could recall any moment of the past. On Titan, it was the future that mattered.

As he walked to the aircraft, carrying his scanty baggage (toilet necessities, a change of underwear, raincoat), Duncan decided that van Hyatt's guess at its age was not too far out. An obvious vertical-lift fusion jet, it probably dated from the turn of the century, and looked as if it had been built to last forever. He guessed that it was designed to operate in the five-thousand-klick range, which meant that it could reach anywhere on Earth in three or four hours. Now he began to understand why all watches had been confiscated; if the flight lasted any length of time, it would be almost impossible to estimate how far they had traveled.

Though the jet was a small one, the score of passengers barely half filled it, and quickly segregated themselves into little groups. Duncan, with some skillful seatmanship, managed to get away from the van Hyatts. He was beginning to suspect that he would see—or certainly hear—more than he wanted of them before the adventure was over.

He snuggled down into the luxurious, though slightly worn, upholstery and tried his luck with the video screen. As he had expected, there was no external view, just continuous loops of canned scenery. And the global viddy channels were all blank. There would be no clues here. . . .

There was, however, a bulky package of literature thoughtfully provided by Enigma, and he settled down to read this. It described, in tantalizingly vague detail, the types of service provided by the organization. As far as Duncan could judge, Enigma seemed to combine many of the functions of travel agency, psychiatrist, nursemaid, procurer, baby-sitter, father confessor, educator, and theatrical impresario. He could understand how Calindy had been attracted to such an enterprise, and was sure that she was very good at her job.

There was a brief announcement from Boss, who had disappeared into the crew quarters.

"Good evening, ladies and gentlemen. Please prepare for take-off. Our flight time will be between one hour and one day, and we shall not be going beyond the orbit of the Moon. Refreshments will be available shortly for those who need them. Thank you."

There was scarcely any change of sound level in the cabin as the jet lifted and began to climb like an elevator. Presently Duncan felt a surge of forward acceleration, but by this time he had already lost all sense of direction, despite a deliberate attempt to monitor his inertial-guidance system. There was no way of telling whether they were flying north, south, east, or west.

He continued to browse through the Enigma literature, glancing from time to time at the fare provided by the video screen. If this was to be believed, they were flying in rapid succession over a desert, over the open sea, over a range of magnificent mountains, over an ice field, over clouds, over the Moon (or Mercury), and over an apparently endless stretch of flat, cultivated fields, laid out in huge squares. This last display was particularly interesting, for Duncan was quite sure that nothing like it had existed for a couple of hundred years. However, he reluctantly dismissed the theory that Enigma Associates had managed to invent a time machine.

Presently, coffee and light snacks were brought around by the inevitable and unchanging stewardesses. Perhaps an hour later—it was amazing how soon one lost the ability to estimate the passage of time when mechanical aids were no longer available —they came around again with a second serving. Almost immediately after this, the aircraft started to descend.

"We'll be on the ground for about fifteen minutes," Boss announced. "If you want to stretch your legs, you're free to do so. But don't get too far away; we're not going to wait for stragglers."

He had scarcely finished when there was a barely perceptible bump, and the whisper of the jets faded away into silence. Almost at once there was a rush to the doors.

The anticlimax was considerable. Wherever they

155

were, it was already night, and all that could be seen was a large shed, lit by flickering oil lamps—oil lamps!—beneath which about twenty people were standing expectantly. The night was so dark and so completely overcast that it was impossible to see beyond the limited range of the lights. The shed was apparently standing in a large field or clearing; Duncan thought he could just see some trees at the limits of vision. There was no sign of any other form of transportation—either of land or air.

"Any guesses?" said the ubiquitous van Hyatt.

"I haven't the faintest idea. Remember—*everywhere* on Earth is new to me."

"We're somewhere in the tropics."

"What makes you think that? It doesn't seem particularly warm."

"It's so *dark*. Remember, this is early summer in Washington—twilight lasts all night, and it never gets really dark."

Duncan was aware of this, somewhere at the back of his mind; but it was theoretical knowledge, which he would never have thought of applying to a practical situation. It was very hard for a resident of Titan to understand all the implications of Earth's seasons.

"So where do you think we are?" he asked.

"Well, we were airborne about two hours . . ."

"As long as that? I would have said not much more than one."

"At *least* two. So we could be anywhere in Africa, or South America. That is, *if* we were traveling at full speed. Perhaps the newcomers will have some ideas."

They turned out to be equally ignorant, having left Los Angeles about two hours earlier in another jet, which had dumped them and taken off again. When he learned this, van Hyatt walked away muttering, "Well, it could *still* be Africa . . . what a pity we can't see the stars.

There were few empty seats when the aircraft took off again, and soon after they were airborne Boss announced: "As this will be a long hop, we'll be dimming the lights shortly so that you can get some sleep."

This was obviously nonsense, and merely intended

to further confuse the now thoroughly disorientated passengers. Nevertheless, Duncan thought it not a bad idea to accept the suggestion. He might need all his physical resources to face whatever ordeals Enigma had in store for him.

He got to sleep more easily than during his first night aboard *Sirius*. But it was a far from dreamless sleep, and after many improbable adventures on a world that seemed neither Earth nor Titan, he found himself trying to reach Calindy, beckoning to him from a mountaintop. Unfortunately, judging by the gravity, he must have been on the surface of a neutron star.

"Wake up," said Boss, "we're there. . . ."

"Out of luck again," grumbled van Hyatt. "If only I could see a few stars . . ."

There was no chance of that; the sky was still overcast. Yet it did not seem quite as dark as at the last stop, even though that was several hours earlier.

Van Hyatt agreed, when Duncan pointed this out. "Either we're overtaking the sun, or we've flown all the way back toward tomorrow morning. Let's see— that would put us somewhere in the Far East."

"Come along, you sluggards!" shouted Boss. "We've got a couple of tons of gear to unload!"

A human chain was quickly formed, and equipment and packages were rapidly shuttled out of the cargo hold. This all had to be carried a hundred meters to avoid the jet blast at takeoff, and his very modest exertions as a porter gave Duncan a chance to examine the landing site.

It was a small, grassy clearing, surrounded by a high wall of trees. For the first time, Duncan began to have serious qualms. He remembered his night at Mount Vernon; he could laugh at his fears, now that he realized how tame and harmless everything had been down on the farm. But this appeared primeval jungle, and there were still dangerous wild animals on Earth. Did Enigma *really* know what it was doing?

Well, it was too late to back out now. With a deep-throated roar, the jet heaved itself off the grass and started to climb into the sky. Duncan turned his back to the blast, and for a minute was whipped by flying debris. The diapason of power faded away into clouds. They were alone in the forest.

For the next hour, however, no one had time to brood over the precariousness of the situation. There were tents to be erected, a small mobile kitchen to be activated, lights to be strung from poles, portable toilets to be set up. . . . All this was done under the supervision of Boss, with the expert help of four assistants and the enthusiastic but far from expert help of a dozen volunteers. Duncan was not one of these; camping was not a recreation that could be practiced on Titan, and he could best serve by keeping out of the way.

However, he found it fascinating to watch the deployment of all this strange technology. The inflatable beds looked extremely inviting, and the collapsible seats, though liable to live up to their name if carelessly handled, turned out to be surprisingly comfortable. Life in the jungle need not be too rigorous —but Duncan was still worried about wild animals. His imagination was full of confused images of carnivorous beasts—lions, tigers, bears, wolves—against whom the flimsy fabric of the tents appeared very inadequate protection.

He felt much happier when the bonfire was lit. Its cheerful glow seemed far more effective than electricity in dispelling the dangers of the night. To Duncan, being able to feel, smell, and throw logs onto a large open fire was a unique experience, and another rare memory to store for the future. For the first time, he could understand what fire must have meant to early man. Looking around at his companions, he could see that many of them were also discovering their lost past. He was not the only stranger here— wherever "here" might be.

Needless to say, Bill van Hyatt had come up with a theory.

"We're not too far from the Equator," he assured Duncan, passing on his way to the fire with an armful of wood. "Probably a couple of thousand meters above sea level, or it would be even warmer. Judging by the distance we must have flown, this could be somewhere in Indonesia."

"But wouldn't it be daylight there?" asked Duncan, somewhat uncertainly. He did not want to reveal his ignorance of geographical details, but he had a vague idea that Indonesia was almost as far from Washington as one could get. And the one fact of which they were sure was that they had left late in the afternoon.

"Look at the sky," said Bill confidently. "It soon will be sunrise. Very quick in the tropics—you know, where the dawn comes up like thunder."

An hour later, however, there was not the slightest sign of the dawn, but no one except Bill van Hyatt seemed to worry in the least. A loud and happy campfire party was in progress, consuming food and drink in amazing quantities. Almost equally amazing was the speed with which forty perfect strangers could become intimate friends. Duncan would never have recognized this uninhibited and noisy group as Terrans. Though he still felt a little apart from the scene, he enjoyed watching it and wandering round the circle listening to the discussions in progress. He was also surprised to discover how much he could eat; something seemed to have happened to his appetite. And there were some splendid wines—all new to him, of course, so it was necessary to do a great deal of research to discover which he liked best.

Presently, singing started, led by an Enigma staff member whose voice—and repertoire—were so professional that he had obviously been selected for this role. In a very short time, he had the whole group rocking and stomping, and joining in choruses describing events most of which were wholly unfamiliar to Duncan. Some seemed to be tragic, though he judged this by the musical treatment rather than the words. He was not quite sure what fate had befallen Darling Clementine, but *that* song was crystal clear compared with one recounting the exploits of Waltzing Matilda. He listened for a few minutes in utter bafflement, then drifted away from the circle of firelight into the semidarkness.

"It's perfectly safe to go as far as the trees," Boss had said. "But if you go *into* them, we can accept no responsibility whatsoever, and the indemnity clause of our contract comes into force."

Duncan would probably not have traveled even as far as this-without the encouragement of the wine but presently he was standing about fifty meters from the edge of the forest, and a considerably greater distance from the songsters. The illumination was roughly that of a cloudy night on Titan, when Saturn was in its crescent phase. Thus he could see general outlines, but no fine detail.

The trees were large and impressive, and he guessed that they were very old. Somehow, he had expected to see the slender palms which were the universal symbol of Earth's tropics—but to his disappointment, there was not a palm in sight. The trees were not very different from those at Mount Vernon; then he remembered van Hyatt's suggestion that they might be well above sea level, where the climate was mild.

Duncan's chemical courage was beginning to desert him; the thrill of standing at the edge of the unknown was rapidly losing its novelty. He turned back toward the now dwindling glow of the bonfire, from which stragglers were slowly departing as they headed to the tents, but had taken no more than a dozen paces when the sound from the forest rooted him to the spot.

Never in his life had he heard anything remotely resembling it. Only a soul in the lowest circle of hell could have produced the wail of anguish that burst from the trees and instantly quenched the festivities at the campsite. It rose and fell, rose and fell, then ululated away into silence. But even in that first moment of sheer terror, when Duncan felt the strength ebb from his limbs, he found himself feeling thankful that at least no *human* throat could have produced that awful sound.

Then the paralysis left him, and he was already halfway back to the camp before he remembered that he was unable to run. Deliberately slowing down was one of the bravest things he had ever done— especially when that nightmare howl echoed once more from the forest.

When he reached the tents, Boss was still trying to restore morale.

"Just some wild animal," he explained soothingly. "After the noise *we've* been making, I'm surprised everything has been so quiet until now."

"What kind of animal, for heaven's sake!" someone expostulated.

"Ask Mr. van Hyatt—*he* seems to have all the answers."

Bill van Hyatt was completely unabashed, and ready as ever to accept the challenge.

"It sounded like a hyena to me," he replied. "I've never actually heard one, but it fits the descriptions I've read."

"I don't see how anyone could describe *that*," somebody muttered.

"Hyenas live in Africa, don't they?" said another voice. "Anyway, they're quite harmless."

"Personally, I don't consider death from heart failure harmless."

"All right, *all right*," Boss interjected. "We've a busy day ahead of us. It's time to go to bed."

Everyone glanced at absent wrist watches, but no confirmation of this fact was really needed. The camp slowly settled down for the night.

Despite maneuverings that had barely stopped short of actual rudeness, Duncan had been unable to avoid sharing a tent with the van Hyatts. Just before he dozed off, he heard Bill remark sleepily to his wife: "I've just remembered—the program said that hard hats would be provided. I wonder why?"

"Because, Bill," said another voice from the darkness, "tomorrow we explore the caves of the man-eating vampire bats of Bongo Bongo. Now for heaven's sake shut up and go to sleep."

26

PRIMEVAL FOREST

To Duncan's surprise, it was already full daylight when he awoke. He decided that the wine must have been responsible, and even wondered if it had been drugged, for all his companions were still sleeping stertorously.

He rolled off the air mattress, and treading carefully over unconscious bodies, opened the flap of the tent. The glare drove him back for his dark glasses, for the sun was now shining from a blue, cloudless sky. As he walked to the portable shower, carrying towel and toothbrush, he scanned the circle of trees. In broad daylight, they seemed much less ominous; but with that infernal howl still echoing in his memory, nothing would have induced Duncan to venture there alone. For that matter, he was not quite sure how many companions he would need to give him any sense of security in the forest—but unless the jet returned for them, that was precisely where they would have to go. At one point he could see what looked like the beginning of a jungle trail, though from this distance it was impossible to tell whether it was made by men or animals. Nothing else was visible; the trees were so high, and so thick, that there could have been a range of mountains a few kilometers away, completely hidden from view.

Duncan ran into Boss on the way back from his toilet. The fearless leader looked as if he could use some extra sleep, but otherwise still seemed in full charge of the situation.

"Did you put something in that wine?" Duncan asked, after they had exchanged greetings. "Usually I dream—but *last* night . . ."

Boss grinned.

"Don't expect me to reveal all Enigma's little secrets. But in this case, we've nothing to hide. You can thank the natural, open-air life for your good night's sleep—though the wine probably helped. Now let's wake up the others."

This took some time, but eventually all the troops were on parade, though in a slightly disheveled condition, with not a few still yawning mightily. Groans of protest greeted Boss's first order.

"We're going for a little safari before breakfast. Coffee will be along in a minute, but that's all you're having now. Your appetites will be all the better when we get back."

"And when will *that* be?" cried half a dozen voices simultaneously.

"It depends how fast you march. Bob—you'll need better footwear than those sandals. Miss Lee—sorry, but in the jungle it's advisable to wear *something* above the waist. And even more advisable below it, Miss Perry. Right, everybody—back here in five minutes, then we start. No breakfast for stragglers."

There were no stragglers, though it must have been more than ten minutes before Boss had everyone lined up in double file. Then he disappeared into his private tent, only to emerge again at once, heavily laden.

Instantly, the babble of conversation stopped. There were sudden gasps of indrawn breath, and Duncan found himself staring at Enigma's latest surprise with a curious mixture of fascination and disgust.

The fascination was undoubtedly there, despite the conditioning of a lifetime. He was ashamed of it —yet, somehow, not as ashamed as he might have been. Duncan had never concealed his impulses from himself; now he recognized the almost irresistible urge to reach out and take one of those monstrous instruments in his hand, to feel its power and weight—and to use it for the only purpose for which it was designed.

It was the first time he had ever seen a gun, and Boss was carrying *two,* as well as a pair of cartridge belts. He handed one gun and belt over to an assistant, who took up his position at the end of the file.

"O.K.," said Boss, just as nonchalantly as if he were unaware of the impression he had created. "Let's go!"

As he walked toward the edge of the clearing, he threw the gun over his shoulder and buckled on the belt of ammunition. It was perfectly obvious that he knew how to handle his armament, but Duncan did not find this in the least reassuring. And judging by the glum silence, neither did anyone else.

The track through the jungle turned out to be surprisingly well kept; when someone commented on this, Boss called back over his shoulder: "We have an arrangement with the local tribes—they're friendly —you'll meet them later."

"That's a giveaway!" whispered Bill van Hyatt in Duncan's ear. "The only primitive tribes left are in the Far East. I *knew* it was Borneo."

They had now walked perhaps a kilometer through the closely packed trees and were already beginning to feel the effects of the day's increasing heat. There was a chorus of relief when Boss abruptly called back: "We're nearly there—close up!"

He stepped to the side of the trail, and let the file walk on past him. Duncan was near the head of the line, and saw that they were approaching a mass of bare rocks which formed a small hillock. Now at last, he told himself, we'll be able to get a good view of the land around us.

Those ahead of him were already scrambling up the rocks, eager to see what lay ahead. Suddenly, there were cries of astonishment, inarticulate shouts. Millie van Hyatt, who had reached the top long before her husband, suddenly collapsed in hysterics. "Borneo!" she screamed. "He said Borneo!"

Duncan hurried to join her as swiftly as he could, in this unaccustomed gravity. A moment later, he reached the top of the little hill, and the vista to the south lay open before him.

Engima had certainly fulfilled its promise. Not more than five kilometers away, gleaming in the morning light, was the most famous structure in the world. And now that all its upstart rivals had long since been demolished, it was once again the tallest.

Even a visitor from Titan could have no difficulty in recognizing the Empire State Building.

"Very clever," said Bill van Hyatt in grudging admiration. "They must have flown us straight back over the same course, when they picked up the second load of passengers. But there are still some questions. That hideous noise last night—"

"Oh, eat your breakfast, Bill. Don't always try to get ahead of the game."

Boss, who was clearly relaxed now that his deception had been successfully carried off, called back from the end of the table: "Surely you've guessed *that* one, Bill?"

"Probably the sound track of an old Tarzan movie."

Boss chuckled and glanced at his watch. All time-pieces and communicators had been returned to their owners, and Duncan no longer felt so naked. He had never been able to stop himself looking at his absent watch, and he realized how cleverly Enigma had managed to disorient him in all four dimensions.

"In about five minutes, Bill, you'll know better."

"In that case, I'd appreciate it if you'd bring up the artillery again."

"No use. The guns were real, but the bullets weren't."

"I see—just another part of the act. Tell me—have you ever used one of those things?"

"Yes."

"On what? Anything big?"

"Fairly."

"Was it dangerous?"

One had to admire Bill's persistence, almost as much as his resilience. It was obvious that Boss was getting tired of this line of questioning, but was too polite to shut it off.

"*Quite* dangerous."

"Could it have killed you?"

"Easily," said Boss, and now his voice had sud-

165

denly become bleak and impersonal. "You see, it was carrying a gun too."

In the ensuing uncomfortable silence, Duncan came to several quick conclusions. Boss was speaking the cold truth; it was no concern of theirs; and they would never learn any more.

Conversation was just getting under way again after this derailment when there was another interruption.

"Hey!" somebody shouted. "Look over there!"

A man was walking out of the "jungle," and he was not alone. Trotting beside him were two enormous animals, attached to leashes which seemed highly inadequate. They were undoubtedly dogs of some kind, though Duncan had not realized that any grew to such a size. There were, he knew, thousands of different breeds, but there seemed something strange about these; they did not fit any of the visual records he had ever seen.

"Of course!" someone exclaimed. "That's Fido and Susie."

There were murmurs of assent, but Duncan was none the wiser. He also thought that he could have chosen more appropriate names.

He was even more certain of this by the time that the monsters had reached the camp. They stood half as high as a man, and must have weighed two hundred kilos.

"What *are* they?" he asked. "Wolves?"

"Yes and no," Boss answered. "They're dire wolves. They've been extinct for about ten thousand years."

Now Duncan remembered. He had heard vaguely of the experiments on genetic reversal that had been taking place on Earth. There had been much excitement a few years ago about something called a passenger pigeon, which had now become such a pest that efforts were being made to control it. And there was even talk of restoring dinosaurs when the technique was perfected.

"Hello, Professor," said Boss. "Your hounds really shook some of us last night. By the way, folks, this is Cliff Evans, head of the department of animal genetics at the Central Park Zoo—have I got that right? And as some of you have guessed, this is the famous Fido and Susie. Is it safe to feed them a few scraps, Cliff?"

The professor shook his head.

"Not on your life; I'm afraid they're not terribly bright. We go to a lot of trouble balancing their diet. I should hate to get human protein mixed up in it."

"Very considerate of you. Now, how's the transport going to work out?"

"I can let you have ten well-behaved horses and five ditto ponies."

"That's only enough for fifteen. We need at least twenty-five."

"No problem. You can also have six miniphants. They can each take two riders, and they're safer than horses. . . ."

While this discussion was in progress, Duncan examined the professor and his pets. The survey did not inspire much confidence; in particular, he did not care for the way in which the scientist was covered from head to heels in smooth leather, with massive reinforcements around the throat and from elbow to heavily gloved hands. It could not have been very comfortable on a hot June morning, and presumably he was not wearing this armor for fun.

However, Fido and Susie seemed sleek, well fed, and even somnolent. From time to time they yawned and licked their chops, with a disturbing display of dentition, but they showed no interest in after-breakfast snacks. In fact, they showed very little interest in anything, and Duncan could see the truth of the professor's remarks about their intelligence. Their narrow skulls obviously contained much smaller brains than those of modern wolves; it was no wonder that they had become extinct. Duncan—himself an experiment in controlled genetics—felt rather sorry for the big, clumsy beasts.

"Attention, everyone!" Boss called. "We're breaking camp in thirty minutes, and then we have a short trip to make—only about six kilometers. You know the restrictions on transport in New York City, so we have the following choices—foot, horse, or miniphant. On a beautiful morning like this, *I'm* going to walk. But it's up to you—who wants to ride horseback? One, two, three—was your hand up, Bill? ... four ... eleven, twelve, thirteen ... that's unlucky —any more? No? O.K., thirteen it is."

"What about bicycles?" somebody shouted.

"Not allowed in the park," said Professor Evans. "Only last year a mad cyclist killed one of my ponies. Unfortunately, *he* survived. If you want a bike, you can go across to Fifth Avenue and hire one. For that matter, you can walk to the 96th Street station and catch the subway. It runs every ten minutes in the tourist season."

There were no takers, but all the miniphants were snapped up. Duncan opted for this mode, on Boss's advice. The rest of the party elected to walk.

Half an hour later, the string of animals arrived at the camping site. To Duncan's astonishment, they were unaccompanied by humans. One large miniphant led the procession, and the other five kept the horses from straying. The two species seemed to be on excellent terms with each other.

"I suppose it's the first time you've seen a miniphant?" said Boss, noticing Duncan's interest.

"Yes—I'd heard about them, of course. Why are they so popular?"

"They have the advantage of the elephant without the handicap of its size. As you see, they're not much bigger than horses. But they're *much* more intelligent, understand several hundred words, and can carry out quite complicated orders without supervision. And with that trunk they can open doors, pick up parcels, work switches—would you believe that they can operate viddies?"

"Frankly, no."

"You're wrong; some of them can, though not reliably yet. They get the right number about eight times out of ten."

The leader ambled up to Boss and raised his trunk in salutation.

"Hello, Rajah—nice to see you again."

Rajah brought down his trunk and wound it affectionately around Boss's wrist. Then he bent his legs and knelt ponderously on the ground, so that his riders could climb easily into the pair of seats arranged sidesaddle on his back. The other five miniphants performed the same act with the timing of a well-trained corps de ballet.

Did a boat feel like this? Duncan asked himself, as he swayed gently and comfortably out of the park. This was certainly the way to travel if the weather was fine, you didn't have far to go, and you wanted to enjoy the view. As all three criteria were now satisfied, he was blissfully content.

The file of animals and humans made its way out of the clearing, through the belt of trees, and past the pile of rocks from which the morning's revelation had been vouchsafed. They skirted the little hill, and presently came to a lake on which dozens of small boats were being languidly paddled back and forth. Each boat appeared to contain one young man, who was doing the paddling, and one young lady, who was doing nothing. Only a few couples took enough notice of the procession wending past to wave greetings; presumably New Yorkers were too accustomed to miniphants to give them more than a passing glance.

After the lake, there came a beautiful expanse of grass, smooth and flat as a billiard table. Though there were no warning signs, not a single person was walking on it, and all the animals avoided it with scrupulous care. Duncan's fellow passenger twisted around in his seat and called over his shoulder: "They say the New Yorkers are getting more tolerant. Last man to walk on *that* wasn't lynched on the spot —they gave him a choice between gas and electrocution." Duncan presumed he was joking, but didn't pursue the matter; this back-to-back seating was not good for conversation.

From time to time Bill van Hyatt, who was riding —quite expertly—a beautiful cream-colored pony, came up to him to deliver snippets of information. Most of these were welcome, even though not always necessary. Of all Man's cities, New York was still the most famous—the only one where all exiles, everywhere in the Solar System, would feel at home. Now that they were clear of the taller trees, it was possible to see many of the midtown landmarks—not only the dominating finger of the Empire State Building, but the slowly orbiting Grand Central Mobile, the shining slab of the old United Nations, the great terraced pyramid of Mount Rockefeller spanning half the island from Fifth Avenue to the Hudson River. . . . Duncan had no difficulty recognizing and naming these, but the more distant structures to the east and west were strange to him. That big golden dome over in—was it New Jersey?—was most peculiar, but Duncan had grown a little tired of exposing his ignorance and was determined to ask no more nonessential questions. He could always look up the guidebooks later.

They reached Columbus Circle and started climbing the ramp up to the bridge over the Grand Canal that now bisected Manhattan. On the level below, bikes, trikes, and passenger capsules were racing silently back and forth; and on the level below *them*, the famous Checker Gondolas were shuttling between the East River and the Hudson. Duncan was surprised to see such heavy traffic so far north of the city area, but guessed it was almost all recreational or tourist.

There was a brief pause at an Eighth Avenue comfort station for the benefit of the horses and miniphants—which, like all herbivores, had low-efficiency, rapid-turnover conversion systems. Some of the passengers also took advantage of the stop, even though the facilities were not intended for them. Remembering his contretemps at Mount Vernon, Duncan tried to imagine what the New York streets must have been like in the days when horses provided the *only* transportation, but failed and thankfully abandoned the attempt.

Now they were skirting the northern flank of Mount Rockefeller, which towered two hundred and fifty meters above them—challenging the Empire State Building in altitude and completely eclipsing it in bulk. With the exception of a few dams and the Great

Wall of China—hardly a fair comparison—it was the largest single structure on Earth. Here had gone all the rubble and debris, all the bricks and concrete, the steel girders and ceramic tiles and bathtubs and TV sets and refrigerators and air conditioners and abandoned automobiles, when the decayed uptown area was finally bulldozed flat in the early twenty-second century. The clean-up had, perhaps, been a little too comprehensive; now the industrial archaeologists were happily mining the mountain for the lost treasures of the past.

The straggling line of men and animals continued south along the wide, grassy sward of Eighth Avenue, skirting the western face of the huge pyramid. Unlike the southern facade, which was entirely covered by the celebrated Hanging Gardens of Manhattan, this side was a montage of frescoes, murals, and mosaics. It would never be completed. As fast as one work of art was finished, another would be demolished, not always with the consent of the artist. The west side of Mount Rockfeller was an aesthetic battlefield; it had even been bombed—with cans of red paint. The terraces and stairways of the man-made hill were crowded with sightseers, and on many of the vertical surfaces craftsmen were at work in swinging chairs suspended by cables. Morbidly conscious as he was of terrestrial gravity, Duncan could only look on these courageous artists with awe-struck admiration.

Nearer ground level, there were hundreds of more informal attempts at expression. One section of wall, four meters high and fifty long, had been set aside for graffiti, and the public had taken full advantage of the opportunity with crayons, chalk, and spray guns. There was a good deal of cheerful obscenity, but most of the messages were totally meaningless to Duncan. Why, he wondered, should he SUPPORT THE MIMIMALIST MANIFESTO? Was it true that KILROY WAS HERE and if so, why? Did the announcement that COUNCILMAN WILBUR ERICKSON IS A YENTOR convey praise or censure? He brooded over these and similar world-shattering problems all the way south to 44th Street.

Here, in a small plaza between Tenth and Eleventh

avenues, they said good-bye to the horses and miniphants. Duncan's mount gently collapsed in slow motion, so that its riders could step off onto terra firma; then, with equal solemnity, it rose to its feet, gravely saluted them with upraised trunk, and headed back toward its home in the Central Park Zoo. The ride had been an enjoyable experience, and Duncan could imagine few nicer ways of sightseeing, in perfect weather such as this. Nevertheless, he was glad to be back on his own feet again. That gentle swaying had been growing a little monotonous. And although he had been in no real danger, he now knew what the first intimations of seasickness must be like.

They were now only a few hundred meters from the elevated ribbon of the West Side Highway and the impressive expanse of the Hudson River, blue and flat in the morning sunlight. Never before had Duncan seen so large a body of water at such close quarters. Though it looked calm and peaceful, he found it slightly ominous—even menacing. He was more familiar with the ocean of space than the realm of water, with all its mysteries and monsters; and because of that ignorance, he felt fear.

There were numerous small villas and cafés and shops along the riverfront, as well as dozens of little docks containing pleasure boats. Although marine transport had been virtually extinct for more than two centuries, water still had an irresistible fascination for a large part of the human race. Even now, a garishly painted paddleboat, loaded with sightseers, was skirting the New Jersey shore. Duncan wondered if it was a genuine antique, or a modern reconstruction.

The three-masted man-of-war with the gilded figurehead could not possibly be the real thing—it was much too new and had obviously never gone to sea. But moored at a dock close to it was the scarred yet still beautifully streamlined hull of a sailing ship which, Duncan guessed, might have been launched in the early twentieth century. He looked at it with awe, savoring the knowledge that it had already finished its career before the first ships of space lifted from Earth.

Boss did not give them an opportunity to linger over these relics; he was heading toward an enormous, translucent half-cylinder lying along more than three hundred meters of the shoreline. It appeared to be a makeshift, temporary structure, quite out of keeping—in scale and appearance—with the careful good taste of everything around it.

And now, as they approached this peculiar building, Duncan became aware of a sudden change in the behavior of his companions. All the way from the park they had been chattering and laughing, completely relaxed and enjoying themselves on this beautiful summer day. Quite abruptly, it seemed as if a cloud had passed across the face of the sun; all laughter, and almost all talking, had suddenly ceased. Very obviously, they knew something that he did not, yet he was reluctant to disturb this mood of solemn silence by asking naïve questions.

They entered a small auxiliary building, so much like an airlock that it was easy to imagine that they were going into space. Indeed, it *was* a kind of airlock, holding rows of protective clothing: oilskins, rubber boots, and—at last!—the hard hats that had been exercising Bill van Hyatt's imagination. Still in that curious expectant hush, with only a few fleeting smiles at each other's transformed appearance, they passed through the inner airlock.

Duncan had expected to see a ship. In this, at least, he was not surprised. But he was completely taken aback by its sheer size; it almost filled the huge structure that surrounded it. He knew that, toward the end, oil tankers had become gigantic—but he had no idea that passenger liners had ever grown so huge. And it was obvious from its many portholes and decks that this ship had been built to transport people, not bulk cargo.

The viewing platform on which they stood was level with the main deck and just ahead of the bridge. To his right, Duncan could see one huge but truncated mast and a businesslike maze of cranes, winches, ventilators, and hatches, all the way up to

173

the prow. Stretching away on the left, toward the ship's hidden stern, was an apparently endless wall of steel, punctuated by hundreds of portholes. Looming high above everything were three huge funnels, almost touching the curved roof of the enclosure. From their spacing, it was obvious that a fourth one was now missing.

There were many other signs of damage. Windows were shattered, parts of the decking had been torn up, and when he looked down toward the keel, Duncan could see an enormous metal patch, at least a hundred meters long, running just below the waterline.

Only then did all the pieces of the puzzle fall into place. Now he understood the awed silence of his companions, and was able to share their emotions of wonder and of pity.

On that day, he had been a boy on a distant world; but he could still remember when, after her three-hundred-and-fifty-year maiden voyage, the *Titanic* had at last reached New York.

27

THE GHOST FROM GRAND BANKS

"They never built another one like her; she marked the end of an age—an age of wealth and elegance which was swept away, only two years later, by the first of the World Wars. Oh, they built faster and bigger, in the half century before air travel closed that chapter for all time. But no ship ever again matched the luxury you see around you now. It broke too many hearts when she was lost."

Duncan could not believe it; he was still in a dream. The magnificent Grand Saloon, with its vast mirrors, gilded columns, and ankle-deep carpet, was opulent beyond anything he had ever imagined, and the sofa into which he was sinking made him almost forget the gravity of Earth. Yet the most incredible fact of all was that everything he saw and touched had been lying for three and a half centuries on the bed of the Atlantic.

He had not realized that the deep sea was almost as timeless as space. "All the damage," the speaker had explained, "was done on that first morning. When she sank, two and a half hours after the spur of ice ripped open the starboard hull, she went down bow first, almost vertically. Everything loose tumbled forward until it was either stopped by the bulkheads, or else smashed through them. By miraculous good luck—and this tells you how superbly she was built—all three engines remained in place. If *they* had gone, the hull would have been so badly damaged that we could never have salvaged her. . . .

"But once she reached the bottom, three kilometers down, she was safe for centuries. The water there is only two degrees above freezing point; the combination of cold and pressure quenches all decay, inhibits all rust. We've found meat in the refrigerators as fresh as when it left Southampton on April 10, 1912, and everything that was canned or bottled is still in perfect condition.

"When we'd patched her up—a straightforward job, though it took a year to plug all the holes and reinforce the weak spots—we blasted out the water with the zero-thrust cold rockets the deep sea salvage people have developed. Naturally, weather conditions were critical; by good luck, there was an ideal forecast for April 15, 2262, so she broke surface three hundred and fifty years to the very day after she sank. Conditions were identical—dead calm, freezing temperature—and you won't believe this, but we had to avoid an iceberg when we started towing!

"So we brought her to New York, pumped her full of nitrogen to stop rusting, and slowly dried her out. No problems here—the underwater archaeologists have preserved ships ten times older than *Titanic*. It's the sheer *scale* of the job that's taken us fourteen years, and will take us at least ten more. Thousands of pieces of smashed furniture to be sorted out, hundreds of tons of coal to be moved—almost every lump by hand.

"And the dead . . . 158 so far. Only a few people were trapped in the ship. Those in sealed compartments looked as if they had been drowned yesterday. In the sections the fish could reach, there were only bones. We were able to identify several, from the cabin numbers and the White Star Line's records. And that story you've heard is quite true: we found one couple still in each other's arms. They were married—but each to someone else. And the two other partners survived; I wonder if they ever guessed? After three and a half centuries, it doesn't much matter. . . .

"Sometimes we're asked—why are you doing this, devoting years of time and millions of solars to salvaging the past? Well, I can give you some down-to-earth, practical reasons. This ship is part of our history. We can better understand ourselves, and our civilization, when we study her. Someone once said that a sunken ship is a time capsule, because it preserves all the artifacts of everyday life, exactly as they were at their last instant of use. And the *Titanic* was a cross-section of an entire society, at the unique moment before it started to dissolve.

"We have the stateroom of John Jacob Astor, with all the valuables and personal effects that the richest man of his age was taking to New York. He could have bought the *Titanic*—a dozen times over. And we have the tool kit that Pat O'Connor carried when he came aboard at Queenstown, hoping to find a better living in a land he was never to see. We even have the five sovereigns he had managed to save, after more years of hardship than we can ever imagine.

"These are the two extremes; between them we have every walk of life—a priceless treasure trove for the historian, the economist, the artist, the engineer. But beyond that there's a magic about this ship which has kept its name fresh through all the centuries. The story of the *Titanic's* first and last voyage

176

is one that has to be told anew in every generation, lest men forget the workings of fate and chance.

"I have talked longer than I intended, and pictures speak louder than words. There have been ten movies about the *Titanic*—and the most ambitious will start production shortly, using the actual location for the first time. But the extracts we want to show you now are from a film made three hundred and twenty years ago. Of course it will look old-fashioned, and it's in black and white, but it was the last film to be made while survivors were still alive and could check its details. For this reason, it remains the most authentic treatment; I think you will discover that *A Night to Remember* lives up to its name."

The lights in the Grand Saloon dimmed, as they had dimmed at two-eighteen on the morning of April 15, 1912. Time rolled back three and a half centuries as the grainy, flickering real-life footage merged into the impeccable studio reconstruction. *Titanic* sailed again, to make her appointment with destiny, off the Grand Banks of Newfoundland.

Duncan did not cry easily, but presently he was weeping.

When the lights came on again, he understood why men had spent so much of toil and treasure to win back what the sea had stolen from them long ago. His eyes were still so misty, and his vision so uncertain, that for a moment he did not recognize the woman who had just entered the Grand Saloon and was standing by one of the ornate doors.

Even carrying a hard hat, and with shapeless plastic waterproof covering her from neck to knees, Calindy still looked poised and elegant. Duncan rose to his feet and walked toward her, ignoring the stares of companions. Silently, he put out his arms, embraced her, and kissed her full on the lips. She was not as tall as he had remembered—or he had grown —because he had to stoop.

"Well!" she exclaimed, when she had disentangled herself. "After fifteen years!"

"You haven't changed in the least."

"Liar. I hope I have. At twenty-one I was an irresponsible brat."

"At twenty-one you should be. It's the last chance you'll have."

This scintillating conversation then ground to a halt, while they looked at each other and everyone in the Grand Saloon looked at them. I'm quite sure, Duncan told himself wryly, that they think we're old lovers; would that it were true. . . .

"Duncan, *darhling*—sorry—I always start talking early twentieth century when I'm in here: Mr. D. Makenzie, please excuse me for a few minutes while I speak to my other guests—then we'll tour the ship together."

He watched her dart purposefully from one group to another, the very embodiment of the efficient administrator, confirming that everything was going as planned. Was she playing another of her roles, or was this the real Calindy, if such a creature existed?

She came back to him five minutes later, with all her associates trotting dutifully behind.

"Duncan—I don't think you've met Commander Innes—he knows more about this ship than the people who built her. He'll be showing us around."

As they shook hands, Duncan said: "I enjoyed your presentation very much. It's always stimulating to meet a real enthusiast."

His words were not idle flattery. While he had been listening to that talk, Duncan had recognized something that he had not met before on Earth.

Commander Innes was slightly larger than life, and seemed to be inclined at a small angle to his fellow Terrans. A world which had put a premium on tolerance and security and safe, well-organized excitements like those provided by Enigma had no place for zealots. Though enthusiasm was not actually illegal, it was in somewhat bad taste; one should not take one's hobbies and recreations too seriously. Commander Innes, Duncan suspected, lived and dreamed *Titanic*. In an ealier age, he might have been a missionary, spreading the doctrines of Mohammed or Jesus with fire and sword. Today he was a harmless and indeed refreshing anomaly, and perhaps just a trifle mad.

For the next hour, they explored the bowels of the ship—and Duncan was thankful for his protective clothing. There was still mud and oil sloshing around on G deck, and several times be banged his head against unexpected ladders and ventilating ducts. But the effort and discomfort were well worth it, for only in this manner could he really appreciate all the skill and genius that had gone into this floating city. Most moving of all was to touch the inward-curling petals of steel far below the starboard bow, and to imagine the icy waters that had poured through them on that tragic night.

The boilers were shapeless, crumpled masses, but the engines themselves were in surprisingly good condition. Duncan looked with awe at the giant connecting rods and crankshafts, the huge reduction gears. (But why on earth did the designers use piston engines *and* turbines?) Then his admiration was abruptly tempered when Commander Innes gave him some statistics: this mountain of metal developed a ludicrous forty thousand kilowatts! He remembered the figure that Chief Engineer Mackenzie had given for *Sirius'* main drive; a trillion kilowatts. Mankind had indeed gone a long way, in every sense of the phrase, during the last three centuries.

He was exhausted when he had climbed back up the alphabet from G to A deck (one day, Commander Innes promised, the elevators would be running again) and was more than thankful when they settled down for lunch in the First Class Smoking Room.

Then he looked at the Menu, and blinked:

R.M.S. "TITANIC"
April 14, 1912

LUNCHEON
Consommé Fermier   Cockie Leekie
Fillets of Brill
Egg À l'Argenteuil
Chicken À la Maryland
Corned Beef, Vegetables, Dumplings

179

FROM THE GRILL
Grilled Mutton Chops
Mashed, Fried, and Baked Jacket Potatoes
Custard Pudding
Apple Meringue   Pastry

BUFFET
Salmon Mayonnaise   Potted Shrimps
Norwegian Anchovies   Soused Herrings
Plain & Smoked Sardines
Roast Beef
Round of Spiced Beef
Veal & Ham Pie
Virginia & Cumberland Ham
Bologna Sausage   Brawn
Galatine of Chicken
Corned Ox Tongue
Lettuce   Beetroot   Tomatoes

CHEESE
Cheshire, Stilton, Gorgonzola, Edam,
Camembert, Roquefort, St. Ivel,
Cheddar

Iced draught Munch Lager Beer 3d. & 6d. a Tankard

"I'm sorry to disappoint you," said Calindy. "We've done our best, within the limits of the synthesizers, but we don't even know what half these items were. The secret of Cockie Leekie went down with the ship, and perhaps it's just as well. But we do have a substitute for the Munich Beer."

Duncan would never have given this ordinary, unlabeled bottle a second thought had he not noticed the extreme care with which it was carried. He looked questioningly at his hostess.

"Vintage '05, according to the wine steward's records—1905, that is. Tell me what you think of it."

With one bottle to forty guests, there was just enough to get a good taste. It was port, and to Duncan seemed just like any other port; but he was too polite to say so. He made vague mumblings of appreciation, saw that Calindy was laughing at him, and added, "I'm afraid we don't have much chance of studying wines on Titan."

"Titan," said Commander Innes thoughtfully. "How very appropriate."

"But hardly a coincidence. You can thank Cal—Miss Ellerman."

"You've no seas on Titan, have you?"

"Only small temporary ones. Of liquid ammonia."

"I couldn't live on a world like that. I can't bear to be away from the sea more than a few weeks. You must go to the Caribbean and dive on one of our reefs. If you've never seen a coral reef, you can't imagine it."

Duncan had no intention of following the Commander's advice. He could understand the fascination of the sea, but it terrified him. Nothing, he was sure, would ever induce him to enter that alien universe of strange beasts, full of known dangers that were bad enough, and unknown ones that must be even worse. (As if one could possibly imagine anything worse than the man-eating shark or the giant squid. . . .) People like Commander Innes must indeed be mad. They made life interesting, but there was no need to follow their example.

And at the moment, Duncan was too busy trying to follow Calindy—without much success. He could appreciate the fact that, having some fifty people to deal with, she could give him only two percent of her time; but when he tried to pin her down to a meeting under less hectic circumstances, she was curiously evasive. It was not that she was unfriendly, for she seemed genuinely pleased to see him. But *something* was worrying her—she was holding him at arm's length. It was almost as if she had been warned that he was bringing deadly Titanian germs to Earth. All that he could extract from her before they parted was a vague promise that she would contact him "just as soon as the season is over"—whatever *that* might mean.

Enigma Associates had not disappointed him, but their vice-president had left him puzzled and saddened. Duncan worried at the problem throughout the thirty-minute ride in the vacuum subway back to

Washington. (Thank God the van Hyatts were staying in New York—he would not appreciate their company in his present mood.)

He realized that there was nothing he could do; if, like some lovesick suitor, he persisted in bothering Calindy, it would merely make matters worse. Some problems could be solved only by time, if indeed they could be solved at all.

He had plenty to do. He would forget about Calindy. . . .

With any luck, for as much as an hour at a time.

28

AKHENATON AND CLEOPATRA

Sir Mortimer Keynes sat in his armchair in Harley Street and looked with clinical interest at Duncan Makenzie, on the other side of the Atlantic.

"So you're the latest of the famous Makenzies. And you want to make sure you're not the last."

This was a statement, not a question. Duncan made no attempt to answer, but continued to study the man who, in an almost literal sense, was his creator.

Mortimer Keynes was well into his eighties, and looked like a rather shaggy and decrepit lion. There was an air of authority about him—but also of resignation and detachment. After half a century as Earth's leading genetic surgeon, he no longer expected life to provide him with any surprises; but he had not yet lost all interest in the human comedy.

"Tell me," he continued, "why did you come yourself, all the way from Titan? Why not just send the necessary biotype samples?"

"I have business here," Duncan answered. "As well as an invitation to the Centennial. It was too good an opportunity to miss."

"You could still have sent the sample on ahead.

Now you'll have to wait nine months—that is, if you want to take your son back with you."

"This visit was arranged very unexpectedly, at short notice. Anyway, I can use the time. This is my only chance to see Earth; in another ten years, I won't be able to face its gravity."

"Why is it so important to produce another guaranteed one-hundred-percent Makenzie?"

Presumably Colin had gone through all this with Keynes—but, of course, that was thirty years ago, and heaven knows how many thousands of clonings the surgeon had performed since then. He could not possibly remember; on the other hand, he would certainly have detailed records, and was probably checking them at this very moment on that display panel in his desk.

"To answer *that* question," Duncan began slowly, "I'd have to give you the history of Titan for the last seventy years."

"I don't think that will be necessary," interrupted the surgeon, his eyes scanning his hidden display. "It's an old story; only the details vary from age to age. Have you ever heard of Akhenaton?"

"Who?"

"Cleopatra?"

"Oh yes—she was an Egyptian queen, wasn't she?"

"Queen of Egypt, but not Egyptian. Mistress of Anthony and Caesar. The last and greatest of the Ptolemies."

What on Earth, Duncan thought in bemusement, has this to do with me? Not for the first time, and certainly not for the last, he felt overwhelmed by the sheer detail and complexity of terrestrial history. Colin, with his interest in the past, would probably know what Keynes was driving at, but Duncan was completely lost.

"I'm referring to the problem of succession. How do you make sure your dynasty continues after your death, on the lines *you* want? There's no way of guaranteeing it, of course, but you can improve the odds if you can leave a carbon copy of yourself. . . .

"The Egyptian Pharaohs made a heroic attempt at this—the best that could be done without modern science. Because they claimed to be gods, they could not marry mortals, so they mated brother and sister. The result was sometimes genius, but also deformity —in the case of Akhenaton, both. Yet they continued the tradition for more than a thousand years, until it ended with Cleopatra.

"If the Pharaohs had been able to clone themselves, they would certainly have done so. It would have been the perfect answer, avoiding the problem of inbreeding. But it introduces other problems. Because genes are no longer shuffled, it stops the evolutionary clock. It means the end of all biological progress."

What's he driving at? Duncan asked himself impatiently. The interview was not going at all in the way he had planned. It had seemed a simple enough matter to set up the arrangements, just as Colin and Malcolm had done, three and seven decades ago, respectively. Now it appeared that the man who had made more clonings than anyone on Earth was trying to talk him out of it. He felt confused and disoriented, and also a little angry.

"I've no objection," the surgeon continued, "to cloning *if* it's combined with genetic repair—which is not possible in your case, as you certainly know. When you were cloned from Colin, that was merely an attempt to perpetuate the dynasty. Healing was not involved—only politics and personal vanity. Oh, I'm sure that both your precursors are convinced that it was all for the good of Titan, and they may well be absolutely right. But I'm afraid I've given up playing God. I'm sorry, Mr. Makenzie. Now, if you will excuse me—I hope you have an enjoyable visit. Goodbye to you."

Duncan was left staring, slack-jawed, at a blank screen. He did not even have time to return the farewell—still less give Colin's greetings, as he had intended, to the man who had created both of them.

He was surprised, disappointed—and hurt. No doubt he could make other arrangements, but it had never occurred to him to go anywhere than to his own point of origin. He felt like a son who had just been repudiated by his own father.

184

There was a mystery here; and suddenly, in a flash of insight, Duncan thought he had guessed the solution. Sir Mortimer had cloned himself—and it had turned out badly.

The theory was ingenious, and not without a certain poetic truth. It merely happened to be wrong.

29

PARTY GAMES

It was well for Duncan that he was now becoming less awed by conspicuous displays of culture. Impressed, by all means; overwhelmed, no. Too strong a colonial inferiority complex would certainly have spoiled his enjoyment of this reception.

He had been to other parties since his arrival, but this was by far the largest. It was sponsored by the National Geographic Society—no, *that* was tomorrow —by the Congressional Foundation, whatever that might be, and there were at least a thousand guests circulating through the marble halls.

"If the roof fell in on us now," he overheard someone remark, rather smugly, "Earth would start running around like a headless chicken."

There seemed no reason to fear such a disaster; the National Gallery of Art had stood for almost four hundred years. Many of its treasures, of course, were far older: no one could possibly put a value on the paintings and sculpture displayed in its halls. Leonardo's *Ginevra de' Benci*, Michelangelo's miraculously recovered bronze *David*, Picasso's *Willie Maugham, Esq.*, Levinski's *Martian Dawn*, were merely the most famous of the wonders it had gathered through the centuries. Every one of them, Duncan knew, he could study through holograms in closer detail than he was doing now—but it was not the same thing. Though the copies might be technically perfect, *these* were the originals, forever unique; the ghosts of the long-dead artists still lingered here. When he returned to Titan, he would be able to boast to his friends: "Yes—I've stood within a meter of a genuine Leonardo."

It also amused Duncan to realize that never on his own world could he move in such a crowd—and be completely unrecognized. He doubted if there were ten people here who knew him by sight; most of them would be ladies he had addressed on that memorable evening with the Daughters of the Revolutions. He was, as George Washington had neatly put it, still one of Earth's leading unknown celebrities. Barring untoward events, his status would remain that way until he spoke to the world on July Fourth. And perhaps even after that . . .

However, his identity could be discovered easily enough, except by the most short-sighted individuals; he was wearing a badge that bore in prominent letters the words DUNCAN MACKENZIE, TITAN. He had thought it impolite to make a fuss about the spelling. Like Malcolm, he had given up *that* argument years ago.

On Titan, such labels would have been completely unnecessary; here they were essential. The advance of microelectronics had relegated to history two problems that, until the late twentieth century, had been virtually insoluble: At a really big party, how do you find who's there—and how do you locate any given person? When Duncan checked in at the foyer, he found himself confronting a large board bearing hundreds of names. That at once established the guestlist, or, to be more accurate, the list of guests who wished to make their presence known. He spent several minutes studying it, and picked out half a dozen possible targets. George, of course, was there; and so was Ambassador Farrell. No point in hunting up *them;* he saw them every day.

Against each name was a button, and a tiny lamp. When the button was pressed, the guest's badge would emit a buzz just loud enough for him to hear, and his light would start flashing. He then had two alternatives. He could apologize to the group he was with,

186

and start drifting toward a central rendezvous area. By the time he arrived—which could be anything from a minute to half an hour after the signal, according to the number of encounters en route—the caller might still be there; or he might have gotten fed up and moved away.

The other alternative was to press a button on the badge itself, which would cut off the signal. The light on the board would then shine with a steady glow, informing the world that the callee did not wish to be disturbed. Only the most persistent or bad-mannered inquirer would ignore this hint.

Although some hostesses thought the system too coldly mechanical, and refused to use it at any price, it was in fact deliberately imperfect. Anyone who wished to opt out could neglect to pick up his badge, and it would then be assumed that he had not put in an appearance. To aid this deception, an ample supply of false badges was available, and the protocol that went with them was well understood. If you saw a familiar face above an innocuous JOHN DOE or MARY SMITH, you investigated no further. But a JESUS CHRIST or a JULIUS CAESAR was fair game.

Duncan saw no need for anonymity. He was quite happy to meet anyone who wished to meet him, so he left his badge in the operating mode while he raided the lavish buffet, then beat a retreat to one of the smaller tables. Although he could now function in Earth's gravity better than he would once have believed possible, he still took every opportunity of sitting down. And in this case it was essential even for Terrans, except those skillful enough to manipulate three plates and one glass with two hands.

He had been one of the early arrivals—this was a folly he never succeeded in curing during his whole stay on Earth—and by the time he had finished nibbling at unknown delicacies, the hall was comfortably full. He decided to start circulating among the other guests, lest he be identified for what he was—a lost and lonely outsider.

He did not *deliberately* eavesdrop; but Makenzies had unusually good hearing, and Terrans—at least party-going Terrans—seemed anxious to spread information as widely as possible. Like a free electron wandering through a semiconductor, Duncan drifted from one group to another, occasionally exchanging a few words of greeting, but never getting involved for more than a couple of minutes. He was quite content to be a passive observer, and ninety percent of the conversations he overheard were meaningless or boring. But not all . . .

I *loathe* parties like this, don't you?

It's supposed to be the only set of genuine antique inflatable furniture in the world. Of course, they won't let you *sit* on it.

I'm *so* sorry. But it will wash out easily.

—buying at one fifty and selling at one eighty. Would you believe that grown men once spent their *entire* lives doing that sort of thing?

—no music worth listening to since the late twentieth century. . . . Make it early twenty-first.

Sorry—*I* don't know who's throwing this party, either.

Did El Greco come before Modigliani? I just can't *believe* it.

Bill's ambition is to be shot dead at the age of two hundred by a jealous wife.

How's the Revolution going? If you need any more money from the Ways and Means Committee, let me know.

Food should come in pills, the way God intended. . . .

Anyone in the room she's *not* slept with?
Well, maybe that statue of Zeus.

188

French is *not* a dead language. At least five million people still speak it—or at least *read* it.

I'm getting up a petition to save the Lunar wilderness areas.
I thought it was the Van Allen Belt.
Oh, that was *last* year.

At that point, Duncan's badge started to hum gently. For a moment he was taken by surprise; he had quite forgotten that it was part of a paging system. He looked around for the rendezvous point, a discreet little banner bearing the notice L-S HERE, PLEASE. Needless to say it was on the far side of the room, and it took him a good five minutes to plow through the crowd.

Half a dozen complete strangers were waiting hopefully under the banner. He scanned their faces in vain, looking for some sign of recognition. But when he got within name-reading range, one of the group broke away and approached him with outstretched hands.

"Mr. Makenzie—how good of you to come! I'll take only a few minutes of your time."

From bitter experience, Duncan had learned that this was one of Terra's great understatements. He looked cautiously at the speaker to sum him up and to guess his business. What he saw was reasonably reassuring: a very neat, goateed little man wearing a traditional Chinese/Indian *shervani,* tightly buttoned up at the neck. He did not look like a bore or a fanatic; but they seldom did.

"That's all right, Mr.—er—Mandel'stahm. What can I do for you?"

"I'd intended to contact you—it was pure luck, seeing your name on the list—I knew there could be only *one* Makenzie—what does the D stand for—Donald, Douglas, David—"

"Duncan."

"Ah, yes. Let's move over to that seat—it'll be quieter—besides, I love Winslow Homer's *Fair Wind,* even though the technique is so crude—you can almost smell the fish sliding around in the boat—why,

189

what a coincidence—it's *exactly four hundred years old!* Don't you think coincidences are fascinating? I've been collecting them all my life."

"I've never thought about it," replied Duncan, already feeling a little breathless. He was afraid that if he listened much longer to Mr. Mandel'stahm, he too would start to talk in jerks. What did the man want? For that matter, was there any way of discovering the intentions of a person whose flow of speech seemed to be triggered by random impulses?

Luckily, as soon as they were seated, Mr. Mandel'stahm became much more coherent. He gave a conspirational glance to check that there was nobody in earshot except Winslow Homer's fisherboys, then resumed his conversation in a completely different tone of voice.

"I promised I'd take only a few minutes. Here's my card—you can use it to key my number. Yes, I call myself an antique dealer, but that covers a multitude of sins. My main interest is gems—I have one of the largest private collections in the world. So you've probably guessed why I was anxious to meet you."

"Go on."

"Titanite, Mr. Makenzie. There are not more than a dozen fragments on Earth—five of them in museums. Even the Smithsonian doesn't have a specimen, and its curator of gems—that tall man over there—is *most* unhappy. I suppose you know that titanite is one of the few materials that can't be replicated?"

"So I believe," answered Duncan, now very cautious. Mr. Mandel'stahm had certainly made his interests clear, though not his intentions.

"You'll understand, therefore, that if a swarthy, cornute gentleman suddenly appeared in a puff of smoke with a contract for several grams of titanite in exchange for my signature in blood, I wouldn't bother to read the small print."

Duncan was not quite sure what "cornute" meant, but he got the general picture quickly enough, and gave a noncommittal nod.

"Well, something like this has been happening over the last three months—not quite so dramatically, of course. I've been approached, in great confidence, by a dealer who claims to have titanite for sale, in lots of up to ten grams. What would you say to that?"

"I'd be extremely suspicious. It's probably fake."

"You can't fake titanite."

"Well—synthetic?"

"I'd thought of that too—it's an interesting idea, but it would mean so many scientific breakthroughs *somewhere* that it couldn't possibly be hushed up. It certainly wouldn't be a simple job, like diamond manufacture. No one has any idea how titanite is produced. There are at least four theories proving that it can't exist."

"Have you ever seen it?"

"Of course—the fragment in the American Museum of Natural History, and the very fine specimen in the Geological Museum, South Kensington."

Duncan refrained from adding that there was an even finer specimen in the Centennial Hotel, not ten kilometers from here. Until this mystery was cleared up, and he knew more about Mr. Mandel'stahm, this information was best kept to himself. He did not believe that burglarious visitors were likely, but it was foolish to take unnecessary chances.

"I don't quite see how I can help you. If you're sure that the titanite is genuine, and hasn't been acquired illegally, what's your problem?"

"Simply this. Not everything rare is valuable—but everything valuable is rare. If someone's discovered a few kilograms of titanite, it would be just another common gemstone, like opal or sapphire or ruby. Naturally, I don't want to make a big investment if there's any danger that the price might suddenly nose-dive."

He saw Duncan's quizzical expression and added hastily, "Of course, now that the profit motive's extinct, I do this for amusement. I'm more concerned with my reputation."

"I understand. But if there had been such a find, I'm sure I would have heard of it. It would have been reported to my government."

Mr. Mandel'stahm's eyebrows gained altitude perceptibly.

"Perhaps. But perhaps not. Especially if it were

found—off-planet. I'm referring, of course, to the theories suggesting that it's not indigenous to Titan."

You're certainly well informed, Duncan told himself —in fact, I'm sure you know far more about titanite than *I* do. . . .

"I suppose you mean the theory that there may be bigger lodes on the other moons?"

"Yes. In fact, traces have been detected on Iapetus."

"That's news to me, but I wouldn't have heard unless there had been a major find. Which, I gather, is what you suspect."

"Among other things."

For a few seconds, Duncan processed this information in silence. If it was true——and he could think of no reason why Mandel'stahm should be lying ——it was his duty as an officer of the Titanian administration to look into it. But the very last thing he wanted now was extra work, especially if it was likely to lead to messy complicatons. If some clever operator was actually smuggling titanite, Duncan would prefer to remain in blissful ignorance. He had more important things to worry about.

Perhaps Mandel'stahm understood the reason for his hesitation, for he added quietly: "The sum involved may be quite large. *I'm* not interested in that, of course——but most governments are rather grateful to anyone who detects a loss of revenue. If I can help you earn that gratitude, I should be delighted."

I understand you perfectly, said Duncan to himself, and this makes the proposition much more attractive. He did not know the Titan law on these matters, and even if a reward was involved, it would be tactless for the Special Assistant to the Chief Administrator to claim it. But his task would certainly not be much easier if—as he gloomily expected—he were compelled to apply for more Terran solars before the end of his stay.

"I'll tell you what I'll do," he said to Mandel'stahm. "Tomorrow, I'll send a message to Titan, and initiate inquiries—very discreetly, of course. If I learn something, I'll let you know. But don't expect too much—or, for that matter, anything at all."

Mandel'stahm seemed quite happy with this arrangement, and departed with rather fulsome protestations of gratitude. Duncan decided that it was also high time that he left the party. He had been on his feet for over two hours, and all his vertebrae were now starting to protest in unison. As he made his way toward the exit, he kept a lookout for George Washington, and managed to find him—despite his short stature—without falling back on the paging system.

"Everything going well?" asked George.

"Yes—I've had a very interesting time. And I've run into a curious character—he calls himself a gem expert—"

"Ivor Mandel'stahm. What did the old fox want from you?"

"Oh—information. I was polite, but not very helpful. Should I take him seriously, and can he be trusted?"

"Ivor is merely the world's greatest expert on gems. And in *that* business, one can't afford even the hint of a suspicion. You can trust him absolutely."

"Thanks—that's all I wanted to know."

Half an hour later, back at the hotel, Duncan unlocked his case and laid out the set of pentominoes that Grandma had given him; he had not even touched it since arriving on Earth. Carefully, he lifted out the titanite cross and held it up to the light. . . .

The first time he had ever seen the gem was at Grandma Ellen's and he could date the event very accurately. Calindy had been with him, so he must have been sixteen years old. He could not remember how it had been arranged. In view of Grandma's dislike of strangers (and even of relatives) the visit must have been a major diplomatic feat. He did recall that Calindy had been very anxious to meet the famous old lady, and had wanted to bring along her friends; that, however, had been firmly vetoed.

It was one of those days when Ellen Makenzie's co-ordinate system coincided with the external world's, and she treated Calindy as if she were actually there. Doubtless the fact that she had a fascinating new novelty to display had much to do with her unusual friendliness.

This was not the first specimen of titanite that had been discovered, but the second or third—and the largest up to that time, with a mass of almost fifteen grams. It was irregularly shaped, and Duncan realized that the cross he was now holding must have been cut from it. In those days, no one thought of titanite as having any great value; it was merely a curiosity.

Grandma had polished a section a few millimeters on a side, and the specimen now lay on the stage of a binocular microscope, with a beam of pseudowhite light from a trichromatic laser shining into it. Most of the room illumination had been switched off, but refracted and reflected spots, many of them completely dispersed into their three component colors, glowed steadily from unexpected places on walls and ceiling. The room might have been some magician's or alchemist's cell—as, indeed, in a way it was. In earlier ages, Ellen Makenzie would probably have been regarded as a witch.

Calindy stared through the microscope for a long time, while Duncan waited more or less patiently. Then, with a whispered "It's beautiful—I've never seen anything like it!" she had reluctantly stepped aside. . . .

. . . A hexagonal corridor of light, dwindling away to infinity, outlined by millions of sparkling points in a geometrically perfect array. By changing focus, Duncan could hurtle down that corridor, without ever coming to an end. How incredible that such a universe lay inside a piece of rock only a millimeter thick!

The slightest change of position, and the glittering hexagon vanished; it depended critically on the angle of illumination, as well as the orientation of the crystal. Once it was lost, even Grandma's skilled hands took minutes to find it again.

"Quite unique," she had said happily (Duncan had never seen her so cheerful), "and I've no explanations—merely half a dozen theories. I'm not even sure if we're seeing a real structure—or some kind of moiré pattern in three dimensions, if that's possible. . . ."

That had been fifteen years ago—and in that time,

hundreds of theories had been proposed and demolished. It was widely agreed, however, that titanite's extraordinarily perfect lattice structure must have been produced by a combination of extremely low temperatures *and* total absence of gravity. If this theory was correct, it could not have originated on any planet, or much nearer to the Sun than the orbit of Neptune. Some scientists had even built a whole elaborate theory of "interstellar crystallography" on this assumption.

There had been even wilder suggestions. Something as odd as titanite had, naturally, appealed to Karl's speculative urges.

"I don't believe it's natural," he had once told Duncan. "A material like that couldn't *happen*. It's an artifact of a superior civilization—like—oh—one of our crystal memories."

Duncan had been impressed. It was one of those theories that sounded just crazy enough to be true, and every few years someone "rediscovered" it. But as the debate raged on inconclusively, the public soon lost interest; only the geologists and gemologists still found titanite a source of endless fascination—as Mandel'stahm had now demonstrated.

Makenzies always kept their promises, even in the most trifling matters. Duncan would send a message off to Colin the first thing in the morning. There was no hurry; and that, he expected and half hoped, would be the last he would hear of it.

Very gently, he replaced the titanite cross in its setting between the F, N, U, and V pentominoes. One day, he really *must* make a sketch of the configuration.

If the pieces ever fell out of the box, it might take him hours to get them back again. . . .

30

THE RIVALS

After the encounter with Mortimer Keynes, Duncan licked his wounds in silence for several days. He did not feel like discussing the matter with his usual confidants, General George and Ambassador Farrell. And though he did not doubt that Calindy would have all the answers—or could find them quickly—he also hesitated to call her. Instinct, rather than logic, told him that it might not be a good idea. When he looked into his heart, Duncan had to admit ruefully that though he certainly desired Calindy, and perhaps even loved her, he did not trust her.

The Classified Section of the Comsole was not much use. When he asked for information on cloning services, he got several dozen names, none of which meant anything to him. He was not surprised to see that the list no longer included Keynes; when he checked the surgeon's personal entry, it printed out "Retired." He might have saved himself some embarrassment if he had discovered this earlier, but who could have guessed?

Like many such problems, this one solved itself unexpectedly. He was groaning beneath Bernie Patras' ministrations when he suddenly realized that the person who could help was right here, pulverizing him with merciless skill.

Whether or not a man has any secrets from his valet, he certainly has none from his masseur. With Bernie, Duncan had established a cheerful, bantering relationship, without detracting from the serious professionalism of the other's therapy—thanks to which he was not merely mobile, but still steadily gaining strength.

Bernie was an inveterate gossip, full of scandalous

stories, but Duncan had noticed that he never revealed names and was as careful to protect his sources as any media reporter. For all his chattering, he could be trusted; and he also had any entrée he wished to the medical profession. He was just the man for the job.

"Bernie, there's something I'd like you to do for me."

"Delighted. Just tell me whether it's boys or girls, and how many of each, with approximate shapes and sizes. I'll fill in the details."

"*This* is serious. You know I'm a clone, don't you?"

"Yes."

Duncan had assumed as much; it was not one of the Solar System's best-kept secrets.

"*Ouch*—have you ever heard of Mortimer Keynes?"

"The genetic surgeon? Of course."

"Good. He was the man who cloned me. Well, the other day I called him, just to—ah—say hello. And he behaved in a very strange way. In fact, he was almost rude."

"You didn't call him 'Doctor'? Surgeons often hate that."

"No—at least, I don't think so. It wasn't really anything on a personal level. He just tried to tell me that cloning was a bad idea, and he was against it. I felt I should apologize for existing."

"I can understand your feelings. What do you want me to do? My rates for assassination are quite high, but easy terms can be arranged."

"Before we get *that* far, you might make some inquiries among your medical friends. I'd very much like to discover why Sir Mortimer changed his mind —that is, if anyone knows the reason."

"I'll find out, don't worry—though it may take a few days." Bernie was obviously delighted at the challenge; he was also unduly pessimistic in his estimate, for he called Duncan the very next morning.

"No problem," he said triumphantly. "Everyone knows the story—I should have remembered it myself. Are you ready to record? A few kilobits of the *World Times* coming over . . ."

The tragicomedy had reverberated around the Terran news services for several months, more than fifteen years ago, and echoes of it were still heard from time to time. It was an old tale—as old as human history, in some form or other. Duncan had read only a few paragraphs before he was able to imagine the rest.

There had been the brilliant but aging surgeon and his equally brilliant young assistant, who in the natural course of events would have been his successor. They had known triumphs and disasters together, and had been so closely linked that the world had thought of them almost as one person.

Then there had been a quarrel, over a new technique which the younger man had developed. There was no need, he claimed, to wait for the immemorial nine months between conception and birth, now that the entire process was under control. If certain precautions were taken to safeguard the health of the human foster mother who carried the fertilized egg, there was no reason why pregnancy should last more than two or three months.

Needless to say, this claim excited wide attention. There was even facetious talk of "instant clones." Mortimer Keynes had not disputed his colleague's techniques, but he deplored any attempt to put them into practice. With a conservatism that some thought curiously inappropriate, he argued that Nature had chosen that nine months for very good reasons, and that the human race should stick to it.

Considering the violence that cloning did to the normal process of reproduction, this seemed a rather strange attitude, as many critics hastened to point out. This only made Sir Mortimer even more stubborn, and reading between the lines Duncan felt fairly certain that the surgeon's expressed objections were not the real ones. For some unknown and probably unknowable reason, he had experienced a crisis of conscience; what he was now opposing was not merely the shortening of the gestation period, but the entire process of cloning itself.

The younger man, of course, disagreed completely.

The debate had become more and more bitter—also more and more public, as it was inflamed by sensation-seeking hangers-on who wanted to see a good fight. After one abortive attempt at reconciliation, the partnership split up, and the two men had never spoken to each other again. A major problem at medical congresses for the last decade had been to ensure that they were not present simultaneously at any meeting.

That had been the end of Mortimer Keynes's active career. The famous clinic he had established was closed down, though he still kept his Harley Street office and did a little consultation. His ex-partner, who had a remarkable gift for acquiring public and private funds, promptly established a new base and continued his experiments.

As Duncan read on, with increasing curiosity and excitement, he realized that here was the man he needed. Whether he would take advantage of the high-speed cloning technique he could decide later; it was certainly interesting to know that the option existed, and that if he wished, he could return to Titan months in advance of his original schedule.

Now to locate Sir Mortimer's ex-colleague and successor. It was lucky that the search did not have to rely on the name alone, for it was one that occurred in some form or other half a million times in the Earth Directory. But he had only to consult the Classified Section—often referred to, for some mysterious reason lost in the depths of time, by the utterly meaningless phrase "Yellow Pages."

And so, on a small island off the east coast of Africa, Duncan discovered El Hadj Yehudi ben Mohammed.

He had scarcely made arrangements to fly to Zanzibar when a small bombshell arrived from Titan. It bore Colin's identification number, but he was unable to make sense of it until he realized that it was both in cipher *and* the Makenzie private code. Even after two processing trips through his Minisec, it was still somewhat cryptic:

PRIORITY AAA SECURITY AAA

NO RECORD OF ANY SHIPMENT TITANITE REGIS-
TERED BUREAU OF RESOURCES LAST TWO YEARS.
POSSIBLE INFRINGEMENT FINANCE REGULATIONS
IF PRIVATE SALE FOR CONVERTIBLE SOLARS NOT
APPROVED BY BANK OF TITAN. PERSISTENT RUMOR
MAJOR DISCOVERY ON OUTER MOON. ASKING HEL-
MER TO INVESTIGATE. WILL REPORT SOONEST.
COLIN.

Duncan read the message several times without any
immediate reaction. Then, slowly, the pieces of the
puzzle began to drift around into new configurations,
and a pattern started to emerge. It was one that Duncan
did not like at all.

Naturally, Colin would have gone to Armand
Helmer, Controller of Resources; the export of minerals came under his jurisdiction. Moreover, Armand
was a geologist—in fact, he had made one small titanite
find himself, of which he was inordinately proud.

Was it conceivable that Armand himself might be
involved? The thought flashed through Duncan's
mind, but he dismissed it instantly. He had known
Armand all his life and despite their many political
and personal differences, he did not for a moment
believe that the Controller would get involved in any
illegality—especially one that concerned his own Bureau. And for what purpose? Merely to accumulate
a few thousand solars in some terrestrial bank?
Armand was now too old, and too gravity-conditioned,
ever to return to Earth, and he was not the kind of
man who would break the law for so trivial a purpose
as importing Terran luxuries. Especially as such
chicanery was always discovered, sooner or later;
smugglers could never resist displaying their treasures.
And then there would be another acquisition for the
impecunious Titan Museum, while the criminal would
be barred from all the best places for at least a month.

No, Armand could be excluded; but what of his
son? The more Duncan considered this possibility,
the more likely it seemed. He had no *proof* whatso-

200

ever—only an array of facts all pointing in one direction.

Consider: Karl had always been daring and adventurous, willing to run risks for what he believed sufficiently good reasons. As a boy, he had taken a positive delight in circumventing regulations —except, of course, those basic safety rules that no sane resident of Titan would ever challenge.

If titanite had been discovered on one of the other satellites, Karl would be in an excellent position to take advantage of it. In the last three years, he had been on half a dozen Titan-Terran surveys. To Duncan's certain knowledge, he was one of the few men who had been to Enceladus, Tethys, Dione, Rhea, Hyperion, Iapetus, Phoebe, Chronus, Prometheus. And now he was on remote Mnemosyne. . . .

Already Duncan could draw up a seductively plausible scenario. Karl might even have made the find himself. Certainly he would have seen all the specimens coming aboard the survey ship, and his well-known charm would have done the rest. Indeed, the actual discoverer might never have known what he had found. Few people had seen raw titanite, and it was not easy to identify until it had been polished.

Then it would have been a simple matter of sending a small package to Earth, perhaps on one of the resupply ships which did not even call at Titan. (What would be the legal situation then? That could be tricky. Titan had jurisdiction over the other *permanent* satellities, but its claim to the obvious temporary ones like Phoebe & Co. was still in dispute. It was possible that no laws had been broken at all. . . .)

But this was sheer speculation. He had not the slightest hard evidence. Why, indeed, had he thought of Karl at all in this context?

He reread the message, still glowing on the Comsole monitor: MAJOR DISCOVERY ON OUTER MOON. ASKING HELMER . . . *That* was what had triggered this line of thought. Guilt by association, perhaps; the juxtaposition might be pure coincidence. But the Makenzies could read each other's minds, and Duncan knew that the phraseology was deliber-

201

ate. There was no need for Colin to have mentioned Helmer; he was sending out an early warning signal.

It was ridiculous to pile speculation upon speculation, but Duncan could not resist the next step. Assuming that Karl was involved—*why?*

Karl might take risks, might even get involved in petty illegalities, but it would be for some good purpose. If—and it was still an enormous "if"—he was trying to accumulate funds on Earth, he must have a long-range objective in mind. The most obvious was the establishment of a power base—precisely as Duncan was doing.

He must also have an agent here, someone he could trust implicitly. That would not be difficult; Karl had met hundreds of Terrans—

"Oh, my God," Duncan breathed. *"That* explains everything. . . ."

He wondered if he should cancel his trip to Zanzibar; no, that took priority over all else, except the speech he had come a billion kilometers to deliver. In any case, he did not see what more he could do here in Washington until he had further news from home.

He was still operating on pure guesswork, without one atom of proof. But there was a cold, dead feeling in the general region of his heart; and suddenly, for no good reason at all, Duncan thought of that solitary iceberg, gliding southward on the hidden current toward its irrevocable destiny.

31

THE ISLAND OF DR. MOHAMMED

El Hadj's deputy, Dr. Todd, was one of those medical men who seem, not always justifiably, to radiate an aura of confidence. This despite his relative youth and informality; for reasons which Duncan never discovered, all his colleagues used his nickname, Sweeney.

"I'm sorry you won't meet El Hadj this time," he said apologetically. "He had to rush to Hawaii, for an emergency operation."

"I'm surprised that's necessary, in this age."

"Normally, it's not. But Hawaii's almost exactly on the other side of the world—which means you have to work through *two* comsats in series. During tele-surgery, that extra time delay can be critical."

So even on Earth, thought Duncan, the slowness of radio waves can be a problem. A half-second lag would not matter in conversation; but between a surgeon's hand and eye, it might be fatal.

"Until twenty years ago," Dr. Todd explained, "this was a famous marine biology lab. So it had most of the facilities we need—including isolation."

"Why is that necessary?" asked Duncan. He had wondered why the clinic was in such an inconveniently out-of-the-way spot.

"There's a good deal of emotional interest in our work, and we have to control visitors. Despite air transportation, you can still do that much easier on an island than anywhere else. And above all, we have to protect our Mothers. They may not be very intelligent, but they're sensitive, and don't like being stared at."

"I've not seen any yet."

"Do you really want to?"

That was a difficult question to answer, for Duncan felt his emotions tugging in opposite directions. Thirty-one years ago, he must have been born in a place not unlike this, though probably not as spectacularly beautiful. If he had gone full term—and in those days, he assumed, all clones did so—some unknown woman had carried him in her body for at least eight months after implantation. Was she still alive? Did any record of her name still exist, or was she merely a number in a computer file? Perhaps not even that, for the identity of a foster mother was not of the slightest biological importance. A purely mechanical womb could have served as well, but there had never been any real need to perfect so complex a device. In a world where reproduction was strictly limited, there would always be plenty of volunteers; the only problem was selecting them.

Duncan had no memory whatsoever of his unknown foster mother or of the months he must have spent on Earth as a baby. Every attempt to penetrate the fog that lay at the very beginning of his childhood was a failure. He could not be certain if this was normal, or whether the earliest part of his life was hidden by deliberately induced amnesia. He suspected the latter, since he felt a distinct reluctance ever to investigate the subject in any detail.

When he formed the concept "Mother" in his mind, he instantly saw Colin's wife, Sheela. Her face was his earliest memory, her affection his first love, later shared with Grandma Ellen. Colin had chosen carefully and had learned from Malcolm's mistakes.

Sheela had treated Duncan exactly like her own children, and he had never thought of Yuri and Glynn as anything except his older brother and sister. He could not remember when he had first realized that Colin was not their father, and that they bore no genetic relationship to him whatsoever. Somehow, it had never seemed to matter.

He appreciated, now, the unobtrusive skills that had gone into the creation of so well adjusted a "family"; it would not have been possible in an earlier age of exclusive marriage and sexual possessiveness. Even today, it was no easy task. He hoped that he and Marissa would be equally successful, and that Clyde and Carline would accept little Malcolm as their brother, just as wholeheartedly as Yuri and Glynn had once accepted him. . . .

"I'm sorry," said Duncan. "I was daydreaming."

"Can't say I blame you; this place is too damned beautiful. I sometimes have to draw the curtains when I want to do any work."

That was easy to believe—yet beauty was not the first impression to strike Duncan when he landed on the island. Even now, his dominant feeling was one of awe, mixed with more than a trace of fear.

Starting a dozen meters away, and filling his field of vision right out to the sharp blue line of the horizon, was more water than he had ever imagined. It was true that he had seen Earth's oceans from space, but from that Olympian vantage point it had been impossible to envisage their true size. Even the greatest of seas was diminished, when one could flash across it in ten minutes.

This world was indeed misnamed. It should have been called Ocean, not Earth. Duncan performed a rough mental calculation—one of the skills the Makenzies had carefully retained, despite the omnipresent computer. Radius six thousand—and his eye was about six meters above sea level—that made it simple—six root two, or near enough eight kilometers. Only eight! It was incredible; he could easily have believed that the horizon was a hundred kilometers away. His vision could not span even one percent of the distance to the other shore. . . .

And what he could see now was only the two-dimensional skin of an alien universe, teeming with strange life forms seeking whom they might devour. To Duncan, that expanse of peaceful blue concealed a word much more hostile, and more terrifying, than Space. Even Titan, with its known dangers, seemed benign in comparison.

And yet there were children out there, splashing around in the shallows, and disappearing underwater for quite terrifying lengths of time. One of them, Duncan was certain, had been gone for well over a minute.

"Isn't that dangerous?" he asked anxiously, gesturing toward the lagoon.

"We don't let them go near the water until they're well trained. And if you *must* drown yourself, this is the place for it—with some of the best medical facilities in the world. We've had only one permanent death in the last fifteen years. Revival would have been possible even then, but after an hour underwater, brain damage is irreversible."

"But what about sharks and all the other big fish?"

"We've never had an attack inside the reef, and only one outside it. That's a small price to pay for admission to Fairyland. We're taking out the big trimaran tomorrow—why don't you come along?"

"I'll think about it," Duncan answered evasively.

"Oh—I suppose you've never been underwater before."

"I've never been *on* it—except in a swimming pool."

"Well, you've nothing to lose. Though we won't complete the tests for another forty-eight hours, I'm sure we'll be able to clone successfully from the genotypes you've given. So your immortality insurance is taken care of."

"Thank you very much," said Duncan dryly. "That makes all the difference."

He remembered Commander Innes' invitation to the Caribbean reefs, and his instant though unexpressed refusal. But those mere children were obviously enjoying themselves, and their confidence was a reproach to his manhood. The pride of the Makenzies was at stake; he looked glumly at that appalling mass of water, and realized that he would have to do something about it before he left the island.

He had never felt less enthusiastic about any project in his life.

The night was beautiful, blazing with more stars than any man could ever see from the surface of Titan, however long he lived. Though it was only nineteen hundred hours—too early for dinner, let alone sleep—the sun might never have existed, so total was the darkness away from the illumination of the main buildings, and of the little lights strung along the paths of crushed coral.

From somewhere in that darkness came the sound of music—a rhythmical throbbing of drums, played with more enthusiasm than skill. Rising above this steady beat were occasional bursts of song, and women's voices calling to one another. Those voices made Duncan suddenly lonely and homesick. He started to walk along the narrow path in the general direction of the revelry.

After wandering down several blind alleys—ending up once in a charming sunken garden, which he left with profuse apologies to the couple busily occupying it—he came to the clearing where the party was in progress. At its center, a large bonfire was lofting a column of smoke and flames toward the stars, and a score of figures was dancing around it, like the priestesses of some primitive religion.

They were not dancing with much grace or vigor; in fact, it would be more truthful to say that most of them were circulating in a dignified waddle. But despite their obvious advanced state of pregnancy, they were clearly enjoying themselves, and were being as active as was advisable in the circumstances.

It was a grotesque yet strangely moving spectacle, arousing in Duncan a mixture of pity and tenderness —even an impersonal and wholly unerotic love. The tenderness was that which all men feel in the imminent presence of birth and the wonder of their own existence; the pity had a different cause.

Ugliness and deformity were rare on Titan—and rarer still on Earth, since both could almost always be corrected. Almost—but not always. Here was proof of that.

Most of these women were extremely plain; some were ugly; a few were frankly hideous. And though Duncan noticed two or three who might even pass as beautiful, it needed only a glance to show that they were mentally subnormal. Had his long-dead "sister" Anitra survived into adult life, she would have been at home in this strange assembly.

If the dancers—and those others merely sitting around, banging away at drums and sawing on fiddles—had not been so obviously happy it would have been a disturbing, perhaps even a sickening spectacle. It did not upset Duncan. Though he was startled, he was prepared for it.

He knew how the foster mothers were chosen. The first requirement, of course, was that they should have no gynecological defects. That demand was easy to satisfy. It was not so simple to cope with the psychological factors, and it might have been a virtually impossible task in the days before the world's population was computer-profiled.

There would always be women who desperately yearned to bear children, but who for one reason or another could not fulfill their destiny. In earlier ages, most of them would have been doomed to spinsterly frustration; indeed, even in this world of 2276, many of them still were. There were more would-be mothers than the controlled birth rate could satisfy, but those who were especially disadvantaged could find some compensation here. The losers in the lottery of Fate could yet win a consolation prize, and know for a few months the happiness that would otherwise be denied them.

And so the World Computer had been programmed as an instrument of compassion. This act of humanity had done more than anything else to silence those who objected to cloning.

Of course, there were still problems. All these Mothers must know, however dimly, that soon after birth they would be separated forever from the child they were to bring into the world. That was not a sorrow that any man could understand; but women were stronger than men, and they would get over it —more often than not by taking part again in the creation of another life.

Duncan remained in the shadows, not wishing to be seen and certainly not wishing to get involved. Some of those incipient Mothers could crush him to a pulp if they grabbed him and whirled him into the dance. He had now noticed that a handful of men —presumably medical orderlies or staff from the clinic—were circulating light-heartedly with the Mothers and entering into the spirit of the festivities.

He could not help wondering if there had also been some deliberate psychological selection here. Several of the men looked very effeminate, and were treating their partners with what could only be called sisterly affection. They were obviously dear friends; and that was all they would ever be.

No one could have seen, in the darkness, Duncan's smile of amused recollection. He had just remembered—for the first time in years—a boy who had fallen in love with him in his late teens. It is hard to reject anyone who is devoted to you, but although Duncan had good-naturedly succumbed a few times to Nikki's blandishments, he had eventually managed to discourage his admirer, despite torrents of tears.

Pity is not a good basis for any relationship, and Duncan could never feel quite happy with someone whose affections were exclusively polarized toward one sex. What a contrast to the aggressive normality of Karl, who did not give a damn whether he had more affairs with boys or girls, or vice versa. At least, until the Calindy episode . . .

These memories, so unexpectedly dredged up from the past, made Duncan aware of the complicated emotional crosscurrents that must be sweeping through this place. And he suddenly recalled that disturbing conversation—or, rather, monologue—with Sir Mortimer Keynes. . . .

That he would follow in the steps of Colin, and of Malcolm before, was something that Duncan had always taken for granted, without any discussion. But now he realized, rather late in the day, that there was a price for everything, and that it should be considered very carefully before the contract was finally signed.

Cloning was neither good nor bad; only its purpose was important. And that purpose should not be one that was trivial or selfish.

32

GOLDEN REEF

The vivid green band of palms and the brilliant white crescent of the perfect beach were now more than a kilometer away, on the far side of the barrier reef. Even through the dark glasses which he dared not remove for a moment, the scene was almost painfully bright; when he looked in the direction of the sun, and caught its sparkle off the ocean swell, Duncan was completely blinded. Though this was a trifling matter, it enhanced his feeling of separation from all his companions. True, most of them also wore dark glasses—but in their case it was a convenience, not a necessity. Despite his wholly terrestrial genes, it seemed that he had adapted irrevocably to the light of a world ten times farther from the sun.

Beneath the smoothly sliding flanks of the triple hull, the water was so clear that it added to Duncan's feeling of insecurity. The boat seemed to be hanging in midair, with no apparent means of support, over a dappled sea bed five or ten meters below. It seemed strange that this should worry him, when he had looked down on Earth from orbit, hundreds of kilometers above the atmosphere.

He was startled by a sudden, distant crash, altogether out of place on this idyllically peaceful morning. It came from somewhere out at sea, and Duncan spun around just in time to see a column of spray slowly falling back into the water. Surely no one would be allowed to set off submarine explosions in this area. . . .

Now there was a jet of vapor, which rose slanting from the sea, hung for a moment in the bright sunlight, and gradually dispersed.

For a full minute, nothing else happened. And then—

Duncan was paralyzed with astonishment. With unbelievable slowness, but with the inevitability of some continent rising from the primordial depths, a vast gray shape was soaring out of the sea. There was a flash of white, as monstrous flukes slammed against the waves and created another cloud of spray. And still that incredible bulk continued to climb, as if defying gravity, until it was completely clear of the water, and hung poised for a moment above the blue ledge of the horizon. Then, still in slow motion, as if reluctant to leave an alien element, it fell back into the ocean and vanished beneath a final geyser of spray. The booming crash seemed to come ages later.

Duncan had never imagined such a spectacle, but he had no need of any explanation. *Moby Dick* was one of the thousands of Terran classics he knew only through repute, but now he understood how Herman Melville must have felt when, for the first time, he saw the sea furrowed by a glistening back as large as an overturned ship, and conceived in the image of the white whale a symbol of the forces that lie behind the universe.

He waited for many minutes, but the giant did not leap again, though from time to time there were brief spouts of vapor, becoming more and more distant until they vanished from sight.

"Why did it do that?" he asked Dr. Todd, his voice still hushed by the lingering aura of departed majesty.

"Nobody really knows. It may be pure *joie de vivre*. It may be to impress a lady friend. Or it may be merely to get rid of parasites—whales are badly infested with barnacles and lampreys."

How utterly incongruous, thought Duncan. It seemed almost an outrage that a god should be afflicted with lice.

Now the trimaran was slowing down, and the sheer strangeness and beauty of the underwater scene captured his attention so completely that Duncan forgot his remoteness from land. The fantastic shapes of the corals, and the colors of the fish that sported or sauntered among them, were a revelation. He had already been astounded by the variety of life on land; now he saw that it was far exceeded by the reckless profusion of the sea.

Something like an antique jet plane went flapping slowly past, with graceful undulations of its spotted wings. None of the other fish took any notice. To Duncan's surprise, there was no sign of the carnage he had expected to witness, in this realm where everything fed on everything else. In fact, it was hard to imagine a more peaceful scene; the few fish that had been chasing others were obviously doing so merely to protect their territory. The impression he had gathered from books and films had been almost wholly misleading. Co-operation, not competition, seemed to rule the reef.

The trimaran came to a halt, the anchor was thrown out—and was followed almost instantly by three rubber dinghies, four doctors, five nurses, and a mass of diving equipment. The scene appeared to Duncan to be one of utter confusion; actually, it was much better planned and disciplined than he realized. The swimmers promptly divided into groups of three, and each trio went off with one of the dinghies, heading in a purposeful manner toward spots that had obviously been chosen in advance.

"If it's so safe," remarked Duncan after the last splashings had died away, "why are they all carrying knives, aand those vicious-looking little spears?"

The trimaran was now almost deserted, its only other occupants besides Duncan being the skipper—who had promptly fallen asleep in front of the wheel—the engineer, who had disappeared below deck, and Dr. Todd.

"Those aren't weapons. They're gardening tools."

"You must have rather ferocious weeds. I wouldn't care to meet them."

"Oh," said Todd, "some of them put up a good fight. Why don't you go and have a look? You'll be sorry if you miss the chance."

That was perfectly true, yet Duncan still hesitated. The water in which the trimaran was gently rocking was very shallow; indeed, it appeared no deeper than the swimming pool at the Centennial Hotel.

"I'll go in with you. You can stand on the diving ladder, until you get the hang of the face mask—and snorkel-breathing should be easy to anyone who's used to a spacesuit."

Duncan did not volunteer the information that he had never worn a genuine spacesuit; nevertheless, a Titan surface life-support system should be good training. And anyway, what could go wrong in a couple of meters of water? Why, there were places here where he could stand with his head above the surface. Sweeney Todd was right; he would never forgive himself if he turned down this opportunity of a lifetime.

Ten minutes later, he was splashing inexpertly but steadily along the surface. Although it had seemed astonishing—and even indecent—to put on clothing when one entered the water, Todd had insisted that he dress from head to foot in a light, one-piece overall of some closely knit fabric. It scarcely affected his movements, but he wished he could do without it.

"Some of these corals sting," the doctor had explained. "It could spoil your day if you backed into one—and you might have an allergic reaction."

"Anything else you can think of?"

"No, that's about it. Just watch me, and hang on to the rubber dinghy whenever you want a rest."

He was now rapidly gaining confidence and beginning to enjoy himself thoroughly. There was obviously no danger whatsoever while he drifted along behind the dinghy, never letting go of the rope dangling in the water. And Dr. Todd, he was reassured to observe, always kept within arm's length; he was being almost ridiculously overcautious. Even if a shark came shooting up out of the depths, Duncan believed he could be aboard the dinghy in two seconds flat—notwithstanding Earth's gravity.

Now that he had mastered the use of the snorkel tube, he kept his head under water all the time, and even essayed shallow dives which involved holding his breath for considerable periods. The panorama beneath was so fascinating that Duncan even occasionally forgot the need for air, and emerged sputtering foolishly.

The first signboard was at a depth of five meters and said, in fluorescent yellow letters: NO UNAUTHORIZED VISITORS BEYOND THIS POINT. The second warning was a flashing holographic display in midwater, which must have been very perplexing to the fish. It announced ominously: THIS REEF IS MONITORED. Duncan could see no trace of the projectors; they had been very cunningly concealed.

Todd was pointing ahead, to the line of divers working along the edge of the reef. So he had not been joking. They really were going through the unmistakable motions of gardeners digging up noxious weeds. And each one was surrounded by a small cloud of brilliantly colored fish, clearly benefiting from all this activity.

The coral formations seemed to be changing shape. Even to Duncan's untrained eye, they looked strange —even abnormal. He had grown accustomed to the branching antlers of the stag-horns, the convoluted labyrinths that looked like giant brains, the delicate

213

mushrooms sometimes meters in diameter. They were still here, but now subtly distorted.

Then he saw the first metallic glint—then another, and another. As he came closer, and the blue haze of distance no longer softened the details of the underwater world, Duncan realized why this reef was cherished and protected.

Everywhere he looked, it glittered and sparkled with gold.

Two hundred years earlier, it had been one of the greatest triumphs of biological engineering, bringing world fame to its creators. Ironically, success had come when it was no longer required; what had been intended to fulfill a vital need had turned out to be no more than a technological cul-de-sac.

It had been known for centuries that some marine organisms were able to extract, for the benefit of their own internal economies, elements present in seawater in unbelievably small proportions. If sponges and oysters and similar lowly creatures could perform such feats of chemical engineering with iodine or vanadium, the biologists of the 2100's had argued, why could they not be taught to do the same trick with more valuable elements?

And so, by heroic feats of gene-manipulation, several species of coral had been persuaded to become gold miners. The most successful were able to replace almost ten percent of their limestone skeletons with the precious metal. That success, however, was measured only in human terms. Since gold normally plays no part in biochemical reactions, the consequences to the corals were disastrous; the auriferous reefs were never healthy, and had to be carefully protected from predators and disease.

Only a few hundred tons of gold were extracted by this technique before large-scale transmutation made it uneconomic; the nuclear furnaces could manufacture gold as cheaply as any other metal. For a while, the more accessible reefs were maintained as tourist attractions, but souvenir hunters soon demolished them. Now only one was left, and Dr. Mohammed's staff was determined to preserve it.

So, at regular intervals, the doctors and nurses took time off from their usual duties, and enjoyed an arduous working holiday on the reef. They dumped carefully selected fertilizers and antibiotics to improve the health of the living corals, and waged war against its enemies—particularly the spectacular crown of thorns starfish and its smaller relative the spiny sea urchin. Duncan floated, perfectly relaxed, in the tepid water, lazily flippering from time to time so that he remained in the shadow of the dinghy. Now he understood the purpose of those sinister knives and spikes; the adversaries they had to deal with were well protected indeed.

Only a couple of meters beneath him, one of the divers was jabbing at a colony of small black spheres, each at the center of a formidable array of needle-sharp spines. From time to time one of the spheres would be split open, and fish would dart in to grab the pieces of white meat that came floating out. It was a delicacy they could scarcely ever have enjoyed without human intervention; Duncan could not imagine that these spiky beasts had any natural enemies.

The diver—one of the nurses—noticed the two spectators hovering overhead, and beckoned Duncan to join her. He had become so fascinated that he now obeyed automatically, without a second's thought. Taking several deep breaths, and partly exhaling on the last one, he hauled himself slowly down the line anchoring the dinghy to its small grapnel.

The distance was greater than he had imagined— more like three meters than two, for he had forgotten the refractive effect of the water. Midway, his left ear gave a disconcerting "click," but Dr. Todd had warned him about this, and he did not check his descent. When he reached the anchor, and grabbed its shank, he felt a tremendous sense of achievement. He was a deep-sea diver—he had plumbed the fabulous depth of three meters! Well, at least two point five . . .

The glitter of gold was all around him. There was never more than a tiny speck, smaller than a grain of sand, at any one spot—but it was everywhere; the entire reef was impregnated with it. Duncan felt that

215

he was floating beside the chef-d'oeuvre of some mad jeweler, determined to create a baroque masterpiece regardless of expense. Yet these pinnacles and plates and twisted spires were the work of mindless polyps, not—except indirectly—the products of human intelligence.

Reluctantly, he shot up to the surface for air. This was easy; he felt ashamed of his previous fears. Now he understood how visitors often reacted to Titan. Next time, when someone politely declined an invitation to take a pleasant jaunt outside, he would be a little more tolerant.

"What are those black things?" he asked Dr. Todd, who was still hovering watchfully above him.

"Long-spined sea urchin, *Diadema* something-or-other. When you see so many, it's a sign of pollution or an unbalanced ecology. They don't really damage the reef—unlike *Acanthaster*— but they're ugly, and a nuisance. If you back into one, the needles may take a month to work their way out. Are you going down again?"

"Yes."

"Good. Don't overdo it. And watch out for those spines!"

Duncan hauled himself down the anchor line once more, and the diver waved him a greeting as he approached. Then she offered him her deadly-looking knife, and pointed toward a small group of sea urchins. Duncan nodded, took the tapering metal blade by the proffered handle, and started jabbing away inexpertly, being careful to avoid those ominous black needles.

Not until then did he realize, to his considerable surprise, that these lowly animals were aware of his presence, and were not relying merely on a static defense. The long spines were swinging toward him, orienting themselves in the direction of maximum danger. Presumably it was only a simple automatic reflex, but it made him pause for a moment. There was more here than met the eye—perhaps the first faint intimations of dawning consciousness.

His knife was longer than the sea urchin's spines, and he jabbed vigorously again and again. The carapace was surprisingly tough, but presently it gave way, and the waiting fish raced in to grab at the creamy white flesh that was suddenly exposed.

And then, with growing discomfort, Duncan realized that his victim was not dying in silence. For some time he had been aware of faint sounds in the water around him—the hammering of the other divers on the reef, the occasional "clang" of the anchor against the rocks. But this noise came from much closer at hand, and was most peculiar—even disturbing. It was a crackling, grinding sound; though the analogy was patently ridiculous, it could only be compared to the crunching of thousands of tiny teeth, clashing in rage and agony. Moreover, there was no doubt that it came from the eviscerated sea urchin.

That faint, inhuman death rattle was so unexpected that Duncan checked his onslaught and remained howering motionless in the water. He had completely forgotten the necessity for air, and the conscious part of his mind had dismissed the mounting symptoms of suffocation as irrelevant—to be dealt with later. But finally he could ignore them no longer, and shot gasping to the surface.

With a profound sense of shock—even of shame— Duncan realized that he had just destroyed a living creature. He could never have imagined, before he left Titan, that such an experience would ever come his way.

One could hardly feel much guilt over the murder of a sea urchin. Nevertheless, for the first time in his life, Duncan Makenzie was a killer.

33

SLEUTH

When Duncan returned to Washington, the second time bomb from Colin was ticking away in the Centennial Hotel. Once again, it was so cryptic that it would have been almost unintelligible, even to an outsider who had succeeded in decoding it.

CONFIRM YOUR OLD FRIEND HAS UNAUTHORIZED ACCOUNT 65842 GENEVA BRANCH FIRST BANK OF ARISTARCHUS. BALANCE SEVERAL TENS OF THOUSANDS SOLARS. THIS INFORMATION NOT TO BE DISCLOSED ANY CIRCUMSTANCES. PRESUME FROM SALE OF TITANITE. MAKING INQUIRIES MNEMOSYNE. MEANWHILE SUGGEST YOU KEEP ALERT. REGARDS COLIN.

Duncan understood perfectly well why this information was "not to be disclosed"; the Lunar banks guarded their secrets well, and heaven alone knew by what prodigies of persuasion or genteel blackmail Colin had managed to get hold of Karl's account number. Even so, he had been unable to obtain a figure for the balance—but it was obviously considerable. Ten thousand solars was far more than anyone would need for the purchase of a few Terran luxuries. And *several* times that was more than the Makenzies held in their own, perfectly legal accounts. Such an amount of money was more than a cause for envy; it was disturbing, especially if it was intended for some clandestine use.

Duncan allowed himself a few moments of wistful daydreaming, imagining what he could do with twenty or thirty thousand solars. Then he put the seductive vision firmly aside and concentrated all his mind upon the problem. While Karl's involvement had been only a vague suspicion, he had been reluctant to waste time on a detailed analysis of how, when, and—above all —*why*. But now that speculation had congealed into certainty, he could no longer evade the issue.

What a pity that the obvious line of approach was out of the question! He could hardly call up the First Bank of Aristarchus and ask for a print-out of Account 65842. Not even the World Government could do *that*, unless fraud or crime had already been proved beyond a shadow of a doubt. Even the most discreet inquiry would trigger an explosion; someone would certainly be fired, and Colin might be faced with most embarrassing questions.

The only *real* problem in life, an ancient philosopher had once said, is what to do next. There was still no link with Calindy—or anyone else. Duncan did not relish playing a role in some sleazy, old-time spy or detective melodrama, and was not even sure how one got started on such an enterprise. Colin would have been much better at it; of the three Makenzies, he was the only one with any flair for subterfuge, indirection, and secrecy. He was probably enjoying himself—especially since he had never liked Karl, being one of the few people on Titan immune to his charms.

But Colin, though he was doing a remarkable job, was more than a billion kilometers away, at the end of an expensive three-hour time-lag. There was no one on Earth in whom Duncan could confide. This was a private Titanian matter, and might yet turn out to be a storm in a teacup. However, if it was serious, the fewer people who knew about it, the better.

Duncan considered, and dismissed, the idea of talking to Ambassador Farrell. He might have to enter the picture later, but not now. Duncan had not been too impressed with Bob Farrell's discretion—and, of course, he *was* a Terran. Moreover, if the Embassy discovered that there was a large amount of masterless money floating around Earth, that would undoubtedly precipitate a tug-of-war. It was true that the rent on Wyoming Avenue had to be paid, but Titan's demands were even more urgent.

And yet perhaps there was one Terran he could

trust—the man who had raised the matter in the first place, and who was equally interested in finding the answer. Duncan tapped out the name on his Comsole, wondering if it would accept that ridiculous apostrophe. (He had managed to misplace the dealer's card, which would have placed the call automatically.)

"Mr. Mandel'stahm?" he said, when the screen lit up. "Duncan Makenzie. I have some news for you. Where can we meet for a private conversation?"

"Are you *absolutely* certain," said Duncan anxiously, "that no one can overhear us?"

"You've been seeing too many historical films, Mr. Makenzie," Ivor Mandel'stahm replied. "This isn't the twentieth century, and it would take a singularly determined police state to bug every autojitney in Washington. I always do my confidential business cruising round and round the Mall. There's absolutely nothing to worry about."

"Very well. It's imperative that this doesn't go any further. I am fairly sure that I know the source of the titanite. What's more, I have a very good idea of the Terran agent—who has apparently already made some substantial sales."

"I've discovered that," said Mandel'stahm, a little glumly. "Do you know *how* substantial?"

"Several tens of thousands of solars."

To Duncan's surprise, Mandel'stahm brightened appreciably.

"Oh, is that all?" he exclaimed. "I'm quite relieved. And can you give me the name of the prime agent? I've been operating through a very close-mouthed intermediary."

Duncan hesitated. "I believe you implied that no *Terran* laws were being broken."

"Correct. There's no import duty on extraterrestrial gems. Everything at this end is perfectly legal—unless, of course, the titanite is stolen, and the Terran agent is an accomplice."

"I'm sure that isn't the case. You see—and it's not really as big a coincidence as you might think—the agent is a friend of mine."

A knowing smile creased Mandel'stahm's face.

"I appreciate your problem."

No you *don't,* Duncan told himself. It was an ex-cruciatingly complicated situation. He was quite sure now why Calindy had been avoiding him. Karl would have warned her that he was coming to Earth and would have advised her to keep out of his way. Yes, Karl must have been very worried, up there on little Mnemosyne, lest Duncan stumble upon his activities.

It was essential to keep completely out of the pic-ture; Calindy must never guess that he knew. There was no way in which she could possibly link him with Mandel'stahm, with whom she was already dealing through her own exceedingly discreet intermediary.

Yet still Duncan hesitated, like a chess master over a crucial move. He was analyzing his own motives, and his own conscience, for his personal and official inter-ests were now almost inextricably entangled.

He was anxious to find out what Karl was doing, and if necessary frustrate him. He wanted to make Calindy ashamed of her deceit, and possibly turn her embarrassment to his emotional advantage. (This was a rather forlorn hope; Calindy did not embarrass eas-ily, if at all. . . .) And he wanted to help Titan, and thereby the Makenzies. All these objectives were not likely to be compatible. Duncan began to wish that titanite had never been discovered. Yet, undoubtedly, there was a brilliant opportunity here, if only he had the wit to make his moves correctly.

Their autojitney was now gliding, at the breathless speed of some twenty klicks, between the Capitol and the Library of Congress. The sight reminded Duncan of his other responsibility; already it was the last week in June, yet his speech still consisted of no more than a few sheets of notes. Overpreparation was one of the Makenzie failings; the "all right on the night" attitude was wholly alien to their natures. But even allowing for this often valuable fault, of which he was well aware, Duncan was beginning to feel a mild sense of panic.

The problem was a very simple one, yet its diagno-sis had not suggested a remedy. Try as he could, Dun-can had still been unable to decide on a basic theme, or any message from Titan more inspiring than the usual zero-content official greetings.

Mandel'stahm was still waiting patiently when they passed the Rayburn Building—now encrusted with a vast banyan tree brought all the way from Angkor Wat; it was hoped that within the next fifty years, this would do the job of demolition at virtually no public expense. There were times when aesthetics took precedence over history, and it was generally agreed that —unlike the old Smithsonian—the Rayburn Building was not *quite* hideous enough to be worth preservation. (But what would that vegetable octopus do next, the professional alarmists had worried, when it had finished this task? Would the monster crawl across Independence Avenue and attack the hallowed dome?)

Now the jitney was cruising past the prone hundred meters of the Saturn V replica lying on what had once been the site of NASA Headquarters. They could not spend all day orbiting central Washington; very well, Duncan told himself with a sigh . . .

"I have your promise that my name won't come out, under any circumstances?"

"Yes."

"And there's no risk that—my friend—may get into trouble?"

"I can't guarantee that he won't lose any money. But there will be no legal problems—at any rate, under Terran jurisdiction."

"It's not a 'he.' I leave the details to you, but you might make some tactful inquiries about the vice-president of Enigma Associates, Catherine Linden Ellerman."

34

STAR DAY

Though he tried to convince himself that he had done the right thing—even the only thing—Duncan was still slightly ashamed. Deep in his heart, he felt that he had been guilty of betraying an old friendship. He was glad that some impulse had kept him from mentioning Karl, and with part of his mind he still hoped that Mandel'stahm—and Colin—would run into blank walls, so that the whole investigation would collapse.

Meanwhile, there was so much to be done, and so much to see, that for long periods of time Duncan could forget his twinges of conscience. It seemed ridiculous to have come all the way to Earth—and then to sit for hours of every day (in beautiful weather!) in a hotel room talking into a Comsole.

But every time Duncan thought he had completed one of the innumerable chores they had given him before he left home, there would be a back-up message reopening the subject, or adding fresh complications. His official duties were time-consuming enough; what made matters worse were all the private requests from relatives, friends, and even complete strangers, who assumed that he had nothing else to do except contact lost acquaintances, obtain photos of ancestral homes, hunt for rare books, research Terran genealogies, locate obscure works of art, act as agent for hopeful Titanian authors and artists, conjure up scholarships and free passages to Earth—and say "Thank you" for Star Day cards received ten years ago and never acknowledged.

Which reminded Duncan that he had not sent off his own cards for this quadrennial occasion. Since '76 was a leap year, Star Day was therefore looming up in the near future—to be precise, between June 30 and July 1. Duncan was glad of the extra day, but it also meant that there would shortly be three days in five where no business could be done. For July 1, being at the beginning of a new quarter, was of course a Sunday; and the Sunday before *that* was only June 28. It was bad enough, in an ordinary year, to have two Sundays at the end of every 91-day quarter, with only a Monday and Tuesday between them—but now to have *another* holiday as well made it even worse.

There was still time to mail cards to all his Terran friends—Ambassador Farrell, the Washingtons, Calindy, Bernie Patras, and half a dozen others. As for Titan, there was really no hurry. Even if they took six months to get there, the cards, with their beautiful gold-leaf Centennial stamps (five solars each, for heaven's sake, even by second-class space mail!), would still be appreciated.

Despite these problems, Duncan had found some opportunities to relax. He had been on personal teletours of London, Rome, and Athens, which was the next best thing to being there in the flesh. Seated in a tiny, darkened cubicle with 360 degrees of high-quality sound and vision, he could easily believe that he was actually walking through the streets of the ancient cities. He could ask questions of the invisible guide who was his alter ego, talk to any passers-by, change the route to look more closely at something that took his interest. Only the senses of smell and touch remained immobile—and even these could be tele-extended for anyone willing to foot the bill. Duncan could not afford such a marginal luxury, and did not really miss it.

He also attended several concerts, two ballets, and one play—all arranged for the benefit of visitors in this Centennial year, and all unavoidable without the exercise of more diplomatic illness, or sheer bad manners, than Duncan felt able to muster. The music, though doubtless magnificent, bored him; his tastes were old-fashioned, and he enjoyed little written after the twenty-first century. The ballet was also a disappointment; to anyone who had spent all his life at a fifth of a gravity, the most remarkable of Terran grands jetés was unimpressive—and also nerve-racking, for Duncan could never quite get over the fear that the dancers would injure themselves. He watched them with envy, but he had no wish to imitate them. It was enough that he could now walk and stand without conscious effort. This achievement was a matter of modest pride, for there had been a time when he would not have believed it possible.

But the play delighted him. He had heard vaguely of George Bernard Shaw, now undergoing one of his periodic revivals, and *The Devil's Disciple* was perfect for the occasion. Though George Washington muttered from time to time in Duncan's ear such comments as "General Burgoyne wasn't the least like *that*," he felt that he at last understood the American Revolution in human terms. It was no longer a shadowy affair of two-dimensional puppets, five hundred years in the past, but a life-and-death struggle involving real people, whose hopes and fears and loves he could share.

Though love, with a capital L, was not a complication that Duncan would welcome during his stay on Earth. He could not imagine anyone ever replacing Marissa, and to have a really serious affair with a Terran would be the stuff of tragedy, since separation would be inevitable when he returned to Titan. He wanted no part of that; he had been through it once before, with Calindy.

Or so it had seemed at the time. Now he realized that the calf love of a sixteen-year-old boy, though it had once dominated all his waking hours, was indeed shallow and transient. Yet its aftereffects still lingered, shaping all his later passions and desires. Although he was annoyed and disappointed with Calindy, that was unchanged; her deliberate avoidance had, if anything, added fuel to his emotions and contributed to some notably fevered dreams.

Bernie Patras, of course, was happy to relieve his symptoms, and had arranged several enjoyable encounters. One cuddlesome and talented young lady, he swore, was his own girl friend, "who only does this with people she *really* wants to meet." She did, indeed, show a genuine interest in Titan and its problems; but when Bernie, as an interested party, wanted to join in the festivities, Duncan selfishly threw him out.

That was shortly before Ivor Mandel'stahm—this time in the Penn-Mass autojitney—totally demolished his peace of mind. They had just left the Dupont Circle Interchange when he told Duncan: "I've some interesting news for you, but I don't know what it means. You may be able to explain it."

"I'll do my best."

"I think I can claim, without much exaggeration or conceit, that I can get to anyone on Earth in one jump. But sometimes discretion suggests doing it in *two,* and that's how I proceeded with Miss Ellerman. I've never had any dealings with her personally—or so I *thought,* until you advised me otherwise—but we have mutual friends. So I got one, whom I can trust without question, to give her a call. . . . Tell me, have you tried to contact her recently?"

"Not for—oh, at least a week. I thought it better to keep out of the way." Duncan did not add, to this perfectly good excuse, the fact that he had felt ashamed to face Calindy.

"She answered my friend's call, but there's something very odd. She wouldn't switch on her viddy."

That certainly was peculiar; as a matter of common good manners, one *never* overrode the vision circuit unless there was a very good excuse indeed. Of course, this could sometimes cause acute embarrassment—a fact exploited to the utmost in countless comedies. But whatever the real reason, social protocol demanded some explanation. To say that the viddy was out of order was to invite total disbelief, even on those rare occasions when it was true.

"What was her excuse?" asked Duncan.

"A plausible one. She explained that she'd had a bad fall, and apologized for not showing her face."

"I hope she wasn't badly hurt."

"Apparently not, though she sounded rather unhappy. Anyway, my friend had a brief conversation with her and raised the subject of Titan—quite legitimately, and in a way that couldn't possibly arouse suspicion. He knew that she'd been there, and asked if she could put him in touch with any Titanians she

226

happened to know on Earth. Actually, he said he had an export order in mind."

"Not a very good story. All business is handled through the Embassy Trade Division, and he could have contacted them."

"If I may say so, Mr. Makenzie, you still have a lot to learn. I can think of half a dozen reasons for *not* going to the Embassy—at least for the first approach. My friend knows that, and you can be sure that Miss Ellerman does."

"If you say so—I don't doubt that you're right. What was her reaction?"

"I'm afraid you're going to be disappointed. She said that she *did* have a good Titanian friend who might be able to help, that he'd just arrived for the celebrations, and he was in Washington. . . ."

Duncan began to laugh; the anticlimax was so ridiculous. . . .

"So your friend wasted his time. We're right back where we started."

"Along *this* line, yes. I thought you'd be amused. But there's rather more to come."

"Go on," said Duncan, his confidence in Mandel'stahm now somewhat diminished by this debacle.

"I tried several other lines of inquiry, but they all came to nothing. I even thought of calling Miss Ellerman myself and saying outright that I knew she was the principal behind the titanite negotiations— without accusing her of anything, of course."

"I'm glad you didn't."

"Oh, it would have been a perfectly reasonable thing to do—she wouldn't be surprised if I found out sooner or later. But as it happened, I had a better idea—one I should have tried in the first place. I checked on her visitors for the last month."

"How," Duncan asked in astonishment, "could you do that?"

"It's the oldest trick in the world. Have you never seen one of those twentieth-century French detective films? No. I suppose not. I simply asked the concierge."

"The what?"

"You don't have them on Titan?"

"I don't even know what they are."

"Perhaps you're lucky. On Earth, they're an indispensable nuisance. Miss Ellerman, as I assume you know, lives in a very luxurious Deep Ten just south of Mount Rockefeller. In fact, she has the basement penthouse—a hankering I've never understood; the farther down *I* go, the more claustrophobic I get. Well, any large complex has a doorkeeper at the entrance to tell visitors who's in and who's out, take messages, accept deliveries—and authorize the right people to go to the right apartments. *That's* the concierge."

"And you were able to get at its memory bank?"

Mandel'stahm had the grace to look slightly embarrassed.

"It's surprising what can be done if you know the right people. Oh, don't misunderstand. There was nothing illegal; but I prefer to omit details."

"On Titan, we're very particular about invasion of privacy."

"So are we on Earth. Anyone who really wants to do so can easily by-pass the concierge. Which, in fact, suggests to me that Miss Ellerman does *not* have a guilty conscience, or anything to hide. But tell me, Mr. Makenzie—didn't you know that she had a Titanian guest staying with her?"

Duncan stared at him open-mouthed, but quickly recovered himself. Of course—Karl might well have prevailed on some trusted friend to act as a courier. That must have been a good many months ago; there had been no passenger ship for six weeks before *Sirius*. Who could possibly . . . ?

That could wait. There was another little matter to clear up first.

"You said *staying with her?*"

"Yes. That is, until only two days ago."

That explained everything—almost. No wonder Calindy had avoided him! In equal measure, Duncan felt jealousy, disappointment—and relief that his maneuverings had, after all, been justified by events.

"Who is this Titanian?" he asked glumly. "I wonder if I know him."

"That's what I'll be interested to hear. His name is Karl Helmer."

35

A MESSAGE FROM TITAN

"That's utterly impossible," said Duncan, when he had recovered from the initial shock. "I left Helmer at Saturn—and I came here on the fastest ship in the Solar System."

Mandel'stahm gave an expressive shrug.

"Then perhaps someone else is using that name, for reasons best known to himself. Miss Ellerman's concierge is not very bright—they seldom are—and incidentally, we were lucky to get at it just before the regular end-of-month memory update. I got hold of the visual recognition coding, and here's the reconstruction."

He handed over the crude but perfectly adequate synthesis. Duncan could identify it as quickly as any robot pattern-detecting circuit.

Without question, it was Karl.

"So you know him," said Mandel'stahm.

"Very well," Duncan replied faintly. His mind was still in a whirl; even now, he could not fully believe the evidence of his eyes. It would take a long time for him to work out all the implications of this stunning development.

"You said he was no longer at Cal—Miss Ellerman's. Do you know where he is now?"

"No. I was hoping *you* might have some ideas. But now that we know the name, I'll be able to trace him —though it may take some time."

And doubtless expense, thought Duncan.

"Tell me, Mr. Mandel'stahm, why are you taking all this trouble? Frankly, I don't see what you hope to get out of it."

"Don't you? Well, it's a good question. I certainly began this out of a pure and honest lust for titanite, and I hope that in due course my efforts will win their just reward. But now it's gone beyond that. The only thing more valuable than gems or works of art is entertainment. And this little caper, Mr. Makenzie, is more interesting than anything I've seen on the viddy for weeks."

Despite his gloomy preoccupations, Duncan could not help smiling. He had been cautious in his approach to Mandel'stahm, but now he was definitely beginning to feel genuine warmth toward the dealer. He was shrewd and perhaps even crafty, and Duncan did not doubt that he would drive a very hard bargain. But he was now quite convinced that George Washington was right: Ivor Mandel'stahm could be trusted implicitly, in all the things that really mattered.

"May I make a modest proposal?"

"Of course," Duncan answered.

"Can you think of any reason at all, now that we've reached this stage, why you should *not* call Miss Ellerman, say that you've just heard from Titan that your mutual friend Mr. Helmer is on Earth—and does *she* know where he is?"

Duncan thought it over; the suggestion was so blatantly obvious that, in his somewhat dazed state, he had completely overlooked it. Even now, he was not sure that he could give it an accurate evaluation.

But the affair was no longer a matter of impersonal tactics and policy, to be worked out like the closing move of some chess game. For his own self-respect and peace of mind, it was time for a confrontation with Calindy.

"You're right," he said. "There's no reason at all why I shouldn't call her. I'll do so, just as soon as I can get back to the hotel. Let's stop off at Union Station and take the express. . . ."

When Duncan reached the hotel twenty minutes

230

later (the "express" was somewhat misnamed) he had the second surprise of the day, though by now it was something of an anticlimax. The longest fax that Colin had ever sent him was waiting in the Comsole.

After the initial quick reading, Duncan's first reaction was, *"This* time, at least, I'm one jump ahead." But even that, he realized, was not quite true. When one allowed for the fact that Colin's message had left Titan two hours ago, it was virtually a photo finish.

> SECURITY AAA PRIORITY AAA
> INQUIRIES MNEMOSYNE DISCLOSE KARL LEFT MID MARCH ON NONSKED EARTH FLIGHT AND ARRIVED APPROXIMATELY TWO WEEKS BEFORE YOU. ARMAND PROFESSES SURPRISE AND TOTAL IGNORANCE. MAY BE TELLING TRUTH. IMPERATIVE YOU LOCATE KARL FIND WHAT HE IS DOING AND IF NECESSARY WARN HIM OF CONSEQUENCES. PROCEED WITH EXTREME CAUTION AS ANXIOUS AVOID PUBLICITY OR INTERPLANETARY COMPLICATIONS. YOU APPRECIATE THE SITUATION MAY BE TO OUR ADVANTAGE BUT DISCRETION ESSENTIAL. SUGGEST CALINDY MAY KNOW WHERE HE IS. COLIN AND MALCOLM.

Duncan reread the message more slowly, absorbing its nuances. It contained nothing that he did not now know, or had not already guessed; however, he did not relish its uncompromising tone. Being signed by both Colin and Malcolm, it had the authority of a direct order—something rare indeed in Makenzie affairs. Though Duncan admitted that it made good sense, he could also detect an underlying note of satisfaction. For a moment he had an unflattering image of his older twins moving in like a pair of vultures, scenting a kill. . . .

At the same time, he was wryly amused to see that Colin had drafted the Telex in a great hurry; it contained half a dozen superfluous words, most offensive to the economical maxims of the clan. Why, there were even "and's" and "the's" . . .

Perhaps, after all, he was not suited for politics.

He felt a growing disenchantment with these machinations. There were, despite genetics, subtle differences between the Makenzies, and it might well be that he was not as tough—or as ambitious—as his precursors.

In any event, his first step was obvious, especially as all his advisers had suggested it. The second move could be decided later.

It was no surprise when Calindy failed to appear on the screen of his Comsole, and he soon had proof that the social convention was justified. Unless there was some excellent reason, it was indeed bad manners to switch off one's viddy circuit. Duncan felt both frustrated and at a serious disadvantage, knowing that Calindy could see him but that he could not see her. The voice alone did not convey all the shades of emotion. There was so many times when the expression of the eyes could contradict the spoken word.

"Why, what's the matter, Calindy?" said Duncan in feigned astonishment. He would feel genuine sympathy if she were indeed hurt; but he intended to reserve judgment.

Her voice was—could it be imagination on his part?—not quite under control. She appeared surprised to see him, perhaps disconcerted.

"I'm terribly sorry, Duncan—I'd rather not show my face at the moment. I fell and hurt my eye—it looks *ghastly*. But there's nothing to worry about—it will be all right in a few days."

"I'm sorry to hear that. I won't bother you if you feel unwell."

He waited, hoping that Calindy could read the concern that he had carefully imprinted on his face.

"Oh, that's no problem. Otherwise it's business as usual—I've just cut out my weekly trip to the office, and now do *everything* by Comsole."

"Well, that's a relief. Now I've got a piece of news for *you*. Karl is on Earth."

There was a long silence before Calindy replied. When she finally answered, Duncan realized, with amused mortification, that he was not really in her league. He could not hope to outwit her for very long.

"Duncan," she said, in a resigned tone of voice, "you *really* didn't know that he was staying with me?"

Duncan did his best to exhibit incredulity, shock, and umbrage—in that order.

"Why didn't you tell me?" he cried.

"Because he asked me not to. That put me in a difficult position, but what was I to do? He said you were no longer on good terms . . . and his business was highly confidential."

Duncan guessed that Calindy was telling the simple truth, if indeed the truth was simple. Some, but not all, of his pique evaporated.

"Well, I'm upset and disappointed. I should have thought you'd have trusted me. Anyway, there's no further need for—*subterfuge*—now that I know he's here. I've an urgent message for him—where can I locate him?"

There was another long pause; then Calindy answered: "I don't know where he is. He left suddenly, and never told me where he was going. He might even have returned to Titan."

"Without saying good-bye? Hardly! And there are no ships to Titan for a month."

"Then I suppose he's still on Earth, or no farther away than the Moon. I simply don't know."

Oddly enough, Duncan believed her. Her voice still had the ring of truth, though he did not delude himself about her power to deceive him if she wished.

"In that case, I'll have to trace him in some other way. It's imperative that we meet."

"I wouldn't advise that, Duncan."

"Why ever not?"

"He's—very angry with you."

"I can't imagine the reason," retorted Duncan, swiftly imagining several. Calindy's voice sounded such a genuine note of alarm that he felt himself responding strongly to her concern.

However, it seemed that this avenue was closed, at least for the time being. He knew better than to argue with Calindy. With a mixture of emotions, he expressed hopes for her continued improvement, and broke the circuit. He hoped that she would interpret his attitude as one of both sorrow and anger, and feel correspondingly contrite.

A minute later, he was looking—with some relief —at a screen that was no longer empty, and could reveal the other party's reactions.

"Did *you* know," he asked Ambassador Farrell, "that Karl Helmer is on Earth?"

His Excellency blinked.

"I certainly did *not*. He never contacted me—I'll see if the Chancery knows anything."

He punched a few buttons, and it was obvious that nothing happened. The ambassador glanced at Duncan with annoyance.

"I wish we could afford a new intercom system," he said accusingly. "They cost a very small fraction of the Titan Gross National Product."

Duncan thought it wise to let this pass, and luckily on the second attempt the ambassador got through. He muttered a few inaudible questions, waited for a minute, then looked at Duncan and shook his head.

"No trace of him—not even a Terran forwarding address for any messages from home. *Most* odd."

"Wouldn't you say—unprecedented?"

"Um—yes. I've never heard of anyone failing to contact the Embassy as soon as they reach Earth. Usually, of course, we know that they're coming, weeks in advance. There's no law *compelling* them to get in touch—but it's a matter of courtesy. Not to mention convenience."

"That's what I thought. Well, if you hear anything of him, would you let me know?"

The ambassador stared back at him in silence for a moment, with the most enigmatic of smiles on his face. Then he said: "What do Malcolm and Colin think he's doing? Plotting a *coup d'état* with smuggled guns?"

After a moment's shock, Duncan laughed at the joke.

"Not even Karl is *that* crazy. Frankly, I'm completely baffled by the whole thing—but I'm determined to locate him. Though there may be half a billion people on Earth, he's not exactly inconspicuous. Please keep in touch. Good-bye for the present."

Two down, thought Duncan, and one to go. It was back to Ivor Mandel'stahm, in his self-appointed, and by no means unsuccessful, role of private eye.

But Ivor's Console answered: "Please do not disturb. Kindly record any message."

Duncan was annoyed; he was bursting to pass on his news, but was certainly not going to leave it stored in a Console. He would have to wait until Mandel'stahm called back.

That took two hours, and meanwhile it was not easy to concentrate on other work. When the dealer finally returned the call, he apologized profusely.

"I was trying a long shot," he explained. "I wondered if he'd bought anything in New York on a credit card. There aren't all that number of aitches, and the Central Billing computer zipped through them in an hour. . . . Alas—he must be using cash. Not a federal crime, of course. But a nuisance to us honest investigators."

Duncan laughed.

"It was a good idea. I've done slightly better—at least I've eliminated some possibilities."

He gave Mandel'stahm a brief résumé of his discussions with Calindy and Ambassador Farrell, then added: "Where do we go from here?"

"I'm not sure. But don't worry—I'll think of something."

Duncan believed him. He now had an almost unreasoning confidence in the dealer's ingenuity, not to mention his influence and his knowledge of the ways of Earth. If *anyone* could locate Karl—short of going to the police, or inserting a personal appeal in the *World Times*—it would be Mandel'stahm.

In fact, it took him only thirty-six hours.

36

THE EYE OF ALLAH

"I've found him," said Mandel'stahm. He looked tired but victorious.

"I knew you would," Duncan replied with unfeigned admiration. "Where is he?"

"Don't be so impatient—let me have my reasonably innocent fun. I've earned it."

"Well, whose concierge did you bamboozle this time?"

Mandel'stahm looked slightly pained.

"Nobody's. I first tried to find all I could about your friend Helmer, by the brilliant device of looking him up in the *Interplanetary Who's Who*. I assumed he'd be there, and he was—a hundred-line print-out. I looked *you* up at the same time, by the way. . . . You rate one hundred fifty lines, if that's any satisfaction."

"I know," said Duncan, with what patience he could muster. "Go on."

"I wondered if it would list any Terran contacts or interests, and again I was in luck. He belongs to the Institution of Electronic Engineers, the Royal Astronomical Society, the Institute of Physics, and the Institute of Astronautics—as well as several Titanian professional organizations, of course. And I see he's written half a dozen scientific papers, and been joint author in others: the Ionosphere of Saturn, origins of ultra-long-wave electromagnetic radiation, and other thrilling esoterica . . . nothing of any use to us, though.

"The Royal astronomers are in London, of course —but the engineers and astronauts and physicists are all in New York, and I wondered if he'd contacted them. So I called on another of my useful friends—a scientist this time, and a most distinguished one, who could open any doors without questions being asked. I hoped that a visiting Titanian colleague was a rare enough phenomenon to attract attention . . . and indeed he was."

Mandel'stahm gave another of his pregnant pauses, so that Duncan could simmer for a while, then went on.

"*This* is what puzzles me. Apart from ignoring the Embassy, and telling Miss Ellerman to keep quiet, he's done absolutely *nothing* to cover his tracks. I don't think that anyone with much to hide would behave in that way. . . .

"It was really very simple. The Electronics people were happy to help. They told us he'd left North Atlan and could be contacted care of the Assistant Chief Engineer, Division C, World Communications Headquarters, Tehran. Not the sort of address you'd associate with gem smuggling and interplanetary skulduggery. . . .

"So over to Tehran—just in time to miss him, but no matter. He'll be at the same location now for a couple of days, and in view of his background, at *last* we've got something that makes a little sense.

"World Com's Division C are the boys who keep Project CYCLOPS running. And even *I* have heard of that."

It had been conceived in the first bright dawn of the Space Age; the largest, most expensive, and potentially most promising scientific instrument ever devised. Though it could serve many purposes, one was paramount—the search for intelligent life elsewhere in the universe.

One of the oldest dreams of mankind, this remained no more than a dream until the rise of radio astronomy, in the second half of the twentieth century. Then, within the short span of two decades, the combined skills of the engineers and the scientists gave humanity power to span the interstellar gulfs— *if* it was willing to pay the price.

The first puny radio telescopes, a few tens of meters in diameter, had listened hopefully for signals from the stars. No one had really expected success from these pioneering efforts, nor was it achieved. Making certain plausible assumptions about the distribution of intelligence in the Galaxy, it was easy to calculate that the detection of a radio-emitting civilization would require telescopes not decameters, but kilometers, in aperture.

There was only one practical method of achieving this result—at least, with structures confined to the surface of the Earth. To build a single giant bowl was out of the question, but the same result could be obtained from an array of hundreds of smaller ones. CYCLOPS was visualized as an antenna "farm" of hundred-meter dishes, uniformly spaced over a circle perhaps five kilometers across. The faint signals from each element in this army of antennas would be added together, and then cunningly processed by computers programmed to look for the unique signatures of intelligence against the background of cosmic noise.

The whole system would cost as much as the original Apollo Project. But unlike Apollo, it could proceed in installments, over a period of years or even decades. As soon as a relatively few antennas had been built, CYCLOPS could start operating. From the very beginning, it would be a tool of immense value to the radio astonomers. Over the years, more and more antennas could be installed, until eventually the whole array was filled in; and all the while CYCLOPS would steadily increase in power and capability, able to probe deeper and deeper into the universe.

It was a noble vision, though there were some who feared its success as much as its possible failure. However, during the Time of Troubles that brought the twentieth century to its unlamented close, there was little hope of funding such a project. It could be considered only during a period of political and financial stability; and therefore CYCLOPS did not get under way until a hundred years after the initial design studies.

A child of the brief but brilliant Muslim Renaissance, it helped to absorb some of the immense wealth accumulated by the Arab countries during the

238

Oil Age. The millions of tons of metal required came from the virtually limitless resources of the Red Sea brines, oozing along the Great Rift Valley. Here, where the crust of the Earth was literally coming apart at the seams as the continental plates slowly separated, were metals and minerals enough to banish all fear of shortages for centuries to come.

Ideally CYCLOPS should have been situated on the Equator, so that its questing radio mirrors could sweep the heavens from pole to pole. Other requirements were a good climate, freedom from earthquakes or other natural disasters—and, if possible, a ring of mountains to act as a shield against radio interference. Of course, no perfect site existed, and political, geographical, and engineering compromises had to be made. After decades of often acrimonious discussion, the desolate "Empty Quarter" of Saudi Arabia was chosen; it was the first time that anyone had ever found a use for it.

Wide tracks were roughly graded through the wilderness so that ten-thousand-ton hover-freighters could carry in components from the factories on the shore of the Red Sea. Later, these were supplemented by cargo airships. In the first phase of the project, sixty parabolic antennas were arranged in the form of a giant cross, it's five-kilometer arms extending north-south, east-west. Some of the faithful objected to this symbol of an alien religion, but it was explained to them that this was only a temporary state of affairs. When the "Eye of Allah" was completed, the offending sign would be utterly lost in the total array of seven hundred huge dishes, spaced uniformly over a circle eighty square kilometers in extent.

By the end of the twenty-first century, however, only half of the planned seven hundred elements had been installed. Two hundred of them had filled in most of the central core of the array, and the rest formed a kind of picket fence, outlining the circumference of the giant instrument. This reduction in scale, while saving billions of solars, had degraded performance only slightly. CYCLOPS had fulfilled virtually all its design objectives, and during the course of the twenty-second century had wrought almost as great a revolution in astronomy as had the reflectors on Mount Wilson and Mount Palomar, two hundred years earlier. By the end of that century, however, it had run into trouble—through no fault of its builders, or of the army of engineers and scientists who served it.

CYCLOPS could not compete with the systems that had now been built on the far side of the Moon—almost perfectly shielded from terrestrial interference by three thousand kilometers of solid rock. For many decades, it had worked in conjunction with them, for two great telescopes at either end of an Earth-Moon baseline formed an interferometer that could probe details of planetary systems hundreds of light-years away. But now there were radio telescopes on Mars; the Lunar observatory could achieve far more with their co-operation than it could ever do with nearby Earth. A baseline two hundred million kilometers long allowed one to survey the surrounding stars with a precision never before imagined.

As happens sooner or later with all scientific instruments, technical developments had by-passed CYCLOPS. But by the mid-twenty-third century it was facing another problem, which might well prove fatal. *The Empty Quarter was no longer a desert.*

CYCLOPS had been built in a region which might see no rains for five years at a time. At Al Hadidah, there were meteorites that had lain unrusting in the sand since the days of the Prophet. All this had been changed by reforestation and climate control; for the first time since the Ice Ages, the deserts were in retreat. More rain now fell on the Empty Quarter in days than had once fallen in years.

The makers of CYCLOPS had never anticipated this. They had, reasonably enough, based all their designs on a hot, arid environment. Now the maintenance staff was engaged in a continual battle against corrosion, humidity in coaxial cables, fungus-induced breakdowns in high-tension circuits, and all the other ills that afflict electronic equipment if given the slightest chance. Some of the hundred-meter antennas had even rusted up solidly, so that they could no longer be moved and had to be taken out of service. For almost twenty years, the system had been working at slowly decreasing efficiency, while the engineers, administrators, and scientists carried out a triangular argument, no one party being able to convince either of the others. Was it worth investing billions of solars to refurbish the system—or would the money be better spent on the other side of the Moon? It was impossible to arrive at any clear-cut decision, for no one had ever been able to put a value on pure scientific research.

Whatever its present problems, CYCLOPS had been a spectacular success, helping reshape man's views of the universe not once, but many times. It had pushed back the frontiers of knowledge to the very microsecond after the Big Bang itself, and had trapped radio waves that had circumnavigated the entire span of creation. It had probed the surfaces of distant stars, detected their hidden planets, and discovered such strange entities as neutrino suns, antitachyons, gravitational lenses, spacequakes, and revealed the mind-wrenching realms of negative-probability "Ghost" states and inverted matter.

But there was one thing that it had not done. Despite scores of false alarms, it had never succeeded in detecting signals from intelligent beings elsewhere in the universe.

Either Man was alone, or nobody else was using radio transmitters. The two explanations seemed equally improbable.

37

MEETING AT CYCLOPS

He had known what to expect, or so he had believed, but the reality was still overwhelming. Duncan felt like a child in a forest of giant metal trees, extending in every direction to the limit of vision. Each of the identical "trees" had a slightly tapering trunk fifty meters high, with a stairway spiraling round it up to the platform supporting the drive mechanism. Looming above this was the huge yet surprisingly delicate hundred-meter-wide bowl of the antenna itself, tilted toward the sky as it listened for signals from the deeps of space.

Antenna 005, as its number indicated, was near the center of the array, but it was impossible to tell this by visual inspection. Whichever way Duncan looked, the ranks and columns of steel towers dwindled into the distance until eventually they formed a solid wall of metal.

The whole vast array was a miracle of precision engineering, on a scale matched nowhere else on Earth. It was altogether appropriate that many key components had been manufactured in space; the foamed metals and crystal fibers which gave the parabolic reflectors strength with lightness could be produced only by the zero-gravity orbiting factories. In more ways than one, CYCLOPS was a child of space.

Duncan turned to the guide who had driven him through the labyrinth of access tunnels on the small, chemically powered scooter.

"I don't see anyone," he complained. "Are you *sure* he's here?"

"This is where we left him, an hour ago. He'll be in the preamplifier assembly, up there on the platform.

You'll have to shout—no radios allowed *here,* of course."

Duncan could not help smiling at this further example of the CYCLOPS management's almost fanatical precautions against interference. He had even been asked to surrender his watch, lest its feeble electronic pulses be mistaken for signals from an alien civilization a few hundred light-years away. His guide was actually wearing a spring-driven timepiece—the first that Duncan had ever seen.

Cupping his hands around his mouth, Duncan tilted his head toward the metal tower looming above him and shouted "Karl!" A fraction of a second later, the K echoed back from the next antenna, then reverberated feebly from the ones beyond. After that, the silence seemed more profound than before. Duncan did not feel like disturbing it again.

Nor was there any need. Fifty meters above, a figure had moved to the railing around the platform; and it brought with it the familiar glint of gold.

"Who's there?"

Who do you think? Duncan asked himself. Of course, it was hard to recognize a person from vertically overhead, and voices were distorted in this inhumanly scaled place.

"It's Duncan."

There was a pause that seemed to last for the better part of a minute, but could only have been a few seconds in actuality. Karl was obviously surprised, though by this time he must surely have guessed that Duncan knew of his presence on Earth. Then he answered: "I'm in the middle of a job. Come up, if you want to."

That was hardly a welcome, but the voice did not seem hostile. The only emotion that Duncan could identify at this distance was a kind of tired resignation; and perhaps he was imagining even this.

Karl had vanished again, doubtless to continue whatever task he had come here to perform. Duncan looked very thoughtfully at the spiral stairway winding up the cylindrical trunk of the antenna tower. Fifty meters was a trifling distance—but not in terms of Earth's gravity. It was the equivalent of two hundred and fifty on Titan; he had never had to climb a quarter of a kilometer on his own world.

Karl, of course, would have had little difficulty, since he had spent his early years on Earth, and his muscles would have recovered much of their original strength. Duncan wondered if this was a deliberate challenge. That would be typical of Karl, and if so he had no choice in the matter.

As he stepped onto the first of the perforated metal stairs, his CYCLOPS guide remarked hopefully: "There's not much room up there on the platform. Unless you want me, I'll stay here."

Duncan could recognize a lazy man when he met one, but he was glad to accept the excuse. He did not wish any strangers to be present when he came face to face with Karl. The confrontation was one that he would have avoided if it had been at all possible, but this was not a job that could be delegated to anyone else—even if those instructions from Colin and Malcolm had allowed it.

The climb was easy enough, though the safety rail was not as substantial as Duncan would have wished. Moreover, sections had been badly rusted, and now that he was close enough to touch the metal he could see that the mounting was in even worse condition than he had been led to expect. Unless emergency repairs were carried out very soon, CYCLOPS would never see the dawn of the twenty-fourth century.

When Duncan had completed his first circuit, the guide called up to him: "I forgot to tell you—we're selecting a new target in about five minutes. You'll find it rather dramatic."

Duncan stared up at the huge bowl now completely blocking the sky above him. The thought of all those tons of metal swinging around just overhead was quite disturbing, and he was glad that he had been warned in time.

The other saw his action and interpreted it correctly.

"It won't bother you. *This* antenna's been frozen for at least ten years. The drive's seized up, and not worth repairing."

So that confirmed a suspicion of Duncan's, which he had dismissed as an optical illusion. The great parabola above him was indeed at a slight angle to all the others; it was no longer an active part of the CYCLOPS array, but was now pointing blindly at the sky. The loss of one—or even a dozen—elements would cause only a slight degradation of the system, but it was typical of the general air of neglect.

One more circuit, and he would be at the platform. Duncan paused for breath. He had been climbing very slowly, but already his legs were beginning to ache with the wholly unaccustomed effort. There had been no further sound from Karl. What *was* he doing, in this fantastic place of old triumphs and lost dreams?

And how would he react to this unexpected, and doubtless unwelcome, confrontation, when they were face to face? A little belatedly, it occurred to Duncan that a small platform fifty meters above the ground, and in *this* frightful gravity, was not the best place to have an argument. He smiled at the mental image this conjured up; whatever their disagreement, violence was unthinkable.

Well, not quite unthinkable. He had just thought of it. . . .

Overhead now was a narrow band of perforated metal flooring, barely wide enough for the rectangular slot through which the stairway emerged. With a heartfelt sigh of relief, pulling himself upward with rust-stained hands, Duncan climbed the last few steps and stood amid monstrous bearings, silent hydraulic motors, a maze of cables, much dismantled plumbing, and the delicate tracery of ribs supporting the now useless hundred-meter parabola.

There was still no sign of Karl, and Duncan began a cautious circumnavigation of the antenna mounting. The catwalk was about two meters wide, and the protective rail almost waist-high, so there was no real danger. Nevertheless, he kept well away from the edge and avoided looking at the fifty-meter drop.

He had barely completed half a circuit when all hell broke loose. There was a sudden whirr of motors, the low booming of great machineries on the move—and even the occasional accompaniment of protesting shrieks from gears and bearings that did not wish to be disturbed.

On every side, the huge skyward-facing bowls were beginning to turn in unison, swinging around to the south. Only the one immediately overhead was motionless, like a blind eye no longer able to react to any stimulus. The din was quite astonishing, and continued for several minutes. Then it stopped as abruptly as it had started. CYCLOPS had located a new target for its scrutiny.

"Hello, Duncan," said Karl in the sudden silence. "Welcome to Earth."

He had emerged, while Duncan was distracted by the tumult, from a small cubicle on the underside of the parabola, and was now climbing down a somewhat precarious arrangement of hanging ladders. His descent looked particularly hazardous because he was using only one hand; the other was firmly clutching a large notebook, and Duncan did not relax until Karl was safely on the platform, a few meters away. He made no attempt to come closer, but stood looking at Duncan with a completely unfathomable expression, neither friendly nor hostile.

Then there was one of those embarrassing pauses when neither party wishes to speak first, and as it dragged on interminably Duncan became aware for the first time of an omnipresent faint hum from all around him. The CYCLOPS array was alive now, its hundreds of tracking motors working in precise synchronism. There was no perceptible movement of the great antenna's, but they would now be creeping around at a fraction of a centimeter a second. The multiple facets of the CYCLOPS eye, having fixed their gaze upon the stars, were now turning at the precise rate needed to counter the rotation of the Earth.

How foolish, in this awesome shrine dedicated to the cosmos itself, for two grown men to behave like children, each trying to outface the other! Duncan had the dual advantage of surprise and a clear conscience; he would have nothing to lose by speaking first. He did not wish to take the initiative and perhaps antagonize Karl, so it was best to open with some innocuous triviality.

No, *not* the weather—the amount of Terran conversation devoted to that was quite incredible!—but something equally neutral.

"That was the hardest work I've done since I got here. I can't believe that people *really* climb mountains on this planet."

Karl examined this brilliant gambit for possible booby traps. Then he shrugged his shoulders and replied: "Earth's tallest mountain is two *hundred* times as high as this. People climb it every year."

At least the ice was broken, and communication had been established. Duncan permitted himself a sigh of relief; at the same time, now that they were at close quarters, he was shocked by Karl's appearance. Some of that golden hair had turned to silver, and there was much less of it. In the year since they had last met, Karl seemed to have aged ten. There were crow's-feet wrinkles of anxiety around his eyes, and his brow was now permanently furrowed. He also seemed to have *shrunk* considerably, and Earth's gravity could not be wholly to blame, for Duncan was even more vulnerable to that. On Titan, he had always had to look up at Karl; now, as they stood face to face, their eyes were level.

But Karl avoided his gaze and moved restlessly back and forth, firmly clutching the notebook he was still carrying. Presently he walked to the very edge of the platform and leaned with almost ostentatious recklessness against the protective rail.

"Don't *do* that!" protested Duncan. "It makes me nervous." That, he suspected, was the purpose of the exercise.

"Why should you care?"

The brusque answer saddened Duncan beyond measure. He could only reply: "If you really don't know, it's too late for me to explain."

"Well, I know this isn't a social visit. I suppose you've seen Calindy?"

"Yes. I've seen her."

"What are you trying to do?"

"I can't speak for Calindy. She doesn't even know that I'm here."

"What are the *Makenzies* trying to do? For the good of Titan, of course."

Duncan knew better than to argue. He did not even feel angry at the calculated provocation.

"All *I'm* trying to do is to avoid a scandal—if it's not too late."

"I don't know what you mean."

"You know perfectly well. Who authorized your trip to Earth? Who's paying your expenses?"

Duncan had expected Karl to show some signs of guilt, but he was mistaken.

"I have friends here. And I don't recall that the Makenzies worried too much about regulations. How did Malcolm get the first Lunar orbital refueling contract?"

"That was a hundred years ago, when he was trying to get the Titan economy started. There's no excuse *now* for financial irregularities. Especially for purely personal ends."

This was, of course, a shot in the dark, but he appeared to have landed on some target. For the first time, Karl looked angry.

"You don't know what you're talking about," he snapped back. "One day Titan . . ."

CYCLOPS gently but firmly interrupted him. They had quite forgotten the slow tracking of the great antennas on every side, and were no longer even aware of the faint whirr of the hundreds of drive motors. Until a few seconds ago, the upper platform of 005 had been shielded by the inverted umbrella of the next bowl, but now its shadow was no longer falling upon them. The artificial eclipse was over, and they were blasted by the tropical sun.

Duncan closed his eyes until his dark glasses had adjusted to the glare. When he opened them again, he was standing in a world divided sharply into night and day. Everything on one side was clearly visible, while in the shadow only a few centimeters away he could see absolutely nothing. The contrast between light and darkness, exaggerated by his glasses, was so great that Duncan could almost imagine he was on the airless Moon.

It was also uncomfortably hot, especially for Titanians.

"If you don't mind," said Duncan, still determined to be polite, "we'll move around to the shadow side." It would be just like Karl to refuse, either out of sheer stubbornness or to demonstrate his superiority. He was not even wearing dark glasses, though he was holding the notebook to shield his eyes.

Rather to Duncan's surprise, Karl followed him meekly enough around the catwalk, into the welcome shade on the northern face of the tower. The utter banality of the interruption seemed to have put him off his stride.

"I was saying," continued Duncan, when they had settled down again, "that I'm merely trying to avoid any unpleasantness that will embarrass both Earth and Titan. There's nothing personal in this, and I wish that someone else were doing it—believe me."

Karl did not answer at once, but bent down and carefully placed his notebook on the most rust-free section of the catwalk he could find. The action reminded Duncan so vividly of old times that he was absurdly moved. Karl had never been able to express his emotions properly unless his hands were free, and that notebook was obviously a major hindrance.

"Listen carefully, Duncan," Karl began. "Whatever Calindy told you—"

"She's told me nothing."

"She must have helped you find me."

"Not even that. She doesn't even know I'm here."

"I don't believe you."

Duncan shrugged his shoulders and remained silent. His strategy seemed to be working. By hinting that he knew much more than he did—which was indeed little enough—he hoped to undercut Karl's confidence and gain further admissions from him. But what he would do then, he still had no idea; he could only rely on Colin's maxim of the masterful administration of the unforeseen.

Karl had now begun to pace back and forth in such an agitated manner that, for the first time, Duncan felt distinctly nervous. He remembered Calindy's warning; and once again, he reminded himself uneasily that this was not at all a good place for a confrontation with an adversary who might be slightly unbalanced.

Suddenly, Karl seemed to come to a decision. He stopped his uncertain weaving along the narrow catwalk and turned on his heel so abruptly that Duncan drew back involuntarily. Then he realized, with both surprise and relief, that Karl's hands were outstretched in a gesture of pleading, not of menace.

"Duncan," he began, in a voice that was now completely changed. *"You* can help me. What I'm trying to do—"

It was as if the sun had exploded. Duncan threw his hands before his eyes and clenched them tightly against the intolerable glare. He heard a cry from Karl, and a moment later the other bumped into him violently, rebounding at once.

The actinic detonation had lasted only a fraction of a second. Could it have been lightning? But if so, where was the thunder? It should have come almost instantaneously, for a flash as brilliant as this.

Duncan dared to open his eyes, and found that he could see again, though through a veil of pinkish mist. But Karl, it was obvious, could not see at all; he was blundering around blindly, with his hands cupped tightly over his eyes. And still the expected thunder never came. . . .

If Duncan had not been half-paralyzed by shock, he might yet have acted in time. Everything seemed to happen in slow motion, as in a dream. He could not believe that it was real.

He saw Karl's foot hit the precious notebook, so that it went spinning off into space, fluttering downward like some strange, white bird. Blinded though he was, Karl must have realized what he had done. Totally disoriented, he made one futile grab at the empty air, then crashed into the guardrail. Duncan tried to reach him, but it was too late.

Even then, it might not have mattered; but the years and the rust had done their work. As the treacherous metal parted, it seemed to Duncan that Karl cried out his name, in the last second of his life.

But of that he would never be sure.

38

THE LISTENERS

"You're under no legal compulsion," Ambassador Farrell had explained. "If you wish, I could claim diplomatic immunity for you. But it would be unwise, and might lead to various—ah—difficulties. In any case, this inquiry is in the mutual interest of all concerned. *We* want to find out what's happened, just as much as they do."

"And who are *they?*"

"Even if I knew, I couldn't tell you. Let's say Terran Security."

"You still have that kind of nonsense here? I thought spies and secret agents went out a couple of hundred years ago."

"Bureaucracies are self-perpetuating—*you* should know that. But civilization will always have its discontents, to use a phrase I came across somewhere. Though the police handles most matters, as they do on Titan, there are cases which require—special treatment. By the way, I've been asked to make it clear that anything you care to say will be privileged and won't be published without your consent. And if you wish, I will come along with you for moral support and guidance."

Even now, Duncan was not quite sure who the Ambassador was representing, but the offer was a reasonable one and he had accepted it. He could see no harm in such a private meeting; some kind of judicial inquiry was obviously needed, but the less publicity, the better.

He had half expected to be taken in a blacked-out car on a long, tortuous drive to some vast underground complex in the depths of Virginia or Maryland. It was a little disappointing to end up in a small room at the old State Department Building, talking to an Assistant Under Secretary with the improbable name of John Smith; later checking on Duncan's part disclosed that this actually was his name. However, it soon became clear that there was much more to this room than the plain desk and three comfortable chairs that met the eye.

Duncan's suspicions about the large mirror that covered most of one wall were quickly confirmed. His host—or interrogator, if one wanted to be melodramatic—saw the direction of his glance and gave him a candid smile.

"With your permission, Mr. Makenzie, we'd like to record this meeting. And there are several other participants watching; they may join in from time to time. If you don't mind, I'll refrain from introducing them."

Duncan nodded politely toward the mirror.

"I've no objection to recording," he said. "Do you mind if I also use my Minisec?"

There was a painful silence, broken only by an ambassadorial chuckle. Then Mr. Smith answered: "We would prefer to supply you with a transcript. I can promise that it will be quite accurate."

Duncan did not press the point. Presumably, it might cause embarrassment if some of the voices involved were recognized by outsiders. In any case, a transcript would be perfectly acceptable; he could trust his memory to spot errors or deletions.

"Well, that's fine," said Mr. Smith, obviously relieved. "Let's get started."

Simultaneously, something odd happened to the room. Its acoustics changed abruptly; it was as if it had suddenly become much larger. There was not the slightest visible alteration, but Duncan had the uncanny feeling of unseen presences all around him. He would never know if they were actually in Washington, or on the far side of the Earth, and it gave him an uncomfortable, naked sensation to be surrounded by invisible listeners—and watchers.

A moment later, a voice spoke quietly from the air immediately in front of him.

"Good morning, Mr. Makenzie. It's good of you to spare us your time, and please excuse our reticence. If you think this is some kind of twentieth-century spy melodrama, our apologies. Ninety-nine times out of a hundred, these precautions are totally unnecessary. But we can never tell which occasion will be the hundredth."

It was a friendly, powerful voice, very deep and resonant, yet there was something slightly unnatural about it. A computer? Duncan asked himself. That was too easy an assumption; in any case, there was no way of distinguishing between computer vocalization and human speech—especially now that a realistic number of "ers," "wells," incomplete sentences, and downright grammatical errors could be incorporated to make the nonelectronic participants in a conversation feel at ease. He guessed that he was listening to a man talking through a speech-disguising circuit.

While Duncan was still trying to decide if any answer was necessary, another speaker took over. This time, the voice emerged about half a meter from his left ear.

"It's only fair to reassure you on one point, Mr. Makenzie. As far as we can ascertain, no Terran laws have been broken. We are not here to investigate a crime—only to solve a mystery, to explain a tragedy. If any *Titanian* regulations are involved, that is your problem—not ours. I hope you understand."

"Yes," Duncan replied. "I assumed that was the case, but I'm glad to have your confirmation."

This was indeed a relief, but he knew better than to relax. Perhaps this statement was exactly what it seemed to be—a friendly plea for co-operation. But it might also be a trap.

Now a woman's voice came from immediately behind him, and he had to resist the impulse to swing around and look at the speaker. Was this quite unnecessary shifting of sound focus a deliberate attempt to disorient him? How naïve did they take him to be?

"To save us all time, let me explain that we have a complete summary of Mr. Helmer's background." *And* mine, thought Duncan. "Your government has been most helpful, but you may have information which is unknown to us, since you were one of his closest friends."

Duncan nodded, without bothering to speak. They would know all about that friendship, and its ending.

As if responding to some hidden signal, Mr. Smith opened his briefcase and carefully laid a small object on the table.

"You'll recognize this, of course," the female voice continued. "The Helmer family has asked that it be handed over to you for safe custody, with the other property of the deceased."

The sight of Karl's Minisec—virtually the same model as his own—was in itself such a shock that at first the remainder of the message failed to get through. Then Duncan reacted with a start and said: "Would you please repeat that?"

There was such a surprisingly long delay that he wondered if the speaker was on the Moon; during the course of the session, Duncan became almost certain of it. With all the other interrogators, there was a quick give-and-take, but with the lone woman there was always this invariable time-lag.

"The Helmers have asked that you be custodian of their son's effects, until disposition is settled."

It was a gesture of peace, across the grave of all their hopes, and Duncan felt his eyes stinging with unshed tears. He looked at the handful of micro-electronics on the table and felt a deep reluctance even to touch it. There were all Karl's secrets. Would the Helmers have asked him to accept this if they had anything to hide? But there was a great deal, Duncan was certain, that Karl had concealed from his own family; there would be much in the Minisec that only he had ever known. True, it would be guarded by carefully chosen code words, some of them possibly linked with ERASE circuits to prevent unauthorized intrusion.

254

"Naturally," continued the voice from the Moon (if it *was* from the Moon), "we are interested in what may be in this Minisec. In particular, we would like any list of contacts on Earth—addresses or personal numbers."

Yes, thought Duncan, I can understand that. I'm sure you must have been tempted to do some interrogation already, but are scared of possible ERASE circuits and want to explore other alternatives first. . . .

He stared thoughtfully at that little box on the table, with its multitudinous studs and its now darkened read-out panel. There lay a device of a complexity beyond all the dreams of earlier ages—a virtual microsimulacrum of a human brain. Within it were billions of bits of information, stored in endless atomic arrays, waiting to be recalled by the right signal—or obliterated by the wrong one. At the moment it was lifeless, inert, like consciousness itself in the profoundest depths of sleep. No—not quite inert; the clock and calendar circuits would still be operating, ticking off the seconds and minutes and days that now were no concern of Karl's.

Another voice broke in, this time from the right.

"We have asked Mr. Armand Helmer if his son left any code words with him, as is usual in such cases. You may be hearing more on the matter shortly. Meanwhile, no attempt will be made to obtain any read-outs. With your permission, we would like to retain the Minisec for the present."

Duncan was getting a little tired of having decisions made for him—and the Helmers had apparently stated that *he* was to take possession of Karl's effects. But there was no point in objecting; and if he did, some legal formality would undoubtedly materialize out of the same thin air as these mysterious voices.

Mr. Smith was digging into his case again.

"Now there is a second matter—I'm sure you'll also recognize this."

"Yes. Karl usually carried a sketchbook. Is this the one he had with him when—"

"It is. Would you like to go through it, and see if there is anything that strikes you as unusual—noteworthy—of any possible value to this investigation? Even if it seems utterly trivial or irrelevant, please don't hesitate to speak."

What a technological gulf, thought Duncan, between these two objects! The Minisec was a triumph of the Neoelectronic Age; the sketchbook had existed virtually unchanged for at least a thousand years —and so had the pencil tucked into it. It was very true, as some philosopher of history had once said, that mankind never completely abandons any of its ancient tools. Yet Karl's sketchbooks had always been something of an affectation; he could make competent engineering drawings, but had never shown any genuine sign of artistic talent.

As Duncan slowly turned the leaves, he was acutely conscious of the hidden eyes all around him. Without the slightest doubt, every page here had been carefully recorded, using all the techniques that could bring out invisible marks and erasures. It was hard to believe that he could add much to the investigations that had already been made.

Karl apparently used his sketchbooks to make notes of anything that interested him, to conduct a sort of dialogue with himself, and to express his emotions. There were cryptic words and numbers in small, precise handwriting, fragments of calculations and equations, mathematical sketches . . .

And there were spacescapes, obviously rough drawings of scenes on the outer moons, with the formalized circle-and-ellipse of Saturn hanging in the sky . . .

. . . circuit diagrams, with more calculations full of lambdas and omegas, and vector notations that Duncan could recognize, but could not understand . . . and then suddenly, bursting out of the pages of impersonal notes and rather inept sketches, something that breathed life, something that might have been the work of a *real* artist—a portrait of Calindy, drawn with obvious, loving care.

It should have been instantly recognizable; yet strangely enough, for a fraction of a second, Duncan stared at it blankly. This was not the Calindy he now knew, for the real woman was already obliterating the image from the past. Here was Calindy as they had both remembered her—the girl frozen forever in the bubble stero, beyond the reach of Time.

Duncan looked at the picture for long minutes before turning the page. It was really excellent—quite unlike all the other sketches. But then, how many times had Karl drawn it, over and over again, during the intervening years?

No one spoke from the air around him or interrupted his thoughts. And presently he moved on.

. . . more calculations . . . patterns of hexagons, dwindling away into the distance—why, of course!

"That's the titanite lattice—but the number written against it means nothing to me. It looks like a Terran viddy coding."

"You are correct. It happens to be the number of a gem expert here in Washington. *Not* Ivor Mandel'stahm, in case you're wondering. The person concerned assures us that Mr. Helmer never contacted him, and we believe him. It's probably a number he acquired somehow, jotted down, but never used."

. . . more calculations, now with lots of frequencies and phase angles. Doubtless communications stuff—part of Karl's regular work . . .

. . . geometrical doodles, many of them based on the hexagon motif . . .

. . . Calindy again—only an outline sketch this time, showing none of the loving care of the earlier drawing . . .

. . . a honeycomb pattern of little circles, seen in plan and elevation. Only a few were drawn in detail but it was obvious that there must be hundreds. The interpretation was equally obvious.

"The CYCLOPS array—yes, he's written in the number of elements and the over-all dimensions."

"Why do you think he was so interested?"

"That's quite natural—it's the biggest and most famous radio telescope on Earth. He often discussed it with me."

"Did he ever speak of visiting it?"

"Very likely—but I don't remember. After all, this was some years ago."

The drawings on the next few pages, though very

257

rough and diagrammatic, were clearly details of CY-CLOPS—antenna feeds, tracking mechanisms, obscure bits of circuitry, interspersed with yet more calculations. One sketch had been started and never finished. Duncan looked at it sadly, then turned the page. As he had expected, the next sheet was blank.

"I'm sorry to disappoint you," he said, closing the book, "but I get nothing at all from this. Kar—Mr. Helmer's field was communications science; he helped design the Titan-Inner Planets Link. This is all part of his work. His interest is completely understandable, and I see nothing unusual about it."

"Perhaps so, Mr. Makenzie. But you haven't finished."

Duncan looked in surprise at the empty air. Then Under Secretary Smith gestured toward the sketchbook.

"Never take anything for granted," he said mildly. "Start at the *other* end."

Feeling slightly foolish, Duncan reopened the sketchbook, then flipped it over as he realized that Karl had used it from both directions. (But he had been badly shaken by those last drawings, and was not thinking too clearly. . . .)

The inside back cover was blank, but the facing page bore the single enigmatic word ARGUS. It meant nothing to Duncan, though it did arouse some faint and unidentifiable association from history. He turned the page—and had one of the biggest shocks of his life.

As he stared incredulously at the drawing that occupied the entire area of the paper, he was suddenly transported back to Golden Reef. There could be no misinterpretation; yet as far as he knew, Karl had never shown the slightest interest in the minutiae of terrestial zoology. The very idea that any Titanian might be fascinated by marine biology was faintly incongruous.

Yet here was a detailed study, with the perspective meticulously worked out around the faintly limned x, y-, and z-axes of the spiny sea urchin, *Diadema*. Only a dozen of its thin, radiating needles were shown, but it was clear that there were hundreds, occupying the entire sphere of space around it.

That was astonishing enough, but there was something even more remarkable. This drawing must have required hours of devoted labor. Karl had dedicated to an unprepossessing little invertebrate—which surely he could never have seen in his life!—all the love and skill he had applied to the portrait of Calindy.

In the bright sunshine outside the old State Department, Duncan and the Ambassador had to wait for five minutes before the next shuttle came gliding silently down Virginia Avenue. No one was within earshot, so Duncan said with quiet urgency: "Does 'Argus' mean anything to *you?*"

"As a matter of fact, yes—though I'm damned if I see how it can help. I still have the remnants of a classical education, and unless I'm very much mistaken, Argus was the name of Odysseus' old dog. It recognized him when he came home to Ithaca after his twenty years of wandering, then died."

Duncan brooded over this information for a few seconds, then shrugged his shoulders.

"You're right—that's no help at all. And I still want to know why these people I met—or *didn't* meet—are so interested in Karl. As they admitted at the start, there's no suggestion that he's done anything illegal, as far as Earth is concerned. And I suspect that he may have only bent some Titanian regulations, not broken them."

"Just a moment—just a moment!" said the Ambassador. "You've reminded me of something." His face went through some rather melodramatic contortions, then smoothed itself out. He glanced around conspiratorially, saw that there was no one within hearing and that the shuttle was still three minutes away by the countdown indicator.

"I think I may have it, and I'll be obliged if you don't attribute this to me. But just consider the following wild speculation . . .

"Every organism has defense mechanisms to protect itself. You've just encountered one—part of the security system of Earth. This particular group, whatever its responsibilities may be, probably consists of a fairly small number of important people. I expect I know most of them—in fact, one voice . . . never mind . . .

"You could call it a watchdog committee. Such a committee has to have a name for itself—a secret name, naturally. In the course of my duties, I occasionally hear of such things, and carefully forget them. . . .

"Now, Argus was a *watchdog*. So what better name for such a group? Mind you, I'm *still* not asserting anything. But imagine the acute embarrassment of a secret organization that happens to find its name carefully spelled out in highly mysterious circumstances."

It was a very plausible theory, and Duncan was sure that the Ambassador would not have advanced it without excellent reasons. But it did not go even halfway.

"That's all very well, and I'm prepared to accept it. But what the devil has all this to do with a drawing of a sea urchin? I feel I'm going slowly mad."

The shuttle was now gliding to a halt in front of them, and the Ambassador waved him into it.

"If it's any consolation, Duncan, be assured that you're in very good company. I'd sacrifice a fair share of my modest retirement benefits if I could eavesdrop now on Under Secretary Smith and his invisible friends."

39

BUSINESS AND DESIRE

There was no way of telling, as Duncan stood at the window of Calindy's apartment, that he was not looking down at the busy traffic of 57th Street on a crisp winter night, when the first flakes of snow were drifting down, to melt at once as they struck the heated sidewalks. But this was summer, not winter;

and even President Bernstein's limousine was not as old as the cars moving silently a hundred meters below. He was watching the past, perhaps a hologram from the late twentieth century. Yet though Duncan knew that he was actually far underground, there was nothing that he could do to convince his senses of this fact.

He was alone with Calindy at last, though in circumstances of which he could never have dreamed only a few days ago. How ironic that, now the opportunity had come, he felt barely the faintest flicker of desire!

"What is it?" he asked suspiciously, as Calindy handed him a slim crystal goblet containing a few centimeters of blood-red liquid.

"If I told you, the name would mean nothing. And if I said what it cost, you'd be scared to drink it. Just taste it slowly; you'll never have another chance, and it will do you good."

It *was* good—smooth, slightly sweet, and, Duncan was quite certain, charged with several megatons of slumbering energy. He sipped it very slowly indeed, watching Calindy as she moved around the room.

He had not really known what to expect, yet her apartment had still been something of a surprise. It was almost stark in its simplicity, but large and beautifully proportioned, with dove-gray walls, a blue *vaulted* ceiling like the sky itself, and a green carpet that gave the impression of a small sea of grass lapping against the walls. There were fewer than a dozen pieces of furniture: four deeply cushioned chairs, two divans, a closed writing desk, a glass cabinet full of delicate chinaware, a low table upon which were lying a small box and a splendid book on twenty-second-century primitives—and, of course, the ubiquitous Comsole, its screen now crawling with abstract art that was very far from primitive.

Even without the force of gravity to remind him, there was no danger that Duncan would forget he was on Earth. He doubted if a private home on any other planet could show a display like this; but *he* would not like to live here. Everything was a little too perfect and displayed altogether too clearly the Terran obsession with the past. He suddenly remembered Ambassador Farrell's remark: *"We* aren't decadent, but our children will be." That would include Calindy's generation. Perhaps the Ambassador was right. . . .

He took another sip, staring at Calindy in silence as she orbited the room. Clearly ill at ease, she moved a chair through an imperceptible fraction of an inch, and gave a picture an equally invisible adjustment. Then she came back to the divan and sat down beside him.

A little more purposefully now, she leaned across the low coffee table and picked up the box lying upon it.

"Have you seen one of these?" she asked, as she opened the lid.

Lying in a nest of velvet was something that looked like a large, silver egg, about twice the size of the real eggs that Duncan had encountered in the Centennial Hotel.

"What is it?" he asked. "A piece of sculpture?"

"Pick it up—but be careful not to drop it."

Despite this warning, that was very nearly what he did. The egg was not particularly heavy, but it seemed *alive*—even squirming in his hand, though it showed no sign of any visible movement. However, when he looked at it more carefully, he could see faint opalescent bands flowing over the surface and momentarily blurring the mirror finish. They looked very much like waves of heat, yet there was no sensation of warmth.

"Cup it in *both* hands," Calindy instructed him, "and close your eyes."

Duncan obeyed, despite an almost irresistible impulse to see what was really happening to the extraordinary object he held. He felt completely disoriented, because it seemed that the sense of touch—the most reliable of all man's messengers from the external universe—was betraying him.

For the very texture of the egg was constantly changing. It no longer felt like metal; unbelievably, it was *furry*. He might have been fondling some small woolly animal—a kitten, perhaps. . . .

But only for seconds. The egg shivered, became

hard and rough—it was made of sandpaper, coarse enough to grate the skin . . .

. . . the sandpaper became satin, so smooth and silky that he wanted to caress it. There was barely time to obey the impulse when . . .

. . . the egg was liquefying and becoming gelatinous. It seemed about to ooze through his fingers, and Duncan had to force himself not to drop it in disgust. Only the knowledge that this could not *really* be happening gave him strength to control the reflex . . .

. . . it was made of wood; there was no doubt of that, for he could even feel the grain . . .

. . . before it dissolved into myriads of separate bristles, each so sharp and distinct that he could feel them prickling his skin. . . .

And there were sensations that he could not even name, some delightful, most neutral, but some so unpleasant that he could scarcely control his revulsion. At last, when within his cupped palms Duncan felt the unique, the incomparable touch of human skin, curiosity and amazement got the better of him. He opened his hands; the silver egg was completely unchanged, though now it felt as if it were carved from soap.

"What in heaven's name is it?" he cried.

"It's a tactoid. You haven't heard of them?"

"No."

"Fascinating, isn't it? It does to the sense of touch what a kaleidoscope does to vision. No, don't ask me *how* it works—something to do with controlled electrical stimulation."

"What's it used for?"

"Must everything have a purpose? It's just a toy—a novelty. But I had a very good reason for showing it to you."

"Oh, I know. 'The latest from Earth.' "

Calindy gave a wistful smile; she recognized that old catch phrase. It brought back vividly to both of them those days together on Titan, a lifetime ago.

"Duncan," she said, so quietly that he could barely hear the words, "do you think it was all my fault?"

They were now sitting two meters apart on the divan, and he had to twist his body to face her. The

263

woman he saw now was no longer the self-assured executive and impresario he had met on the *Titanic,* but an unhappy and uncertain girl. He wondered how long the mood of contrition would last, but for the moment it was genuine enough.

"How can I answer that?" he replied. "I'm still completely in the dark. I don't know what Karl was doing on Earth, or why he came here."

This was only partially true; Karl's Minisec had begun to reveal its secrets. But Duncan was not yet prepared to discuss those with anybody, least of all with Calindy.

She looked at him with an air of faint surprise and answered: "Do you mean to say that he never told you—in fifteen years?"

"Told me *what?*" said Duncan.

"What happened on that last night aboard *Mentor.*"

"No," replied Duncan, with painful slowness. "He never talked about it."

After all these years, that betrayal was still a bitter memory. He knew now, of course, that it was absurd for two young adults like Karl and Calindy, obsessed by their own grief, to have given any thought to the feelings of the boy who adored them both. He could not blame them now; but in his heart he had never forgiven them.

"So you didn't know that we used a joy machine."

"Oh, *no!*"

"I'm afraid so. It wasn't *my* idea. Karl insisted, and I didn't know any better. But at least I had sense enough not to use it myself. Well, only at very low power . . ."

"They were illegal even in those days. How did one get aboard *Mentor?*"

"There were a lot of things on *Mentor* that no one ever knew about."

"I'm sure of that. What happened?"

Calindy got to her feet again and began to pace nervously to and fro. She avoided Duncan's eyes as she continued.

"I don't like to think about it. Even now, it frightens me, and I can understand why people get hopelessly addicted. I'm sure your fingers have never

264

touched anything as—well, I suppose —*palpable* is the only word—as that tactoid. The joy machine is just the same; it makes real life seem pale and thin—and Karl, remember, used it at full power. I told him not to, but he laughed. He was confident that he could handle it. . . ."

Yes, thought Duncan, that would be just like Karl. Though he had never seen an emotion amplifier, one was kept under proper supervision at the Oasis Central Hospital. It was a very valuable psychiatric tool, but when the simple, portable versions quickly christened "joy machines" had become available around the midcentury, they had spread like a plague over the inhabited worlds. No one would ever know how many immature young minds had been ruined by them. "Brain burning" had been a disease of the sixties, until the epidemic had run its course, leaving behind it hundreds of emotional husks. Karl had been lucky to escape. . . .

But, of course, he had not escaped. So this was the truth about his "breakdown," and the explanation of his changed personality. Duncan began to feel a cold anger toward Calindy. He did not believe her protestation of innocence; she must have known better, even then. But part of his anger was not based on moral judgments. He blamed Calindy because she was alive, while Karl lay frozen in the Aden morgue, like some splendid marble statue defaced by time and carelessly restored. There he must wait until the legal complications involved in the disposal of an extraterrestrial corpse were unraveled. This was another duty that had fallen upon Duncan; he had done everything he believed necessary before saying farewell to the friend he had lost before his death.

"I think I see the picture," continued Duncan, so harshly that Calindy looked at him with sudden surprise. "But tell me the rest—what happened then?"

"Karl used to send me long, crazy speeches—sealed, special delivery. He said he would never be able to love anyone else. I told him not to be foolish, but to forget me as quickly as he could, since we'd never be able to meet again. What else could I have said? I didn't realize how absolutely useless that advice was—like telling a man to stop breathing. I was ashamed to ask, and only discovered years later what a joy machine does to the brain.

"You see, Duncan, he was telling the literal truth when he said he could never love anyone else. When they reinforce the pleasure circuits, joy machines create a *permanent,* almost unbreakable pattern of desires. The psychologists call it electro-imprinting. I believe that there are techniques to modify it now, but there weren't fifteen years ago, even on Earth. And certainly not on Titan.

"After a while, I stopped answering; there was nothing I could say. But I still heard from Karl several times a year. He swore that sooner or later, he would get to Earth and see me again. I didn't take him seriously."

Perhaps not, thought Duncan; but I am sure you weren't wholly displeased. It must have been flattering to have held in your hand the soul of someone as talented and beautiful as Karl—even if he had been enslaved accidentally, with the aid of a machine. . . .

He saw very clearly now why all Karl's later liaisons and marriages had exploded violently. They had been doomed to failure at the start. Always, the image of Calindy would have stood, an unattainable ideal, between Karl and happiness. How lonely he must have been! And how many misunderstandings might have been averted if the cause of his behavior had been realized in time.

Yet perhaps nothing could have been done, and in any case it was futile to dream about missed opportunities. Who was the old philosopher who had said: "The human race will never know happiness, as long as the words 'If only . . .' can still be spoken"?

"So it must have been a surprise, when he finally *did* turn up."

"No. He'd dropped several hints—I'd been half expecting him for a year. Then he called me from Port Van Allen, said he'd just arrived on a special flight, and would be seeing me as soon as he'd completed his gravity reconditioning."

"It was a Terran Survey supply ship, going back empty—and fast. Even so, it took him fifty days."

And it couldn't have been a very comfortable trip, Duncan added to himself—fifty days inside one of those space trucks, with minimal life-support systems. What a contrast to *Sirius!* He felt sorry for the officers who had innocently succumbed to Karl's persuasion, and hoped that the current Court of Inquiry would not damage their careers.

Calindy had recovered some of her poise. She stopped pacing around, and rejoined Duncan on the divan.

"I was not sure whether I really wanted to see him again, after all these years, but I knew how determined he was; it would have been useless trying to keep him away. So—I suppose you can say I took the line of least resistance."

She managed a wry smile, then continued: "It didn't work, of course, and I should have known it. Then we saw in a newscast that you'd just arrived on Earth."

"That must have been a shock to Karl. What did he say?"

"Not much; but I could see that he was upset and very surprised."

"Surely he must have made *some* comment."

"Only that if you contacted me, I was not to tell you that he was on Earth. That was the first time I suspected something was wrong, and started to worry about the titanite he'd asked me to sell."

"That's a trivial matter—forget about it. Let's say it was just one of the many tools that Karl used to reach his objective. But I'd like to know this—when we met aboard *Titanic,* was he still with you?"

Another hesitation, which in itself supplied half the answer. Then Calindy replied, rather defiantly: "Of course he was. And he was very angry when I said I'd met you. We had a bad row over that. Not the first one." She sighed, slightly too dramatically. "By that time, even Karl realized that it wouldn't work —that it was quite hopeless. I'd warned him many times, but he wouldn't believe me. He refused to face the fact that the Calindy he'd known fifteen years before, and whose image was burned in his brain, no longer existed. . . ."

Duncan had never thought that he would see tears

in Calindy's eyes. But was she weeping for Karl, he wondered—or for her own lost youth?

He tried to be cynical, but he did not succeed. He was sure that some part of her sorrow was perfectly genuine, and despite himself was deeply touched by it. And more than touched, for now, to his great surprise, he found that sympathy was not the only emotion Calindy was arousing in him. He had never realized before that shared grief could be an aphrodisiac.

This was a development that he did nothing to discourage, but he did not want to hurry matters. There was still much that he hoped to learn and that only Calindy could tell him.

"So he was always disappointed when we made love," she continued tearfully, "though at first he tried to conceal it. I could tell—and it wasn't pleasant for me. It made me feel—inadequate. You see, by this time I'd learned a good deal about imprinting and knew exactly what the trouble was. Karl's case isn't unique. . . .

"So he got more and more frustrated—and also violent. Sometimes he frightened me. You know how strong he was—look at this."

With another theatrical gesture, she slipped open her dress, displaying the upper left arm—not to mention her entire left breast.

"He hit me *here,* so hard that I was badly bruised. You can still see the mark."

With the best will in the world, Duncan could discover no trace of a bruise on the milky-white skin, smooth as satin, that was exposed before his eyes. Nevertheless, the revelation did not leave him unmoved.

"So that's why you switched off the viddy," he said sympathetically, and edged closer.

"Then Ivor's friend called me, with that query about Titan. I thought it was an odd coincidence . . . you know, Duncan, that was an unkind trick to play on me."

She sounded more sad than angry; and she did not

move away from him. Almost half of the sofa was now unoccupied.

"And then everything started to happen at once. Did you know that Terran Security sent two of its agents to interview me?"

"No, but I guessed it. What did you tell them?"

"Everything, of course. They were very kind and understanding."

"And also clumsy," said Duncan with deep bitterness.

"Oh, Duncan, that was an *accident*! You were an important guest—you *had* to be protected. There would have been an interplanetary scandal if something had happened just before you were going to address Congress. But you should never have gone after Karl, in such a dangerous place."

"It wasn't dangerous—we were having a perfectly friendly discussion. How did I know that trigger happy idiot was lurking in the next antenna?"

"What was he to do? He'd been ordered to protect you at all costs, and had been warned that Karl might be violent. It looked as if you were starting to fight— and that laser blast would only have blinded Karl for a few hours. It was all a terrible accident. No one was to blame."

Perhaps, thought Duncan; it would be a long, long time before he could view the whole sequence of events dispassionately. If there was blame, it was spread thinly, and across two worlds. Like most human tragedies, this one had been caused not by evil intentions, but by errors of judgment, misunderstandings. . . .

If Malcolm and Colin had not insisted that he have a showdown with Karl, confronting him with the facts . . . if he had not *wanted* Karl to prove his innocence, and deliberately given him the opportunity to assert it, even to the extent—unconsciously, but he was aware of it now—of putting himself in his power . . . Perhaps Karl had been really dangerous; that was something else he would never know.

It seemed as if they had both been enmeshed in some complex web of fate from which there had never been any possibility of escape. And though the scale of that disaster was so much greater that the very comparison appeared ludicrous, Duncan was again reminded of the *Titanic*. She too had been doomed, as if the gods themselves conspired against her, by a whole series of apparently random and trivial chances. If the radioed warnings had not been buried under greetings and business messages . . . If that iceberg had not sliced so incredibly through all those watertight compartments . . . If the radio operator on the ship only twenty kilometers away had not gone off duty when the first of all SOS signals was flashed into the Atlantic night . . . If there had been enough lifeboats . . . It was like the failure of a whole series of safety devices, one by one, against incalculable odds, until catastrophe was inevitable.

"Perhaps you are right," said Duncan, trying to console himself as much as Calindy. "I don't really blame anyone. Not even Karl."

"Poor Karl. He really loved me. To have come all the way to Earth . . ."

Duncan did not answer, though for a moment he was tempted. Surely Calindy did not believe that this was the only reason! Even a brain-burned man, imprinted by one of those diabolical joy machines, was driven by more than passion. And Karl's main objective had been so awesome that, even now, Duncan could scarcely believe the picture that was slowly emerging from his sketchbook and the guarded portions of his Minisec.

Karl had had a dream—or a nightmare—and Duncan was the only man alive who even partially understood it. How utterly baffled and bewildered the Argus Committee must be! That thought gave Duncan a heady sense of power, though there were times when he wished that the burden of knowledge had reached him in some other way, or had not come at all. . . .

For power and happiness were incompatible. Karl had reached for both, and both had slipped through his fingers. How Duncan could profit by the lesson he did not yet know; but it would be with him for all the years to come.

But if happiness was perhaps unattainable, at least pleasure was not beyond his grasp, nor was it to be despised. For a few moments he could forget the affairs of state and turn his back upon an enigma far more profound than any of those that Calindy peddled to her clients.

It was strange how the wheel had gone full circle. Fifteen years ago, he and Karl had turned to each other in shared sorrow for the loss of Calindy. Now he and Calindy were mourning Karl.

And presently Duncan knew, though it could be only a faint shadow of that unassuageable hunger, something of the disappointment Karl must have experienced. How true it was that one could never quite recover the past. . . .

It was almost as good as he had hoped, but one thing was lacking.

Calindy no longer tasted of honey.

40

ARGUS PANOPTES

So they had the wrong Argus. If this were a time for humor, Duncan would have felt like laughing.

Colin had put him on the track, with one of his usual economical Telexes. It should not have been necessary to go all the way to Titan to check such an elementary point.

WHICH ARGUS DO YOU MEAN? Colin had asked. THERE WERE THREE.

A couple of minutes with the Comsole's ENCYCLOPEDIA section had confirmed this. As Ambassador Farrell had recalled, Argus was indeed Odysseus' faithful old watchdog, who had recognized his master when the wanderer returned from exile. The name was certainly appropriate for a secret intelligence organization, though now that Duncan had started making inquiries, it turned out that the Argus Committee was not as secret as it might have wished. Bernie Patras (needless to say) had heard of it; so had George Washington, who admitted with some embarrassment: "Of course they've asked me questions. But there's nothing to worry about."

Ivor Mandel'stahm had been more forthcoming— even a little sarcastic.

"I'm used to secrecy in my business, and I could teach these people a thing or two. They wouldn't have lasted five minutes under Stalin—or even the old czars. But I suppose they're necessary. Society will always need some warning system to spot malcontents before they can cause real trouble. I only doubt if *any* system will really work, when it's needed."

The second Argus had been the builder of Jason's mythical—or perhaps not so mythical—ship, the *Argo*. Duncan had never heard of the Golden Fleece, and the legend fascinated him. Argo would be a good name for a spaceship, he thought; but even this association had nothing to do with Karl Helmer's notes.

He wondered how Karl had ever come across the third Argus; his inquisitive mind had wandered down many byways of fantasy as well as science. And now that he had the key, Duncan understood why the project that had clearly dominated Karl's later years could have only one name—that of the all-seeing, multiple-eyed god, Argus Panoptes, who could look in every direction simultaneously. Unlike poor Cyclops, who had only a single line of vision . . .

There had been a delay of almost thirty hours before the legal computer on Titan could probate Karl's will. Then Armand Helmer reported that, as Duncan had hoped, it contained a list of obvious code words —presumably the keys to the Minisec's private memories.

Armand had been perfectly willing to Telex the codes, and Duncan had stopped him just in time.

Thanks to recent experience, the naïve young Makenzie who had arrived on Earth only a few weeks ago had now developed a mild paranoia. He hoped that it would not become obsessive, as sometimes seemed to be the case with Colin. Yet perhaps Colin was right. . . .

Not until the Argus Committee had, with some reluctance, handed over Karl's Minisec did Duncan allow Armand to radio the codes from Titan. Now it would not matter even if they were intercepted. He alone could use them.

In all, there were a dozen combinations, with identical formats. Each began with the G/T or GO TO instruction, followed by the six binary digits 101000. That might be an arbitrary number, but it was more likely to have some mnemonic association. A common trick was to use one's day or year of birth; Karl had been born in '40, and Duncan was not surprised at the answer when he converted 101000 to base ten —though he was a little disappointed at so obvious a subterfuge.

Yet the code was secure enough, for the chances were astronomically remote that anyone, in a random search, would ever hit upon the alphabetical sequences that followed. Though they were easy to remember—at least for a Titanian—they were safe from accidental triggering. Each was a name spelled backward—another old trick, but one which never lost its effectiveness.

The list began with G/T 101000 SAMIM and continued with G/T 101000 SYHTET, G/T 101000 SUNAJ, G/T 101000 ENOID, G/T 101000 EBEOHP. Then Karl grew tired of moons, for the next, unsurprisingly, was G/T 101000 DNAMRA. That would certainly be a personal message—and so, of course, would be G/T 101000 YDNILAC. . . .

There was no G/T 101000 NACNUD. Though it was unreasonable to have expected it, Duncan still felt a momentary flicker of regret.

A few more family names, but he scarcely noticed them, for his eyes had already caught the final entry: G/T 101000 SUGRA. The search was ended.

But it was not yet successful; there could be one last barrier. Most men had some secrets that they wished to preserve inviolate, even after death. It was still possible that unless these codes were used correctly, they might trigger an ERASE instruction.

Possible—but unlikely. Karl had clearly intended these memories to be released, or he would not have left the codes in his will, with no warning attached to them. Perhaps the wisest move would be to Telex Armand again, just in case Karl had left any further instructions that his distraught father had overlooked.

That would take hours, and it might still prove nothing. Duncan scanned the list again, looking for clues and finding none. The sequence 101000 *might* mean ERASE. He could speculate forever, and get nowhere.

There was no # or EXECUTE sign at the end of the sequences, but that proved nothing at all, for few people bothered to write down anything so obvious; nine times out of ten, it was omitted as understood. Yet one of the standard ways of canceling a secret ERASE order was to hit EXECUTE twice in quick succession. Another was to do so with a definite interval between the two keyings. Did Karl's omission have any significance, or was he merely following the usual convention?

The problem contained its own solution, though emotion rather than intelligence pointed the way to it. Duncan could see no flaw, though he explored every possibility that he could imagine. Then, feeling a faint trace of guilt, he tapped out G/T 101000 YDNILAC, pausing for a fraction of a second before he completed the sequence with #.

If he was wrong, Calindy would never know what she had lost. And though Karl's last message to her might have been erased, none of the other stored memories would be placed in hazard.

His fears were groundless. Duncan heard only the opening words—"Hello, Calindy, when you hear this, I shall be . . ."—before he hit the STOP key and the Minisec became silent again. He was after bigger game. Perhaps one day, when he had the time—no, *that* was a temptation he would be strong enough to resist. . . .

And so, in the secluded luxury of the Centennial Hotel, with a DO NOT DISTURB block on all visitors and incoming messages, Duncan keyed G/T 101000 SUGRA #. For two days he canceled his appointments, and had all meals sent up to his room. Occasionally, he made an outgoing call to check upon some technical point, but most of the time he was alone, communing with the dead.

Finally he was ready to meet the Argus Committee again, on his own terms. He understood everything —except, of course, the greatest mystery of all. How delighted Karl would have been if he had ever known about Golden Reef. . . .

The room had not changed, and perhaps the invisible audience was the same. But there was now no trace of the slightly uncertain Duncan Makenzie who, only a few days ago, had wondered if he should opt for diplomatic immunity.

They had accepted, without any dispute, his explanation of the word "Argus," though he did not imagine they were much impressed by his suddenly acquired knowledge of classical mythology. He could tell from the brief questioning that there was a certain disappointment; perhaps the Committee would have to find some other justification for its existence. (Was there really an organized underground movement on Terra, or was it merely a joke? This was hardly the right time to ask, though Duncan was tempted.)

Yet, ironically, there was a small conspiracy, in this very room—a conspiracy mutually agreed upon. The Committee had guessed that he now appreciated the significance of the name Argus to Terran security —and he knew that *it* knew. Each side understood the other perfectly, and the next item of business was quickly adopted.

"So what was Mr. Helmer's Argus?" asked the woman whom Duncan had tentatively placed up on the Moon. "And can you account for his odd behavior?"

Duncan opened the stained notebook to display

275

that astonishing full-page sketch which had so trans-
fixed him at its first revelation. Even now that he
knew its true scale, he could not think of it as anything except a drawing of a sea urchin. But *Diadema*
was only thirty or forty centimeters across; Argus
would be at least a thousand kilometers in diameter,
if Karl's analysis was right. And of that, Duncan
no longer had any doubt, though he could never give
his full reasons.

"Karl Helmer had a vision," he began. "I'll try to
pass it on as best I can, though this is not my field
of knowledge. But I knew his psychology, and perhaps I can make you understand what he was trying
to do."

You may be disappointed again, he told himself
—you may dismiss the whole concept as a crazy
scientist's delusion. But you'll be wrong; this could be
infinitely more important than some trivial conspiracy
threatening your tidy little world. . . .

"Karl was a scientist, who always hoped to make
some great discovery—but never did. Though he was
highly imaginative, even his wildest flights were always soundly based on reality. And he was ambitious. . . ."

"If it were so," murmured a quiet voice from the
air beside him, *"it was a grievous fault. And griev-
ously hath Caesar answered it.* Sorry—please continue."

The reference was unfamiliar to Duncan, and he
showed his annoyance at the interruption by pausing
for a few seconds.

"He was interested in everything—*too* many things,
perhaps—but his great passion was the still un-
solved CETI problem—communications with extraterrestrial intelligence. We used to argue about it for
hours when we were boys; I could never be quite sure
when he was completely serious, but I am now.

"Why have we never detected radio signals from the
advanced societies which must surely be out there in
space? Karl had many theories, but in the end he
settled on the simplest. It's not original, and I'm sure
you've heard it before.

"We ourselves broadcast radio signals for only

about a hundred years, roughly spanning the twentieth century. By the end of that time, we'd switched to cable and optical and satellite systems, concentrating all their power where it was needed, and not spilling most of it wastefully to the stars. This may well be true of all civilizations with a technology comparable to ours. They only pollute the universe with indiscriminate radio noise for a century or two—a very brief fraction of their entire history.

"So even if there are millions of advanced societies in this Galaxy, there may be barely a handful just where we were three hundred years ago—still splashing out radio waves in all directions. And the laws of probability make it most unlikely that any of these early electronic cultures will be within detection range; the nearest may be thousands of light-years away.

"But before we abandon the search, we should explore all the possibilities—and there's one that has never been investigated, because until now there was little we could do about it. For three centuries, we've been studying radio waves in the centimeter and meter bands. But we have almost completely ignored the very long waves—tens and hundreds of kilometers in length.

"Now of course there were several good reasons for this neglect. In the first case, it's impossible to study these waves on Earth—they don't get through the ionosphere, and so never reach the surface. You have to go into space to observe them.

"But for the *very longest* waves, it's no good merely going up to orbit, or to the other side of the Moon, where CYCLOPS II was built. You have to go halfway out to the limits of the Solar System.

"For the Sun has an ionosphere, just like the Earth's—except that it's billions of times larger. It absorbs all waves more than ten or twenty kilometers in length. If we want to detect these, we have to go out to Saturn.

"Such waves have been observed, but only on a few occasions. About forty years ago, a Solar Survey mission picked them up; it wasn't looking for radio waves at all, but was measuring magnetic fields between Jupiter and Saturn. It observed pulsations that must have been due to a radio burst at around fifteen kilohertz, corresponding to a wavelength of twenty kilometers. At first it was thought that they came from Jupiter, which is still full of electromagnetic surprises, but that source was eventually ruled out, and the origin is still a mystery.

"There have been half a dozen observations since then, all of them by instruments that were measuring something else. No one's looked for these waves directly; you'll see why in a moment.

"The most impressive example was detected ten years ago, in '66, by a team doing a survey of Iapetus. They obtained quite a long recording, rather sharply tuned at nine kilohertz—that's thirty-three kilometers wavelength. I thought you might like to hear it. . . ."

Duncan consulted a slip of paper and carefully tapped out a long sequence of numbers and letters on the Minisec. Into the anechoic stillness of that strange room, Karl spoke from the grave, in a brisk, businesslike voice.

"This is the complete recording, demodulated and speeded up sixty-four times, so that two hours is compressed into two minutes. Starting *now*."

Across twenty years of time, a childhood memory suddenly came back to Duncan. He recalled listening out into the Titanian night for that scream from the edge of space, wondering if it was indeed the voice of some monstrous beast, yet not really believing his own conjecture, even before Karl had demolished it. Now that fantasy returned, more powerful than ever.

This sound—or, rather, infrasound, for the original modulation was far below the range of human hearing—was like the slow beating of a giant heart, or the tolling of a bell so huge that a cathedral could be placed inside it, rather than the reverse. Or perhaps the waves of the sea, rolling forever in unvarying rhythm against some desolate shore, on a world so old that though Time still existed, Change was dead. . . .

The recording, as it always did, set Duncan's skin crawling and sent shivers down his spine. And it brought back yet another memory—the image of that mightiest of all Earth's creatures, leaping in power and glory into the sky above Golden Reef. Could there be beasts among the stars, to whom men would be as insignificant as the lice upon the whale?

It was a relief when the playback came to an end, and Karl's surprisingly unemotional voice commented: "Note the remarkably constant frequency—the original period is 132 seconds, not varying by more than point one percent. This implies a fairly high Q— say . . ."

"The rest is technical," said Duncan, switching off the recording. "I merely wanted you to hear what the Iapetus survey team brought home with them. And it's something that could *never* have been picked up inside the orbit of Saturn."

A voice he had not heard before—young, rather self-assured—came out of the air behind him.

"But this is all old material, familiar to everyone in the field. Sandemann and Koralski showed that those signals were almost certainly relaxation oscillations, probably in a plasma cloud near one of Saturn's Trojan points."

Duncan felt his façade of instant expertise rapidly crumbling; he should have guessed that there would be someone in his audience who would know far more about this subject than he did—and possibly, for that matter, even than Karl.

"I'm not competent to discuss that," he replied. "I'm only reporting Dr. Helmer's opinions. He believed that there was a whole new science here, waiting to be opened up. After all, every time we have explored some new region of the spectrum, it's led to astonishing and *totally unexpected* discoveries. Helmer was convinced that this would happen again.

"But to study these gigantic waves—up to a million times longer than those observed in classical radio astronomy—we must use correspondingly gigantic antenna systems. Both to collect them—because they're very weak—and to determine the directions from which they come.

"*This* was Karl Helmer's Argus. His records and sketches contain quite detailed designs. I leave it to others to say how practical they are.

"Argus would look in all directions simultaneously, like the great missile-tracking radars of the twentieth century. It would be the three-dimensional equivalent of CYCLOPS—and several hundred times larger, because it would need to be at least a thousand kilometers in diameter. Preferably ten thousand, to get good resolving power at these ultralow frequencies.

"Yet it need contain much less material than CYCLOPS, because it would be built in Deep Space, under weightless conditions. Helmer chose as its location the satellite Mnemosyne, outermost of Saturn's moons, and it seems a very logical choice. In fact the only choice . . .

"For Mnemosyne is twenty million kilometers from Saturn, well clear of the planet's own feeble ionosphere, and also far enough out for its tidal forces to be negligible. But most important of all, it has almost zero rotation. Only a modest amount of rocket power would cancel its spin entirely. Mnemosyne would then be the only body in the universe with *no* rotation at all, and Helmer suggests that it might be an ideal laboratory for various cosmological experiments."

"Such as a test of Mach's principle," interrupted that confident young voice.

"Yes," agreed Duncan, now more than ever impressed by his unknown critic. "That was one possibility he mentioned. But back to Argus . . .

"Mnemosyne would serve as the core or nucleus of the array. Thousands of elements—little more than stiff wires—would radiate from it, like—like the spines of a sea urchin. Thus it could comb the entire sky for signals. And incidentally, the temperature out around Mnemosyne is so low that cheap superconductors could be used, enormously increasing the efficiency of the system.

"I won't get involved in the details of switching and phasing that would allow Argus to swing its antenna spines electrically—without moving them *physically*—so that it could concentrate on any particular region of the sky. All this, and a great deal more, Helmer had worked out in his notes, using techniques evolved with CYCLOPS and other radio telescopes.

"You may wonder—as I did—how he ever hoped to get such a gigantic project started. He planned a simple demonstration, which he was certain would provide enough evidence to prove his theories.

"He was going to launch two equal, massive weights in exactly opposite directions, each towing a fine wire, several hundred kilometers long. When the wires had been completely deployed, the weights would be jettisoned—and he would have a simple dipole antenna, perhaps a thousand kilometers long. He hoped that he could persuade the Solar Survey to do the experiment, which would be quite cheap, and would certainly produce *some* results of value. Then he was going to follow it up with more ambitious schemes, shooting wires out at right angles, and so on. . . .

"But I think I've said enough to let you judge for yourselves. There's much more I've not had time to transcribe. I hope you can be patient, at least until after the Centennial. For that, as you are well aware, is what I really came for—and I have work to do. . . ."

"Thank you for your moral support, Bob," said Duncan when he and His Excellency the Ambassador for Titan had emerged into the bright sunlight of Virginia Avenue.

"I never said a word. I was completely out of my depth. And I kept hoping that someone would put the question I'm still anxious to see answered."

"What's that?" Duncan asked suspiciously.

"How did Helmer think he could get away with it?"

"Oh, *that,*" said Duncan, mildly disappointed; this aspect of the matter seemed so unimportant now. "I think I understand his strategy. Four years ago, when we turned down his project for a simple long-wave detecting system—because we couldn't afford it, and he wouldn't say what he was *really* driving at—he decided he'd have to go directly to Earth and convince the top scientists there. That meant acquiring funds, somehow. I'm sure he hoped that he'd be vindicated so quickly that we'd forget any minor infraction of the exchange laws. It was a gamble, of course, but he felt it so important that he was prepared to take risks."

"Hmm," said the Ambassador, obviously not too impressed. "I know that Helmer was a friend of yours, and I don't want to speak harshly of him. But wouldn't it be fair to call him a scientific genius —and a criminal psychopath?"

Rather to his surprise, Duncan found himself bristling at this description. Yet he had to admit it contained some truth. One of the attributes of the psychopath—a term still popular among laymen, despite three hundred years of professional attempts to eradicate it—was a moral blindness to any interests but his own. Of course, Karl could always produce a very convincing argument that *his* interests were for the best of all concerned. The Makenzies, Duncan realized with some embarrassment, were also skilled at this kind of exercise.

"If there were irrational elements in Karl's behavior, they were at least partly due to a breakdown he had fifteen years ago. But that never affected his scientific judgment; everyone I've spoken to agrees that Argus is sound."

"I don't doubt it—but why is it *important?*"

"I'd hoped," said Duncan mildly, "that I'd made that clear to our invisible friends."

And I believe I have, he told himself, to at least one of them. His most penetrating questioner was certainly one of Terra's top radio astronomers. *He* would understand, and only a few allies at that level were necessary. Duncan was certain that someday they would meet again, this time eye to eye, and with a pointed lack of reference to any prior encounter.

"As to why it's important, Bob, I'll tell you something that I didn't mention to the Committee, and which I'm sure Karl never considered, because he was too engrossed in his own affairs. Do you realize what a project like Argus would do to the Titan economy? It would bring us billions and make us the scientific hub of the Solar System. It might even go a long way to solve our financial problems, when the demand for hydrogen starts to drop in the '80's."

"I appreciate that," Farrell answered dryly, "especially as my taxes will go toward it. But let nothing interfere with the March of Science."

Duncan laughed sympathetically. He liked Bob Farrell, and he had been extremely helpful. But he was less and less sure of the Ambassador's loyalties, and it might soon be time to find a replacement. Unfortunately, it would again have to be a Terran, because of this infernal gravity; but that was a problem Titan would always have to live with.

He could certainly never tell his own ambassador, still less the Argus Committee, why Karl's brainchild might be so vital to the human race. There were speculations in that Minisec—luckily, there was no hint of them in the sketchbook—which had best not be published for many years, until the project had proved itself.

Karl had been right so often in the past, seizing on truths beyond all bounds of logic and reason, that Duncan felt sure that this last awesome intuition was also correct. Or if it was not, the truth was even stranger; in any event, it was a truth that must be learned. Though the knowledge might be overwhelming, the price of ignorance could be—extinction.

Here on the streets of this beautiful city, steeped in sunlight and in history, it was hard to take Karl's final comments seriously, as he speculated about the origin of those mysterious waves. And surely even Karl did not *really* believe all the thoughts he had spoken into the secret memory of his Minisec, during the long voyage to Earth. . . .

But he was diabolically persuasive, and his arguments had an irresistible logic and momentum of their own. Even if he did not believe all his own conjectures, he might still be right.

"Item one," he had murmured to himself (it must have been hard to get privacy on that freighter, and Duncan could sometimes hear the noises of the ship, the movements of the other crew members), "these kilohertz waves have a limited range because of interstellar absorption. They would not normally be able to pass from one star to another, unless plasma clouds act as waveguides, channeling them over greater distances. So their origin *must* be close to the Solar System.

"My calculations all point to a source—or sources —at about a tenth of a light-year from the Sun. Only a fortieth of the way to Alpha Centauri, but two hundred times the distance of Pluto . . . No man's land—the edge of the wilderness between the stars. But that's *exactly* where the comets are born, in a great, invisible shell surrounding the Solar System. There's enough material out there for a trillion of those strange objects, orbiting in a cosmic freezer.

"What's going on, in those huge clouds of hydrogen and helium and all the other elements? There's not much energy—but there may be enough. And where there's matter and energy—and Time—sooner or later there's organization.

"Call them Star Beasts. Would they be alive? No —that word doesn't apply. Let's just say—'Organized systems.' They'd be hundreds or thousands of kilometers across, and they might live—I mean, maintain their individual identity—for millions of years.

"That's a thought. The comets that we observe— are they the corpses of Star Beasts, sent sunward for cremation? Or executed criminals? I'm being ridiculously anthropomorphic—but what else can I be?

"And are they intelligent? What does *that* word mean? Are ants intelligent—are the cells of the human body intelligent? Do all the Star Beasts surrounding the Solar System make a single entity—and does It know about us? Or does It care?

"Perhaps the Sun keeps them at bay, as in ancient times the campfire kept off the wolves and saber-toothed tigers. But we are already a long way from the Sun, and sooner or later we will meet them. The more we learn, the better.

"And there's one question I'm almost afraid to think about. Are they gods? OR ARE THEY EATERS OF GODS?"

41

INDEPENDENCE DAY

Extract from the *Congressional Record* for 2276 July 4. Address by the Honorable Duncan Makenzie, Special Assistant to the Chief Administrator, Republic of Titan.

Mr. Speaker, Members of Congress, Distinguished Guests—let me first express my deep gratitude to the Centennial Committee, whose generosity made possible my visit to Earth and to these United States. I bring greetings to all of you from Titan, largest of Saturn's many moons—and the most distant world yet occupied by mankind.

Five hundred years ago this land was also a frontier—not only geographically but politically. Your ancestors, less than twenty generations in the past, created the first democratic constitution that really worked—and that still works today, on worlds that they could not have imagined in their wildest dreams.

During these celebrations, many have spoken of the legacy that the founders of the Republic left us on that day, half a thousand years ago. But there have been four Centennials since then; I would like to look briefly at each of them, to see what lessons they have for us.

At the first, in 1876, the United States was still recovering from a disastrous Civil War. Yet it was also laying the foundations of the technological revolution that would soon transform the Earth. Perhaps it is no coincidence that in the very year of the first Centennial, this country brought forth the invention which really began the conquest of space.

For in 1876, Alexander Graham Bell made the first practical telephone. We take electronic communications so utterly for granted that we cannot imagine a society without them; we would be deaf and dumb if these extensions of our senses were suddenly removed. So let us remember that just four hundred years ago, the telephone began the abolition of space —at least upon *this* planet.

A century later, in 1976, that process had almost finished—and the conquest of interplanetary space was about to begin. By that time, the first man had already reached the Moon, using techniques which today seem unbelievably primitive. Although all historians now agree that the Apollo Project marked the United States's supreme achievement, and its greatest moment of triumph, it was inspired by political motives that seem ludicrous—indeed, incomprehensible —to our modern minds. And it is no reflection on those first engineers and astronauts that their brilliant pioneering effort was a technological dead end, and that serious space travel did not begin for several decades, with much more advanced vehicles and propulsion systems.

A century later, in 2076, all the tools needed to open up the planets were ready to hand. Long-duration life-support systems had been perfected; after the initial disasters, the fusion drive had been tamed. But humanity was exhausted by the effort of global rebuilding following the Time of Troubles, and in the aftermath of the Population Crash there was little enthusiasm for the colonization of new worlds.

Despite these problems, mankind had set its feet irrevocably on the road to the stars. During the twenty-first century, the Lunar Base became self-supporting, the Mars Colony was established, and we had secured a bridgehead on Mercury. Venus and the Gas Giants defied us—as indeed they still do— but we had visited all the larger moons and asteroids of the Solar System.

By 2176, just a hundred years ago, a substantial fraction of the human race was no longer Earthborn. For the first time we had the assurance that whatever happened to the mother world, our cultural heritage would not be lost. It was secure until the death of the Sun—and perhaps beyond. . . .

The century that lies behind us has been one of consolidation, rather than of fresh discovery. I am proud that my world has played a major role in this process, for without the easily accessible hydrogen of the Titanian atmosphere, travel between the planets would still be exorbitantly expensive.

Now the old question arises: Where do we go from here? The stars are as remote as ever; our first probes, after two centuries of travel, have yet to reach Proxima Centauri, the Sun's closest neighbor. Though our telescopes can now see to the limits of space, no man has yet traveled beyond Pluto. And we have *still* to set foot on far Persephone, which we could have reached at any time during the last hundred years. . . .

Is it true, as many have suggested, that the frontier has again closed? Men have believed that before, and always they have been wrong. We can laugh now at those early-twentieth-century pessimists who lamented that there were no more worlds to discover—at the very moment when Goddard and Korolev and von Braun were playing with their first primitive rockets. And earlier still, just before Columbus opened the way to *this* continent, it must have seemed to the peoples of Europe that the future could hold nothing to match the splendors of the past.

I do not believe that we have come to the end of History, and that what lies ahead is only an elaboration and extension of our present powers, on planets already discovered. Yet it cannot be denied that this feeling is now widespread and makes itself apparent in many ways. There is an unhealthy preoccupation with the past, and an attempt to reconstruct or relive it. Not, I hasten to add, that this is *always* bad —what we are doing now proves that it is not.

We should respect the past, but not worship it. While we look back upon the four Centennials that lie behind us, we should think also of those that will be celebrated in the years to come. What of 2376, 2476 . . . 2776, a full thousand years after the birth of the Republic? How will the people of those days remember us? *We* remember the United States chiefly by Apollo; can we bequeath any comparable achievement to the ages ahead?

There are many problems still to be solved, on all the planets. Unhappiness, disease—even poverty —still exist. We are still far from Utopia, and we may never achieve it. But we know that all these problems *can* be solved, with the tools that we already possess. No pioneering, no great discoveries, are necessary here. Now that the worst evils of the past have been eliminated, we can look elsewhere, with a clear conscience, for new tasks to challenge the mind and inspire the spirit.

Civilization needs long-range goals. Once, the Solar System provided them, but now we must look beyond. I am not speaking of *manned* travel to the stars, which may still lie centuries ahead. What I refer to is the quest for intelligence in the universe, which was begun with such high hopes more than three centuries ago—and has not yet succeeded.

You are all familiar with CYCLOPS, the largest radio telescope on Earth. That was built primarily to search for evidence of advanced civilizations. It transformed astronomy; but despite many false alarms, it never detected a single intelligent message from the stars. This failure has done much to turn men's minds inward from the greater universe, to concentrate their energies upon the tiny oasis of the Solar System. . . .

Could it be that we are looking in the wrong place? The wrong place, that is, in the enormously wide spectrum of radiations that travel between the stars.

All our radio telescopes have searched the short waves—centimeters, or at most, meters—in length. But what of the long and ultralong waves—not only kilometers but even *megameters* from crest to crest? Radio waves of frequencies so low that they would sound like musical notes in our ears could detect them.

We know that such waves exist, but we have never been able to study them, here on Earth. They are blocked, far out in the fringes of the Solar System, by the gale of electrons that blows forever from the Sun. To know what the universe is saying with these vast, slow undulations, we must build radio telescopes of enormous size, beyond the limits of the Sun's own billion-kilometer-deep ionosphere—that is, at least as far out as the orbit of Saturn. For the first time, this is now possible. For the first time, there are real incentives for doing so. . . .

We tend to judge the universe by our own physical size and our own time scale; it seems natural for us to work with waves that we could span with our arms, or even with our fingertips. But the cosmos is not built to these dimensions; nor, perhaps, are all the entities that dwell among the stars.

These giant radio waves are more commensurate with the scale of the Milky Way, and their slow vibrations are a better measure of its eon-long Galactic Year. They may have much to tell us when we begin to decipher their messages.

How those scientist-statesmen Franklin and Jefferson would have welcomed such a project! They would have grasped its scope, if not its technology—for they were interested in every branch of knowledge between heaven and Earth.

The problems they faced, five hundred years ago, will never rise again. The age of conflict between nations is over. But we have other challenges, which may yet tax us to the utmost. Let us be thankful that the universe can always provide great goals beyond ourselves, and enterprises to which we can pledge our Lives, our Fortunes, and our sacred Honor.

Duncan Makenzie closed the beautifully designed souvenir book—a masterpiece of the printer's art, such as had not been seen for centuries and might never be seen again. Only five hundred copies had been produced—one for every year. He would carry his back in triumph to Titan, where for the rest of his life it would be among his most cherished possessions.

Many people had complimented him on his speech, enshrined forever in these pages—and, much more accessibly, in library memories and information banks throughout the Solar System. Yet he had felt em-

289

barrassed to receive those plaudits, for in his heart he knew that he had not earned them. The Duncan of a few weeks ago could never have conceived that address; he was little more than a medium, passing on a message from the dead. The words were his, but all the thoughts were Karl's.

How astonished, he told himself wryly, all his friends on Titan must have been, when they watched the ceremony! Perhaps it had been slightly inappropriate to use such a forum as this for what might be considered self-serving propaganda—even special pleading on behalf of his own world. But Duncan had a clear conscience, and as yet there had been no criticism on this score. Even those who were baffled by his thesis had been grateful for the excitement he had injected into all the routine formalities.

And even if his speech was only a seven-day wonder to the general public, it would not be forgotten. He had planted a seed; one day it would grow—on barren Mnemosyne.

Meanwhile, there was a slight practical problem, though it was not yet urgent. This splendid volume, with its thick vellum, and its tooled leather binding, weighed about five kilograms.

The Makenzies hated waste and extravagance. It would be pleasant to have the book on the voyage home, but excess baggage to Titan was a hundred solars a kilo. . . .

It would have to go back by slow boat, on one of the empty tankers—UNACCOMPANIED FREIGHT, MAY BE STOWED IN VACUUM. . . .

42

THE MIRROR OF THE SEA

Dr. Yehudi ben Mohammed did not look as if he belonged in a modern hospital, surrounded by flickering life-function displays, Comsole read-outs, whispering voices from hidden speakers, and all the aseptic technology of life and death. In his spotless white robes, with the double circlet of gold cord around his headdress, he should have been holding court in a desert tent, or scanning the horizon from the back of his camel for the first glimpse of an oasis.

Duncan remembered how one of the younger doctors had commented, during his first visit: "Sometimes I think El Hadj believes he's a reincarnation of Saladin *and* Lawrence of Arabia." Although Duncan did not understand the full flavor of the references, this was obviously said more in affectionate jest than in criticism. Did the surgeon, he wondered, wear those robes in the operating theater? They would not be inappropriate there; and certainly they did not interfere with the feline grace of his movements.

"I'm glad," said Dr. Yehudi, toying with the jeweled dagger on his elaborately inlaid desk—the two touches of antiquity in an otherwise late-twenty-third-century environment—"that you've finally made up your mind. The—ah—delay has caused certain problems, but we've overcome them. We now have four perfectly viable embryos, and the first will be transplanted in a week. The others will be kept as backups, in case of a rejection—though that is now very rare."

And what will happen to the unwanted three? Duncan asked himself, and shied away from the answer. One human being had been created who would never otherwise have existed. *That* was the positive side;

better to forget the three ghosts who for a brief while had hovered on the borders of reality. Yet it was hard to be coldly logical in matters like this. As he stared across the intricate arabesques, Duncan wondered at the psychology of the calm and elegant figure whose skillful hands had controlled so many destinies. In their own small way, on their own little world, the Makenzies had played at God; but *this* was something beyond his understanding.

Of course, one could always take refuge in the cold mathematics of reproduction. Old Mother Nature had not the slightest regard for human ethics or feelings. In the course of a lifetime, every man generated enough spermatozoa to populate the entire Solar System, many times over—and all but two or three of that potential multitude were doomed. Had anyone ever gone mad by visualizing each ejaculation as a hundred million murders? Quite possibly; no wonder that the adherents of some old religions had refused to look through the microscope. . . .

There were moral obligations and uncertainties behind every act. In the long run, a man could only obey the promptings of that mysterious entity called Conscience and hope that the outcome would not be too disastrous. Not, of course, that one could ever know the *final* results of any actions.

Strange, thought Duncan, how he had resolved the doubts that had assailed him when he first came to the island. He had learned to take the broader view, and to place the hopes and aspirations of the Makenzies in a wider context. Above all, he had seen the dangers of overreaching ambition; but the lesson of Karl's fate was still ambiguous and would give him cause to wonder all his life.

With a mild sense of shock, Duncan realized that he had already signed the legal documents and was returning them to Dr. Yehudi. No matter; he had read them carefully and knew his responsibilities. "I, Duncan Makenzie, resident of the satellite Titan presently in orbit around the planet Saturn" (when did the lawyers think it was going to run away?) "do hereby accept guardianship of one cloned male

292

child, identified by the chromosome chart herewith attached, and will to the best of my ability. . . ." etc., etc., etc. Perhaps the world would have been a better place if the parents of normally conceived children had been forced to sign such a contract. This thought, however, was some hundred billion births too late.

The surgeon flowed upward to his full commanding two meters in a gesture of dismissal which, from anyone else, would have seemed slightly discourteous. But not here, for El Hadj had much on his mind. All the while they had been talking, his eyes had seldom strayed from the pulsing lines of life and death on the read-outs that covered almost one whole wall of his office.

In the main hall of the Administration Building, Duncan paused for a moment before the giant, slowly rotating DNA helix which dominated the entrance. As his gaze roamed along the spokes of the twisted ladder, contemplating its all-but-infinite possibilities, he could not help thinking again of the pentominoes that Grandma Ellen had set out before him years ago. There were only twelve of those shapes—yet it would take the lifetime of the universe to exhaust their possibilities. And here was no mere dozen, but billions upon billions of locations to be filled by the letters of the genetic code. The total number of combinations was *not* one to stagger the mind—because there was no way whatsoever in which the mind could grasp even the faintest conception of it. The number of electrons required to pack the entire cosmos solid from end to end was virtually zero in comparison.

Duncan stepped out into the blazing sunlight, waited for his dark glasses to adjust themselves, and set off in search of Dr. Todd, guide and friend of his previous visit. He would not be leaving for another four hours, and there was one major item of business still to be settled.

Luckily, as Sweeney Todd explained, there was no need to go out to the Reef.

"I can't imagine why you're interested in those ugly beasts. But you'll find some on a patch of dead coral at the end of that groin; not much else will live there. The water's only a meter deep—you won't even need flippers, just a strong pair of shoes. If you *do* step on a stonefish, your screams will bring us in time to save your life—though you may wish we hadn't."

That was not very encouraging, but ten minutes later Duncan was cautiously walking out into the shallows, bent double as he peered through his borrowed face mask.

There was none of the beauty here that he had seen on the approach to Golden Reef. The water was crystal clear, but the sea bed was a submarine desert. It was mostly white sand, mingled with broken pieces of coral, like the bleached bones of tiny animals. A few small, drably colored fish were swimming around, and others stared at him with anxious, unfriendly eyes from little burrows in the sand. Once, a brilliantly blue creature like a flattened eel came darting at him and, to his great surprise, gave him a painful nip before he chased it away. It was every bit of three centimeters long, and Duncan, who had never heard of cleaning symbiosis, worried about poison for a few minutes. However, he felt no pangs of imminent dissolution, so pushed his way onward through the tepid water.

The concrete groin—part of the island's defense against the ceaseless erosion of the waves—stretched out for a hundred meters from the shore and then disappeared beneath the surface. Near its seaward end, Duncan came across a pile of jumbled rocks, perhaps hurled up by some storm. They must have been here for many years, for they were cemented together with barnacles and small, jagged oysters. Among their caves and crevices, Duncan found what he was seeking.

Each sea urchin appeared to have hollowed out its own cavity in the hard rock; Duncan could not imagine how the creatures had performed this remarkable feat of burrowing. Anchored securely in place, with only a bristling frieze of black spines exposed to the outer world, they were invulnerable to all enemies—except Man. But Duncan wished them no harm, and this time had not even brought a knife. He had seen enough of death, and his sole purpose now was to confirm—or refute—the impression that had haunted him ever since he had set eyes on that drawing in Karl's notebook.

Once again, the long black spines started to swing slowly toward his shadow. These primitive creatures, despite their apparent lack of sense organs, knew that he was there, and reacted to his presence. They were scanning their little universe, as Argus would search the stars. . . .

Of course, there would be no actual physical movement of the Argus antennas—that was unnecessary, and would be impossible with such fragile, thousand-kilometer-long structures. Yet their electronic sweeping of the skies would have an uncanny parallel with *Diadema's* protective reaction. If some planet-sized monster, which used ultralong radio waves for vision, could observe the Argus system at work, what it "saw" would be not unlike this humble reef dweller.

For a moment, Duncan had a curious fantasy. He imagined that he was such a monster, observing Argus in silhouette against the background radio glow of the Galaxy. There would be hundreds of thin black lines, radiating out from a central point—most of them stationary, but some of them waving slowly back and forth, as if responding to a shadow from the stars.

Yet it was hard to realize that even if Argus was built, no human eye could ever see it in its entirety. The structure would be so huge that its slender rods and wires would be totally invisible from any distance. Perhaps, as Karl had suggested in his notes, there would be warning lights dotted all over the millions of square kilometers of the spherical surface and strung along the six principle axes. To an approaching spaceship, it would look like some glittering Star Day ornament.

Or—and this was more appropriate—a discarded toy from the nursery of the Gods. . .

Toward evening, while he was waiting for the shuttle back to the mainland, Duncan found a secluded corner of the coffeeshop-cum-bar which overlooked

295

the lagoon. He sat there thoughtfully, sipping from time to time at a Terran drink he had discovered—something called a Tom Collins. It was a bad idea, acquiring vices which could not be exported to Titan; on the other hand, it could equally well be argued that it was foolish not to enjoy the unique pleasures of Earth, even if one had to relinquish them all too soon.

There was also endless enjoyment in watching the play of wind over the water protected by the barrier of the inner reef. Some stretches were absolutely flat, reflecting the blue of the unclouded sky as if in a flawless mirror. Yet other areas, apparently no different, were continually quivering so that not for a moment was the surface still; it was crossed and criss-crossed by innumerable tiny wavelets, no more than a centimeter in height. Presumably some relationship between the varying depth of the lagoon and the velocity of the wind was responsible for the phenomenon, quite unlike anything that Duncan had ever before seen. No matter what the explanation, it was enchantingly beautiful, for the countless reflections of the sun in the dancing water created sparkling patterns that seemed to move forever down the wind, yet remained always in the same spot.

Duncan had never been hypnotized, nor had he experienced more than a few of the nine states of consciousness between full awareness and profound sleep. The alcohol might have helped, but the scintillating sea was undoubtedly the main factor in producing his present mood. He was completely alert—indeed, his mind seemed to be working with unusual clarity—but he no longer felt bound by the laws of logic that had controlled all his life. It was almost as if he was in one of those dreams where the most fantastic things can happen, and are accepted as matter-of-fact, everyday occurrences.

He knew that he was facing a mystery, of the sort that was anathema to the reputedly hard-headed Makenzies. Here was something that he could never explain to Malcolm and Colin; they would not laugh at him—or so he hoped—but they would never take him seriously.

Besides, it was so utterly trivial. He had not been vouchsafed some blinding revelation, like an ancient prophet receiving the word of God. All that had happened was that he had come across the same very unusual shape in two quite independent contexts; it might have been a mere coincidence, and the sense of *déjà vu* pure self-delusion. That was the simple, logical answer, which would certainly satisfy everyone else.

It would never satisfy Duncan. He had experienced that indescribable shock a man may know only once in a lifetime, when he is in the presence of the transcendental and feels the sure foundations of his world and his philosophy trembling beneath his feet.

When he saw that careful drawing in Karl's sketchbook, Duncan had recognized it at once. But now it seemed to him that the recognition came not only from the past, but also from the future. It was as if he had caught a momentary glimpse in the Mirror of Time, reflecting something that had not yet occurred—and something that must be awesomely important for it to have succeeded in reversing the flow of causality.

Project Argus was part of the destiny of mankind; of this, Duncan was now sure beyond any need for rational proof. But whether it would be beneficent was another question. All knowledge was a two-edged sword, and it might well be that any messages from the stars would not be to the liking of the human race. Duncan remembered the dying cries of the sea urchin he had killed, out there on Golden Reef. Were those faint but sinister crepitations wholly meaningless—an accidental by-product? Or did they have some more profound significance? His instincts gave him not the slightest clue, one way or the other.

But it was an act of faith to Duncan, and to those he had worked with all his life, that it was cowardice not to face the truth, whatever it might be and wherever it might lead. If the time was coming for mankind to face the powers behind the stars, so be it. *He* had no doubts. All he felt now was a calm content-

Part IV

Titan

43

HOMECOMING

It was over. All the good-byes had been said to crew and passengers, all the formalities had been completed, everything he had brought from Earth was already moving along the conveyor belt. Everything, that is, except for the most important gift of all.

He could walk through that door marked TITAN CITIZENS, and he would be home. Already he had forgotten the crippling gravity of Earth; that—and so much else—was fading into the past like a dissolving dream. This was where he belonged and where his life's work would be done. He would never again go sunward, though he knew there would be times when some remembered beauty of the mother world would drive a dagger into his heart.

The family must be waiting, there in the reception lounge; and now, with only seconds before the moment of reunion, Duncan felt a reluctance to face the whole Makenzie clan. He let the other travelers go hurrying past him, while he stood irresolutely, trying to pluck up his courage and clutching his precious bundle awkwardly to his chest. Then he moved forward, under the archway, and out onto the ramp.

There were so many of them! Malcolm and Colin, of course, Marissa, more beautiful and desirable than even in his most restless dreams, now free of Calindy forever; Clyde and Carline—could she really have grown so much, in so short a time? And at least twenty nephews and nieces whose names he knew as well as his own, but just couldn't recall at the moment.

No—it was impossible! But there she was, standing a little apart from the others, leaning heavily on her cane, yet otherwise completely unaltered since he had last seen her on the cliffs of Loch Hellbrew. Much else had changed indeed if Grandma Ellen had returned to Oasis for the first time in fifty years.

As she saw Duncan's astonished gaze, she gave a barely perceptible smile. It was more than a greeting; it was a signal of reassurance. *She already knows,* thought Duncan. She knows and approves. When the full fury of the Makenzies breaks upon my head I can rely on her. . . .

There flashed into his mind an old Terran phrase, whose origin he had long ago forgotten: the Moment of Truth. Well, here it was—

They all crowded eagerly around him as he drew back the shawl. For an instant only he felt regret; perhaps he should have given some warning. No, it was better this way. Now they would learn that he was his own man at last, no longer a pawn of others—however much he might owe to them, however much he might be *part* of them.

The child was still sleeping, but normally now, not in the electronic trance that had protected it on the long voyage from Earth. Suddenly it threw out a chubby arm, and tiny fingers gripped Duncan's hand with surprising strength. They looked like the pale white tentacles of a sea anemone against the dark brown of Duncan's skin.

The little head was still empty even of dreams, and the face was as void and formless as that of any month-old baby. But already the smooth, pink scalp bore an unmistakable trace of hair—the golden hair that would soon bring back to Titan the lost glories of the distant Sun.

ACKNOWLEDGMENTS AND NOTES

My first thanks should go to Truman Talley, who in the early '50's made what was then (and for that matter still is) a most generous offer for this book, on the strength of the title and one conversation. I have often wished that I could remember what I said then; it might have saved me much trouble, twenty years later. I now have no idea if this book bears the slightest resemblance to that early concept, but "Mac's" initial encouragement kept me from abandoning it.

Like many other addicts, I was introduced to polyominoes by Martin Gardner's *Scientific American Book of Mathematical Puzzles and Diversions,* which, however, fiendishly refrains from giving the solution to the 20 X 3 rectangle. In his definitive book *Polyominoes,* Solomon W. Golomb takes mercy on his readers. In the hope of preventing a few nervous breakdowns, I reproduce his answer herewith:

U X P I L N F T W Y Z V

Anyone who wishes to construct this rectangle from the twelve pentominoes should have no difficulty in matching them with the letters they (sometimes approximately) resemble. It is easy to see that the second of the (only) two solutions is obtained by rotating a seven-element central portion.

Dr. Golomb, who is now professor of Electrical Engineering and Mathematics at the University of Southern California, has also invented an ingenious game called *Pentominoes®* (distributed in North America by Hallmark Cards and in Europe by Zimpfer Puzzles). It has more openings than chess. In an earlier version of *2001: A Space Odyssey,* Stanley Kubrick shot Hal playing this game against the astronauts.

I am indebted to Dr. Robert Forward of the Hughes Research Laboratory, Malibu, for introducing me to the fascinating concept of mini black holes, and for making such encouraging noises about the somewhat outrageous propulsion system of S. S. *Sirius* that I am almost inclined to patent it. . . .

Dr. Grote Reber, the father of radio astronomy and builder of the world's first radio telescope, started me thinking about the extent of the heliosphere and its possible consequences. I am grateful for his comments on cutoff frequencies, but he is in no way responsible for my wilder extrapolations of his ideas. Dr. Adrian Webster, of Cavendish Laboratory's Mullard Radio Astronomy Observatory, also gave much vital information, and he too is not to be blamed for my use of it.

I am especially indebted to Dr. Bernard Oliver, vice-president and director of research of Hewlett-Packard, not only for hospitality at Palo Alto but also for an advance copy of the Project CYCLOPS Design Study (NASA/Ames CR 114445), which he directed. And I hope Barney will forgive me for the assumption—which in fact I regard as highly improbable—that CYCLOPS would *not* have detected intelligent signals, even after two hundred years of operation.

Indignant antenna designers who feel that Argus would not work as specified are invited to contemplate ABM search radars, and to Think Big. All I will say in self-defense is that the Argus elements would be superconducting, active, and divided into many switchable subsections, perhaps with cross-connections between the "spines." I leave minor practical details (as in the case of the Asymptotic Drive) as an exercise for the student.

The "exasperated" remark in Chapter 21 was made to me at a NASA conference by Professor Neil Armstrong in July 1970. I hope it is the last word on some famous first words.

I am deeply grateful to my old friend William MacQuitty, producer of *A Night to Remember,* for much material concerning the *Titanic*—including the menu in Chapter 27. Collectors of unlikely coincidences may be interested to know that just *three hours* after I had decided to incorporate it in the text, I read in the May 1974 *Skin Diver* that the Titanic Enthusiasts of America had served this menu at their Annual Dinner. . . .

Some readers may feel that the coincidences—or "correspondences"—that play a key part in this story are too unlikely to be plausible. But they were, in fact, suggested by far more preposterous events in my own life; and anyone who doubts that this sort of thing *can* happen is referred to Arthur Koestler's *The Roots of Coincidence.* I read this fascinating book only after completing *Imperial Earth,* though that fact itself now seems somewhat improbable to me.

Even more improbable is the fact that when, on July 24, 1975, I appeared as a witness before the House of Representatives Subcommittee on Space Science (in the very building libeled and demolished in Chapter 33!), I was able to quote extensively from Duncan's address to Congress in Chapter 41. Thus the House of Representatives' hearings now contain extracts from the *Congressional Record* for July 4, 2276, which should cause confusion among future historians.

The curious acoustic behavior of the spiny sea urchin, *Diadema setosum,* was observed by me on Unawatuna Reef, off the south coast of Sri Lanka. I have never seen this recorded elsewhere, so it may be my one original contribution to marine biology.

Finally, my speculations about conditions on Titan were triggered by a series of papers that Dr. Carl Sagan was good enough to send me. Needless to say, I am also indebted to Carl for many other stimulating ideas, which any properly designed universe would be very foolish to ignore. "For if not true, they are well imagined. . . ."

ARTHUR C. CLARKE

Cinnamon Gardens, Colombo
January 1974—January 1975

ADDITIONAL NOTE

Several expert readers have accused me of grave error by assuming that Malcolm would pass on the Makenzie defect to his clones. Though I was well aware of this problem (and tried to avoid it by being carefully unspecific) I did not go into the matter as seriously as I should have done. I am still hoping that some ingenious geneticist will be able to contrive a solution; unfortunately, I doubt if I will be able to understand it.

Meanwhile, for those biologists who refuse to be placated, I can only fall back upon what is known in the trade as Bradbury's Defense, viz:

One dreadful boy ran up to me and said:
"That book of yours, *The Martian Chronicles?*"
"Yes," I said.
"On page 92, where you have the moons of Mars rising in the East?"
"Yeah," I said.
"Nah," he said.
So I hit him.*

ARTHUR C. CLARKE

Colombo, June 1976

---

* *Mars and the Mind of Men* (Harper & Row 1973.)